LOVE HER MADLY: A DARK MAFIA ROMANCE

MAFIA KINGDOM, BOOK 2

JESSICA RUBEN

Visit my website at www.jessicarubenauthor.com
Cover Designer: Sarah Hansen, Okay Creations
Editor: Jovana Shirley, Unforeseen Editing, www.unforeseenediting.com
Editor: Nicole Bailey, Proof Before You Publish
Publicity: Autumn Gantz, Wordsmith Publicity

Paperback ISBN: 978-1-7334751-3-6

E-book ISBN: 978-1-7334751-2-9

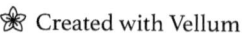 Created with Vellum

There is a secret world of sexual exploitation in the Middle East. Some Shia clerics use a controversial practice of nikah mut'ah, or sigheh—meaning temporary pleasure marriage—to take vulnerable girls and young women and pimp them out. This book is dedicated to those women.

While Love Her Madly is a work of fiction, for which I have taken fictional liberties, I tried to keep facts regarding nikah mut'ah and Shia Islam as accurate as possible.

Before the Iranian Revolution, my family immigrated to America from Tehran. May freedom, free speech, and equality for women reign again!

BLURB

From International Bestselling author Jessica Ruben comes a passionate romance. From India to Iran, and Paris to New York City, buckle up for a journey you won't forget.

Darius is a man with power and control.
As a child in the Mumbai slums, living among lethal street gangs, all he cared about was his safety and where he would find his next meal. That is, until the Madam of the most famed brothel in India finds him, offering him a life he can't refuse.

As an intelligent, beautiful woman raised in a small mountain village, Gini never would have imagined that a place like The Mansion exists. Stolen by Darius into a dark underworld where the famed Mullah Omar arranges pleasure marriages to the highest bidder, Gini fights for survival.
At first frightened by the dangerous man who keeps her prisoner, Darius slowly becomes the one light in her dark world.

The Madam. The Mullah. The Protector. The Beauty. Who will win when money reigns supreme and power is everything?

TERMS

Allah: Refers to God, in Islam
Arabic: Language of the Arab world
Ayatollah: A Shiite religious leader in Iran
Burka: A garment covering a woman from head to feet, worn in public by Muslim women
Caliphate: An Islamic state
Caste: Hereditary classes of Hindu society
Farsi: Language spoken in Iran
Halal: Meat prepared as prescribed by Muslim law
Haram: Forbidden by Islamic law
Hijab: A head covering worn by Muslim women
Imam: Title of many Muslim leaders
Jihad: The fight against the enemies of Islam
Khan: In Farsi, when speaking to a man of nobility, the speaker will use the word "Khan" at the end of the nobleman's name.
Kutta: Dog, in Hindi
Mafia Shqiptare: Albanian Mafia
Mahr: An obligation in the form of money or gifts to be given by the groom to the bride at the time of Islamic marriage
Mut'ah: An Arabic word meaning pleasure

Mullah: A religious title used for a man educated in Muslim theology

Nikah Mut'ah (Arabic), or **sigheh (Farsi):** A verbal marriage contract practiced in Shia Islam, made between a man and an unmarried woman, in which both the period the marriage shall last and the amount of money to be exchanged must be specified

Odalisque: A female slave in a harem

Saalam: An Arabic word meaning hello

Sharia law: Islamic law based on the teaching of the Qur'an, prescribing religious and secular duties

Shia or Shiite Islam: A branch of Islam that relies heavily on the words of their ayatollahs

Shqipe: Slang for Shqiptare, which means people of Albanian origin

Taarof: A Persian word describing a social etiquette of politeness

Takhte or takhte nard: Backgammon, the game

Tawaif: a sophisticated courtesan who caters to the nobility of India

Urdu: Official language of Pakistan, and also commonly spoken in parts of India

Zoroastrian: A religion centered on the cosmos

1

Gini

EARLIER TODAY, when the moon was shining full in the dark, star-littered sky and my first round of water buckets were filled, but not yet deposited in the house, my father told me I'd be leaving our small village in the foothills of Aja Parvat to become a maid in the big city of Mumbai.

"As you know, you've become expensive to feed and house, particularly as your siblings continue to grow," he said. "And as no man will ever come forward to marry you, leaving is a true blessing." He opened his hands, smiling, giving me his words like an offering of hope.

A man named Mr. Shah had heard from a friend in my village that I was a hard worker. Mr. Shah then offered to take me as a maid and pay a fee. "Which we need. And he'll even pay you monthly for your work!" Father tilted up on his toes, this news as incredible to him as the first rain of the season.

I was so shocked that I almost dropped the water buckets in my hands. I couldn't even reply with words. Countless nights, I'd begged for an answer to my prayers, and now, a reply had arrived.

By the way Father's mouth slightly gaped and the excitement in his wide eyes, I knew that he expected me to be joyous. This was the best result I could have hoped for. A maid in the magical city of Mumbai!

As the reality set in, a smile broke out onto my face. I set the buckets down, trying to keep my poise despite the thrumming in my chest. "Will I need to pack?" My voice shook just as my body shuddered from anticipation. I adjusted my long green sari, thinking, *A new life awaits!*

"You'll need nothing." Father blinked with relief, his eldest daughter finally having a course.

Two matters principally occupied my father's mind at all times: the state of our crops and upcoming religious ceremonies—namely, the weddings of his children. Everything else, such as the fact that no husband could be procured for me, was in the universe's domain and, therefore, not ours to worry over. He had been right.

"Finish your chores," he added, smiling wide. "Mr. Shah will be here after the sun rises."

I'M NOT worthy in this lifetime to have a husband. Still, I have always been Father's favorite of his seven children. It's because I'm the beautiful one. In a sea of dark brown skin and darker brown eyes, I'm who he calls *golden girl.* The day of my birth, he declared my name to be Gini because of my petite frame and fine features. My coloring is light sand, and my eyes are grayish-blue, like rain clouds. The only feature I share with my parents and siblings is my hair; it's jet-black and straight as a pin.

On her deathbed, my mother told me, "Beauty and luck do not go hand in hand."

My grandfather—name unknown—had been in the British military, stationed in India. He used my grandmother against her will for sexual pleasures until it was time for him to return to his home in London. For a long while, the village decided to pretend that none of that had happened—an extraordinary kindness shown to my grandmother. Two generations later, I was born with skin and eyes lighter than they should have been. With my arrival came the return of the village's memory, and the buried family shame became like dirty laundry, hanging out to dry in the midst of a monsoon.

I am the reminder that in our family history is rape. Anyone who sees me knows this. My face is a stamp of disgrace for my family and village. My leaving will certainly be a relief to them all. Although they do like to come over in the dead of night, knocking on my door and asking for various herbal substances to help with maladies. I have always obliged, of course, as medicinal work has become my calling in recent years. But their rudeness to my face in the daylight will definitely not be missed.

I quickly make my way down to the well, the soft black dirt padding my steps as I move to refill my water buckets. Arriving, I find Sumita, one of the elderly from our village, pulling up water. Of course, she has known me since my birth. Our village has only forty homes. Everyone can trace their descendants back hundreds of years. Still, she turns her head away from me as I greet her. I want to remind her that I delivered her grandson three days ago, but I bite my tongue.

If I could have one wish, I would wish to have dark eyes and skin. A normal face that no one would ever blink twice at.

Mother often pointed out, "As the visual descendent of sin, what else can you expect?"

My elder brother Aadi used to get angry when we walked to school together. Boys stared at me with their mouths hanging open before pinching me, chasing me, and pulling my hair. They claimed to only tease, but everyone knew what happened to girls who spoke or touched any boy other than her father or brothers. My reputation was already soiled by virtue of my skin, and I never wanted to add to it. I would run off when I saw the boys coming, hiding in bushes or taking alternate routes, even if that meant lateness to school.

I trusted that if I was good enough in this life and treated the ones around me with kindness, the universe would reward me in the next.

But Aadi didn't think that way. He would yell at the boys,

screaming and shouting to get away from his sister. He would throw rocks from the side of the road, telling them to get lost.

But that's just the way Aadi is.

I'm not that way.

I straighten my back, looking at the well before forcing a smile on my face. I cannot let Sumita's dismissal deter me from acting kindly. The elderly must be respected at all times.

Setting my buckets aside, I take the buckets from her wrinkled hands and fill them, one at a time. When they are full, I hand them back.

She grunts what sounds like, "Thank you," keeping her eyes averted.

When my own buckets are refilled, I stare up at the brightening sky and the mountains to the north before leaning down to touch a patch of dewy green grass. *Father will be glad to see the weather is turning.*

Despite my busy mind, I force my legs to pick up their pace. Each trip to the well takes approximately thirty minutes, and I have five more trips to make. I've never been more thankful for the labor; it keeps my mind focused on the task at hand instead of whirling with anxiety and excitement of what's to come.

I'm in the hands of the universe, I tell myself on repeat, barely believing that, in short order, I'll be leaving to Mumbai.

I do know that Mumbai is large and busy, although I only know this through Aadi. He travels between our village and Mumbai to sell our mangoes and other wares.

Once, he told me, "Mumbai is so loud and dirty. The streets are filled with motorcycles and buses, men on foot, and children begging to eat. Lights are on the streets, so the evening is still bright as day. It's so many people; you feel like a bug waiting to be crushed. You have to run to keep up with everyone."

To me, it sounds exciting! A colorful world with sounds I've never heard and scents my nose have never smelled. So many people, none of who know me and my past.

I want to find Aadi now to ask if he's ever seen the maids or how large the homes are, but he is not around.

I continue moving forward, my cheeks widespread from smiling. At this hour, most of my siblings have either left for school or are working the fields, transplanting paddy seedlings. We all do what we ought to do.

Sweat pours down my face as red flies swarm around my head, speaking to each other in buzzing sounds. Luckily, the bugs are friends of mine. I listen to their conversation and hum as though I were part of it.

It has begun to rain. I glance around and notice everything turning green. The world is opening. Singing a tune, I smile at my youngest brother, who is brushing his teeth before washing his face in the outhouse.

He calls out to me, and I shout, "Hello," my hands too full to wave. *Next time I see him, I will bring him a gift!*

I use my elbow to open my front door, my arms straining from the weight.

"Here she is," Father shouts from the floor, sitting cross-legged on our rug with two strangers beside him. His eyes brim with tears. "Just as beautiful as I said, yes?" He chuckles, putting out his hand and gesturing for me to come to him. "She will make an excellent worker. Perfect temperament. Strong, too."

I walk over, careful to set the buckets beside us before taking my place next to my father. He touches the sides of my face with his fingertips, and suddenly, I feel my own tears welling up.

Oh, Father. Leaving? How? Who will bring your water? Fetch your tea? Cook your meals? Yes, my sisters are growing. But they are still in school. My younger sister Aashi will have to stay home then.

All of this I try to convey without words. He understands, nodding, his dark hands caressing the skin on my face like I am precious.

With a soft but shaking voice, he tells me, "Put the water out back and then come here."

I do as he said, standing up and adjusting my sari before

breathing deeply and moving the buckets behind the door. Sitting beside my father, I finally take a look at the men in my home.

One man is middle-aged with sparse black hair and sallow skin. His scalp, like grease, shines.

The other is younger. He looks up at me, raising his eyebrows. He glances between Father and me, his eyes calculating.

His cheekbones are high, as though they were carved from rock. His dark brown eyes pause in their assessment of Father before locking with mine.

A hard swallow moves down my throat. I'm mesmerized by him.

The back of my brain tells me, *He does not look Indian.*

In fact, I have never seen a man who looks as he, with such a clear, angular white face and large, dark eyes. His hair is pulled up and wrapped high in a twist. It's a hairstyle I have seen on many men, and yet he is nothing like the others. Maybe it's because of the color, like darkly burned wheat. Lips so full. My skin buzzes.

My father shifts, and it breaks my trance. Looking down, I notice the younger man's plate is empty. Of course it is. I must cook. But the water hasn't been fully collected. I'll need to finish gathering water more quickly then. I look back to the door when the older man clears his throat. My gaze swings to him, catching his crooked smile. Bumps rise on my arms, like pebbles. I want to speak, but speaking to an elder before spoken to is intolerable. I blink, drop my head, and wait for instruction from my father.

Did the younger man notice my gawking? Embarrassment makes my blood heat.

I need to calm down. I exhale, noticing the older man's shoes are clean leather and polished black. They gleam. I look at my own bare feet, gray from clean earth.

"Hello, Gini." His voice is slick.

I lift my face to the voice. The older stranger's yellow teeth peek between scrawny lips. He pulls out a thin cigarette from a rectangular silver case, lighting it up with a match. I catch the glint of a heavy-looking watch around his wrist. Gold.

"Come." Father nods, tapping the space beside him and nodding his head like he has a great surprise for me. His mood is lifting. "This, here, is Mr. Ishaan Shah." He points to the older man. "And beside him is his son, Viraj. They will bring you to your new home, where you will live and work. You will receive a weekly salary and a room of your own." He tries not to sound overjoyed, but it's unstoppable.

My own stomach flutters as I press my side flush against my father. I turn, and we lock eyes, our happiness radiating against each other. My nerves are temporarily forgotten.

I risk another look at Mr. Shah's son. He sits up taller, and I notice that he's big. Huge, broad shoulders. I can't tell how old he is, but he has a man's eyes. They're full of something. Like he sees what others don't.

Mr. Shah tilts his head, trying to catch my gaze, but I drop my face and look down, something telling me to hide.

"Obedient." He chuckles, blowing smoke to the center of the table.

My body shudders. A chill has the ability to wreak havoc through the insides, and for some reason, Mr. Shah worries me. If my father notices my fear of this man, he doesn't say anything.

"I told her the good news earlier," my father explains, turning back to me. "Gini will prepare breakfast now. She'll gather the vegetables from the field and then cook outside. She really makes the most delicious idlis." Turning to me, he whispers, "Don't think about the water. Aashi will finish fetching it."

I nod. "Yes, Father."

Aashi will be taking my place, as woman of the house. My mind whirs, imagining how she will fare.

"I would like to come," Viraj pipes up, his deep, gravelly voice settling into my chest. Rough, dark stubble circles his jaw and the sharp planes of his face.

I blink and turn to my father, confused, as the blood rushes through my body once again.

Father laughs. "I'm sure, to a man like you, growing up in the big city, being here in the country is something of a novelty." He gestures around our room. "If you would like to go with Gini to see the vegetables, please do." He happily bobbles his head from side to side, our way of conveying understanding.

With a nod, Viraj stands to move next to me. His size dwarfs mine. Suddenly, I can barely breathe. Every square inch of this man is intense.

"Enjoy the field, son." Mr. Shah lifts his hand.

I drop my head, swallowing hard. He smells so different from the men here. It's so good. Like a warm spring day and sweet tobacco. And something else that I cannot pinpoint. I want to look up at him, but I won't. Can't.

I take my thatched basket by the door before we silently make our way into the vast field. Although I know these grounds like the back of my hand, somehow, I'm the one following *him*. I quicken my pace and move toward the cucumbers. I pull one out of the ground and put it into my basket, trying to focus on my task and ignoring the strange pulse that has taken up residence inside my stomach. Lower even.

I want to speak to him, but any words that come into my mouth turn to static. As each quiet second passes, the pressure to speak increases. He bends down alongside me, touching the vines. His heavy leg brushes against mine. I hold my breath, wanting to touch him again so badly and yet I'm so afraid. If I speak, he might stop. Maybe I should stay silent and pretend like I don't feel him. I don't want it to end.

I move toward the potatoes, and he bends down again, his left side grazing my right. I pull up the roundest potatoes I can find, keeping my head down. I'm somehow shrinking in his presence, my head lowering and lowering. Maybe he thinks I'm just too busy to talk. Maybe he thinks—

"Everything you eat is fresh, from this field?" He stands up to his full, enormous height as he gazes, assessing.

I wish the grounds were already fresh and green and not dusty or burned. *Does he think our field is good?* I bite my lip, worried. I can't imagine what he must be comparing my life to. Well, that's not entirely true. I know there is a huge world that exists outside of this one, even though I've never seen it. I've read about sights and sounds and smells that exist in other places. There are things called televisions, where you can watch images. Or radios, where you can hear faraway voices.

Once, a couple from a place called California came to visit. They were very kind and gave me a book about cities in America. My brother brings me books from the library in Mumbai, too. I've read classics, and I even saw a science book once. It was in English, so I couldn't understand it, but I saw the photographs.

I risk a look to his face and see straight white teeth. Brown eyes that glow. Hair shining in the sun. Something within me melts. My mouth opens and closes, not unlike a fish on its way to death. He's just so handsome.

He tilts his head and raises his eyebrows, not unkindly, and I realize he is waiting for an answer.

"Oh, y-yes. We have everything we need. I have been cooking since I was old enough to heat water. With my mother. She taught me everything. She used to tell me, 'If a woman has hands, they must be used to cook. And clean. And work. Working is important in this life'." I have to bite my tongue to stop rambling.

He smiles, a small laugh leaving his lips. I wait for actual words, but he stays silent. The awkwardness pushes me into action, and I go back to choosing and picking vegetables. He lifts an onion and brings it to his nose.

He's so sure of himself in a way I've never seen. I want to ask him where he's from. Why he's the one to pick me up and bring me to Mumbai. If I will be working for him or someone he knows. Is the house I will clean large? But I do no such thing. Without words, we continue to gather.

He clears his throat, and I try not to jump.

"Where is your mother?"

"She died during childbirth." I shrug.

We all miss her, but death is part of life.

"Do you have a best friend here? Anyone in particular who matters to you, above all others? A man, perhaps?"

I blush at his insinuation. "Oh no, of course not. Only my father and siblings. I do wish I could have made more friends, but my circumstances make it difficult." I bite my lip, hoping he'll take my response and not ask for more.

"Circumstances?" he presses.

I exhale. "Yes. All the people in my village can trace their ancestry back to their beginnings. But as you can see"—I point to my eyes —"there is a break in mine."

"Ah." He nods, something clearly passing over his face. "And what is your favorite color?" His eyes sparkle.

"Yellow. Definitely yellow. Like the sun." I cannot help but smile. "How about you?"

"Black." He smirks.

"Oh no."

"Oh yes." He nods, holding back a large smile. "And do you know your birthday?"

"I am twenty-two."

I don't want to ask his age, but I'm also dying to know. I have never spoken to a man who is not my family so freely, but it feels so good.

Our eyes lock, and something inside my chest opens.

I've never dared myself to dream about a life with a husband. *Maybe Viraj will call on me when I get to the city. Maybe he will not care about my past the way the village cares.*

Aadi always told me that in the city, there is a different sort of freedom. The thought has my heart pounding.

Or maybe he is the owner of the house where I will work. Would he even marry below his caste?

When we have what we need, I set the ingredients for our meal on the floor behind the house. Viraj watches, standing above me, as I peel the vegetables with a small knife. I can't help but want to show off for him. I want him to see that I am capable.

The women from the homes next to me are laughing, cooking together, but they quiet when they see a man is in their midst. I do not let their presence deter me. I act like I don't realize their silence and stares, and I drop the vegetables in one of the buckets of fresh, cool water. Using my hands, I rinse them. I have good hands. *Does he notice?* I can feel the hope bubbling in my insides. *Could he like me? Would he marry me?* I keep working, wanting to be efficient. But my thoughts won't quiet down.

I pause, moving my hair to the side. I see village girls do this when they are around men. I look up shyly. He is staring, but his face is unreadable.

Am I pleasing him? I bite my bottom lip, hoping to redden it, before pursing it out. I turn my eyes again and see his long, heavy legs, corded in muscle. *How can a man be so handsome and well built?*

I look at my neighbors and wonder, *Is this the last time we will cook side by side?* I try to swallow back my emotion.

They look down upon me, but at least they know me, and I them.

But what about the world outside? Who will know me, and who will I know in return?

"Will you be there?" I finally look up at Viraj. The way he is standing and looking at me now, I would imagine he never took his eyes off me.

"Where?"

I realize that it might be presumptuous of me, but for some reason, I need to know. "At the home where I shall be a maid?"

He nods. "You might see me from time to time." His answer is cryptic.

I turn back to my work.

Finally, I blurt, "I do other things, too."

"Other things?"

"Oh, yes." I nod, slicing vegetables. "I help the sick. I collect herbs. Also, I deliver babies."

"Is that right?" he asks, cocking his head to the side. "You learned from one of the other women, I suppose?"

"Mmhmm," I reply casually, hoping that this news pleases him.

A few minutes later, my neighbors stand up and reenter their own homes. I am now alone with Viraj watching over me with his dark, looming eyes. My previous interest and excitement turn into fear. His demeanor is aggressive.

Why is he watching me like this?

He might be silent, but it's like a storm brews behind his calm exterior. I can feel it; he is a predator.

The world has chosen my fate.

It is a good fate, I remind myself.

I continue my work, as I have always done. Clean. Cook. Combine.

My last meal here.

I manage to put aside the fact that Viraj is still here, watching my every move.

I set fire to the small stove and warm a pot of water as I rinse the rice, washing it three times before putting it inside the boiling water. After brewing tea, I roll out the dough for bread. When the vegetables and rice are cooked, I set it on plates. I lift up the knife again to peel another set of vegetables. Viraj clears his throat, and my hands falter. My small knife drops, piercing my skirt and my upper thigh. My mouth falls open in pain. But I can't seem to yell. Or cry out.

He's in front of me in an instant, hands around my thigh so enormous and frightening. My blood pulses. He looks savage right now with his jaw clenched and eyes focused. With one hand, he raises my sari. Warm air rushes across my legs. I'm not sure if I should moan or scream.

We both freeze, staring at my straight wound as blood pools and drips at my skin's surface. Red stains my pale, white thigh. He looks back up, eyes on fire. My impulse is to run. To yell, *Indecent!* But I can't speak. He presses down on the cut with this thumb, smearing red across my skin. A sensation like a buzzing heat moves from his hand into my skin and somehow straight to my heart. He's so firm and yet gentle.

"It's nothing. Just a surface wound." His voice is dark and low with a hint of something careful. Like an animal, careful not to show too much of its strength too soon.

But I know that if he wanted to, he could hurt me. Maybe we both know.

My mouth circles in a gasp as his hands continue to graze my thigh, higher, caressing me with the pads of his fingers. His brown eyes are now practically black as he dares me to say a word about what is happening.

I can do what I want to you, he silently says.

My entire brain shuts down as the thought leaves my head and enters somewhere deep and low in my stomach, pounding, asking for more of this. It's a dark heat, but I don't want it to end.

"Good girl," he whispers, inching higher up my thigh and moving his own heavy body closer.

I can feel the rough calluses on his fingers against my skin. His lips come near mine, and all I want to do is breathe. Breathe him inside me and chain him in.

He's so close now. Breath at my neck as he caresses me. I look at his heavy, muscled arms. His hands. Anything but his eyes. Suddenly, he drops my skirt back down, leaving me quivering and shocked. He steps away, like he himself is surprise by what happened.

A few seconds pass before I say, "You sit. I will serve you." My head falls forward, face pulsing. I might faint.

He stands tall, impossibly tall, and nods calmly before pivoting, walking back inside the house with long, masculine strides. I can feel the stare of my neighbor straight through the back of my head. I turn around to find her eyes on me.

Did she see what he did?

She stands up and walks over to where I sit. Her spice-stained yellow forefinger points at my chest. "Your honor is what you will die with. Never be alone with a man who is not your father or husband. You should know better," she admonishes. Looking behind me at my home, she adds, "Especially with a man whose hands could snap a snake. He must be twice the size of any man in this village. Dangerous." She shudders. "Are you okay, Gini?"

Her public kindness is almost too much. I've yearned all my life to feel this friendship with my neighbors. And now, it is too late. I try not to let my tears show.

"I should have stopped him," I exclaim.

She is right. I should not have let him come alone with me.

Not unkindly, she adds, "This is the nature of men. Beware of them. All of them." And then she goes back to her kitchen.

I can hear the men chatting inside, but I tune them out. My ears buzz as I spoon some yogurt into small bowls, continuing my work.

She saw what she saw; nothing can be done to erase her vision.

How could he have raised my skirt? Is this the way they treat maids in the big city? The thought has my throat tightening.

My face burns. He saw my thigh. *Bare.* Touched me.

Should I have screamed? And then what would have happened? I'd have lost my chance at a job. Disappointed my father.

One dish at a time, I bring the food to the floor atop our mat inside the house, willing my body to stop shaking.

He's still there, strong and tall, sweat from the humidity encasing his skin. He glistens.

I turn my face to my father, who looks at me and smiles, the corners of his dark brown eyes crinkling.

What would he say if he knew how Viraj had just treated me? What would he think if he knew how much I had liked it?

"Perfect." He smiles, nodding to me.

I try to keep steady.

First, I fill my father's plate, wishing I could erase Viraj from the table. I feel dizzy, hands clammy.

I take a seat as his gaze assesses me. This time, I don't drop my head. Rage slowly fills my chest. It starts slow but then begins to rumble, like boiling water. Viraj's eyes move to each portion of my face, almost calculating. He's watching to see my reaction. I keep my outward composure and cling to my dignity. I won't let him see that what he did has shamed me.

Still, I'm not used to being watched in this way. It's unnerving, and somehow, it makes me more conscious of myself.

What does he see? Can he tell, just like the village, that my ancestry is impure? Is this why he took the liberty in lifting my dress?

But it didn't feel dirty. It felt so good.

My stomach churns. I'm already twenty-two years old. Without a husband or a path, I will stay with my father and work here until I die. I cannot live this way. What seemed tolerable last night, staying and living and breathing this village life, is now completely impossible. I must make sure these men take me with them.

"The trip is not short, Gini. Make sure to eat well." Mr. Shah stuffs his mouth with bread, chewing loudly.

I do as instructed, dipping my bread in yogurt and taking a bite.

Viraj shifts, and my gaze lifts to his.

"Very good," he says, seemingly content with the food.

I don't reply but swallow thickly, my face blossoming pink beneath his deep stare. Likely, I will barely see him once I reach my destination. And if I see him more often than not, then I will handle it.

Or maybe he will still want me?

He didn't leave my side for some time. Maybe he actually likes me. The way he touched me ...

He doesn't seem to be thinking less of me.

But ...

He puts more food through his full lips and chews. He swallows, and I finally force my eyes away.

Before I know it, my father is shaking hands with Mr. Shah and Viraj. For the first time in my life, I notice how frail my father is. And small. His teeth are crooked, and his deeply tanned skin is lined from work under the sun. And then my heart expands with love for him.

I look down, noticing my plate is still filled with food. *Did time move so quickly?*

Father has work to do, and I must change into a fresh sari before I leave. I move into the back and choose my red one, reserved for holidays. I do not know what awaits me, but I assume I should look my best. I fist my red skirt but then pause, refusing to do anything that might make one think I'm a woman of less than stellar virtue. After what happened between us, I feel the need to be extra conservative. I refold it and instead choose my blue sari before pulling off and folding my current clothing and placing it in the corner of my room. Aashi can use it. The fresh clothes feel good against my warm skin. They will have to do.

When I reenter, Father says, "Gini," in that warm way of his. He holds my shoulders in his strong and rough palms. The tears refill his dark eyes.

In a rush, I tell him I don't even have time to find my siblings to say good-bye.

"I will tell them. This is your path. They will be happy for you, Gini. A job in the city. Your own future, just like you've dreamed. Think about all those books your brother brings for you to read. It's time to live your own life. The world has a plan, Gini. Take it in stride and be grateful."

I feel an immense pride for my father. He is dutiful and good. And he wants my happiness. This job will be wonderful. I must make him proud.

"You're off to a better life, Gini," he swears, kissing my hands. "Make sure to do just as they say. Always accept their word."

Tears fall down my face as I nod. I force the words, "I'm so happy!" through my lips. It settles him.

And then, I'm ushered by Mr. Shah into a small white car.

"It's written," Father calls out. "Your life is beginning!"

As soon as I sit, the car doors slam shut. Mr. Shah takes the driver's wheel, and Viraj sits beside him. The wheels kick across the dirt road.

Suddenly, a swarm of children, not yet school-aged, knock on the glass of the windows, screaming happily and saying, "Bye, bye, bye!"

I put my hand up to the glass, a smile breaking my face. *Good-bye!*

2

Darius

SHE STARES out the open window with her pink rosebud mouth slightly parted, not saying a word or making a sound.

In English, Ishaan tells me, "Normally, I need to drug the girl a few minutes into the ride, but seeing as she trusts you, drugs are not necessary." He chuckles. "Good move, by the way, trailing her like that. Keeping her under your vision while she picked the food. You're a careful man, Darius. I appreciate that quality."

I ignore him and take another glance at her before imagining her gorgeous creamy thigh, encased in a light dusting of golden hair. One thing I can say for certain is that Gini is built with perfectly long legs, a small waist, and breasts that would overflow in my palms. All men have different tastes. But to me, this woman is perfection.

The last thing I was supposed to do was touch her. But it all happened too fast. I got worried for her when the knife dropped—a feeling I hadn't felt for another person in a long time. I checked her leg to make sure she hadn't truly hurt herself. And then that thigh ... a place on her body that no man had probably ever seen. I see women nude. It's a fact of my life. But this one? She perplexes me.

I didn't have to follow her out to the field or watch her cook, but something about her made me want to keep an eye on her. I had to see if she was merely an act or if she really was as virtuous as she had seemed at first glance. Just the way she looked at her father when she came into their shack, carrying those heavy water buckets like they weighed nothing at all, I could see love and respect shining from her eyes. There was so much emotion between them, the likes of which I had never seen.

Something about how she gathered her vegetables with so much care and ease showed she took her simple life in stride. She focused on her task of cooking, ignoring the women from the house beside hers, who were obviously gossiping about us. Her movements were all done with attention.

I turn back again, taking another look. Hands down, she is stunning. Her black hair is long and thick. And those eyes? A dusty blue with silver flecks. And skin like warm cream. That entire village must have been in love with her, but she doesn't seem like the kind of girl who would use her beauty to get what she wanted in life. That is something she will have to change.

I face forward again, trying to get comfortable in this small seat. Hopefully, she won't be too difficult to break when the time comes. When she finds out what's really happening. I rub the center of my chest. Each time she called me by my false name, Viraj, I wanted to spit on the ground.

Ishaan lifts his eyes to the rearview, enjoying the view of Gini, her thighs pressed together in the back. I clench my teeth, and Ishaan smirks.

In English, he tells me, "She'll fetch a good price, don't you think? Men would line up across the country to have a taste of that. Might be the best I've ever gotten." He licks his lips, like the sick fuck he is.

I stare at him hard until he notices my anger. He looks alarmed at my mood and refocuses back on the road.

Good.

I'm not sure where my emotions are coming from, but something heavy has settled into my chest, making it difficult to breathe. I exhale through my nose, expelling the emotion.

Ishaan is good at his job, but that doesn't excuse the fact that he acts like an animal with no thoughts outside of his own personal survival. I hate him.

I want to plant some doubt in his head. "If she's unsoiled, then she'll fetch a good price. Otherwise, not so much."

I crack my neck, watching Ishaan's forehead wrinkle and feeling good about that. I like it when he squirms like a rat.

Truth is, I know perfectly well that Amma, who oversees and runs The Mansion, is going to love this girl. She's beautiful and without baggage, a clean slate—just the type Amma loves to mold. Young and innocent but also not a child.

I already questioned Gini and can assess her value to the rupee. Everything about this girl says, *I will bring in money*. The fact that she is a virgin is more obvious than Ishaan's filthy face.

The game between Ishaan and The Mansion works simply enough. Ishaan pays a tiny fee to a village family for a single daughter to work as "a maid in the city." If Amma and I want her, I will negotiate the price with Ishaan. If we don't want her, Ishaan will have to go to the whore district and sell her to one of the houses for a price that will cover his costs. This is the first time I've come to pick up cargo. But after the last girl Ishaan brought came to us close to death because of his complete and utter disregard for her welfare, I decided it would be best for me to come and ensure a safe passage. A father-and-son team, I thought, would be less frightening to a young girl about to leave her home. If she's less skittish and nervous, less force is necessary. Amma agreed, of course.

"The girls coming in without drugs or binds make for a much better situation. Easier," Amma said.

Ishaan laughs loudly, like a hyena, and I turn to see if Gini is catching any of our discussion.

Her thick black lashes barely blink as she stares out the window. She's likely never been this far out before.

"If she is unsoiled?" he scoffs. "Her village has no electricity! The nearest railway station is over seven kilometers away. She has no idea about Facebook or the internet. Sex before marriage is completely impossible in her village. Trust me, she is as pure as they come."

I ask, "No school for her, either?"

"Nearest school is forty-five minutes away. According to her neighbor, Gini used to go to school, but when the boys began bothering her due to her beauty, her parents made her stay home, worried that her honor would be compromised." Ishaan laughs, shaking his head. "She'll be compromised soon enough, eh?"

I don't reply to him. Instead, I ask, "Age?"

"Twenty-two." He shrugs. "A little older than we like, of course, but with that face, what can a man not forgive?"

That feeling settles into my chest again. Gini is truthful. She is also ten years younger than me.

"She'll fetch a real good price," Ishaan adds excitedly. "A face like hers is impossible to buy in this country. The Middle Eastern men will go insane for her. Russians, too. She looks almost Iranian with that olive skin tone. Actually"—he squints his eyes—"her coloring is like water. It's smooth and adaptable. If The Mansion can clean up her Hindi accent and teach her English well enough, she could pass for a native of any country. And if she has half a brain behind those gorgeous eyes, she might end up as the most profitable woman in your house."

He pulls out a cigarette from the dash and lights up, taking short, choppy inhales before exhaling a long flow of smoke. He knows he's won the lottery, and the bastard is happy as fuck. I should be, too. Gini could do very good things for my business.

I want to look back at her again, but I don't. Instead, I wipe my sweaty palms on my legs.

"You see, Darius," he continues, "I only get the best. You will give me great money for this one." He nods his stubby, square-shaped head, mind made. "And you'd better make sure Madam is on board. You know, I expect you to support me. That bitch might be tough, but I have become an important man in your business chain. Do not forget that I'm the reason this girl is here. You must—"

My hand moves straight to his throat, squeezing. Brakes slam as his cigarette drops into his lap, singeing his pants. With men like Ishaan, you have to assert dominance quickly and swiftly.

"Don't you ever threaten me, Ishaan. I am not here to be your fucking sidekick. I am only here to ensure the girl arrives in one piece. After the shitshow you dealt us last month, we're not going to take any risks." I loosen my grip but continue, "Madam and I will decide the price for the girl, if she is deemed worthy after an inspection. And then you'll go back to that shitty little rathole you crawled out of until you hear of another alleged diamond in the rough."

I let go of his neck, and he coughs, having the decency to try to hide the pain.

I turn back again to find Gini's large eyes square on me, full of shock and fear. A normal man might feel bad about pulling a girl from her home and forcing her into prostitution. But I'm not a normal man.

I glare at her, strengthening my armor to give my insides time to recover. Her beauty and innocence are disarming. Clenching my fists, I will my emotions to turn into anger. There is no place for feelings, not in this life. But from the moment I saw her today, it was like the world slowed down. I blink, imagining her sitting beside her father. The look of adoration passing between them. It wasn't twisted or sexual. It was honest. I shake my head, turning away, and crack my knuckles.

As a child, I forced myself to act like a tough guy. I spoke like a man who was not to be messed with, regardless of the fact that it was an utter lie. I remember standing in front of the mirror in the dance hall at The Mansion, puffing my chest, while Madam—who I've always called Amma—stood behind me.

HER WHITE FACE *shone above mine in the mirror. "You aren't Indian, Darius. You'll have to be tougher, then, to show those street thugs you're even more dangerous than they are."*

"If I am not Indian, what am I?"

"You're mine."

"But where did I come from? Before this?"

I already knew that babies were born from a woman, but a man's seed was necessary to start its creation.

"The gutter." She combed my hair with her sharp nails, grazing my scalp.

"What about before the gutter?"

"There was no before." She waved her hand in the air, dismissing my question. "History is meaningless. You're going to be the king of this house one day, Darius. That is who you are meant to be. You will be the strength behind my word. With you by my side, we will be untouchable."

"What if I don't want to be the king here?"

Laughter. "Silly boy. This is your future. Allah has chosen it."

AMMA WOULD TELL me if I ate my dinner, I'd grow into the strongest man in Mumbai. I not only ate it, but also took seconds. Thirds. Anything to finally get out on the streets and grow. Be the man Allah wanted me to be.

When I was a child, the women in The Mansion adored me. They would hug me often, bringing me chocolates. They would fight over whose lap I could sit on and who could brush my hair. When learning dances, they would have me dance with them. But when groups of men came for entertainment, I would always make myself scarce. Amma used to frighten me, threatening with a laugh that if one of the men saw me and wanted me, she would have no choice but to hand me over. I still remember the way I would hide when any man entered.

ON MY WAY TO bring Avni, the beautiful tawaif with lightened hair, a pink ribbon, I bumped into a man. He was huge and dark, leaning against the wall in the bedroom hallway with a cigarette hanging from his mouth. She stepped out of her room just in time to find us staring face-to-face, with me shaking from fear.

"Where did he come from?" the man asked Avni.

She laughed, telling him to quit being funny and to come join her in her room. "He's no one. Just a child born in the brothel."

He paused, looking at me, eyes full of questions. "The brothel? Are you sure? He looks to be from another country. Look at him."

"Oh, well, men of all kinds and from all places come here. He must take after his father then."

"No." The man shook his head. "He has no Indian blood in him. In fact, he looks just like—"

Before he could say another word, I ran. Piss dripping down my legs, soaking my pants.

I SLEPT in a ditch under the house for days. Avni found me, pulling me out. Giving me hot tea with loads of sugar. Singing songs until I fell asleep in my own bed, downstairs in the basement.

The same room Gini will stay in.

As I got older, Amma sent me with some of the tough crews to walk the outskirts and find the youngest and best-looking girls with no choices or options. I held my first gun. I learned my knife skills. I saw how some kids lived and others died. The slum life had no patience for weakness.

Amma sold flesh, but the girls were not unhappy beneath our roof. Most of them were relieved to have a home with food and safety. And it was the natural order of things that I went from their baby to their protector.

My thirteenth birthday was when my future was solidified.

WE WERE IN THE SLUMS, *a girl locked beneath Raffi's arm. He was the leader of an opposing crew who wanted this girl for himself.*

"She'd make a great beggar," Raffi said. "Beautiful and pathetic. Can you imagine her with one arm? Americans feel sorriest for beauty that was never realized."

One of his boys tucked his right arm inside his shirt, limping and closing one eye. The entire crew laughed.

But who would win her? Amma had specified that she wanted a girl with a heart-shaped face and small bones, and this girl had it.

Raffi started cackling. Someone kicked trash my way—an empty soda bottle. Raffi brought out his gun and told me he'd maim her. Maybe maim me, too. He raised a brow.

I was threatened, but my heart didn't quicken.

Arman, my closest childhood friend, whispered, "Do it. Do it now, Darius."

I aimed and took a shot. Raffi's head burst open. Oily guts everywhere. My friends cheered, and I came home with the girl, who became my prize. She thanked me when she was taken into her room, telling me she had heard of Madam's house and prayed to land here. After her parents had died, she'd had no more choices. At least here, no one would kill her or gouge out her eyes. She hugged me, tears streaking her beautiful face.

With shaking fingers, she asked, "Can I thank you?"

She pulled the thin shirt over her head and gave me everything.

IT DIDN'T TAKE LONG for me to grow into *him*. The man who could slit a throat without batting an eye. The man who took girls from their homes to sell to the highest bidders.

That man is me.

Life is full of turns we never see coming. The choice is in how we deal with them. If Gini is smart, she will eventually come to realize that I gave her a gift. The world is about to open to her in a way she can't imagine. Sure, she'll have to use her body as payment for everything from basic survival to diamonds and vacations. But what is free? The answer is simple: nothing. All of the women in Madam's house understand this to be true. Gini's success depends on it.

I turn to the window, unwilling to respond to the worry etched all over her face. I'm not a nice man. But I like to consider myself a fair one. I've seen hundreds of girls like her. Maybe more. So long as she submits, she will not have a problem.

Two hours later, we pull the car to the side of the road, taking a break beside a field. The dirt, burned from the summer heat, goes a great distance. As far as my eyes can see, there is nothing but bare, red-colored earth and small patches of green. I light up a smoke before opening her door. Tentatively, she steps outside.

Her eyes widen with relief as she bends down, touching the tips of dry dust with her fingertips. Her long skirt brushes the ground. Exhaling, she rises. I swallow hard, unable to move my eyes from her form. For a girl from one of the lowest castes, she has an amazing amount of elegance. It's in the way she moves. There is something fluid in her mannerisms. It's hard to take my eyes away. Impossible almost.

She stands beside the car, shifting from foot to foot. She must have to relieve herself. I walk to the trunk and let my fresh cigarette dangle from the corner of my lips as I take out a large, colorful blanket and a package of tissues. I tilt my head, telling her with my body language to follow me.

We're far enough away from Ishaan and the car when I say, "I won't look. But I'm armed, Gini." I raise my shirt to show her my pistol, and she steps back, her breath catching. "I will shoot you in the leg if you attempt to run. You are my property now."

I notice her bare feet. My eyes travel upward to the small sliver of stomach peeking through her sari. My body stirs of its own accord, and I promptly shut down my thoughts. I pull the burning cigarette from my mouth and throw it onto the road.

Her face turns to some far-off place, like she is contemplating her situation. She is beautiful.

"I am here to ensure your passage to your new home. You aren't to leave my sight, Gini." My stare tells her, *Don't fucking move.*

She nods her head, shifting. I can see the fear and confusion in her eyes. Her silence is frustrating me. Still, I know that bodily functions will always trump feelings such as embarrassment.

"I will not look," I repeat firmly. "Take this." I hand her the tissue. "Now."

I lift the blanket up high, giving her privacy and staring into the cloudless sky. My world and Gini's are completely different, and yet we both live beneath the same clouds. When she is finished, I lower the blanket. She keeps her head turned away from me in shame, biting her full bottom lip. Her village has almost nothing, but she has maintained her modesty.

I exhale, knowing she'll have to be broken of her shyness.

Together, we walk back to the car as I fold the blanket into a square, putting it back into the trunk.

Her eyes move between Ishaan and me. He is on the phone, screaming at his wife about something.

"Who are you?" Her voice cracks. Clearly, she knows something is awry.

I sigh, agitated, all seriousness channeled toward her. "I am Darius."

She looks as though she's been slapped by my hand. Yes, a lie was told. But how far does it go? Soon, she'll know. I pull out a fresh smoke from my back pocket and light up, blowing upward in the air that's tinged with damp heat.

Realizing that she isn't going to learn anything more from me, she looks down. Everything about this girl is natural. Guileless. She looks up again and licks her lips, and my eyes follow the trail of wetness her tongue left behind. We stare at each other in silence, the smoke from my cigarette wafting between us like a net. The story we told her father will soon clash with the facts. But still, she doesn't falter. She does not cry like another girl in her place might do.

Staring at her face and then letting my eyes trail down to her full breasts, flat abdomen, and long legs, I am nothing if not certain she will fetch the highest price. The thought has my stomach twisting—a feeling completely foreign to me.

"We should get going." I arch my back before opening the car door for her.

She enters without protest, and I slam it shut, hitting the window for good measure. The safety of our cargo must be the priority.

Finally, Ishaan returns to the car. He's still angry from his conversation, and he hits the gas with fervor. The car jerks, and Gini plunges forward. She yelps and then sits back, gripping the edge of the seat.

In English, I say, "Ishaan, calm the fuck down. You're scaring the shit out of this girl."

"And you? Showing her your fucking pistol and making her take a piss in front of you?" he scoffs. "You act like I'm the only monster. I've heard of your reputation, Darius. I like it. Men like us are rare."

"Don't lump me with you. Ever. You and I are not alike." I grit my teeth, feeling sickened by him.

He laughs like I'm joking. I want to bash his face in, but with this girl in the back, I need to stay calm.

I lower my window to let the breeze in and shut my eyes, leaning my head against the chair and drifting off into a half-sleep. The warm wind moves in and out of the car. My body rests, but I have one ear open and alert. Other than the breeze, not a sound is made until we reach our destination.

Once arriving in the bustling city of Mumbai, I sit up and look behind me. Gini's eyes are glued out the window. I can see by her body language that she is in shock. From silence and peace to a wild city, the adjustment isn't small. In her home, there was not even refrigeration. Here, the world is alive. Men shout, selling food from carts on the street. Beggars are everywhere, camped out on sidewalks beneath trees. Children run barefoot, calling out to each other. Like ants, they gather and then separate. There might be millions of them. A few fancy cars, like rare gems, sparkle against the dirt streets. Uber rich and destitute, we all live together in a strange sort of harmony.

She looks interested but also frightened. Mumbai is a circus.

We pull into a long, private road and drive up half a mile until we arrive at The Mansion. I exit the car before opening her door. She gets out slowly, and I secure her arm in my grip. I can feel her shaking.

Her head turns to me. "A maid, right? A maid to clean?"

I don't reply, my face feeling more like a dark mask than a normal man with emotion. This is the way it has to be.

"Please." Her bare feet, firmly planted on the ground, refuse to move. "Is this where I will work? Please ..."

I squint my eyes and tighten my hold on her upper arm. "You must come with me—either by will or by force."

Ishaan steps to her other side, grabbing her free arm. I want to tell him to get his dirty hands off of her but decide against it. Together, we practically drag the girl up into the home of the most famous brothel in Mumbai.

3

Gini

MY MIND IS HAVING difficulty computing my situation. And while I couldn't understand anything between Ishaan and Darius, their conversation sounded bad. Really bad. The men dumped me in this room and told me to get on my knees and wait. I'm doing just that.

I drop my head onto the rug, my body curled down, as though in prayer. The carpet beneath me feels silken. My fingers roam up and down the fibers as I breathe in and out, trying to keep my composure. Dark hair like a curtain, it covers my face.

When I meet whoever is coming, I must put my best foot forward. *What would my father say if I returned home?* The money I will send back will make a big difference in my family's life. I have to calm down and make sure to stay here.

Maybe he goes by two names—Viraj and Darius. Maybe there is nothing so bad to come.

Gathering my wits, I sit up on my knees and straighten my hair behind my shoulders. I look around, taking stock of the room. It looks like a palace with gold and silver candlesticks sitting atop golden, round tables. There are more than I can count surrounding the room. I want to stand up and roam, touch the walls and the furniture, but what if someone comes in? They might think I'm a snoop. Still, my eyes can scan. I crawl forward, just a few feet, wanting to get to the wall so I can feel it. It's blue with gold stripes. There is one enormous carpet spanning the entire room, the size of which I never knew was possible. It's navy, red, gold, and green. I flip over the corner to see the back, noticing the hand-woven loops. How small the fingers must have been to create this masterpiece.

White statues frame each window. I squint my eyes, wondering if my vision is failing me. The statues are all ... nude women. One in the back corner sits in a kneeling position, her hands forward and breasts high. Another is of a woman cupping her own breasts. I turn my head, noticing a statute of a woman whose hands caress her most intimate place, her mouth parted. I look back down to a glass table between the couch and chairs, but the table is not being held up by legs. Instead, it looks like a marble woman on her back with her hands and feet holding up the glass. Her mouth is agape, and her head is tilted back, breasts pointing upward.

What?

My heart pounds. A raw feeling gnaws at my stomach.

I should run. Something isn't right here.

No. There is nothing to fear. So long as I do my job and keep my head down, it will be okay.

Finally, the door opens. A woman enters the room along with a man, who is dressed in the garb of a *mullah*. He holds a board, a pen, and what looks like a black rectangle. The woman, however, is old and short, her teeth darkened yellow, like Mr. Shah's.

"Lift your dress." Her words are clipped as she stops in front of me.

I blink, unsure if I heard correctly. Before I can speak, she raises her hand and slaps me right across the face. The sound bounces off the walls, like an echo. While I am in absolute disbelief, she lifts me to my feet and raises my skirt, jamming her fingers straight up deep inside me. My face throbs, and my entire core contracts.

"Intact," she grunts.

The mullah writes something down, a smirk marring his cruel face.

The woman seems to wait for me to gather myself, but the mullah wants no such thing.

He shouts, "What are you waiting for? She's nothing but property. Treat her like it!"

The woman grunts, "Turn around."

Swiftly, she pushes my right shoulder so that my back is to her. My tears stream down my face as she raises the back of my skirt up to my neck, roughly pinching my backside and sliding her cold, clammy hand down my shoulder blades.

"Clean."

She walks around me. Opens my mouth. Looks inside, as though I were an animal, and stretches my lips left and right while examining my teeth. Something in the back of my head tells me to scream, but I know it'd be useless.

"Clean," she states.

He laughs, and the shame hurts almost as much as the woman's ministrations. "I knew this one could be something special. How much dirt did we sift through until we found gold?"

My entire body fills with shame as the woman pushes me back onto the floor and examines my long, thick hair. Pulling and twisting the strands from my scalp until my face is water-filled, every crevice pouring in silent pain.

The mullah simply stares at me now, assessing. And then he lifts the black rectangle, and flashes of light go off. "Let me see your backside."

After I am forced into different positions, they turn on their feet and leave. I don't take a breath until the door is closed.

I curl my quaking body on the silk carpet, my knees to my chest. *They must make sure I am clean. How could they employ me in their home if I were not? Maids need to be clean, of course.* I shiver, swallowing back the bile rising from my stomach.

Memories of just this morning filter across my eyes. I want to wail.

But there is no point in that. What's done is done. The worst should be behind me, shouldn't it?

I spend the next period of time staring at the ceiling, wondering what exactly will become of me if I do not pass their test.

Sometime later, the woman returns. I hold my breath, afraid that the mullah is back with her.

"I am alone, child." She lifts me up from beneath my arm. "Come with me," she says, this time not unkindly. "My name is Narmada. I run the house details and make sure all the workers do their jobs."

She opens up the door, and with sudden haste, she rushes me toward the back of the grand mansion, where the floor is dark wood and the walls are rough white with gray patches. We continue moving until she opens another door. This one painted black. She pushes it wide open and touches something on the wall. A dim glow illuminates a set of stairs, and I pause in utter surprise. I look up and see a light glowing from the ceiling. *Is this what my brother described as electricity?* The stairs are illuminated, almost purple. She grunts, and I stumble forward, walking downward.

"Your room," she states, pulling on a long, thin chain dangling from the center of the ceiling.

Another light comes on, making my jaw drop.

We walk to the back of the room, where she slides a door open. "You can clean and relieve yourself outside. I'm sure this won't be a problem for you."

It's a concrete square with high walls but without a roof, where I can see the clear blue sky. There are two empty water buckets and a small plate for cooking.

"If you try to climb this wall, your skin will be torn to shreds. There is barbed wire at the top, see?"

I shiver. "Where do I gather my water?"

She opens her eyes widely, surprised I have a voice. I bite my tongue, wishing I hadn't spoken.

"You will not be leaving the compound. One of the maids will bring water for you each week, and you'll have to use it sparingly to cook and clean yourself. You can take care of your private matters in the empty bucket. The girls upstairs use running water, of course, but that won't be available to you." Her eyes roam my body. "Yet."

She continues, "Here is the stove. You will get the leftover vegetables the ladies do not see fit to eat. Be aware, there is mold on much of the unfit foods. You'll have to peel that away before you cook it."

I can do nothing but blink.

"Your duties will begin tonight, and you must wear this garment." She points to a set of brown clothes neatly folded on the mattress. "A bell will ring when it is time. When you come upstairs, you will wait by the door until Madam greets you. The girls will need you during meals, and you will clean up after them. Some will also have mending for you to do ..." Her voice trails off for a moment. "As well as other things. This evening, you will also meet the one you will shadow."

She waits silently until I reply, "Yes, ma'am."

I am having trouble understanding what she is talking about, but it is obvious that, soon, I will know. I keep my face passive, my mouth wordless. Part of me knows that my destiny is not something I can question. Still, the fear of what is to come thrums within every part of my body.

I want to ask her, *What was the religious man doing in that room?*

Narmada whispers, "Things will not be easy. But if you do your job to the best of your ability, you will rise. When you meet Madam, do not stare at her! Keep your head bowed low, and for your own sake, do not speak. Oh, one more thing. Your name, until you rise above this station, will no longer be Gini. You will answer to *Kutta*."

They want me to answer to the word dog? Normally, I would shy away from an insult as bad as this, but all I feel now is blank. I can tell something awful is coming, but I refuse to come to terms with it. Not yet and not now. I can answer to Kutta if it means money for my family and a new life, full of potential, for me.

Luckily, she doesn't wait for my reply. She leaves, closing the door behind her.

I take a moment to review my lodgings. There is a small mattress with gray sheets and a brown blanket. The floor is bare and walls a broken white. I remove my clothes and fold them, placing them at the edge of the bed, and I put on the clothing given to me. It feels like a sack to store onions. Scratchy.

The room is not too bad, although I do wish there were natural light. This electricity is astonishing, but I do not understand it.

I lift on my toes to touch the light. *Hot!*

I take a seat on the mattress and bounce up and down a few times. I think I'd prefer the floor. Looking down, I see some mice scurrying into a corner. They do not look like the mice I know, pink and smooth. These are dark and large, full of gray hair. I swallow hard, wondering if maybe the mattress is the better option.

I think about how my father is faring. I rub my hands, asking the world to give me the strength to be the best maid I can be.

I close my eyes, letting my heart and brain drift to the image of clear skies and reflection. Just this morning, I was bringing water. The grass turning green. And Darius. His height and his heavy body. My heart flutters, although it shouldn't. He was so difficult. So strong and dominant. The way he became so worried when I dropped the knife. The heat in his eyes and his hands when he saw my thigh. And the warmth he showed me in the field. He asked me questions and seemed to listen to my answers. Never in my life had I seen a man like him. But then ... the change in him. The moment I found out that he was someone else.

A bell rings, and my heart jumps. *The alarm!*

I tentatively pull down the rope, and the light turns off. *Miraculous!*

My eyes adjust to the darkness as I open the door and slowly make my way up the hard steps. My fingers glide against the crumbling wall, keeping me steady.

At the top step, I open the door to find a woman, like a long, lean tree, waiting. A smile is painted liquid red on her frozen skin, as though it were covered in clay. Eyebrows drawn in dark. Frazzled hair in a creamy-white color—something I have never seen. Ears filled with golden rings, shimmering like shooting stars. I want to scream in fear and run back downstairs, but my inner self tells me not to say a word or move a muscle. I'm so startled by her appearance, my mouth hangs open.

"Those eyes." She tilts my chin upward, focusing on my face and studying me. I do my best to keep myself still. "How old are you?" Her voice is surprisingly melodic.

"I have twenty-two years." I swallow, the water in my throat turning to sand.

Her hands glide across my arms and breasts. "A little older than I would like, but you do look and feel youthful." She stops, her eyes focusing in on mine.

"When you do not behave, we will have you beaten. You haven't been brought here to clean toilets, although you will do that, at first. You will also scrub the rooms, sweep the floors free of dirt, and wash all of the clothing. There is a cook, although you are not entitled to eat anything but the leftovers. If you do as you're told and you learn the arts, you will become a *tawaif*." She raises her head, as though this were something to be proud of.

"My girls are the most sought after in the world for *nikah mut'ah*, also known as a pleasure or temporary marriage, although they also entertain men who are not of the religious variety. You will learn to dance. Sing. Seduce. You will learn to please men, of all kinds and types. In return, we will clothe and feed you. Once you have paid back the fee we spent buying you, we will give you a percentage of your earnings.

"Nikah *mut'ah* will bring you the most money, particularly ones that last longer than an evening. If you are lucky enough, a man will decide to sign a long-term contract for you. He might take you with him to travel. Or"—she presses her lips together—"take you with him back to his country and buy you a home. He will pay me an incredible sum as well as pay you a dowry. But this is only the hope. If you are not very good, no man will sign for you for longer than is necessary."

I feel faint but manage to stay on my feet.

"The men who come here who aren't religious are often just businessmen looking for the most beautiful women our country has to offer. We will entertain them for the evening, and all ladies who partake will get a fee.

"But first"—she lifts a bony finger in the air—"you must rise to the level of tawaif, and then you will be eligible for both nikah mut'ah or evenings with secular businessmen. We won't allow you to tarnish our reputation of excellence by starting before you have acquired your skills, of course." She pauses, straightening her back. "And so, before we allow you into the parties as a tawaif, you must earn your keep by serving the other women. You will work and learn from Roshan."

My breath feels labored, but I can't give in to tears. Not yet.

"And one more thing." She slowly looks me up and down. "If you are unable to learn the arts or if you are deemed tainted or unworthy with your virginity not intact, you will be sent to one of the many Indian brothels famed for their dirty whores. You will suck a cock for mere rupees and learn to be thankful for it. There, the women sleep and rut in dirt stalls. Remind yourself, when you feel sad, that you have actually hit a pot of luck." She smiles coyly, opening her hands. "You have been given a gift!" Her smile widens and then falls. Coldly, she says, "Now, follow me."

Behind her, I drift forward in something like a trance. My throat tightens, but my mind sits in staunch refusal. It's like a cement curtain has risen between reality and my brain.

It just can't be.

I walk, and yet it's as though I'd lost my legs. She expects me to become a tawaif, who then enters into short-term marriages.

As I remember the boys in school joking, a tawaif is a prostitute. And pleasure marriages are something I have heard of, too—quite often.

The people in my village talked about what might happen if the farming ever stalled. A father who could not feed his daughter might sell her to a wealthy man for a marriage for a specified period of time. People liked to say that the father had no other choice, as he could not feed his family, and the wealthy man, in return, was doing the family a favor. However, it was known that when the contract was over, the girl would return home, buried in shame.

I look up at the walls, gilded in gold. Without a shadow of a doubt, I know my life will never be the same.

We enter an enormous dining room with a long, rectangular table and huge lights sparkling above. My hands shake like leaves as I take in the magnificent scene. The view clashes with what I have just learned. A huge feast sits on the table, the likes of which I've never imagined. But then I notice the girls sitting around it. They are quiet and watching me with pursed lips and straight faces. I should drop my head, but I cannot. They are all startlingly beautiful. Amid all of my fears, their beauty has me in a trance. Backs straight, hair long and in varying shades of brown and black. Their perfection is astonishing.

Behind them, standing against a wall and chewing on a small stick of some kind, is Darius. *He is still here!* But he looks ... angry to see me. His jaw is tightly clenched. He changed his clothing and now wears a white T-shirt. It frames his broad chest. I want to run to him and beg him to take me out of here. Demand answers. Ask him, *Why?*

"This is our new kutta," Madam says, bringing me back to the moment and introducing me to the table. "Roshan will be her mentor."

She nods at a woman with long black hair, braided to the side of her head like a silken rope. Her eyes are shaped like two large, brown almonds. Even her lips are perfectly full and almost red against pale white skin. For the first time, I recognize the power of beauty and the confidence this woman possesses because of it. I'm dirty and tired, like a dried grape. Everyone here knows I am worthless. And Roshan? She looks like the sun.

"Go," Madam orders. "Sit beside her, on your knees." She points to a spot on the floor beside Roshan, her scrawny finger directing me.

I go forward with Madam and all the women gazing at my back. I am used to stares and awful comments, but this feels tremendously worse.

When I get to Roshan's side, Madam screams, "Down."

I sink onto the cold white floor, my knees brushing against the freezing tiles.

"Good girl." Madam pats my head before putting her fingers into my hair, tugging downward, her nails snagging in my knots. Like with a claw, she pulls.

Tears fall from my eyes but she doesn't stop. Not until she reaches the ends.

The conversation continues around the table in a language I cannot understand, and Madam moves to take her seat at the head of the table. The food smells delicious, and my stomach rumbles. My mouth is dry, as well. I want water and food, too. Instead, I swallow my tears, embarrassment stinging my chest as the roots of my hair burn.

I miss my father. My siblings. My clothes.

Is Darius watching me on the floor like this? He must see me as lower than dirt. And I will be—soon. A whore. A prostitute for men to use. A contract will be signed for me so that a man can use me at his will.

I will find a way to run. I must!

Every emotion in my body is on fire. As the time ticks by, my limbs turn to jelly. I used to believe that I was nothing, unfit to live the way others lived. Now, I know that I am even less than that.

I imagine my father finding out what has become of me. A tawaif, used for pleasure marriage! At the news, his heart would twist in anguish. The shame it would bring upon my family is horrifying. My tears drip down onto the cold floor, making a small pool at my feet. I cry as they all ignore me and continue speaking, silver clinking against plates. I don't want to show my emotions like this, but what choice do I have?

A small voice in the back of my head tells me I should do what Madam asked of me and never let my family know, so as to spare them the shame. Another part of me knows that I need to run.

Finally, the women all stand, pushing their chairs out behind them.

Madam points to me as she stands. "You can finish Roshan's plate or anyone else's."

My heart skips for a moment at the thought of food, but then a few of the girls giggle.

A tall woman with hair the color of black ash bends over, spitting on her plate. All of the others follow suit. I can only stare in shock as they spit with relish, ruining any possibility of me eating. Roshan, however, does no such thing. I see that she has left a small square of food, that looks as though it was untouched, on the corner of her plate. In Urdu, she tells me, "When you finish eating, go back to your quarters." She leaves without another glance at in my direction, the rest of the women following suit.

I look behind me, feeling a pair of eyes. Darius continues to stand, his eyes in slits. I turn my head to face the table, wishing he weren't watching me.

"Eat," he says behind me.

I do as Darius commanded, too exhausted to do anything else, and inhale the food Roshan set aside for me. It's not enough, but it will have to do.

I find some water left in a pitcher. I lift it, noticing how considerable the weight of it is. I pour it into Roshan's empty glass, filling it to the brim. Swallowing it down, I feel relief. Finished, but still hungry, I wipe my mouth with the back of my hand. I take a step back. He's here, sitting at the head of the table, opposite from where Madam sat. His plate is full of food. Four large platters surround him, steaming. Otherwise, we are completely alone.

I watch as he cuts a thick piece of meat with a sharp knife. My pulse skyrockets as he continues this mundane act of eating. Swallowing, his throat bobs. His forearms are corded in muscle.

He met my father and watched me cook in the back of my home. I wish I didn't know him. I wish I'd never met him! He brought me to this disgrace. And yet, he's the only one I know.

He takes large, generous bites of food. It looks amazing and juicy.

"Is it good?" I barely realize I spoke until it's too late.

"Yes. Now, come here." His voice is an order.

Slowly, I walk toward him. *Should I be afraid?* He's stone.

"Sit." He gestures to the seat next to him. "This"—he gestures between us—"will never happen again. Tonight, it's fine. We must speak about some rules."

He pours a cup full of a red liquid and hands it to me. "Wine. One Islamic law I continuously break."

I stare at his eyes and down to his full lips and back up again before taking the glass. I take a sip and swallow, trying not to wince. It's awful.

He smirks, putting food onto a plate for me. White rice first, covered in chole masala. The chickpeas are steaming. On the side, he gives me some bhatura. I hesitate, watching the food. Slowly, I lift the bread, ignoring the fact that I was instructed by Madam not to eat from anything other than the ladies' food. I scoop up the rice with the stew, savoring the feeling of hot food in my mouth. It's different from what I'm used to, but it's so delicious.

"You like meat?" His voice is slow and measured.

I nod my head, whispering, "Yes. My father has always spoken about vegetarianism, but it wouldn't be possible among my caste."

"Tonight, I want you to speak to me. If you have something to say, do not hold your voice back. I want to know who lurks behind those eyes."

He stares at my face until I nod my head.

His tongue slides against his teeth. "Rogan josh." In a bowl, he pours a few ladles full.

I lift it to my nose to smell it, noticing the heavy scent of lamb with turmeric and garam masala. There are other spices in here I have never eaten.

"It is very good. Cook's specialty." He cuts more of his meat before gesturing to my food. "Eat."

I go ahead, dipping my bread inside and lifting a large piece of meat into my mouth. I can barely contain my moan; it's delicious. Chewing, I notice him staring at every part of my face. He did this earlier today, too. My emotional self is conscious of the way I must look to him, dirty and tired, and yet the instinct in me keeps my head up high. I don't want to show my fear.

"Make sure to eat well," he states. "You will be hungry often. Also, be sure to keep yourself clean. It won't be easy, but you can get sick if you aren't careful. This isn't your quiet village with clean dirt. The dirt here is ... dirtier."

I eat, his quiet allowing me to shut all thoughts out from my head. My father. My home. The village. Everything I have been torn from. When my stomach is finally full, I stop and stare at the room around me. Darius finishes his meal as though it were just another evening. And I guess, for him, it is. I look around at the opulent surroundings and the large lights dangling from the ceiling.

How can they be sure it won't fall?

"They are hung very carefully."

I glance at him, wondering how he's reading my mind.

"It is called a chandelier. Many things will be surprises to you, at first. But as you will see, everything becomes normal soon enough. Humans have a way of quickly getting used to things. Now, say it in English." He points up to the light on the ceiling. "*Shan-da-leer.*"

I repeat the word. It sounds so foreign to me, twisting my tongue.

"Good girl. The language you heard the women speaking is English. You will need to learn that in order to speak with the men who frequent here. They hail from all over the world. Mostly Iran. Iraq. Saudi Arabia. I insist the women only speak English during mealtimes, so they can practice."

He takes another sip of his drink, gesturing for me to do the same. It was awful, but I wouldn't dare say no. When I finish it, he pours another glass full.

My feet, which were so cold earlier, suddenly feel warm. I lean back into my chair, finding it hard to sit upright. "The light is really bright," I tell him, smiling. "And those women are so beautiful."

"The wine has loosened your tongue." He smiles, not unlike a vicious animal. "I'm glad it was that easy."

"Has it?" I put my hand over my mouth, noticing my tongue actually feels quite heavy.

He lets out a laugh, and I find myself laughing with him. I want to ask him to take me away from here. And he did just say I should speak my mind, didn't he? What do I have to lose?

"Darius," I start, clearing my throat. "I think a mistake has been made. I'm not the girl for this place." I lean forward, and as if in conspiracy, I whisper, "I couldn't possibly live this life. I've never even been with a man. How could I—"

"I know you haven't. That is what makes you so prized."

"But once I am used, I will never be able to find a husband. I will be a-a greater shame than I already am." My voice stutters, along with my heart.

"You were unable to find a husband anyway." He shrugs, like my circumstances are meaningless. "You are already twenty-two. In village life, you are practically a spinster." He might be correct, but it still stings. He must see my thoughts working because he says, "Accept your fate, Gini."

"I cannot accept this." I shake my head, pushing the plate away from me.

"You must." He places his elbows on the table and I notice his strong forearms flexing. "We are all dealt a hand. This is yours."

"But my hand was already dealt, and I acted to the best of my ability. I cannot accept the shame of being a tawaif, given for pleasure marriages. Never!"

"Here"—he motions around the room—"you will have things the people in your village have only read and dreamed about. Electricity and running water are just the beginning. You will have money. Diamonds. You will travel the world."

"How?" My voice comes out more forceful than I intended.

"I am sure Madam discussed it with you already, but let me make it clearer." He sits back, so calm. "A woman works here, learning the trades of the body as well as the arts. If she's lucky, a man will be procured, who is willing to enter into a nikah mut'ah for a specified period of time. He will buy her from our home and give her a dowry before taking her away. He will give her a home filled with gifts. She will satisfy him. And when he tires of her, which he always does eventually, she will leave with the gifts he gave her. If she fails in her duties, he will cut the marriage short, and she will return here to enter again into another marriage. There are also nonreligious businessmen who frequent here, who just want an enjoyable evening. You will engage in those, as well—for a fee."

The tears won't come. They sit in the center of my chest, beneath rage. "Why me? This isn't fair. I-I cannot!"

"Why you?" He shrugs. "Why not you?" His voice booms.

"I never did anything to deserve this." I look up at the ceiling, wondering, *How, how, how?*

"Gini, you must understand, your level of beauty is known far and wide. You are the most gorgeous girl to enter these doors in years. Many men would pay top dollar to keep you. That is a good possibility, is it not?"

"No. These women who are already here, they're the most beautiful I've ever seen. This isn't me. I can barely look at my own nudity. No." I shake my head. "This cannot be—"

"You do not see yourself. You do not know what I know. What Madam knows. What the mullah knows. You are a diamond in the rough. Your eyes. Your skin. Your—"

A darkness moves past his eyes, as though he didn't mean to speak those words. I want to think more about it, but my mind hazes over.

"Everyone is a cog in the world machine. You can grow within this world, Gini. You might end up as a kept woman with a ninety-nine-year contract. With diamonds and rubies. A fully furnished apartment. If you saw the things that women could get, you would change your mind about this life. I know there is shame around the concept of mut'ah marriage here in India. But in countries that follow *Sharia law*, not as much."

"No." I vigorously shake my head. "Material things mean nothing to me. What you see as poverty, I see as simplicity. I'm not hungry for more or for bigger. I only want a peaceful life with respect and dignity. Do I see the beauty in this home and the ease of electricity? I'm not blind or dumb. But I don't care. I would rather have my small home, sharing a bed with my siblings and sleeping and waking according to the sun and the moon. This life isn't right. I understand that many in Shia Islam agree to these types of marriages, but I ... I don't want to agree to this." I don't sound like myself, but my mouth continues to move. "I don't have to agree."

"It is sanctioned by our religious law, Gini. And you must agree. Otherwise, you will be sent out, and you will have no choice but to prostitute yourself in a situation that has no support. Nothing is perfect in this life, but this is the one you've been given." He raises his eyebrows. "You'd better start learning how to reprioritize your wants. This life will be much easier to bear if you put riches at the height of your pyramid. The world is a magnificent place. If you play your cards correctly, you might even get to enjoy some of it. Haven't you yearned for travel? These men will put you on a plane and take you to see the wonders of the world. All you must do is sign the contract and give your life and body to the man who chooses you."

"No. I-I can't." I cross my arms, trying not to shake. "You seem to be a decent man who is wrapped up in this life. What brought you here? Why do you do this?"

"That is none of your concern. And, Gini, do not ever look at me and see decency. I'm a hard man, and you'd do well to understand that." He drops his head, digging back into his food and shutting me out.

"I will find a way out. I will leave here." My words come out as a threat, and I guess they are.

He sits back and licks his lips. My stomach sinks when he begins to speak. "There was word that the most beautiful girl with a tainted history lived in a small Indian village. No one would go near her. She was a village burden, they said, but valuable. With eyes like the ocean and skin like creamy sand. A body that had made men insane since her eleventh birthday. Her father tried to keep her under cover. Stopped sending her to school. But one day, he was approached. Two men arrived with a partial truth. She was to work for money. He could have asked more questions, but he did not. Instead, he sent her off, relieved."

"No!" I exclaim. "How would he have known? My father, he is trusting. He has no reason to be—"

"That father," he continues, "was a grown man with his own

mind. And he was happy to send this girl into the big world. But"—he pauses, lifting a finger in the air—"once she was taken, she had a choice. Embrace her future or fight it. She could work hard and do what was asked of her, only to rise up, or she could rage against her fate. What did she do, Gini? Did she trust in the heavens and take her fate in stride? Or did she run?"

"She ran away." My heart speeds up, mouth drying.

"She ran, did she? In that case"—his voice moves to a dark whisper—"I will tell you how her story ended. She was caught. Caught by one of the many goons who worked under the enforcer's hand. Goons who answered to a man named Darius." His tongue glosses across his straight white teeth. "And those men sliced the tip of her tongue with a knife and tore her clothes before dumping her into the dirtiest brothel they could find. And there was no running water or a well. There were only the smells of sex and sweat. Men rutting with women like animals. And she became like an animal, too."

I shake my head, fear racking my body. "What if she hadn't run? Wh-what if she'd accepted her fate?"

He chuckles. "Good girl, Gini. Good girl. Now, drink some more. That girl is someone else, isn't she? The one who ran?"

"Someone else," I repeat, my stomach curling up within itself.

I finish the glass of wine and he stands tall. I do the same, but swaying. The room is spinning! I grip the bottom of the table, and he laughs.

"Time for bed." Darius puts a hand behind my back, leading me out of the room. "Hopefully, the drink will help you sleep deeply."

"I want to go home." I hiccup, starting to cry again. "I don't want you to cut my tongue."

"Don't speak, or I will punish you," he whisper-yells. "Make yourself quiet, Gini."

Like a ghost, my footsteps are completely silent as we make our way down the hallway. Again, the earth turns. I stumble, propping myself up against the wall.

Before I know it, he lifts me up, as though I were a feather. "Wrap your arms around me."

Into his neck, I whisper, "Darius, are you going to cut me up?"

"No, I won't do that. Just do as you're told."

"I miss my father."

"I know." He continues walking. His body is so solid and straight.

"I've never left my family before. I miss them."

I lean my head against his muscled chest. Aadi is definitely not this ... hard. Darius pulls me to him, and I try to inhale his scent. Can I still smell my field on him or the food I prepared for our lunch? I try so hard to catch the scents of home, but I can't. Still, he smells so, so good. I bury my face harder into his neck, wondering what his skin would taste like. All of the awful things he said during dinner seem to disappear from my brain, replaced by his hardness. We walk down the stairs, and I press my nose against his throat, inhaling, inhaling. Then, slowly, I let my tongue peek out with a warm exhale. His skin is so hot.

He pauses, still gripping me against his chest. "Gini," he growls. "What are you doing?"

"Did today really happen? Maybe this is all a dream. Are you a dream?"

I look up into his deep, dark eyes, wondering if maybe none of this is real. Darius is too handsome to be real. Too cruel.

"I can assure you, Gini, that I am no ghost."

How did I get myself in this mess? I have heard of this happening to other girls, from other villages, but I never imagined it would happen to me. To become a tawaif. To learn the art of seduction. To be forced to have sexual relations with men for a prescribed period of time, for a fee. Shame burns through my face.

Feeling strangely emboldened, I ask, "Wh-what about earlier? You spoke to me. You laughed with me. You ... looked at me. You touched my thigh. Was that all a test? A game?"

"That shouldn't have happened." He moves his face away from mine, opening the door to my bedroom. He turns on the light and unceremoniously drops me onto the bed. "It was a moment in time that must be forgotten."

"I've never been touched before, in that way. Is that how all the men will soon touch me?"

He stands before me, huge and looming. I should be afraid of this man, but for reasons my heart cannot comprehend, I am not. What a baby I was, thinking he and I had something. I lie down, turning away from him, wishing I had never seen him. Wishing I'd never felt his hands on me. Wishing that the fire he'd ignited in my heart could be doused in water. I cannot see him, but I can feel him standing tall in my small room.

"Are you comfortable?"

I start to laugh, although nothing about this situation is funny. "No." This is my first night sleeping all alone. Normally, my siblings and I all curl up together in the room in the back, my father on the other side of the wall, sleeping on his mat. "My life is over. I'm in a dungeon with no stars or air. Where is hope? Allah has forsaken me."

He moves to the side of the bed I am facing so that I can no longer hide from him. His normally straight back softens, and I know the monster from dinner is gone. This is the man with warm eyes that I saw in my field.

"This house and the laws of Shia Islam are now the masters of your fate," he whispers. "There is nothing you can do about it. Just as you were born in that tiny village without a choice, you will now be reborn in this house. You must allow it. The more you fight the change, the more difficult it will be for you. Accept your circumstances. Learn the ancient ways of the tawaif. And when Madam believes you to be ready, sign your first contract, knowing Allah is on your side. When you pay back your debts to the house, you will begin to make money. More money than you can imagine." His words are hard, but his voice is gentle.

I close my eyes.

"I used to sleep in this room. It has been a long time since I have returned."

"You did?" I want to sit up, but I can no longer move. My entire body feels weighted.

"Yes. But I would not sleep here." He stands and scratches the back of his head, as though remembering something important. "Come, Gini."

I do as he said, finding the strength within my body to rise. The room whirls, but I manage to stay upright as Darius pulls the mattress from the floor and takes me to the small outdoor space. Immediately, I feel better. The air smells different from home. Thicker and without the sweet scent of grass. But still, it's improved. He leans the mattress against the wall before moving the water buckets to the corners.

"I will arrange that you have more than this."

He drops the mattress down onto the ground, sliding the sheets on top of it. He is making my bed beneath the stars.

"The ground is concrete," he says. "It is not soft, but it stays strong. Go ahead, Gini. Lie down on the mattress I set up for you."

I do as he said. Around me are walls, but when I look up, I see stars. They twinkle. I lift my arm and close one eye, imagining I could touch one.

"Are they speaking to you?" He sits on his haunches beside me, no longer the wolf.

"Yes," I whisper, turning to him. "They tell me that the world is big. Bigger than this small life I am living. They tell me that my father is watching the same stars. He is wondering if I will live." A tear rises to the corner of my eye.

"You will be okay, Gini. You will not die. You will survive this."

"How do I know that?"

"Because I am here. And wherever I am, you will be safe."

He leans forward, and for a moment, I think his lips are about to touch mine. I hold my breath, waiting.

But he stands, bringing the sheet and laying it over my body. "This is better?"

I swallow hard. I want to tell him, *Yes*. I want to say, *Thank you*. I want to ask, *Do you feel that pull between us, too?*

Instead, we simply stare at each other. His brown eyes shine so brightly that I can feel the blaze in the pit of my stomach. I want to touch his skin. I want his hands on me, like they were in my home.

Home. The word ricochets against my heart, the ache like nothing I've ever felt before.

I close my eyes, willing my life to return to what it was. I can hear his footsteps on the floor of the room, and then, I hear nothing.

I open my lids. "I miss you, Father."

I close my eyes again, picturing my entire family is next to me. One by one, I say good night to each of them. I imagine kissing my youngest brother Aarush on the nose. I visualize the small birthmark by Aashi's ear, where I always tickle her. My sister Amee asks me to tell a story, and so I tell them all about Sleeping Beauty. And finally, I fall asleep.

4

Darius

I ENTER the room at the end of their conversation, but it appears to have gone well. Amma smirks with both mischief and relief, sitting tall in her pink silk armchair, taking a sip of her newest obsession—Turkish coffee. The brew is a new novelty for us, brought here by one of The Mansion's frequent clients.

Amma sits smugly, like the queen of her castle, likely extremely satisfied by what Gini will bring.

Mullah Omar sits beside her in a matching chair, his face sinister and dark despite the crisp white turban wrapped neatly around his little head. He only visits on two occasions. The first is when new cargo arrives. He makes sure that photos of the girl are taken, along with detailed notes on her virginal status, among other things. The second is when he has a client looking for a specific type of woman, and he wants to see the girls face-to-face. Not least, he loves to lecture Amma and me about what is expected of the particular chosen girl.

Mullah Omar is one of the chief clerics in the city of Tehran, over-seeing nikah mut'ah, or *sigheh*. These pleasure marriages must be done in the name of Shia Islam. When wealthy Shia Islamic plan to travel abroad to Mumbai for business, but seek pleasure, Mullah Omar is the one they find. Amma and I must, therefore, keep him happy, as he is the gatekeeper of this arrangement between us and the men who seek temporary wives.

For years, The Mansion has been the leader in bringing the most beautiful women of India to men who can afford them. Our girls fit the criteria for a temporary pleasure marriage: The bride must not be married, she must attain the permission of her legal guardian if she has never been temporarily married before, and she must be either Muslim, Jewish, Zoroastrian, or Christian. She may act independently if she is Islamically a non-virgin or she has no guardian.

Still, our status as "the best of Mumbai" can change quickly, if Mullah Omar decides to soil our name or to stop bringing wealthy men to our door.

My gaze moves to Amma, whose face and chest are, as always, painted shades lighter than her natural skin. The color is in stark contrast to the black chador she wears exclusively for the benefit of Mullah Omar. It covers her neck and head like a shroud, and is required.

She keeps her face completely still, as she never likes to smile or move her face much, out of fear that her painted mask will crack. But I saw it—the moment Gini entered the home, her face lit up with lines. She is so happy about this girl that she is barely fussing over Mullah Omar. She knows she has something he wants.

Sitting on the window's ledge, I turn away from their scene and stare at the long driveway filled with trees.

Since I first saw Gini, there has been a feeling in my stomach. It's a tightness that has forced me to be more often silent when I used to speak. I've tried to bury her face, but all I see are her gorgeous gray-blue eyes staring back at me in the rearview mirror. Her beautiful, strong body against mine as I carried her to her room on the evening she arrived. When she licked me, I had to swallow back my groan. Countless women have been in my bed, but none have ever elicited this level of both desire and hunger to know what exists behind the beauty. I can finally admit to myself that while I followed her into the fields that morning to keep an eye out, that was simply an excuse. I wanted to be near her. I wanted to know her, and I didn't want to let her go.

I've seen some terrible and sick things in my life, but seeing Gini lying on the ground, in the space where I used to sleep, was a kick to my gut. She thought I'd left the room, but I hadn't. I watched her speak to her family, her soft voice hanging in the dark night. I heard her tell a bedtime story, which must have been an attempt at self-soothing. I wanted to sink down beside her, hold her hand, and tell her it would be all right.

As a child living alone in the slums, I used to do similar things. I would sit inside my cardboard home and speak to my mother, who I could barely remember—and still cannot. I would imagine a conversation with her, where she told me she was out shopping for food for me to eat and would be back soon. I would speak out loud, hoping that my words would enter the universe and reach her.

I had forgotten all of that—or so I thought. But seeing Gini, it came back. Who am I? Where was I, before the gutter?

I can feel the subtle change in me. It's not even simply wanting Gini. With her arrival, certain questions, which have always been looming around my head, have set themselves front and center. I used to swallow the realities of life, whereas now, I'm wondering why it has to be this way for not only her, but for myself, as well.

I want to rage at Mullah Omar and ask, *Why are you and the other clerics the ones who decide what is right and what is wrong? Why do you decide who deserves to live and who dies? Who obtains riches and who will be thrown into the streets? Why is it the case that this life of legalized prostitution is the only option for these women?*

I have thirty-two years on this earth, and I have always known that to question the Islamic authority is to become an infidel. I have always outwardly practiced Islamic law in public, but in my heart, my belief system is filled with cracks. *How can I believe what I am not allowed to question?*

When Gini asked, "Why me?" I wanted to point to my own chest and ask the same question. *Is this the life I'm set to live from here on out, forever? And if I ever left, where would I go?* This is all I know.

Not least, Mullah Omar has a cousin who is a *marja*, a source of emulation in Twelver Shia Islam. Mullah Omar is also considered an expert in Islamic law. His political power is vast. Without a doubt, he would have me killed within minutes if I ever disobeyed him. As a direct descendent and disciple of President Rafsanjani of Iran, Mullah Omar can reach every corner of the world with just one simple decree. Amma might run the day-to-day operations of The Mansion, and I might be the man who carries out her wishes and protects the property in our home, but Mullah Omar is the man who allows our lives to run. He is the one who brings the men to our parties, sets them up with our women for mut'ah marriages, and collects a portion of payment. He is also the one who makes sure the marriages are followed by Shia Islamic law. Without him, we would cease to exist. The Mansion could never run solely on evening parties with nonreligious men.

"Thank you, Madam." Mullah Omar stands, and we quickly rise in deference. "And, Darius"—he nods—"that girl, Gini. Madam will explain what it is we need from her. She is perfect for my newest client." He claps happily. "Allah forces me to believe. Why, you ask? Because I asked him for a girl like Gini, and now, she is mine!" He claps again. "*As-salāmu ʿalaykum wa-raḥmatu-llāhi wa-barakātuh.*"

He waves to the both of us and exits.

The moment the door is closed, Amma tears off her black head covering, forcing her sharp eyes to me. "You feel bad for the poor rat, Darius? Ever since she came here, you've been quiet." Amma tilts her head to the side, dark eyes squinting in that way of hers when she's trying to read me. "Look at you, in full contemplation mode. You feel sorry for her, is that it? Taking her away from her poor village, where girls shit behind trees, and bringing her into this beautiful home?"

I can practically feel the clash of her teeth against each other. That's how hard she's clenching.

I chuckle, like I don't notice the fire that's been lit in Amma's stomach. "She is fine," I reply nonchalantly, cracking my knuckles.

"She'll do well here." My voice is steady. The last thing I need is for her to believe I have any interest in any of the girls, other than making sure they stay alive and out of harm's way.

Her eyes turn to slits. "Yes, she will do well. Mullah Omar already has someone in mind for her, but she will have to speak English. Not simple English, either. She needs to understand the nuances of the language. She is headed for Iran in the next year or so and will need to learn how to survive there. If she wants to live, she must learn." Amma exhales, smiling.

"His name is Navid Soltabian. He is richer than Croesus. He constantly travels between Iran and New York, and he needs a wife to travel with him. She must sit with him during dinners with men from other countries. She can't be a twit, either. She must be able to converse in a decent manner." She takes another sip of her coffee. "If Soltabian buys her for ninety-nine years, our home will be stronger than ever. Possibly, we will not have to be at Mullah Omar's mercy any longer. But for that to work"—she clears her throat—"Gini will need to be molded just for him. We have to do our best, Darius. The better she is, the longer the duration of the contract. If Soltabian doesn't like her, Omar will find another girl—God forbid, one who is not from our house. That would be disastrous."

I swallow hard, my mind racing. My mind roves back to Gini in the fields. Her gentle nature does not lend itself to this life. The tightness in my stomach becomes stronger.

Amma stares up at me and then away with that faraway look of hers. She shifts, straightening her shoulders. "Years ago, when I was the most sought-after tawaif in all of India, men came from all over the world to listen to me sing and watch me dance. And, of course, pay for my time. Italy loves to think about their courtesans. But those girls had nothing on me. And now, I am the queen of The Mansion." She looks me up and down with her side-eye, wanting to make sure I'm listening.

"Before you touched your first bite of meat, I made you kill and skin the animal yourself, did I not? The difference between us and the wealthy we serve is, they've weakened themselves. Prostrated themselves. They eat but do not know how the food got to their table. What would become of them without all the people they employ? They'd fall. Most of these men we know, they need our help, even with taking a woman for a night," she exclaims. "But not us. Not you and me. You and I see a problem, and we find a fix, using our own hands.

"Our girls are doing well, but not well enough in this world we live in. This new girl, she could be our answer. But"—she trains her eyes directly on me—"if it is beginning to hurt your sensibilities to see where these girls arrive from and how we get them, then maybe I've spoiled you. Are you weak, Darius?"

"I have no sensibilities, Amma. Nothing can offend me." I sit straighter, telling her what she wants to hear. I see her body tightening with my submission.

"Just don't forget where I found you," she continues, wanting to hammer home her point. "In the gutter. Dirty and racked with disease." She lifts her thin, bony chin. "I might not have had you in my womb, but don't forget how you were on death's door when I saved you. Your life is mine, Darius. And selling this girl to Soltabian is how we shall stay alive. Feeling bad for her or having any interest in her, other than ensuring her growth for that man, is a waste of your energy. For our survival, she must be kept pure and then immediately sold. If you want a plaything, the city is at your disposal. But not this girl, Darius. Let her learn and become the best. I will have Roshan teach her the arts, and you must give her the English. And you must watch her like a hawk. Do not let her out of your sight. Not even for a moment. If any of these men get any ideas, the answer is no. She will be molded for Soltabian alone."

"I have pledged allegiance to this house." I stand up, walking toward her.

A tremor moves through her hand, although her posture doesn't falter. Amma is the toughest woman in Mumbai, and she has years of emotional training under her belt to keep herself visibly strong in the face of fear. But a man well over six feet tall, with aggression in his eyes, always causes a ripple within even the strongest of souls. I fold my body down, holding the arms of her chair and bringing us face-to-face. It's becoming increasingly difficult for me to submit to this woman, but I bring myself to do it. It's what I know.

"I brought the girl here." I grit my teeth. "And I will make sure she stays here and learns everything she needs to learn. And once she is taught, she will be safe so that we can sell her for all she's worth. No one matters to me but us."

Lie, my brain says.

Amma's smile forces my eyes back to hers. She exhales her relief. Rubbing the back of my shoulders, she purrs, "That's good, Darius. I did raise a good man, didn't I?" She licks her lips while moving her hands up and down my back. Chills rise on my arms. "This exercise you're doing? It is doing well for you. I think you've grown even stronger. Make sure to see that girl again soon. Jaya, is it? And her twin sister, too? Let them help you with your stress." She smirks. "Otherwise, you can always knock on my—"

Before she can finish her sentence, I excuse myself and walk upstairs. Once in my private quarters, I lock the door. I curse Amma before picking up my phone, texting Arman. I need to walk. I need to think, have a few drinks, and get these ridiculous ideas out of my head. Before I get into the shower, Arman replies, telling me he'll be here to pick me up in thirty minutes.

The shower is hot. I lean against the wall, wishing the water would clear my head. Instead, Gini's face flashes in my mind's eye. The way she picked vegetables and cooked with so much focus. Her absolute innocence, flushing in my presence. She had no idea the life I was about to pull her into. Somehow, she trusted me.

I know my reputation is a dangerous one, and it's well deserved.

I've killed. I've abused. I've taken what isn't mine.

I've been a thief.

I've committed adultery, using women who are already married and taking them for all they are worth.

I've taken many women at one time.

I've used guns to bring fear into those around me and shot dead those who refused to listen.

I stole food when I was hungry. And even when The Mansion gave me food, I continued to steal.

I've helped to buy and sell women under the guise of religiously sanctioned prostitution. And I have told myself that it is acceptable, even while my morality tells me that it isn't so.

I know I am undeserving of love. But I want it. From Gini, I want it all.

I take a deep inhale, suddenly feeling angry. Turning off the water and wrapping a fresh towel around my waist, I say to myself, *How dare she force me to question my life!*

We all have to survive the best way we can, don't we?

I drop onto my bed and cover my face with my hands. She does not matter to me. Gini is only a woman about to be sold. She is nothing and will always be nothing to me. I must continue my life as it always has been, as it always will be. There is no other choice.

I change as quickly as I can into a black button-down shirt and dark jeans. Jogging downstairs, I leave the premises. It feels good to get out.

After I wait at the bottom of the driveway for a few minutes, Arman pulls up in his shiny, new black BMW. I get into the car without a backward glance.

"What's up?" He smiles, his crooked teeth and dimple on full display.

He's a cheeky fucker. Some of the tawaifs assume I was born in The Mansion. What they don't know is that Arman, who helps me out when the parties get too large, is the one who was actually born in one. Not in The Mansion, of course, but in one of the dingy whorehouses in Kamathipura—Mumbai's notorious red-light district. As children, we played together in the slums. He would sneak me into the brothel where his mother sold herself and give me grain from their stash. Amma never minded it; she thought it would teach me to appreciate the life we gave our girls.

I would bring Arman into our home, too—of course, where he saw what constitutes as "the good life". Still, Arman and I built forts out of garbage and cardboard, ran with crews who stole food from markets, and begged when convenient. It was a strange sort of double life.

Our paths diverted when I stayed to fulfill my destiny as the man of Madam's house and Arman was pulled into a street gang. What began as petty thievery and bootlegging turned into something bigger when he joined Devan Ibrahim's D-Company. Arman now runs operations in the Mumbai docks, where hashish is trafficked, among other black-market items.

He and I? We're tight.

"Let's get to a bar. I need a stiff drink." I lean forward before leaning back, uncomfortable in my own skin.

"You look like fucking shit, man"—he laughs—"which is saying a lot." Patting me on the back, he presses on the gas. "I already called. Aer is holding our usual table for us."

He turns up the music, and it's still not loud enough. I adjust the volume so that it's blasting, and a new song begins to play. It's "Daddy" by Blueface. The girls have been dancing to this song for the last few weeks. I roll my eyes at the lyrics, which are dirty and poetic about how women will do whatever it takes for the designer clothes and bags. My mind tells me that there is a difference between a woman who chooses a life of sex for money and a woman who is forced into it.

Then again, what do I know?

"Listen," he starts, pulling the car into a side street and parallel parking between two white cars. "I've got some good news for you. It will lift your mood." He slides his tongue over the top of his teeth—a tic he's had for years.

"Yeah?"

We get out of the car, walking to the Four Seasons Hotel. Aer, a new bar that recently opened on the hotel's rooftop, is our newest favorite place. Arman and I have been frequenting for months now.

"The Mafia Shqiptare is coming in a few months to do some business with us. Devan wants both of our crews to meet up in neutral territory—The Mansion. Just a fun night to relax everyone."

He lifts his eyebrows up and down, and I shake my head. The

girls love the *Mafia Shqiptare*. I have heard about them nonstop, ever since they came last January.

"Last time the Shqipe came to Mumbai, their boss was regrettably absent. This time"—Arman pauses—"Nico will be there." He rubs his hands together.

"What do I care about him?"

We step off the street and into the beautiful hotel, patting the two shiny golden retrievers who serve as hotel guard dogs. Why the hotel believes these sweet dogs would make good guards is anyone's guess. After waving to the hotel receptionist, we push the silver button for the elevator. It immediately opens, and we walk inside, standing with our backs against the wall.

"Oh, you'll be happy. One of the men in his crew is hoping to pick up one of your girls. They had a good time together last time they visited. He wants to buy her freedom. If Nico is comfortable with her, he'll let the union happen."

"Which girl?"

"Roshan. You know, the one with those huge eyes and even bigger tits—"

"Yes, of course. So, how much do they want to pay? Madam is going to want a pretty penny for someone as excellent as Roshan. For her freedom?" I scoff. "They'd better be ready to empty their pockets."

"Nico's crew is loaded, Darius. The Shqipe will pay any price you ask."

"Why doesn't he just sign a contract for ninety-nine years? Cheaper that way."

"These Albanians follow Islam, but they are not very extreme. Their practices are generally minimal. Anyway, they aren't interested in contractual mut'ah marriages."

I lick my bottom lip and crack my knuckles. "Better that they aren't. But Mullah Omar will still want to take a cut."

Angrily, Arman says, "Why the fuck should he? The girls are your property, not his."

The door opens to the deck, and we step out.

"And if it's not a mut'ah marriage, it's out of his domain." Arman hates Mullah Omar—always has.

The rooftop glows in neon lights with white couches and tables spread around the perimeter. And with a perfect view of Mumbai, it's a magnificent spot.

"Hello, Darius," the hostess greets, stepping away from her small podium. She is wearing a long-sleeved white jacket with a belt. She is technically covered, but I'd bet money she has nothing on beneath. "I wish you would let me know when you were coming. I would have made sure your drink was ready. Remember how I used to do that, just for you?"

She isn't a bad girl, but her desperation grates on my nerves.

Arman steps forward, clearly annoyed. "*I* called you, didn't I?"

She hisses under her breath, "Well, I didn't know you'd be with him." Arman rolls his eyes as she says, "Follow me."

"For you, they take out the fucking red carpet, eh?" Arman jokes. "Too good-looking for your own good."

I ignore the comment about my looks. I know women are interested. I used to care, and under normal circumstances, I'd flirt with the hostess. But now—and for a blue-eyed reason I don't want to think about—I don't. We sit at our usual corner table, and we immediately order our drinks.

When the waitress disappears, I turn back to him. "So, about Omar. Unfortunately, the girls he finds, he keeps. He found and paid for Roshan himself, and he sees her as his own cargo. He will want to be compensated for her leaving."

"Motherfucker," he exclaims. "I hate that dirty fuck! Selling girls under the guise of religion. If you're going to do it, do it. Don't fucking lie and hide behind Muhammad."

"I hear you, brother." I swallow the lump in my throat.

"Listen," he says, leaning forward. "Your business has potential. Cut that motherfucker Omar loose. I've been thinking about The Mansion. You know, Devan loves your girls. All of D-Company does."

"True." I think back to all the business Devan and his crew have brought to The Mansion. A lot of their work gets done there.

"Problem is, Omar has us in his back pocket. I hate it, too. But the money is too good to pass up. Madam is worried that if we cut him out, we'll fall under."

"Convince her otherwise. I can set up a meet for you with Devan. There are possibilities, my friend."

"Maybe if I had a strong partner who could bring in some cash, we wouldn't need to use Omar anymore." I raise an eyebrow, liking this idea.

"Listen." He smiles. "There are no promises. But think about how much business of ours is done on The Mansion's turf. Becoming a partner would be excellent for us. And with our money and support, The Mansion wouldn't have to be at Omar's mercy. Speak to Devan. See what can happen."

I nod, and we fall into a comfortable silence.

"So, about Roshan"—he nods—"they don't want a marriage contract. They just want to buy her outright, so they can date and maybe eventually get married. Or not. Regardless, the Albanian Mafia doesn't like other men touching what is theirs."

The drinks are given to us, and he takes a sip.

"What is he like, the boss?"

"Nico is tough as fuck. In the 1990s, with all the fighting in Kosovo, he was at the top of the Kosovo Liberation Army. When shit settled, he left to London. And using his contacts, he grew the toughest gang in the fucking world. I wouldn't fuck with that guy or his Mafia Shqiptare for anything."

"No shit." I light up a smoke, shocked to hear this from Arman. "Coming from you? They must be terrifying."

"They are. Full-on stomped on any other gang that even attempted to outrun them. And it's all Nico. The man has got brains. Money laundering all around the globe. Every politician in his back pocket. But from what I've heard, a straight shooter. Fair—in his own fucked up way."

"Yeah. Just like Omar, huh?"

Arman laughs out loud. "Cut from the same cloth? Sure."

For the first time in a while, my heart feels somewhat lighter.

Arman was right, after all. This news is definitely good. Outwardly, I tell him I'm glad we'll get the cash from the sale. Amma will be thrilled. But in my chest, relief expands. Roshan is a good girl. She deserves to be out of this life.

Arman and I spend the rest of the night laughing about dumb shit from our past. And for a little while, I relax.

5

Gini

AFTER MY MORNING chores are complete, Narmada tells me to get in the corner on my knees and not to move. "Roshan will be here shortly," she says curtly. "You're lucky she was chosen for you. Listen to every word!"

Over the last few days, I have gotten a course in cleaning the house, filling water using the sink, and cleaning the women's clothes and undergarments by hand in a special tub. Mostly, I have learned about the many cleaning methods available. Bleach and special dusters and mops. On my word, I have never seen floors shine like they do after I clean with these methods. I know that I am meant to wish for the cleaning to be over, but I do not mind it in the least. This is what I assumed I would be doing. Maybe part of me is hoping that if I do a good enough job, they will keep me as the maid.

Narmada slaps my back. "Keep your back straight, Gini. Show off your assets." She points to my breasts. "Don't curl forward as though they were an embarrassment to you. Women would give their arms for breasts like yours."

"Yes, ma'am." I drop my face, raising my back.

Suddenly, Roshan walks toward me in a long white sari. It drifts behind her, dancing at her feet. Her long black hair is loosely tied with a pink ribbon. "Stand up. Follow me."

We walk up the grand staircase, carpeted in red, and down a dim, long hallway littered with doors. She opens the fourth one on the right, gliding inside. Like a lamb with no other choice but to follow its master, I go along. There is a large and beautiful bed in the center of the room, filled with colorful pillows. A wooden desk sits on the right with glass vials and bottles in many colors.

"Makeup, creams, and perfumes," Roshan says. "I will teach you how to apply everything." A large mirror hangs above her desk. She picks up a small bottle and opens the top. "Smell."

I do as she said, bringing my nose forward. It's jasmine with a hint of rose water. The scent is beautiful, just like Roshan. She sits on the edge of her bed and pats the side, motioning for me to sit with her.

"This week will be about survival," she starts.

"Survival?"

"Yes." She nods. "There are two things you will need to learn as soon as possible. One is how to stay safe within these walls, and the other is to learn Iranian culture. The weeks after will be about learning the craft of seduction."

"Iran?"

"Oh, yes." She nods excitedly. "There is someone Mullah Omar has chosen for you. He is a very important man! You will go to Iran to live with him and travel with him. I do not know the contract duration, but God willing, it will be long. As a tawaif, you will act as a sophisticated woman who can dance, sing, and seduce. You cannot be a simple peasant. I will help you prepare for him."

"Sh-should I fear him?"

She shrugs. "The truth is, some men can be quite vicious. But do not imagine that to be possible. Assume you are going on a trip, where you will see parts of the world you never knew existed. And then, in time, you will figure out your long-term place within his life. I have always believed that if you satisfy a man's deepest desires, he will want to treat you as his queen."

"What if I don't want to learn how to become a tawaif? What if I just stay here and not go to Iran?"

She stands up and runs to shut her door, seemingly to make sure that no one overhears the conversation. "Never speak that way!" she admonishes. "Your emotions will follow your speech. If you speak happily, you will slowly begin to feel it. If you speak negatively, not only will it hurt you, but if Madam catches on, there will also be hell to pay."

"But I don't understand this life. I can't sell myself." I begin to pant, my mouth drying out. This is all too much.

She places an arm around my shoulders. "You will. You will because no other choice exists for women like us."

"There is always a choice," I reply sadly.

"Death? Death is not an option, Gini. Not when you can find a way to live a good life within the confines we've been given."

"I'm—"

She lifts an eyebrow, shutting me up. I can smell her breath, like mint.

"I came from a small village, about four hours from Mumbai, just as you did. And over time, I have come to learn that this fate that has been bestowed upon me is not so bad. In fact, it has been pleasing, too. I learned our trade. Among all the women of The Mansion, my dancing skills are the most known."

I nod my head, listening intently.

"Additionally"—she pushes her hair over her shoulder—"I have had the longest-term mut'ah marriages. I was in Iran and know all about it. The men are mostly decent. They want to have a woman of their own who is separate from the world in which they live. All you must do is make yourself lovable in the way your man needs to love. If he needs a woman to be dominant, you will become his master behind closed doors. If he wants a woman like a servant, you will bow and kiss his feet when he enters the home. The key is to figure out who he is and what he wants. Madam has told me that this Iranian man lives under strict Sharia law. Typically, when a man like that comes here to take one of us, it is because he wants a woman who, secretly, will be vocal. The women he is used to barely leave the home. He wants you because he wants something different."

"Different? But I am a simple village girl—"

"When he sees you, he will believe you to be a modern woman of the world. Before you meet him, you will learn to dance. You will speak English. You will walk and speak and move like a goddess."

I find myself laughing, although nothing about this conversation is funny. "How?"

"Because I will teach you the arts. We will make sure he goes crazy for you." She smiles. "And then the world will open. Travel. Parties. Jewels. Once you learn to see the good in him and you give him what he yearns for, he will be good to you in return."

"But what about the other parts? I know nothing of those things."

"The sexual relationship is not difficult to learn." She shrugs. "Sometimes, it is wonderful. With the right man, it can be"—she sighs—"mind-blowing."

"And with the wrong man?"

"With the wrong man, you close your eyes and imagine Darius." She giggles. "Works like a charm!"

My throat burns as I picture him. The way he touched me did, in fact, make my mind feel blown. But the idea of a different man, a man who doesn't make my heart beat? A man who isn't Darius? It sickens me.

"Let's put the stressful things aside and let me tell you what it is like when men come for one evening, for a regular party." She moves closer to where I sit. "They come here in groups, always with people from their own country. Typically, they are businessmen who are here in Mumbai for work. Religion is a nonissue. No cleric. No contracts. We put on a themed event for them. We always begin each evening with a group dance, which we learn prior to the men arriving. And then each one of us performs on our own, in a designated space, by playing an instrument or singing or simply relaxing and eating."

"Eating?"

"Oh, yes." She nods. "You would be surprised how the act of

eating can make men wild. Wait right here." She leaves the room, and a few moments later, she returns with a bowl of grapes.

Slowly, she plucks a fat purple grape off its vine and drops it into her mouth. Closing her eyes, she moans as she chews, like nothing has ever been more delicious than this tiny piece of fruit. Then, she opens her eyes, and she's back to being smiley Roshan. "See?"

"Uh-huh."

"So, the men walk around and enjoy the view of us—sometimes joining us, other times laughing between themselves and having a drink while watching. And then, if one of the men likes what he sees, you"—she pauses—"go off with him. Engage in sex."

I can feel my eyes popping wider. "Is this how it will work when the Iranian comes?"

"That's a little different." She exhales. "When men come through because of Mullah Omar, they expect us to sign a contract for nikah mut'ah marriage. It is how they feel comfortable engaging in sex with a stranger under Shia Islam. There is a duration of time written out, and money is exchanged. It's the same as a regular marriage, except there is an end point."

I nod, doing my best to follow along.

She shrugs. "Those men normally aren't allowed to drink alcohol because it's forbidden, but when they come here, they act totally free. The parties with them are actually the wildest. Mullah Omar is the one who comes with those men and acts as a cleric. Once papers are signed, he leaves. And then it's as though all bets are off. They're *crazy*."

I want to respond, but I'm in too much of a shock.

"I believe they are coming in a few months. The Iranian will likely watch you, and if he likes what he sees, things will proceed. You will sign, and then after some fun, he will take you home. At least, that's how it normally happens."

"And if he doesn't like me?"

"He will." She nods. "Remember when you first came here, Mullah Omar took ... photographs of you? Maybe you saw a flashing light or Mullah Omar lifting something that looks like this?" She lifts up a black rectangle with a clear circle on the upper right corner.

I think back, remembering my agony when flashes went off. The man with the white turban—it must be him. Chills rise on my arms. Was that what happened?

"He must have sent the pictures of you to the Iranian. With phones, like mine, it might have taken him mere seconds to show photographs of you. I would assume that he already saw you and was very happy."

"Do the photographs still exist? Do they stay like they do in books?"

She bites her lip, nodding her head.

"If he can only take me when the contract is signed, what if I refuse it? Will he not be able to take me?"

She looks at me sadly. "If Mullah Omar wants this to happen, you have no choice but to sign. If you make Mullah Omar upset ..." She lets her voice trail off. "He has a temper, Gini. A bad one. He has been known to inflict punishment on any girls he sees fit. I heard about one woman who refused to sign. Mullah Omar burned her face. It's in your best interest to find the positive in this situation. That's what I do."

"Roshan, I don't think I can handle this." I grip the sheet, worry tearing my chest apart. My mind cannot even imagine what these parties must be like.

I can feel my heart pounding. The women in my village often stressed the importance of keeping one's virginity. Once it is taken by a man, I will be soiled. A prostitute. I want to inhale, but the breath is stuck in my throat, drying out.

She takes my hand. "You are still untouched by a man, and so no one will be allowed to speak to you or touch you. The Iranian must be your first, and Darius's job will be to ensure your life and your virtue. You will not be any man's property until the contract is signed."

Slowly, I nod.

"You will shadow me, and I will teach you everything you need before leaving for Iran. During the parties, you will stand near me and watch how I speak and act with the men. Darius will always be near, making sure no man takes any liberties with you. They might touch me or grope me, but not you. You'll be safe."

"Darius is the one to keep my safety?"

"Oh, yes. He is the protector of the house. When religious men come to us, they want to do business only with a man. He scares most of the men who come here because he's so big and dangerous-looking!" She laughs out loud. "And while he is those things, he's actually the best man on earth. And have you seen his body yet?" She leans back on the bed, exhaling. Her long hair fans out around her, pink lips pursed. "Perfect. Also, he's really smart."

I find myself humming in understanding. Roshan has feelings for Darius. My stomach twists.

"He has been with Madam all his life, although it's unsure if he is her blood relative. Some say he was born in this brothel. From a tawaif who has since died."

"Oh." I lift the hem of my shirt, rubbing it back and forth between my forefinger and thumb.

I wasn't sure what I expected, but it wasn't that. Then again, he does not look Indian. Maybe, just like me, he has a tainted birthright.

"But he makes sure that each man who attends our parties acts properly. And you, as the newest girl, are prized. When I first came, he didn't let me leave his sight. I shadowed Sophia, who has since been taken by a Saudi man who lives in London. I believe he has three wives, but he is so rich that he fills his home with any number of beautiful women for pleasure."

"D-do you think she is okay?"

"Oh, sure." She nods happily. "Most men who come here are married to at least one woman. He put Sophia in her own apartment and takes care of everything. Food. Clothes. Maids. The works!"

"Wow."

"The men who come here for mut'ah marriages are extremely wealthy. But just remember, the marriage term only lasts as long as the man chooses. It could be an hour, or it could be years. Keeping him on his toes and managing his interest in you is part of what you will learn as a tawaif. The longer you stay with him, the better off you will be, and the more money you and The Mansion stand to make. Sophia lives a life of luxury. She wants to keep it that way."

"I'm sure." Although, the truth is, I'm not sure.

"Desire between you and a man will always be in your control. Remember that. And if he is kept satisfied, he will make sure you have a beautiful place to live with clothes and jewels. These men are not typical street men. They are important."

She hops up out of her bed and opens a drawer, bringing out a large black box that looks soft to the touch.

"Are you ready?" The smile on her face shines.

I am nervous, but curiosity takes the best of me. I nod.

She opens the box. It's a necklace with a gold chain and a huge circular diamond in the middle. It sparkles like nothing I have ever seen. "This is from Abdyl. He sent this for me a few weeks ago." She is so happy that she is practically vibrating. "He's part of the Mafia Shqiptare, which is the Albanian Mafia. They control the under-ground across countries, which sounds scary but he's so good to me." She sighs. "They came here to do business with some men in India and stopped at our home for some enjoyment. No mut'ah marriage. No Mullah Omar. Just pleasure. Abdyl and I hit it off that evening.

"At first, I tried to be who he wanted me to be. But then we were together in my bed. And we began to talk. Really talk. And he asked me so many questions, and for the first time in my life, I wasn't afraid to answer."

Her eyes? They sparkle.

"He held me. Loved me, even. He promised he would come back for me. He sent me a mobile, so we could stay in touch. I haven't seen him in a few months, but we've been texting constantly."

I tilt my head to the side. "Text?"

"Oh, yes." She lifts the black rectangle. "This is a mobile phone. You can make calls with it to anyone in the world. See?" She hands it to me, and I look closely, noticing a background of flowers and then lines of small squares. "There is also a camera to take photographs.

And something called text messages. You type a message and choose who you want to send it to, and then—*voilà*—it's sent!"

She is speaking Urdu, and yet I feel like I'm in some sort of alternate world.

She doesn't seem to notice my distress.

She flips her hair to the side and continues, "It was hard, at first, to type, but I've gotten good at it. And then, last week, he sent me this gift! I hope he comes back soon. And I wouldn't mind another gift, too." She giggles.

She places a warm hand on my shoulder. "In time, you'll understand that it's not so bad. Follow my lead, and I will teach you everything, just as I've been taught. If it's any consolation, Sophia—who taught me—the woman who taught her, and so on have all been taken out of this house for long-term mut'ah marriages. Life is always a pattern. They were bought, and so we shall be! And until then, we'll try to get as much as we can from these men, won't we?" She smiles wide.

I find myself nodding. "And what happens after the marriage is done? Or when we no longer hold ... appeal?"

"Let's not think about that. You're young and beautiful. Now, let's get back to work on these house details, so we can get to the arts more quickly." She hands me a notebook, opening to the first page. It's a picture of a beautiful woman, tan with long black hair. "This is Shaina. She's the one you'll have to watch out for ..."

After learning everything possible about the other girls and what I'll need to do to make sure they're comfortable during my time as the house slave, Roshan brings me to the kitchen, and we discuss the value of forks, spoons, and knives.

"I know you've been taught to scoop food with bread, but the men who come here would see you as unsophisticated if you did not use utensils."

She hands me the fork in my left hand and knife in my right, and we painstakingly go over how to hold them and then how to cut and push the food with the knife onto the fork. Once I master that, we work on how to actually get the food into my mouth. I remember

Darius eating this way. It does look graceful. Still, it is difficult. It helps to be focused on these tasks.

When we are done with that, we move on to brewing and carrying chai. She insists that I will have to learn how to hold as many as six full cups of steaming tea on top of a silver tray with my back straight.

"Making good tea is an important asset, particularly in Iran," she swears.

At first, she has me holding the platter with empty cups. They topple over again and again, but eventually, I learn the stance that enables me to keep balanced.

While she shows me how to brew the perfect pot of chai, she asks about my family. I find myself opening up, telling her about my siblings and my father. I also tell her about the herbs I used to collect. How I delivered babies.

"Does Madam know what you are able to do?"

"I don't think so."

"Well, if she does, she might find use for you. Darius gets terrible headaches from time to time. They debilitate him for days."

"Oh no." I feel the furrow in my eyebrows.

"We've tried to give him different medications, but nothing ever works."

"I'm sure I could figure something out."

A man in the village used to get blinding headaches. One of the elder women taught me special massage techniques to soothe his pain.

She puts her arm around my shoulders. "When you are contracted out of The Mansion, you will send your family so much money that they won't even know what to do with it all! With Allah's help, it shall be. Do not worry, Gini. Follow my lead."

I nod as tears stream down my face.

THAT EVENING, when the sky is dark and my head is flat on the mattress, I finally consider what life has brought me. Roshan sees herself as something special. She travels the world with men and receives expensive gifts. Because of this life, she now speaks English as well as Urdu. Apparently, Darius is the teacher, as well as the protector.

After reviewing all of the women who stay here, I notice some clear patterns. All of them are beautiful. They don't seem to be miserable or crying. They're happy enough, and they seem to be friends with each other. A sisterhood, of sorts. Roshan told me many of the women here at The Mansion were sold directly by brothers or fathers who could no longer feed them. Others, like myself, were simply stolen. Apparently, pretending to take a girl as a maid is a common ruse.

The truth is, spending time with and watching Roshan makes my agony easier to bear. She is kind and genuine and seems to have embraced this world with open arms.

Darius's face floats into my mind. We've barely spoken, but I can't remove his body or face from my vision. He is so tall and strong. Intimidating. And now, I finally know what it is he does here. It's obvious Roshan has feelings for him. Likely, all the women do.

Slowly, so slowly, to visions of Darius in my field, picking vegetables and smiling, I drift off to sleep.

MORNING COMES, and I rinse my face and hands in the cool water bucket. Walking upstairs into the kitchen, I'm set to begin my chores. I am used to labor, but I wish I could be in the fresh air. No matter how large this home is, I still feel suffocated.

Suddenly, Darius enters the kitchen. I stand tall, my back against the wall, and gaze forward. He takes a fresh apple from a basket sitting on the counter. Taking a hard, large bite and chewing, he takes a seat at the table and begins to read a newspaper. I'm not sure why I'm afraid today, but I am.

"Gini," he calls, "bring me water."

I put down my bucket and fill a glass with water from the sink, placing it beside him. Running water is quite a wonder.

Before I can turn around, he takes my wrist, keeping me beside him. "How are you?" He lowers his eyebrows, looking both genuine and serious.

"I am okay." I lick my lips, trying to force my gaze elsewhere.

He points out, "You are a terrible liar. You will need to work on that. Next time I ask how you are, say, *Fine, praise God*. This is English. You will also say, *Bi-khayr, al-Hamdu lillah*, which means the same in Arabic." He stares at me expectantly. "Repeat it."

Painstakingly, I repeat the phrase in both English and Arabic. He stops me countless times, making me repeat sounds over and over again. By the time I get it right, my face feels as though it had been lit on fire.

He shakes the paper and brings it back up to his face. I should leave his side, but I don't want to. Aadi always brought a newspaper home when he returned from Mumbai. After he and my father finished reading, I'd always read it, too. Slowly, I raise my head, hoping to catch the headline.

He growls, "What are you staring at?" He waits expectantly.

"Your paper." My voice comes out smaller than I would have hoped.

He lowers it, so I can see him. "Can you read, Gini?" He tilts his head to the side.

"Yes," I reply, stronger this time. "I wasn't able to go to school for long, but I went long enough. And then my brother would bring books home for me. I read well." I stand up taller, feeling proud of myself. "The title of the article is 'With Brutal Crackdown, Iran Is Convulsed by Worst Unrest in 40 Years'."

He might see me as a simpleton from the village, but I'm not illiterate.

"That is correct." He nods, a smile on his face.

"So," I start, gathering courage, "what happened? In Iran?" I shouldn't be informal with him, but I can't seem to help myself.

"Most recently, the problem began with a rise in gas prices. People demonstrated their anger, calling for an end of the Islamic Republic. Security opened fire on the protestors and killed them all."

"My brother told me that, once, Iran was a center of culture. But then, with the fall of Shah Pahlavi, the Islamic revolutionaries took over the country."

"Your brother is knowledgeable," he admits. "What he said is all true. There used to be nightclubs and co-educational schools for boys and girls. During the Pahlavi dynasty, women were granted the right to vote. After the revolution in the late 1970s, everything changed. The country is now governed by Sharia law. The morality police roam the streets, looking for citizens who cause infractions. For women, a veil is compulsory. It is not unknown for a woman wearing lipstick to have it removed with a razor blade. It is important to know this because Iranian men behave a certain way toward women in their country, and when you are there, you will be expected to follow suit. Publicly, that is. In private ..." He pauses, hesitating. "In private, what he will want from you is a different matter."

My heart beats. It beats so hard that I feel faint.

He continues, "When those same men—who rule the land and are entitled to four wives, plus an infinite amount of temporary partners—come to The Mansion?" He chuckles. "They are like children in a store of candy. They want to talk to the women. They want to see and touch their hair and ankles. They want to hear their voices. They want the women to have knowledge and to speak freely. They couldn't care less about reputation or appearances, which is extremely important in their homeland. The Iranian man will want to dance, sing, and drink without any constraint. This is why these men come here, Gini. Because Madam's tawaifs can do it all. So, you will learn to play both roles. Dutiful and obedient on one hand, free-spirited and knowledgeable on the other. In public, you will drop your head and bow to your husband. In private, you will act like a Western woman who reads the newspaper and drinks coffee. Now, come behind me and read above my shoulder. You should learn."

"What if I cannot manage that?"

A shadow passes over his face. "If you want to live, you will find a way. Now, come here, like I told you, and read."

I move behind him as he raises the paper.

"Come closer," he whispers.

I step forward. Shutting my eyes, I inhale his scent. He smells so fresh and clean. I reopen my eyes, thankful that he cannot see my face flushing behind him.

My mind whirs with what is to come when I hear, "Kutta!"

Shaina is by the kitchen door, her evil glare shaking me out of my trance. She stands by what I have now learned is called a refrigerator. With one long leg in front of the other, wearing nothing but a short black silken robe tied at the front with a sash, she looks impossibly gorgeous—and cruel.

"Come here!" she screams, stomping a bare foot.

I scurry to her, keeping my head down. From Roshan, I've already learned of Shaina's impossible temper and anger at being the oldest tawaif in the house. She is sour because of her circumstances, and the fury seeps from her pores. Roshan explained that after four years as a tawaif, if you are not bought for a long-term pleasure marriage, the chances of ever leaving become slimmer and slimmer. The longer you are taken by various men, the less valuable you become.

"The floor is full of grime, Kutta. Get on your knees and clean it. Now." Shaina points to a random spot on the floor.

I grab the sponge and bucket from the corner and bend down. Before I can start cleaning, I hear the grate of a chair pushing against the floor. Darius is beside me in a blink.

"Get up!" he growls, bending down to my face. "Sit down and finish that paper."

My jaw drops open as he grabs Shaina by the upper arm, dragging her to the corridor. I want to look up and tense my ears to listen, but Darius's voice is so low that I can barely catch a word.

I go back to the table and lift the paper, wanting to do exactly as he said. But I can't manage to focus on even one letter. It doesn't take long for me to give in to my curiosity and raise my face. Darius is speaking to her quite seriously. His eyes? They hold fire. She talks back, at first, in an angry whisper, but then she's silent as he begins to berate her, his voice becoming louder.

She drops her head. Apologizing? Her long hair hangs in waves down her back. She steps up to him before looking up, her eyes coy. Nails, sharp like claws, rub against his hard chest. She moves to her tiptoes, trying to get closer to his height. She is quite tall, but he is much taller.

He turns his face away from her, like he's finished. She finally exits, practically running off, and I exhale a breath I didn't know I was holding.

That is when Darius and I lock eyes. It only lasts a split second, but I felt it. His gaze has my heart pounding. I lift the paper to show him that I plan to read it. He nods and then turns away.

Suddenly, I hear Roshan clap, calling, "Ladies, it's time for dance!"

I repeat her words over and over in a whisper, trying to get accustomed to English. It sounds funny, coming from my mouth.

The women practice their dances each morning and each afternoon. Between sessions, they work on their specialties, like singing and piano. I've never watched them, but I see how flushed and exhausted they are by the end of their study.

"Come with me," Roshan states plainly, nodding. "You must watch, so you can learn. It's time."

I stand up, brushing down my brown cloth shirt, and follow her lead into an enormous, empty room. There are some large black objects in the corner on the far end. The floor is bare wood, and large mirrors are placed along the left side of the room. The girls line up in two horizontal rows with Roshan front and center. When everyone is in the right position, Roshan skips to the front of the room and touches a button on a black rectangular box. Sound blasts, and I try not to gasp.

"This is our last day to practice, so let's get it right. And you"—she points to me, not unkindly—"sit by the music box. Hit the button shaped like a square when I say stop. And hit the left button, shaped like a triangle, when I say play. If I say rewind, hit the arrow going left, and if I say go forward, hit the arrow going right."

I scurry to the front of the room and sit on the floor beside the music player. I look down, noticing the arrows. *Please don't let me mess this up!*

"Rewind!" she shouts.

I hit the backward button.

"Stop!"

I hit the square.

"Quick learner! Good job."

Some girls chuckle, and the others shrug. Shaina glares at me as though she had just smelled something awful.

"Now, play!"

The song begins. It's in a language I've never heard. It has a deep, beautiful beat. I think I recognize some of the instruments, but before I can think on it, the girls start to move in perfect tandem. My jaw drops open as I watch this dance. It's sexy and slow, both proper and incredibly improper. Something in the look in their eyes as they move. Each girl brings a uniqueness to the dance, and it's astounding. Again and again, I'm told to rewind, stop, and play. They practice the dance until I am sure they can do it in their sleep.

After the song is completed, a new song begins. This one is also foreign. Each girl now does a solo dance, taking up portions of the song. This section is a lot sexier than the previous. The moves are slower, and the women are sultrier, if that is even possible. I handle the music to the best of my ability, not wanting to anger anyone. After maybe the fiftieth time of playing the song, I see a large figure entering the far end of the room. Darius. I just saw him not too long ago, but that doesn't stop my heart from soaring at the sight of him.

I swallow hard as he steps forward, commanding the entire space and shrinking it with his presence.

Roshan yells, "Stop!"

With a shaking finger, I press the square. Darius walks up to her, saying words I cannot hear.

Smiling and breathless, she seems to ask him if he wants to dance with her. He replies, and I hear the word exercise.

"Please, just for a few minutes? We love when you join us." She turns to me without giving him a chance to respond, yelling, "Play!"

I push the button, and the music starts. The girls dance as they have been, in perfect sync. But this time, Darius is here. He changes everything. His muscles flex as he lifts Roshan, and she slides from his waist, downward, her body pressed against his until she's on her knees before him. Suddenly, she pops up with the music, twirling as his hands move to her behind, sliding across her slim hips. His hands are so large that they surround her entire waist. Roshan spins around again and again before dropping down to the ground, this time into a perfect split.

I gasp because I can't help it. Luckily, no one notices or hears. I've seen beautiful dancing. But this? This is something else entirely.

She rises, and their chests touch. His eyes stare directly at hers. I can't help but touch my own chest with my hand. Darius and Roshan are mere inches apart, seemingly so entwined that even their breathing is in sync. I feel a pressure tugging into my soul. Watching this is ... hurting me. *Is there something between them?* They are perfect together.

I look down at my own brown clothes, the sack for potatoes. Where I grew up, these differences between people were never possible. We all wore the same clothes. We slept in similar homes. We farmed. We worked. We helped each other. But here is a true hierarchy, like animals. And I'm at the lowest rung.

The song finishes. My breaths are labored, as though I were the one who had been dancing.

"Good work, Roshan." Darius gives her a small nod with his head and moves to the corner of the room, not far from where I sit with the music machine.

The ladies pause to drink some water. My gaze follows Darius, noticing a silver bar across the doorway and a blue mat on the floor. He jumps up, both hands holding the bar so his legs dangle an inch off the ground. Crossing his legs together, he pulls up until his chest is in the middle of the bar, his back and arms flexing with the movement, and then he brings himself down again. After a few minutes, he jumps down to the mat on the ground, pushing himself off the floor with his hands and then lowering himself.

Roshan comes next to me. "He's something, huh? Those are pull-ups and push-ups. Darius does a lot of exercise."

I can't even respond. It's physically hard to do anything but watch.

"He's a good man. An incredibly handsome one, too. But you must stay away. Falling for Darius is a very bad idea." She looks at me pointedly.

"He is a good dancer."

She nods. "Oh, yes. He has been dancing for years, which is why he is so good. Practice makes perfect. Speaking of which, let's do the dance a few more times."

"Yes, Roshan."

The girls continue the dance, doing it over and over again until a bell rings.

"Finally, lunch!" one of the ladies exclaims.

Roshan waves me over to follow her. She tells me to go into the kitchen to help the staff as she and the other women enter the dining room.

I scurry into the kitchen.

"Take one of the pots into the dining room," one of the maids says.

Before I can take hold of the handles, Darius materializes out of nowhere, putting out his hand and saying, "No."

I step back, shocked. *When did he come in here?*

"These handles will burn your hands. They are extremely hot." He pulls out two rags from a drawer, handing them to me.

My heart starts to pound as something like defiance rises into my chest. "My hands can handle the heat. I'm not delicate, Darius. I used to do field work. Cooking, too! You remember when you came into my home?" I want to kill him right now for bringing me into this world.

His eyes fill with surprise at my outburst and then flash in such a way that I can hardly breathe. It's not anger though. I can feel the look shoot straight through my bloodstream. I felt this heat from him the first time we met. It's arousal.

"Your hands can no longer show your past as a laborer." His voice is rough but kind. He continues, lifting my hand in his and staring at my palm, "Calluses and burns are not for a woman like you. You are no longer a village girl, Gini. Your skin should not show traces of sun and work. You need to look like a kept woman." He gently lets go before giving me the rags again.

He is being decent. I use them to lift the pot.

He nods. "Better."

I swallow, my bravado from a moment ago gone.

After lunch is served, the ladies eat, and then a huge screen lights up.

Roshan calls me over to her, whispering that it is called a television. "The news in the world is oftentimes very important. When certain groups of men arrive, the ladies must know what it is they are going through in their countries. If there is a war brewing, the men want a specific type of woman. And when things are peaceful, they might be interested in another type. Darius makes sure we watch at least a few times a week. And read. Oh, he's always making us read."

"Oh," I whisper, turning toward her.

I stare at this television in a trance when Madam walks into the room.

"Kutta!" she yells, her shoes clicking against the floor. "Get on your knees. You are not equal to Roshan to stand beside her." The entire room takes a collective turn, staring at me. "This television isn't for you to watch. If you are finished serving, you sit, as you've been told to sit. Do you suffer from memory loss?"

I can hear Shaina's laughter as I drop downward.

"Actually," Madam says, "take your shirt off." She crosses her arms in front of her chest.

I look up at Roshan, but she immediately averts her eyes.

"You will need to learn to be less bashful. Now is a good time. In this house, nudity is normal. It's time for you to get used to that."

Her face is frozen in its mask, but mine must be betraying me. Fear and embarrassment course through every inch of my body.

"Now," she whispers, close to my face, low and dark.

I look up, sweat pouring from my temples as I shiver. I pull the cloth around my body tighter as a sense of impotence barges into my chest. Darius is here, leaning against the wall. His face is hard, jaw clenched. I can't undress. I can't, not in front of him! Girls are chuckling, and Shaina shrugs, like I'm getting my due. I hear a door open and watch Darius exit the room. Sparing me?

"Now!" Madam yells, slapping me across the face. She grabs the back of my hair, pulling until my head snaps back. "I will make you sleep in a ditch. You are my property, do you understand? When I tell you to get naked, you strip. When I tell you to watch one of the women suck a cock, you'll do that, too. Every word of mine is your command. Do you hear me? Now, take off your shirt!"

With shaking fingers, I lift it above my head. My nipples instantly turn cold, peaking. The cool air rushes over me, and I want to die. There is no way I can stay in this home. I refuse. I will play their game for as long as necessary, and then I will find a way out of here. The thought of running has me raising my chin. I stare forward. I imagine blades of grass against my feet and the air so fresh. Which vegetables are ready to be picked? I think about my father and his *come sit with me* smile. Cooking beside my neighbors. My siblings—I miss them so much. My memories are untouchable. I swear that I will find a way to freedom. Roshan is kind, and I'm glad she has made this life work for her. But she is not me.

Roshan clears her throat, and I glance at her.

You're okay, she mouths. It's not a question, but a statement meant to strengthen me.

I will miss her. Never have I had a friend outside of my family. She is different. With Roshan, I laugh.

"I'm okay," I reply, slightly nodding.

There is a new strength inside me, the likes of which I've never known. I will not accept this fate. The moment Madam steps away from me, I cover my breasts with an arm and sink lower, hoping my privacy is not seen.

From the front of the room, Madam calls out, "Continue watching the news, ladies. The Albanians are coming soon, and I want everyone's English to be clear. Your newest dance is ready, I assume."

A cheer goes through the room, and Roshan drops her head, an enormous smile filling her face. She is excited.

Finally, the women quiet down, watching the English news channel.

I glance around the room, relieved to see that all the women are enraptured. My nudity isn't an issue. It is more about the degradation of me than seeing my skin. I exhale, covering my nudity with both arms. I won't let them win.

6

Darius

ENTERING one of the brothels set in Kamathipura, I scan the girls, who each sit in their own square concrete stall with a dirty, old cot in the center. I find one woman on her knees before a fat man, who looks more like a pig than a human. He grips her long hair in his hand, moaning. I try to look away from the scene. It disgusts me more than I would like to admit. I want to cover my nose, but I won't shame these girls any worse than their circumstances already do.

As I walk, some women glance at me, baring themselves in an attempt to entice. Full breasts dangle low. Others fearfully press themselves against the gray concrete wall, trying to hide. Divya brings me to the last stall, where a tiny girl sits, huddled in a corner, her knees up to her chest and head downcast.

"Her family is all dead. One of our boys found her alone, sleeping inside the trash. Pretty, huh? She is still a virgin. I checked."

I swallow hard. She looks emaciated and frightened with nothing but a dirty black skirt hanging on her tiny waist.

"How old?"

"You think I know? I doubt she even knows!" She swats a fly from her face. "Listen, enough small talk. Are you going to buy her or not? I'm sure that your righteous mullah would love this one. We can easily say she's nine, if you want to use her for one of those mut'ah marriages. She's very thin."

"Do you think she's even nine?"

"What do I look like, an oracle reader?"

I give her a glare, and she rolls her eyes, laughing like this is a joke. I have known Divya since I was just a child. She isn't a bad woman, but she does what she must. The world isn't ideal, but it's what we have been given.

Many years ago, Divya and I made a deal. She promised that when she found a diamond, she would call me. In return, I agreed to pay her a pretty sum. I've made this agreement with most of the brothels in the red-light district. They are more than happy to take my money. After all, the men who frequent these types of establishments are not exactly picky. The brothels make more money selling a girl to me than if they were to sell her to men. No matter how beautiful, a woman here will never command more than a few rupees.

One might imagine a competition between us all, but Indians are not this way. Most of us are simply trying to be the best we can be with what the heavens have bestowed upon us.

"All right, Darius. How about you give me a small kiss, eh? Otherwise, I'll tell people how you come here like that Robin Pood character, and they will all know you are not as hellish as you want them to believe." She smiles a semi-toothless grin, bobbing her head from side to side.

"You mean, Robin Hood?" I try not to laugh.

"Kiss!" she demands, tapping her round cheek.

Allah, give me strength. I bend down, kissing her. She smells like raw onions and sweat.

"Take as long as you need," she calls, leaving me and the girl alone.

I get down on my haunches, careful not to get too close. "Do not be afraid, dove. Tell me, what is your name?"

She presses her stomach against the wall, keeping her face and body away from me.

"I will not touch you." I raise my hands up, and she finally turns her head, giving me a sidelong glance.

From her side alone, I can tell she will be a beauty. Her nose is straight and sits between large, oval-shaped brown eyes.

"There is another house. You will be safer there."

"Safer?" Her voice is so small that I wonder if maybe she has less than nine years.

I take a step closer. "Yes. I am there. I will make sure you are fed. Clothed. Have a place to sleep that is cleaner than this. Fresh water to drink. You can start out as a maid. Would you like that?"

She nods, nervously biting a fingernail before turning her back completely to me. I can see the outline of her spine beneath tanned skin.

"You will clean, mend, and learn to cook. The women will also teach you how to dance and sing. When it is time, you will become a tawaif. Do you know what that is—to be a tawaif?"

She shakes her head, and her long black hair sways down her back.

"A tawaif is a woman who caters to men. She entertains them by singing and dancing, among other things." There's no reason to give her the dirty details now. Not when those parts won't happen to her for a few years yet. "Now, tell me"—I move closer—"what is your name?"

"Aisha." Her voice is truly like a baby's.

It sickens me to think what a man might do to her.

"Do you know who Aisha was?" I smile, trying to keep my tone gentle. "She was the third and youngest wife of Muhammad. She was intelligent and spread his word to the people. She was praised for her vast knowledge in medicine and poetry. Maybe you will be like her, is that right?" I press my lips together, hoping her family was Islamic. It's always easier when a girl already believes the Word.

Aisha nods, finally pivoting and turning her face to mine. Covering her bare chest by wrapping her arms around herself, she graces me with a tentative smile. Immediately, I notice a missing front tooth.

"When did you lose it?" I point to mine. Teeth can tell a lot about age.

Hesitant, she says, "At first, it was loose. I bit an onion, and it fell out of my mouth." Tears fall from her eyes.

"Was it a small tooth that fell?"

Hiccuping, she nods.

"Don't fret. It will grow back. Will you come with me?"

After a few moments, she looks around at her surroundings. A woman moans loudly from the stall beside hers, and she seems to notice that anything is better than here. "Yes."

"Just give me a moment, little dove. I will return."

I find Divya by the front door and hand her the cash payment. I could bargain, but for some reason, I don't want to. She happily takes it, counting bills like she's hit the jackpot.

Grumbling, I say, "Give me something for the girl to wear."

"She is barely developed. Nipples like grapes. Who cares if she has a shirt?" She pushes the wad of bills between her heavy, sweaty breasts.

"I care." I clench my teeth and rub the back of my head. I feel a headache coming on.

She must notice my irritation because she stops arguing and leaves to walk upstairs. The steps are so old and weak. It's a miracle they haven't collapsed beneath her weight.

I step outside and lean against the ramshackle house, taking out a cigarette to smoke. I haven't had a headache in a few months. The pounding in the back of my head usually means I have a day or so before the pain becomes a full-blown migraine. Until then, I have things I should take care of. I need to review the books one more time this month.

By the time my smoke is finished, Divya returns with an old blue T-shirt. "It's torn, but you can wrap it around her." She hands it to me before saying, "Now, give me one of your fancy cigarettes. My throat is dry."

I throw the tiny cloth over my shoulder before holding up my pack for her. It's so hot today. The sun pounds against our faces.

"And one more kiss?" She tilts her head as I light her up.

"Only one kiss per diamond you find, Divya." I light up a second cigarette for myself and blow the smoke upward as she puffs.

"You're too handsome for this, Darius. Bollywood wouldn't be good enough for you. You can go to Hollywood!" She happily shakes her head from side to side.

"Anything else I should know, Divya? About the girl."

She purses her lips, annoyed that I'm not flirting back. "Yes. She is hungry. I gave her some food yesterday, but she refused."

"And today?"

"What about today?"

"Did you offer her food today?"

"I didn't! She said no the first time. I'm not going to insist. What am I, her mother?" She laughs jokingly.

I throw the half-smoked cigarette onto the dusty floor and turn around, heading to the stall to find Aisha. "Stand up, dove, and turn around."

She does as I said. I wrap the shirt around her tiny chest and neck, ensuring that she is covered. When she turns back around, I put out my hand. She takes it, shaking like a leaf, but she walks out with me into the daylight.

I buy her a vada pav and cola from a vendor a few paces from the brothel. When I hand the food to her, she looks uncertain.

"Go ahead. It is potato, bread, and pepper. The drink is—"

She quickly takes it from me, as though fearful I will change my mind. Within four bites, the food is finished. I pop the top of the soda, and she grabs it from my hand. She drinks it down in a few long, deep swallows. When she is done, she lets out a long burp with a smile.

I tell her, "Let us go now."

She looks up at me in a daze, the black grime on her face more obvious in the sunlight. "W-will you tell me more about Aisha?"

And so I do. I tell her about all of the kindness and intelligence Aisha possessed.

When we get home, I hand her to Amma, who immediately screams for Narmada to come to the kitchen.

Pointing to the young girl, Amma makes her expectations known. "You will clean the house and serve the women. In a few years, we will train you to become a tawaif. But only if you grow as beautiful as it seems you will be. Otherwise, you will stay as a maid. But remember this"—she clicks her tongue, lifting a finger in the air—"if you are bad, if you steal, if you try to touch what isn't yours, if you grow ugly, if you are stupid and cannot learn, Darius will send you back to the hole you came from."

Aisha bows her head, legs quaking. Within minutes, Narmada swoops in and takes her out of our sights.

"I love when they come so young." Amma smiles. "Much easier to mold when they grow up in our life, understanding the rules."

I nod, relieved that Aisha will now live in relative safety.

Opening up the refrigerator, I pour myself a glass of fresh orange juice. Narmada is tough, but she makes the sweetest fruit juice. I lean back against the counter as some of the girls walk in. Shaina is with them in her signature short black silk robe. She tightens it, showing off the slight curve of her waist, before saying hello to me.

"My French has been getting weaker," she whines. "How about we do some more lessons?"

"Your French is fine, Shaina." I blink a few times, feeling a pulse in the back of my head. I grit my teeth, noticing the pace of my headache is increasing. This is always how it starts.

Unfortunately, Shaina doesn't get the memo that I'm not in the mood to speak. When migraines overtake me, I wind up in bed for days with a cold compress over my eyes and the blinds drawn. The pain is unspeakable. Hearing her voice is making it worse.

"I'm not so sure you're right, Darius," she flirts, glancing up. "The group lessons we do just aren't enough."

Shaina is a beautiful girl, but unfortunately for her, her blatant sex appeal landed her as the one who performs acts onstage during parties, in front of all to see. The first time Amma decided to add live sex to our shows, we were both hesitant. But this was what the important brothels were doing throughout Germany, and Amma isn't one to be left behind. Because of this designation, Shaina is never requested for mut'ah marriage or anything that lasts longer than a night or two. But she definitely adds excitement. Ever since she began fucking onstage, we've had more repeat clients than ever. What can I say? Extreme sells.

I'm not sure how much longer I can stand here. She blinks up at me, waiting for me to reply. But I can't speak without increasing the pain. I've learned that gritting my teeth makes it worse, but it's hard to stop. At this point, even worse than the throbbing is the fear of what is to come. Sweat beads at my temples.

She presses, still not getting it, "How about a movie maybe? In French?"

I momentarily look up at the ceiling. My level of annoyance is reaching a breaking point. When I bring my gaze downward, I see Gini on all fours, scrubbing the floor. For weeks now, I've watched her work. She's considered the house dog until she earns her stripes as a tawaif, and the girls work her like their personal slave. But in this moment, seeing her on her hands and knees, it's twisting my gut. It's beneath her, and I can't stand to see it.

"Gini," I call out, not too loudly. "Stand up and stop cleaning."

Slowly, she rises, turning to me before bowing her head. I want to pull her against me and tell the other women to get the fuck out of the room. But I can't speak. I can barely move. She raises her eyes and my gaze locks on hers. Yearning builds in my chest like a storm.

"Cleaning is done." The words hurt, but they have to be said. This is way out of my bounds, but fuck that.

The girls start murmuring.

"What. Are. You. Complaining. About?" I punctuate my words,

not as a fear tactic, but because speaking in full sentences at this point has become impossible. I've got to get up to my room.

"Well, we need her to mend our clothes," Shaina starts. "And my toilet needs to be washed. All of ours do."

"No," I whisper darkly.

Her face turns red as she turns to Gini. "The toilets are your job, Kutta. I want to see my bowl sparkling tomorrow." With gritted teeth, she makes an exit.

The other girls awkwardly look between Gini and me before following Shaina out of the kitchen.

"Darius, why—"

I drop my head, inhaling and holding in my breath as I grip on to the table. My headache is now a legitimate pound. Spots dot my vision.

I feel a soft hand at my back.

"A-are you okay? Are you about to be sick? Come, let's go to the toilet."

I want to push her away, but my head spins. I can barely walk. She lets me lean on her, and slowly, we make our way to the bathroom.

As I drop to my knees, I manage to scream, "Get out!"

She hesitates for only a moment before leaving. Immediately, I throw up, the acid burning my insides. Black spots dot my vision.

Fuuuck. I rest my head against the toilet.

Seconds pass. Minutes maybe.

I have to get upstairs.

And then the door slowly opens.

"Darius?" Her voice is so quiet, like a gentle whisper. Her hands glide to my back. "I used to gather herbs in my village. I was training under one of the village women to be a doctor."

I close my eyes, the pain radiating through my temples.

"You are having a bad headache, yes? Roshan mentioned to me that you suffer from migraines. I will tell her the herbs I need, so I can combine them for you. They will help. But until then, let me bring you to your bed."

She takes me by the middle, and with a strength I'm shocked to see she possesses, she lifts me up. Together, we walk upstairs. I crawl on all fours into my sheets.

"Cold wa-washcloth," I manage to spit out.

I hate that she's seeing me like this, but there's nothing I can do.

She flutters around the bedroom, closing the curtains. Although my eyes are shut, I can see the darkness overtake the room. It's a minor relief. I hear the water turn on. Finally, she comes back, putting the cold cloth over my eyes. I feel her fingers at the top of my jeans, unbuttoning before sliding them down my legs. Years ago, I was knifed in the arm while trying to take a girl from one of the gangs. Right now, it's like I've been slashed behind my eyes.

Her hands find the top of my head, and she presses downward, massaging. I want to fight it—tell her not to touch me, that I don't need the help—but I can't. It feels too good. Her fingers settle into different spots around my face and scalp, and the nausea and pain slowly numb. My eyes flash open when she presses against my temples. Somehow, my pain has quieted.

I exhale in relief, "My God."

"There we go, Darius." Her voice is a melody. "I'm glad you're so responsive to massage. This is a good thing."

"Don't leave." I want to cry at her feet.

How she knows to do this is anyone's guess.

She lets go of my head, and I momentarily panic.

She takes my hand. "I'm not leaving you. Trust me."

Her fingers find the soles of my bare feet. It's as though there were an invisible line between my body parts because the pounding in my head lessens even more. The pain is still there, but the slamming has stopped. She moves between my head and my feet, a rhythm so soothing that I could sleep from the relief. She gets up, and I grab at her wrist. With this cloth over my eyes, all I can see is her outline. But there is no way I'm letting her go. Not when she's the answer to my pain.

"Another cold compress, Darius."

She comes back, replacing the cloth I have with a much colder one. It feels so good.

I'm in and out of sleep, but each time I open my eyes, I can see Gini's outline. She's at my feet now, rubbing and pressing. Taking care of me in a way I've never known. A shiver runs through me.

Eventually, I have the strength to take the compress off my face. Her hands must be exhausted.

"Gini," I whisper, pulling her closer. I do not know what I'm doing, but my body has its own ideas.

She fits herself into the crook of my chest, right beneath my chin, and for the first time in my life, I feel a complete satisfaction. Like I'm exactly where I was always meant to be. And it isn't this room. And it isn't this bed. It's the girl.

Her body is rigid, at first, but slowly, she softens. A tenderness hits me as I inhale her. She fits so perfectly at my side, her legs between mine.

We lie together for a while in silence.

"Thank you," I croak. I lift her hand, splaying it across my chest. *How many more ways can I connect us?*

"I will make you a special medicine. Whenever you feel the pain in your head beginning, you must take it."

I listen to her voice. Look at her body and her face. I need to tell her to leave, so I can get a rein on my feelings. *What has she done to me?*

"Darius?" She tilts her head to the side, her fingers moving to brush my hair aside. "What is it you want to say? You keep opening and then closing your mouth."

I clear my throat, finding it impossible to stop this force between us. I bring her face to mine, kissing her forehead. She lets out a soft exhale.

I whisper, "Look at you," and kiss her eyes. "Gini, my beautiful girl. You saved me. The pain I feel from the headaches."

"I'm so sorry you feel it. But I will help you, for as long as I can."

I chuckle sadly, unsure of how long that is.

Her eyes flit to the ceiling. "I heard you are to teach me English soon."

Her words hit me like a gunshot. It's reality.

"Yes. Soon."

"Why English, if you plan to send me to Iran?"

"English is considered an international language." I shuffle to sit up, keeping her at my side. What we're doing right now shouldn't be happening, but I can't let her go. Not yet. "Many men come here from various countries. It would be too complicated to learn all of their languages. I will teach you basic phrases you will need in Arabic and Farsi, but English is the primary concern. After you master it, we can move on to others."

"You speak many languages, Darius?"

I nod. "I can speak seven."

"Seven?" she repeats, her eyes practically popping.

I smile. "Yes. Urdu. English. Arabic. Farsi. French. Spanish. Italian."

"How?"

"Languages just come very easily to me. They always have."

She licks her lips. "The women watch television in English, yes?"

"Exactly. They watch the news and different shows to keep them fluent."

She should leave. My headache has settled. There's no reason for her to stay.

"Do you think you can handle bathing?" She swallows hard. "Some cool water on your wrists might help. And don't eat anything with heat. Only cool foods for the next few days. Cucumbers and watermelon."

I nod. "Okay."

Her gaze takes in every inch of my face. I finally look down, noticing I'm in nothing but my underwear and a white T-shirt. When I'm sick and Amma comes in to help me, she has never once done anything to make me more comfortable. She just walks in and out, changing the cloth over my eyes and telling me to be a man and get a grip. In the past, I've stayed in this darkened room for days, begging any god who would listen to take my pain away. It isn't until now that I notice I've never been taken care of. Not ever. Not until now.

"When did you first begin getting the headaches?"

"It started when I was a child. But they've gotten worse." I notice she is no longer flush against me, her hands no longer on my chest. "Shh." I pull her back into my side, forcing our bodies to meld. "Don't move."

Time passes with us just like this.

How much time do we have before she leaves? Days? Months? I swallow hard, my throat drying.

"Darius," she whispers, "tell me how you ended up here. Some of the girls say Madam is your mother. But I don't believe that." Her fingers gently caress my neck.

The memories hit me like a current.

"I'll tell you."

And the truth is, right now, I would tell her anything.

"*Are you an angel?*"

She was the most beautiful thing I had ever seen. With her white hair and skin like pale cream, never had I seen a human look as she did.

She looked at my shirtless torso, her mouth turned downward. "You are so thin. But I can see your skeleton is heavy. You will be a strong man one day. If you come with me, I will feed you."

"I can't leave," I told her, looking around. "My mother and father are here." I always used this line just to be safe; saying I was alone could get me killed.

I couldn't remember my parents, but the elders had told me that I came from two people—a man and woman.

"Your mother and father?" She laughed loudly, like I had told her a funny joke. "We both know you have no father or mother. But"—she lifted a beautiful finger, nail painted red, like blood—"in The Mansion is safety. Would you like a life with baths, clean water, and food? Where I live, there is water running all the time. Unless"—she paused, her eyes getting small —"you would rather one of the crews cut off your hands and turn you into a beggar?"

I looked at my hands, caked with dirt. I had friends who, for the promise of bread, had left with men who chopped their fingers or blinded their eyes, just as this woman had said. I moved my arms behind my back, knotting my hands together.

That will never happen to me!

"No, I am not coming."

"Hmm, maybe I can change your mind."

"H-how did you find me?"

"I found you like I find everyone who comes into The Mansion. I heard of you. A handsome boy roaming the slums, tall and strong with hair like a raven. The children follow him around, they said. A leader." She smiles. "There will be food. And a place to sleep. And a roof that does not leak. Safety."

"Are you rich?"

I tilted my head to the side, noticing stones in her ears that sparkled. Her sari was a color I'd never seen before, similar to red but softer.

"Oh, yes." She smiled, white teeth glowing. Putting her hand in her pocket, she pulled out a dark brown square. "This is called chocolate. It's a special candy. Take it and eat it."

I took it from her hand and felt its weight. Bringing it to my nose, I smelled. Sweet. Finally, I licked it. It was ... delicious.

"Tell me this, boy, if there are seven birds in the tree and three of them fly off, how many are left?"

"Four birds."

"That is correct. If there are four cars in my driveway, how many wheels are there in total?"

"Sixteen." I put the chocolate in my mouth. It melted on my tongue. I had to shut my eyes for a moment. That was how good it was. When I finally opened my eyes, I saw the woman smiling. "Do you have more?"

"There is only one small task that you must complete. If you want to come to my home, you must find the prettiest girl you know and bring her to me now."

"I know someone," I told her excitedly, thinking about Aabha. She, too, lived without parents, just like me. And she was beautiful.

"I will wait. Now, hurry along!"

I ran out, my bare feet used to the pebbled, dirt floor. I skipped over *trash and ran through the rows of small cardboard houses with their silver roofs shining beneath the sun, and a smile stretched across my face.*

A mansion and food! I've gotten lucky!

I found Aabha and called to her, quickly telling her about the angel with white hair who wanted to save us.

"Are you sure?" she asked, biting her lip. "What if she wants to hurt us?"

"Oh, no. She is too beautiful to be mean!"

Excitedly, Aabha picked up her favorite doll, perfect if not for her missing arm, and ran with me. We laughed together, as we always did, skipping across muddy puddles.

The lady was just where I'd left her but standing to her full height. Both of us stopped in front of her in awe.

"Let me see you."

Aabha stood straight, her huge eyes blinking in curiosity.

"Turn around. Shake each leg and each arm. I want to make sure they work."

Aabha listened, showing off her strong limbs.

"Teeth?"

Aabha opened her mouth, and the woman looked inside.

"Do you see, boy?" The woman held Aabha in her hands. "This girl you brought me is good and strong. When you live with me, you will have to find girls just like her and bring them to me. Understand?"

I nodded my head, not seeing why that should be too hard. I knew most of the girls here.

"That's a good boy. Tell me, what do you call yourself?"

"Darius."

"Hmm." She smiled approvingly. "You know, Darius was a Persian king."

"Yes, one of the men told me. One day, I want to be a king and rule the world."

She laughed. "That might come to pass. How many years do you have?"

I shrug. "Enough. Don't you want to see my arms and teeth?"

"Sure I do." She smiled.

I showed her my bicep, and she felt it with her fingers.

"Very nice. You will be big and strong one day, and I will need a man by my side. Unfortunately, in this world, a woman needs a man to stand with her. A king."

"I can be king!" I exclaimed.

"Not yet. But one day, you will be. Until then, you shall be my son. Would you like that?"

I stood tall, unsure. Still, I liked what she was offering. And I had been without a mother for so, so long.

"Okay." I nodded. "What shall I call you?"

"Amma."

"Amma," I repeated. Mother.

"OH, DARIUS."

I feel wetness gathering on my chest.

"Don't feel bad for me. It was the path written for me." I close my eyes, feeling exhausted and yet, somehow, relieved.

Arman knows my history, and so does Amma. But neither of them is Gini.

"Your headaches will get better. Do you need more massage?"

"Maybe. But you should rest now." I sink deeper into the mattress. "The first time I saw you, Gini ... I knew it."

"What did you know?"

"How good you'd be. Sweet. Your skin has a special glow. Your eyes, guileless."

"I have a good father," she says. "He's a decent man."

I push the hair out of her face. She responds with a look—a yearning mixed with sadness. I want to comfort her. Take care of her the way she did me. My brain tells me this shouldn't be happening. But I refuse to listen to the warnings.

"Gini," I rasp, "your inside is so incredibly beautiful."

She replies by curling deeper into me, and at once, I feel peace.

"You are ..." She doesn't complete her sentence.

A warmth settles between us. Like the sun.

Time passes. I can't tell what's happening outside of this room, and I wish I didn't ever have to. In this bed, with this woman, it's like the earth has stopped shifting. Amma. Omar. The girls here, spending all of their hours learning how to be more desirable to men. The girls who are starving in the slums. Selling them. Collecting money. The cycle. They all stop turning, and all there is, is Gini.

Eventually, she asks, "What will the women say since I'm not cleaning for them today?"

"They will say nothing. None of them would dare." Another kiss on her head. My eyes adjust to the darkness. I want to keep them open. I don't want to miss a moment because I know that none of it can last.

She swallows hard, saying a million things with her silence. I catch them all, *feeling* them all. She wants out of this place. She's afraid of the women and the life.

The truth? She should be.

She's leaving soon enough ... unless, somehow, I can find a way to stop it.

7

Gini

THE SOUND of a knock on my door makes me jump off the floor. My heart skips as he comes into view. He's wearing his usual outfit of low, loose jeans and a white T-shirt. His hair looks wet and darker than usual, wrapped up in a neat bun. He must have just washed.

I press my lips together, wondering what he's doing here. Over the last few weeks since the headache, I have seen him all over the house. But whenever we get too close, he dismisses me or walks away, like he wants to forget what we shared. I've begun to avoid him, too. Partly because I'm afraid of him and the closeness we have, and partly because he's too glorious to stare at for too long.

Seeing him here now, in front of me, I realize how much I've missed his voice. I quickly brush out my hair with my fingers, tucking the front behind my ears. I bow my head.

"Don't lower your face from me." His voice is stern as he crosses his arms over his thick chest, muscles heavy.

I curse the fact that my mouth is drying, watching him. This is a different side to Darius than the one I took care of just a few weeks ago. This is the man who people fear. *What has changed?*

"Let's sit together. It's time to learn English." He lifts a black bag up. "Language books and also an Urdu-English dictionary for translation." Opening the zipper, he pulls out the books.

Sitting on the floor so his long legs are stretched before him, he leans back against the wall, seemingly waiting for me to sit beside him. From a yellow folder, he pulls out a sheet that looks like it might be the alphabet, along with a stack of papers, blank if not for lines.

I bring myself down to the floor. There is a small amount of space between our legs.

"Here is the letter *A*." He points to the letter with two lines forming a vertical peak and a horizontal line connecting them. "As you copy the letters, say the letter you are writing—*ei*—and add its sound. Do it below mine, so you can make sure they match."

I hold the pencil, unmoving. *Is he going to mention what happened between us?*

After he felt better, we held each other for almost the entire night. Eventually, he brought me back downstairs, placing me on my mattress outside. I pretended not to notice, but I saw him watching me from his bedroom window. For how long he stood there, I do not know.

"Well? Begin."

One by one, I copy each letter of the English alphabet. I listen to the sounds he makes and repeat them, doing my best to write as he does. The letters are a bit easier for me to write than to speak. I remember when my teachers would compliment me on my pencil grip. I smile from the memory.

"You are doing well. We will go through the entire alphabet just like this, and after I leave, you should continue on your own. Just keep the light on until you are finished. Soon, you will be able to put sounds together and read. After that, we will move to conversational English."

He's so learned.

"How do you know how to speak and write English?" I tilt my head to the side, curious.

He exhales, as though questioning whether or not he should

speak. After licking his lips, he begins, "There was once an American woman, Claire, traveling around the Middle East when she found herself in love with a man from Iraq. After weeks of dating in secret, he asked if she would marry him. Her money was running out, and he told her he would take care of her. She thought the whirlwind romance was dreamy." He chuckles and shakes his head, a sneer forming on his face. "Within a week, they were officially married by a cleric."

"Oh," I whisper. I find myself leaning into him, wanting to hear every word out of his mouth.

"It was a mut'ah marriage, simply short-term and for pleasure. There was an end date, of course, but she didn't know that." Darius nods. "After a blissful few weeks in a hotel room, he disappeared. She found herself alone and abandoned, living in a country where she had zero rights. She returned to the cleric who had married her, demanding answers. He told her there was no use in trying to search for the man, as the marriage had since ended. Still, she had no money left. She felt used and mortified. Soon enough, he began finding men to have sex with her. 'Just for a little while,' he said. 'You have to eat, no? And as you are not a virgin, what does it matter?' She knew the reality, of course. She had no money and no place to go."

"There was no real choice," I add.

He shakes his head. "She signed so many contracts, she could barely keep track. Some men were only for a few hours and some for weeks. One day, Mullah Omar was introduced to her. You see, Gini, she had this long blonde hair. Men in this part of the world go crazy for blondes." He looks far away, as though imagining her face. "Omar recognized that she could fetch a much higher price here, in Mumbai, with us. He arranged for her to study under Madam and learn the arts. She had a beautiful voice. She would sing, and men would pay to listen. Of course, she continued to sell herself, and Mullah Omar was able to make a lot from her."

A million questions battle in my mind, but I bite my tongue. I want to hear the rest.

"I was still young when she arrived in the house, and she always wanted to be near me. She taught me English on her nights off. To Amma's surprise, English was quite useful when men would arrive here from other countries. The men flocked to her because they could communicate. Amma realized how beneficial it would be if the other girls could speak, too. She had her teach them. It sets our home apart from the other brothels and makes us much more valuable."

"What happened to her?" I hold my breath, waiting for his reply.

He drops his head before raising it up again. "She took her own life after one of the longer-term contracts. One of the men Mullah Omar had hand-picked due to his heavy pockets. Six months in Saudi. She came home rattled."

I imagine a woman just like me, taking her life; I shudder. If I didn't understand the severity of my circumstances before, I know it now.

"I was the one who found her, floating in the bathroom tub." He swallows hard, his throat lifting up and then down.

All thoughts of myself are gone when I see the pain marring his face. I lean in toward him, unsure about this overwhelming feeling inside me. It's clear he doesn't want to think about the night we had, but I want to comfort him. I lift my arms and place them around his shoulders. I reassure him just as I would with one of my brothers when one of them were sad. Darius's body is tight and strong, completely unyielding. But still, he doesn't shift. After a few seconds, I let go. Before I can turn away, he pulls me back to his chest. We're ... embracing. Before my mind can comment, I drop my head into the crook of his neck, and he does the same, inhaling my scent. We've done this before, and it's just as miraculous as I remember. A rush of blood pulses through me. I can hear the thrum of his heart. I'm shaking. Or is it him? In this moment, we're one.

I should move away, but with Darius, I seem to lose all sensibility.

This warmth ... before Darius, did I ever feel something so perfect? I swear to all that is holy, I wish this would never end.

"Will that be my fate, Darius? I know I must sign the contract if I want to keep my life. Roshan mentioned to me that Mullah Omar is extremely dangerous. That he would kill me if I disobeyed him."

"Women do not exactly have freedom to choose, Gini ..." His voice trails off.

"Here, you might be right. But there are other places where freedom is possible. America, maybe, where that woman was from. Have you ever been outside of Mumbai?"

"Yes." Darius nods. "I have been to London and Paris."

"How was it? I've heard of those cities."

"Oh, it was definitely different. Paris is best." His eyes, usually dark, have yellow rings around them. I let myself stare. "The women who live in Europe wear clothes similar to menswear. Pants and shirts." He gestures to his own clothing. "They also wear shorts when the weather is warm. Shorts are like pants but cut to here." He motions to his mid-thigh. "There are women who wear modest dress, too. But what's so great is, anything goes. And for the most part, no one seems to care."

"Anything?"

"Yes. You can date someone and go to dinner and films in public. You can get married. You can get divorced. You can live together and have children, even without marriage. You can even study and learn in countless universities." He looks at me long and hard. "It's beautiful, but this is home."

Whispering, I say, "I want to go there."

I look at the door, wondering what it would be like to have that sort of freedom. To be with Darius under no superseding law. Or The Mansion. *Why does it have to be the way it is? Why can't we get away from here and live somewhere else?*

We're both silent, asking the same questions with our eyes. How do I know he's thinking this? Because I just do. I can *feel* it.

Talk about change. When I arrived, I was terrified of Darius. He had taken me from my home and forced me into this life. I know that it's his fault I'm here. But somehow, over the last weeks, I have found myself longing for him. In the beginning, it was his looks. His hair and his eyes and his build. But the truth is, Darius is the epitome of decency. That first night, he fed me. And since then, he's added water buckets to my room, making sure they are changed more often than they should be. From the corner of my eye, I've seen him swapping out old vegetables for fresh ones to be sent to my room for me to cook. I've witnessed him in the hallways, inquiring after each and every woman in the house. Asking how she's feeling. How she's faring. Of course, the women are always talking about him, too. How he saved them from awful lives and brought them here to The Mansion, where there is food to eat and the possibility of *more*. I'm not like them, though. My life wasn't hell before this place.

He sits up with something like sadness in his eyes. "Maybe the Iranian will take you. In fact, I'm sure he will. Madam tells me that he will want to bring you with him when he travels for business. He will likely hand you cash and tell you to shop."

A sense of urgency to find a way out of my situation fills my heart. I need to stop this. I need to make him see that *we* could be something.

"What if I don't want to shop?"

"There are museums. Restaurants, too. With all kinds of foods."

A plan takes hold in my head. "Maybe you could meet me."

He laughs out loud, as though I were joking. "That would be something."

I ignore his tone. "We could arrange to meet at one of the large museums. Or shops. Or even a library. At a certain date and hour. Roshan got a mobile phone. She told me about this ... text message."

"Text message," he repeats, trying not to smile. "You've been learning."

"Yes, I have." I press my lips together, willing him to be serious. This is good. If I could just get him to understand what could be. "You could give me a phone," I continue. "And we could message while I was there, in Iran. I could tell you that I'd be in a certain library. And then maybe you could take a trip. And visit me."

He cocks his head to the side, as though trying to figure something out. "Are we friends now, to be visiting each other?" His voice is hard.

I bite my lip. His anger worries me that I overstepped. "W-we could be," I continue. "Maybe. It would be nice. Maybe even, you could pick me up. Take me somewhere. We could leave," I finally admit. "Together to Paris. Or America. Or anywhere."

He swallows hard, eyebrows lowering. "Maybe, in a different world, we could. But we aren't in that world. We're in this one."

"Why?" I swallow back the dryness in my throat. I want to push him. I want to scream. *Why won't he acknowledge what he already knows?* "Why are we living in this one?"

"Why?" He laughs. "Because my job is to sell you, Gini. To sell you again and again and again until you're no longer of use." He grits his teeth. "It's my job to find men to pay for you. Whether it's one night or one year or one hundred fucking years!"

"Why do you look so upset then?" I stand up, pushing against his chest. "I thought it was all okay because Muhammad said so. It's a good thing, isn't it? It's *halal*?"

He stands up, grabbing my wrist. "You're misinterpreting—"

I press, trying to get my hand free, "Am I?"

"Yes!"

"So, why do you look so distraught?" I shake my hand from his grip. "Why did you suffer over the death of Claire?" I've never seen this side of myself before, but I have to make him see! "And why are you yelling if that's what you believe?"

He drops his head in his hands. "Gini, we shouldn't be talking like this. This is life. This is how it is." He turns his face from mine, like he can't bear to look at me.

"But you told me about Paris. That's not how it is *there*. Things are different *there*. Why do we have to keep doing this? Let's just—"

"This is what I know. This is who I am. I was bred to be the man I've become. Don't fucking tell me who I am or what I should or shouldn't do. You think I can waltz into another country and do, what, sell groceries as a clerk? What would I do to make money? To feed you?"

"Stop talking like this!" I exclaim, my passion overtaking reason. "This isn't who you have to be. I don't want this life. Let's choose a different one. Together. Darius, you and I keep passing each other in the hallways. Since the moment we met, we've had something real. It's like nothing else—"

He grips my arm so tightly that I shut up. "There is no you and me." His voice is so low, it's practically cruel.

But I remember when he was sick with his headache and he needed me so badly. He lets me go, and I pace to and from the window, knowing in my gut that he just can't see past his situation.

I turn back to him, opening my palms. "Darius, please ..."

And then, without a word, he pivots to leave. "We're done here." His voice is gravelly. "Continue studying until you have finished the alphabet at least one more time."

I look at him expectantly. I am not sure what I am anticipating, but I am not ready for him to go. This argument can't be over.

"Darius, what about the fact that Claire died? What if that winds up being me?"

"Stop speaking, Gini. I am here as the protector of this house and to make sure you leave here, armed with knowledge to survive." He raises his chest, and it's like another man has just inhabited his body.

"Survive? But, Darius, I'm not cut out for this life. I couldn't possibly ..." I swallow hard, feeling defeated. "P-please. Let's not fight. Come back. Help me learn." I look straight into his face, my body trembling. I'm giving in to him, but what option do I have?

He moves closer to me, like a predator coming after his prey. "If you make errors with the Iranian, death will be your end. All he would have to say is that you were disrespectful about Allah, and no one would blink an eye. Vigilante justice is accepted in Iran. And that is where you are going. To Iran. This situation you're in? It's serious."

I nod my head, taking hold of his hand. "Okay."

"No!" His arm cuts through the air before he steps close to me, wrapping his hands around my arms. I'm sure that, tomorrow, I will bruise. I can feel his hot breath against my skin. "There is no possibility of anything other than this. You think you can change me? Do you even know who you're dealing with? You have feelings for the wrong man, Gini."

He lets me go, and I try not to crumple onto the floor.

"Wh-what if it's too difficult for me to speak English? What if I cannot do it?" I keep my head high, pushing him harder. For some reason, I won't back down.

"Too difficult?" He laughs. "First of all, we both know how quick you're learning and how intelligent you are. English is the language you must learn to be able to converse with the Iranian and his associates. Your life depends on learning this language." He squints his eyes. "You will learn, Gini. And you will go to Iran. And you will please him. Do you think Mullah Omar and the Iranian are the only men who can kill or throw acid at a woman's face?" He laughs.

I shake my head, swallowing back tears. "W-will you be here nightly?" I clear my throat. "To teach me? And then to send me off to my death?"

"You will not die. If you listen to me, I will make sure you know everything there is to know. If you know how to behave, you will live."

"But if I cannot learn English, will I still have to leave for Iran? Maybe Madam will decide that I can't handle this life, and she'll have you send me to a different brothel. Right? But instead of doing that, you can set me free—"

He throws his hands up in the air. "Enough!" he yells. "Iran is where you must go. I will never, ever help you escape. This is the life Allah has chosen for you to live. You cannot go against what he has chosen for you. When Mullah Omar decides a match, you have no choice but to follow his word. You cannot get out of this circumstance. Ready or not, the Iranian is coming for you. And I have no problem with killing any woman who fails to listen. You will go to Iran with a smile on your face and do everything your husband asks of you, to the letter. You do not talk back. You do not question!"

"And if he is disgusting or cruel?"

He presses his hand against my lips, silencing me. It hurts. "According to Aisha, Mohammad's third and youngest wife, a young girl came to the prophet and said, 'O Messenger of God, I am a betrothed girl, but I detest marriage. What are the husband's rights from the woman?' He replied, 'Were he covered with pus from the tip of his head to the soles of his feet and were she to lick him, she would not compensate him enough.' "

"I do not want to go," I beg, dropping to my knees. "I am afraid! So afraid, Darius. Please. Listen to me." I drop down to my hands and feet, crawling to take hold of his ankles and sobbing.

He doesn't move. Erect like a statue, completely turned to stone.

He shakes me off, so I no longer touch him. "You want me to tell you that I am not actually this angry, lethal man. But that would be a lie. I'm a monster. I stole you from your family, and I would do it again. I put you in this house so that I can make money from you selling your body. I have killed. I have maimed." He grits his teeth. "I know that you feel something for me. I see it in every single word you utter and in every move you make around this damn house. Still, this dream of yours—that we can leave together, be together—must be eradicated from your mind. You must banish those thoughts. Your future husband will expect submission and gratitude. And when he expects something else, you will give him that, too."

"You don't care? You don't care at all?" The tears stream down my face. "This goes both ways. I felt it the first time we met, outside of my home while I cooked. And I see it all over you, too. It's here, in the way you look at me. Care for me. I know how you try to make my life better." I lift my hands in prayer, begging him to admit what he feels. "And the night we shared when your head ached—"

"Forget that night." His hands ball into fists, but I can tell he is battling with his own emotions.

The look inside his dark eyes has me melting. My heart moves to a slow beat as he stares, his armor seemingly disappearing. I'm beginning to question my own sanity. Warring emotion pours from him. He hears me, but will he ever give in?

"Oh, Darius—"

My words seem to wake the monster within him. "You will be stronger than this. I will not hesitate to drag you by the hair, force-feeding you English until you can see nothing other than the ABCs. This man in Iran, he will expect complete submission. And it is my job to make sure you are groomed for him. While you are under my roof, you will do as I say. If you do not listen, I will not hesitate to beat you. And when you leave here and go to Iran, you will do what your husband says."

He grabs the back of my hair, pulling it back so that my neck opens to him. Slowly, so slowly, he brings his face to my neck. I'm shaking so hard, it's a miracle I don't collapse. His words are awful, and yet I don't believe them. How can I when he—

Oh ...

My mouth opens and closes, but no words leave me.

He whispers behind my ear, "Do as I say, Gini. If you care for me at all, you will not force my hand against you. It's a strong, strong hand." He is so close, but he isn't close enough.

His tongue, like velvet, licks a path across my neck. My eyes close, the heat strumming through my body too much to bear. He rears back and turns away from me, strutting to the doorway.

He stops, turning around to face me again. "There is a party in one week, with the Albanians. The dance the girls were practicing will be performed that evening. Follow Roshan. Listen to her. Watch her. Learn to do and to act as she does. It is the only way to be safe. Without armor and knowledge, you would be a lamb to the slaughter. Promise me, Gini. Promise me you will do your very best to learn everything we teach you."

I swallow hard. I want to tell him no. I want to scream and shout. But the look on his face is too desperate.

Against my will, I nod.

And then he's gone.

OVER THE COMING WEEK, I work hard, cleaning the home and taking care of mending for the women. I assume most of the clothes I touch are costumes of some sort for the parties. The colors are some I have never seen.

I follow Roshan's guidance and keep my head bowed when speaking to certain women. My meetings with her continue, and she teaches me how to apply hair oils to give my strands more shine, and powder on my face to even out my skin tone. It took me days to learn how to walk with shoes that had stilts attached to their bottoms. They are called high heels.

Darius wasn't joking when he told me to be careful of the skin on my hands.

"Being a woman in this house means taking impeccable care of one's body," Roshan said. "It means always staying clean and keeping oneself above the wives and sisters and daughters of this world who sweat and engage in labor. When men come to see us, they do not want to smell the spices of their home. They want something unique. Something fresh." She handed me a special cream to put on my hands and face each evening, telling me it would lighten my skin.

Our dance lessons began, too. She was happy with the way my hips moved but told me I must learn to relax and make my movements more fluid and natural.

"With practice, it will come," she insisted, hands holding my hips, pushing them around in circles.

It hasn't been easy, but it hasn't been awful, either. In some ways, I'm coming to terms with my new life.

Darius has spent each evening teaching me how to read English and finally how to put sounds together. It's more exciting than anything I've ever done. I have tried to speak with him in Urdu to get him to open up to me as he did the first night of learning, but he always refuses. He tells me that we will speak together in English only. He even gave me a book that he wanted me to read—*The Da Vinci Code*. It is quite thick, but each evening, I try to get through a few pages. Already, it is interesting!

He has also begun tutoring me in Islamic and Iranian traditions. We reviewed the concepts of halal and haram—or what is permissible under Islamic Law or forbidden—which led us to so much laughter. He tries to be serious, insisting how important it is for me to understand the differences, but we often find ourselves snickering at the fine line between what is or is not permitted.

Yesterday, we practiced understanding the concept of *taarof*, since apparently, it is something I will see firsthand. Essentially, it's a Persian tradition of extreme politeness. For example, if the Iranian offers me something, I must tell him no, even if I want to say yes, so that he can insist. Only when his insistence becomes great enough can I accept.

We role-played together, so I could learn. We sat on the floor, facing each other, the small ceiling light shining above us. I love sitting like that because I can stare at him without hiding. And I love electricity because it allows me more hours to stay awake to learn and be with Darius.

"TAKE A BANANA." *He handed me the long, ripe fruit, a smile on his gorgeous face.*

I shook my head, replying, "Oh, no," in English, feeling proud of my simple language skills. Feigning refusal, I put my nose in the air.

"Yes, please, take it." He pressed it against my hand, slightly more insistent. "It is good for your health."

I put my hands to my chest. "I can't. I food too much for breakfast." I had to bite my cheek to stop myself from laughing.

Seriously, he replied, "No, Gini. You say, 'I ate too much at breakfast.' Repeat it."

"I ate too much at breakfast."

"That's better." He smiled. "Now, you must take the banana. I had one this morning from the same bunch, and I know that you will love it," he practically begged, pushing the banana against my chest. "It's delicious." Slowly, he peeled it. "Here, have a bite."

I leaned forward. "Okay." Closing my eyes, I took a large bite of the banana. "Mmm. Delicious."

I opened my eyes to see him almost frozen to the spot. I chewed and swallowed, but still, it felt like the fruit was stuck in the center of my throat. His stare was so heavy. Full.

"Okay, that's enough," he finally said, his voice gruff. "And what is it you put on your skin?"

"The smell?" I lifted my hand, rubbing my neck.

"Yes, the scent."

"It's a special perfume. Roshan gave me a few different oils, and I combined them. Is it nice?"

"Don't use perfume. It's unnecessary," he said. "Makeup, too. Keep your skin as clean as possible. Nothing should cover it." He touched my face with the side of his hand, whispering, "For you, natural is always better."

MY LIFE MIGHT BE ENDING SOON. Before it does, I want to spend it with Darius.

8

Darius

I WALK DOWN the steps to enter Gini's room, a movie in my hand. Earlier today, I had one of the girls bring a television set down to her room. Watching films often helps to learn a foreign language, so I am hoping it increases her fluency. She is definitely intelligent and learning much faster than I assumed she would.

The fact that I'm teaching her to speak with a man who isn't me? Makes me sick. But there is no other option.

I open the door to see her sitting against the wall, *The Da Vinci Code* open alongside the Urdu-English dictionary. My breath catches as her scent hits me. She smells incredible. Like the wildflowers in her field, fresh and clean and so natural. I close my eyes, inhaling deeper. My body stirs, recognizing that the very essence of Gini just does it for me. Just the thought of her has my feet faltering. Staring at her like this, I know the truth. I'm completely falling for this woman.

I clench my fist, throwing my feelings to the wall and hoping they stay put. It's either that or let myself fall into a tailspin, and that's something I swore I wouldn't let myself do. I've spent the last months trying to pull my emotions and mind off Gini, which is quite a test of character since I see her every single night to teach English and often when she's cleaning around the house or fetching things for the girls. Keeping her from speaking Urdu helps, since limiting her language makes it harder for her to communicate with me. But my heart. *Fuck!*

All of the questions she asked me that evening, the first time I came to teach her English, haunt me. All the whys and why-nots. All the couldn't-it-bes and the why-shouldn't-it-bes. I have been alive for over thirty years, and these questions have always sat quiet in my chest. Gini has pried me open. Forced them out. Made me wonder about things I should not be wondering about. Making me *feel*.

I grit my teeth. The reality is in black and white. She is getting ready for a nikah mut'ah with one of the wealthiest men in Iran, and I am here to protect her and teach her while she lives under this roof. If I love her, I must be even surer that she is secure and ready for what might come.

And yet, according to the stirrings of my soul, she is mine.

She is so engrossed in her work that she still hasn't noticed me. I take it as a blessing and turn away, walking back up the steps, my feet padding quickly but quietly. I need to leave The Mansion and have a drink—or four. I pull out my phone, texting Arman.

I can feel that nervous rush beginning to filter through me. Anger pushes into the forefront of my mind. It's everyone and everything. The world, for putting me in this mess. For bringing forward a woman to test my strength. For Amma, for putting the weight on my shoulders. Omar, for the power and control he possesses over me and The Mansion. What I need is a night out and a reconnection with something I've loved since the age of fourteen—sex.

With shaking fingers, I type.

Let's party tonight.

Arman: Come to me. A group of Bollywood girls are coming over. Fun times.

Please, stop with the smiley face. It's fucking weird.

Arman: What's fucking weird is how you live with the hottest asses in the country and you don't fuck them. Maybe it's me you really want? LOL

Ha.

Arman: Anything is possible ...

No denial on that.

Arman: You get stir-crazy when you haven't fucked in a while. Come here. Get laid. Feel better.

I'm on my way.

THE INSIDE of my car is hot. I turn on the engine as sweat rises to my skin and hit the gas. I pull down the windows, the air from outside still thick and warm. I make it to Arman's sea-view flat in a matter of minutes.

Mumbai has one of the largest billionaire populations in the world, and in these parts, it's obvious. I park my car on the street and walk toward his building. I see some kids on a dark corner, laughing and passing around a smoke. Even though I've been living in Amma's Mansion since I was a kid, I, too, would hang out on street corners, just like them. They're barefoot but happy. Full of soot. Instead of entering Arman's building, I pause to watch them. Taking out a cigarette, I see their carefree laughter, and for reasons I can't understand, it angers me.

"Hey," one of them calls out. "Can we have one of your smokes?"

Without speaking, I lift the pack, offering it to them.

They run over to where I stand, smiles on their faces. They have everything to cry and complain over, but here they are, smiling.

"Thanks!" they exclaim, all four boys pulling their own stick.

One of the kids shuffles his feet, taking one only after the rest do. The others lean in, trying to get closer. The street is so dark, mixed with our collective smoke. I clench and unclench my fist, wanting to break something. *And these kids are fucking happy?*

The tallest one speaks first, "Are you part of any crew?"

"You could say that." My voice comes out like gravel.

"Yeah, I thought so. You're really big."

I don't reply. Just inhale and exhale, staring at him. Truth is, I can be a maniac. I should tell these kids to get away from me before I beat their asses for no other reason than the fact that I feel like shit. I wish I were with Gini now, watching that film. Instead, I'm here, where I don't want to be. There will be international women at Arman's, but none of them will ever be able to fulfill the need inside me. I've already fucked more of them than I care to admit. They're beautiful faces and tight bodies. But I want none of it. Right now? I'm dangerous.

"So ..." A kid's voice trails off. "If you ever need any help doing anything, you could call us."

"Call you?" I repeat, trying not to laugh.

They're all thin. Likely hungry. And they think they can help *me*?

"Yeah." He nods. "We do some small time. You know Arman, at the docks?"

My jaw twitches. "Maybe."

"Sometimes, we take care of things for him. He sells drugs, you know. The best. We peddle them."

"Is that so?" My temper rises. I step closer, grabbing his throat with one hand and lifting him up so his feet dangle a few inches from the ground. "Listen, motherfucker. You don't ever mention anyone's name. What if I were the police, huh? You could have gotten someone very important in trouble with your big fucking mouth!"

I let go, and he crumples onto the floor, coughing weakly. I step back before kicking him hard in the ribs. That's my friend he could have buried! I kick again and again, and yet my temper is barely soft-ening. He's lucky I'm not packing my gun tonight.

The scent of urine permeates the air. I pause, sweat dripping down my head.

They all run off into the night, dragging their friend with them. I crack my knuckles, still shaking with anger. I could chase the kid down, but what would that accomplish?

I shake out my shoulders, angry, walking a few feet before stopping.

Gini. I'm getting ready to sell her. She, too, was happy, even though she had nothing. My stomach turns sour, and suddenly, I feel like throwing up. She showed me herself. Her kindness. And I ignored her. Refused to listen to her cries because she was afraid. I always knew how bad I was, but now, my sins are like a freight train running over me.

I turn around and walk, the heat in my veins bursting through my skin. I was able to rationalize the girls I bought and sold in the past, as I really believed they had a better life in The Mansion than they would otherwise. And I still think, for most of them, it's true. But not Gini. And it's not just because I want her. But because she was okay before. She had a father who loved her and could afford to feed her. *How could I do this to her?*

I wander the streets in circles, chain-smoking, until I find myself back in front of Arman's building. From where I stand, I have the perfect view of his balcony. The music is so loud, I can hear it from all the way down here. People are spilling from the apartment, laughing. Glasses of champagne in hand. Skirts that sparkle. Before Gini, I would have gone straight to that party. Taken one or two girls to the guest room in the back and enjoyed their bodies. Now? The thought has my stomach turning.

In one square mile, there is impoverished, and there is uber-wealthy.

Who am I in this machine of life? Who the hell am I? My heart pounds harder, legs turning numb. I drop down to the ground and empty the contents of my stomach.

Getting back into my car, I begin the drive back to The Mansion. My phone buzzes with what I assume are multiple texts from Arman, but I ignore them. I feel like shit, my stomach cramping. Instead of going down the correct road, I drive toward the slums. I've studied the geography of other big cities, and no others have their slums bordering their beautiful high-rise buildings quite like Mumbai. It's unique.

I park the car and walk toward the mountains of trash. I shouldn't be here because I don't have to be, but for some reason, I feel like I should. I sit on the ground, pulling my knees up, and look around. A few feet from where I sit, the rows of tin shacks begin. In that exact spot, I fall asleep.

I FEEL something at my shoulder. I reach into my pants, searching for a knife, before opening my eyes and training it on the person who dared to touch me. It's a weathered woman, who looks likely fifty years older than her actual age. I can tell it's morning from the temperature, but darkness still looms.

The lady invites me into her home for some rice and dal. I shake my head, not wanting to talk or eat. Right now, I just want some peace. She takes my hand, insistent and strong, and drags me into her hut, where four young children sit, along with an adult male. He looks tired, toothless, too. Seeing as the shack is near the road, I have to assume that both husband and wife are construction workers. The mountain roads are always in need of maintenance. Still, the work is backbreaking. All day, until nightfall, they smash the large rocks with hammers, breaking them down to stones. Often, they get hit by trucks speeding down the roads.

The husband gives me a genuine smile while wobbling his head from side to side. Obviously, despite the struggles of his life, he is happy to be with his family. The woman introduces me as a strong man who was sleeping alone, and takes a seat on the floor, tapping the space beside her. After introducing myself properly, I sit and take some food, not wanting to be rude. There is no question that the entire slum is cramped, but the sense of community here is great.

The youngest of the children is a girl, likely around four years of age. She has black eyes the size of dinner plates and a tiny mouth, like a rosebud.

"Hello," she greets me, putting food in her mouth. "Can you be my daddy?"

The entire family laughs, the older children giggling.

"But he's your papa," her brother says, pointing to his father.

"No." She shakes her head. "I want him to be my papa." She looks to me, her brown cheeks turning pink.

I laugh, making light of her compliment.

They ask me my heritage and admit that, at first, they assumed I was a foreigner.

"No," I reply. "I am Indian."

After thirty minutes and a full stomach, their father asks me to walk with him, alone. We go outside, among their neighbors.

"My youngest daughter is growing older, but I am finding it difficult to feed her. I have heard of you. Many of us talk. Some even remember you here, as a boy. You find women for The Mansion, correct?" His clothes are beige, torn, and full of grime.

I look into his kind eyes and nod my head, although my stomach sinks lower. I have no help for his daughter.

He claps in joy. "Would you consider taking her? Maybe you can find a husband for her there, at The Mansion. Even if it's a temporary marriage, that works for us, too. I have asked around in the community, but of course, no one here is rich enough to take a bride. The *imam* tells me that Mullah Omar works with you, and he might find a match for her. She could be a second or third or even fourth bride. If The Mansion has space—"

"As of now, there is no room for more girls. Why don't you give me your name, and I will come back if anything changes?"

"No. You don't seem to understand." He smiles again but swallows hard with it. "My daughter looks about four years of age, but in reality, she is nine."

I keep my face straight, knowing he lies.

"She is old enough for pleasure marriage. And we don't have enough to feed her. Please"—he shakes his head side to side—"take her. We won't charge you too much of a dowry, although that would help us. Something small would be sufficient for her." He opens his hands to me, but there is nothing I can do.

"Like I said"—I clear my throat—"let me speak with Madam and see if we have space for her. I know where to find you."

I reenter the home to bid the family my farewell, feeling like my brain has been stomped on. I know there is no place for her. She isn't beautiful enough for The Mansion.

I get back into my car and turn on the engine. In this moment, I despise Amma and the burden she set on my back.

Could I just up and leave everything behind?

As though driving in a trance, I find myself in The Mansion's driveway without remembering ever making a turn. I walk straight up to my room, ignoring the girls calling me to sit with them in the kitchen. Gini is there, cleaning dishes in the sink. All it takes is one glance at her face for my entire body to react.

I get into my room and immediately strip my clothes and get into bed, shifting onto my back. With a groan, I palm my rock-hard erection. My rational brain tells me that I should deny myself this pleasure. After the night I had, who knows why I'm as horny as I am? Oh, who the hell am I kidding? I saw Gini. And when I see Gini, think of Gini, imagine Gini ... denying my cock becomes impossible.

Images of us having sex in this very bed flash in every part of my brain, front to back. Her nude, above me, moaning and murmuring in my ear. My teeth against her slim throat. Stroking her in places she has never been touched—wet, forbidden heat. In a soundless cry of my own, I can feel my cock heating up, ready to go off. Her breasts, round and perky, bouncing above my face. *Oh, yeah, it's here.* My balls tighten, and I flip to my side, coming so hard that it's practically shocking. My body slows down as I breathe into my pillow, sweat soaking my skin.

It's official; there is no amount of jerking off to rid this woman from my thoughts.

I exhale, needing to gather myself, but failing. I should be used to her by now. Instead, my feelings continue to deepen. With an iron will, I force myself to picture Gini leaving the house. The Iranian coming to take her away after she signs her agreement. My body might refuse to listen, but maybe my head finally will.

No!

I stand up, sliding my boxers back on before pacing around my room like a caged beast. No other woman can fill this void. Just the thought of someone other than Gini has my stomach turning. Maybe if I open up to her, it will stop this pulsing desperation from taking me over. If I let the truth free, maybe I will finally be able to come to terms with the reality. She's leaving, and there is nothing I can do to stop her.

AT MY DESK, I review the house's finances. We're not doing well enough. Without Gini's impending marriage, we would sink. I stand up, looking out my room's window. I can see Gini's small outdoor space from my window. It's set neatly with four large tubs of water in the corner, next to a cooking station. Not for the first time, I'm glad I had Narmada put out extra barrels of water. She was annoyed to do it, but of course, she listened to my direction. The girls who come here start out with basically nothing. But I couldn't watch Gini suffer in that way.

She shuffles outside and washes her face, dipping her hands in the water and bringing it up to her cheeks and eyes. I smile as she cleanses herself with so much care.

Ever since the night I spent in the slums, I have been avoiding Gini at all costs. I'm just not sure which way to turn. I haven't even taught her English, although I know she has been studying on her own. Most evenings, before the sun sets, she sits outside and reads her books.

I try not to watch her, but I can't help myself.

Eventually, I leave my room and walk down the steps, swallowing hard as I open her bedroom door. I have to put my own shit aside and teach her. Without me, she won't learn fast enough. I find her outside, reading.

I clear my throat, putting on my mask of disinterest. "Hello."

She jumps. "Oh, Darius. It's you. I didn't hear you come in."

She spoke in Urdu, but I won't correct her. Not now. I need to hear her voice. I missed her so much that my chest squeezes.

She puts her hands over her hair, trying to fix it.

I smile. "No use. It's hopeless."

Her face falls, and I find myself laughing out loud.

"Don't be silly, Gini. Your hair is fine."

She looks at me, tilting her head to the side, questioning.

"It's better to read out loud." I lean against the crumbling wall. "It helps to hear the sounds." I pull a piece of mint gum from my pocket, opening it and putting it in my mouth. I stuff the wrapper back in my pocket.

"When I have no teacher, I do what I can."

"Oh?" A combination of shock and pride move through me at her words. She is so strong.

She shrugs, her steam seeming to settle. "So, where have you been?"

When she looks up at me with those big gray-blue eyes, I feel like a king. There is no way I can leave her now.

"It's been so long since you've come downstairs. Or taught me."

"Listen, Gini, about what's been happening between us." I exhale, the truth pulsing to be freed. "I've been thinking. I have no answers." I move closer, wanting so badly to confide in her. To have just one person in my life who I can trust, to open my heart to.

"Okay." She gives me a sidelong glance.

"I'm unsure how to change the hand that we've been dealt. Things are complicated. Mullah Omar is a very powerful man. I do not know how to change my fate or yours without incurring death for us both. He and Madam wouldn't just let me walk away. Still"—I pause, taking her hand and rubbing my thumb across her knuckles—"I can't stop myself from wishing the circumstances were different. Everything I said that night ... all of the emotions you think you see and feel ... they are all true. I don't want to hide myself from you." I swallow hard, feeling as though I were sinking in water.

I want this woman so badly, but I can't see past our situation. I am selfish for wanting her in this limited capacity, but I can't help it.

She puts her hand on my chest. "Somewhere in my days here, I moved away from the path of finding my way out of this life and into the mindset that you are somehow meant for me. I want you, Darius. Not for a day or a night or even ninety-nine years. I want forever. Please, think of something."

"Oh, Gini." I put my forehead on hers, and we breathe each other's breaths. I want to tell her yes, but my brain knows it isn't going to happen. It's impossible. Not if we want to live. Instead of telling her the truth, I ask, "Want to watch a movie? We will use something called subtitles, which means that Urdu will be written on the bottom of the screen so you can follow along. It will help teach you conversational English."

"So, we will continue learning ... as though I'm leaving?"

"What other choice is there?" I touch her full bottom lip. "We can have each other in this limited capacity. But only if you swear to avert your eyes from mine when we are not alone."

"Avert?"

"No one can know or even imagine that anything exists between us."

"Of course—"

"Even the idea that there might be something could mean the end of your life."

"Okay." She nods. "I get it. I will always keep my gaze from yours."

"We must keep a distance."

She nods solemnly. "So, I won't press my lips to your lips, as I wish I could."

I nod my head so slowly, watching her perfect mouth. She shifts, and it shakes me out of my trance.

"To turn on the television, we use a remote. It is a device that controls what you watch." I stand up, taking the movie and the remote from the top of the box. I will let her watch it alone. This way, she can learn, and I can create some much-needed space. After our conversation, time apart would be good.

Lifting the movie in my hand, I ask, "Have you ever seen one?"

She shakes her head. "But I've heard of movies, of course. One time, my neighbors learned this Bollywood dance. I watched them practice. It was so beautiful."

"Well, this is a famous American movie. It's called *Pretty Woman*. All Indians love it."

"What is it about?" She brings her knees up to her chest.

"It's about a girl who sells herself but then falls in love with one of the men who buys her."

She starts to smile. "Interesting."

I laugh freely in a way I don't think I ever have. "We can start watching tonight. We'll do about thirty minutes each evening. And when we've finished, you can watch it again and again, on your own."

I want to tear my tongue out. But I simply cannot leave her. I put in the tape, and press play.

Her leg moves beside mine. Her innocent touch is enough to heat my blood.

That night, I sleep better than I ever have. Finally, she knows.

9

Gini

THE FOLLOWING DAY, I notice a new maid cleaning up the kitchen. She is a tiny slip of a girl, wearing a dress similar to mine. Her beauty is definitely something to notice. She looks like an angel.

I call to her in Urdu, "Hello."

By her size, I would guess she is the same age as my youngest sister. It makes my heart lurch.

She looks up at me with her huge brown eyes and smiles, a missing front tooth in her tiny rosebud mouth. "Hello," she replies happily, bowing her head to me.

"When did you arrive here?" I want to make small talk and keep her near. She's just simply adorable.

"Weeks ago. I was saved by a man. He found me in the stalls and brought me into this beautiful mansion." She smiles so brightly, as though being here is her luck.

I shift, hesitating. Darius brought her from one whorehouse to this one. Clearly, her beauty called to him. But she is too young for this. *How could he?*

"Today," she continues, interrupting my thoughts, "I'm learning how to clean the bedrooms and bathrooms. They will teach me to dance, too. And maybe even sing."

"Dance?" My heart skips a beat, not wanting to imagine this child moving so seductively. My mouth suddenly dries out.

"Oh, yes." She nods, completely unaware of my distress. "One day, I will be the most famous tawaif in all of Mumbai! And every man in the world will come to see me."

The girl is set in happiness. I can't be the one to take it from her.

She bounces on her toes. "Breakfast was so delicious. Did you eat? I've never seen so much food in all of my life!"

"Oh, sure." I clear my throat. "Ar-are you okay here? Do you have enough water?"

"This place is heaven," she replies easily. "This is the life Allah chose for me. I must have done something very good in my last life to wind up here!"

She skips off, following one of the other maids, when Narmada moves next to me.

"That girl will be bred to be a valuable tawaif. Lucky for her, starting so young, she will have excellent skills by the time she is ready. She will catch a good husband when her day comes. Our home used to sell girls as young as her, but when Darius became a man, he decided against it."

The relief I feel on behalf of the girl is palpable. I lick my lips, asking, "Madam allowed Darius to make that choice?"

Narmada laughs. "He raised hell over it. He told her that when we use girls so young, we soil them too quickly. A girl who becomes a woman first, plus three years, has a much longer shelf life." She shrugs. "The girl will be a maid for at least a few years. She has yet to have her menstrual cycle, although it could be because she is still so thin. After we fatten her up a bit, we'll know where we stand."

I hum in understanding and think about Darius, who tries to maneuver rules of The Mansion for the benefit of the women. Knowing that this little girl will not be bought for years is a relief.

Narmada curiously looks me up and down. "Why are your cheeks reddening? Is it because I mentioned Darius?"

"Of course not!" I exclaim a little too loudly.

"You aren't the only girl here to fall under his charm. But remember, just as he bought you, he shall sell you."

"I—"

"Shut your mouth and listen," she commands, gripping the edge of the sink. "You think that because Darius is kind, he cares. But you are misreading him. Darius has been in this life from childhood, just like that little girl he brought here. Earlier, even. And he will continue in this life. You play a part, as well. The part you play is to get on your back and make the men who buy you happy. With that money, The Mansion eats and continues to prosper."

I drop my head, not wanting her to see the pain welling up inside me.

"Never forget this. And if you even dream of something different, Madam will smell it on you. And if she senses you aren't going to do well by The Mansion, she will sell you off. Not necessarily to one of these brothels in the area, either. She can send you across an ocean, if she chooses."

I lift my head. "I understand."

"Do you?"

"Yes." And the truth is, I do.

They want me to obey these rules and live the life that has been set in motion for me. To disobey is death.

"When we call you Kutta, it is because you are nothing but one. Even when they eventually call you Gini, you'd better remember that a kutta is all you truly are. This is what Allah has ordained for you."

The tears drip down my face, and I wipe them away with the side of my arm. "Why has he given me this life?"

"Aren't you tired of giving in to your tears? The why-me? The what-if? You need to put that away and face the music. We all get used to our stations. Why should you be any different? Be the best whore you can be, and maybe, in your afterlife, you will rise."

～

"No one has ever died from wearing high heels."

Roshan and I are getting dressed together this evening. Her makeup is dark and sultry with full blood-red lips and eyes lit with shadow like shimmering smoke. She wears the diamond necklace given to her by Abdyl. Putting her hand over the stone, she closes her eyes, lips moving in prayer. I hope she gets what her heart yearns for.

We walk out into the room, and I press my lips together, trying not to tumble. These heels, which are so easy for the other girls to walk in, are torture on my feet. And yet, I have no choice but to learn how to walk. I straighten my back, the pain reminding me to keep my spine upright. Small steps. One foot in front of the next.

The evening's party is done like a Turkish harem with the ceilings covered in colorful fabrics and circular couches, like beds, lining the room. There are so many pillows, all silvers and golds and oranges. It looks like a dream, really.

The girls are dressed as, what I've been told are, *odalisques*. Roshan told me that an odalisque is a female slave in a Turkish harem. I was confused because why would you dress up as something you already are? Apparently, my question was funny. She laughed so hard and told the others, who also seemed to think it was hilarious.

My skirt is long and pale pink with beautiful golden birds sewn into the fabric, hiding the shoes that give me extra height. The blouse is pink and gauzy with a sheer, billowy fabric for the arms. A low-dipping neckline accents the private area between my breasts, paler than the rest of my body. The whiteness of that skin makes the outfit even more forbidden, as it's obvious this part of my body never sees sun. It's one of Roshan's old dresses that she first wore after arriving at The Mansion. I guess it's a tradition of sorts.

I look up at the high white ceiling, reminding myself to keep my back erect. If I were to bend, the men would get an eyeful of my breasts. Of course, this is by design. Even I can recognize the truth. I look ... enticing. And that makes me more afraid than I've ever been. Some of the girls are already in position, relaxing on large pillows with their breasts on display.

Alisha, one of the younger tawaifs, sits back on a green chaise, posing just like a Turkish chambermaid might have done. Her dark nipples point outward from her perfectly round, heavy breasts. She raises her eyebrows, smirking at me. I immediately turn away, embarrassed. Madam was serious when she told me to get comfortable with nudity.

Ananya, who looks like a doll, walks around, holding a silver bowl full of bright red apples, dazzling. Her breasts are tiny with pink nipples that remind me of spring flower petals. Red jewels are sewn into the curls of her hair.

Suddenly, the chatter quiets down. I look behind me, and there he is. Darius. He struts forward, eating a cluster of red grapes as he talks with Madam, seemingly joking about something. His hair. *Oh my.* For the first time, it's down. Chin-length and jet black. Low-slung black pants and a white shirt. He's warm and tan, skin encasing muscle. He turns his back to me, and I exhale, frozen to the spot and staring. He pivots, sauntering closer to where I stand, chewing.

"Hello." He smirks before popping a plump grape into his mouth. Raising his eyebrows, he asks, "Want some?"

I blink, so nervous from beauty that I can barely stand it. "N-no, thank you."

The smile on his lips wipes away so quickly that it's as if it never existed. "Wrong answer." He lowers his hands, face turning to stone. "When you walk into this room, you are no longer the girl you once knew. If any man asks you if you'd like a grape, you drop your head and do not respond. Roshan will reply for you. Do not give any of these men even a sliver of your voice. You don't give so much as a smile. Or a word. Or a sip of offered water unless you want them to tear your dress to shreds before dragging you onto the floor. Do you understand?"

I can only nod. I know that in front of everyone in The Mansion, we must act like we should—he's the master, and I'm the slave. But does he have to be so convincing?

"Oh, Darius." Roshan walks over, putting a hand on his shoulder. "Were you this tough with me? I don't think so. Please, calm down.

We will enjoy tonight! The Albanians and the Indians. I love this combination." She claps.

"Tell me, Roshan," he starts, pretending like I've disappeared, "have you heard of this Nico?"

"I hear he is dangerous. Even worse than you," she adds with a smile. "Cruel but fair. Abdyl tells me that Nico's word is like ... gospel. Am I saying the words right?"

He nods. "Do you know what Gospel is? It is the teaching of Jesus Christ, who is the central figure of Christianity. When people say someone's word is gospel, they mean their word is absolute truth."

She laughs, rolling her eyes. "Always the teacher! I am going to put on more perfume. Do I smell okay?" She worriedly steps to Darius, lifting her neck to his face. In the shoes she's wearing, she is close to his enormous height.

"You smell nice, but more would be better."

She spins, leaving for her room.

Darius looks around, and I do the same. No one is near.

He exhales, like he's glad for it. "Tell me, Gini, how are you? Are you nervous for tonight?"

I want to cry with happiness that he is speaking in Urdu. That he is no longer mean.

I want to tell him I'm more afraid than I've ever been. But I also know that there is no way to change what is to come. Gathering my wits, I tell him in English, "I am fine, praise God." After giving him a huge smile, I switch to Arabic, wanting to impress him. "*Bi-khayr, al-Hamdu lillah.*"

"You've been practicing?"

He can barely contain the smile on his face. And if I said it didn't cause a wave within my chest, I would be lying.

"Yes."

"Good girl, Gini. Very good."

"He will be happy when I use these words, my Iranian?"

It's like a black cloud passes through Darius's face. *Oh no. I did not mean that.* Of course, the Iranian man is not mine. My words came out wrong. I want to backtrack and explain. I simply meant, *the*

Iranian man. I was hoping to make Darius happy. But before I can speak, he starts.

"Your Iranian, eh?" he sneers. "Get one thing straight, Gini. At this point in time, you should assume that you will be his pleasure slave. Your job will be to keep him interested for as long as humanly possible. If you ever speak to him like an equal or with any kind of ownership, he will crucify you. There is no equality. No ownership by you, of him."

I lift my hands in surrender, trying not to become hysterical. It hits me. I'm scared to death of my situation. I'm afraid of where I'm going. What am I going to do? "Okay, okay."

"And as of now, you are mine." He points to his wide chest. "Under *my* watch. Beneath *my* gaze. No one has control over you other than *me*. A man so much as breathes in your direction tonight, and I will snap his neck."

The rational side of my mind knows where he is coming from. I am property. I want to get on my knees and beg him to stop this. "I understand, Darius. Please, be reasonable."

"Say it in English," he commands. "I. Un-der-stand."

I repeat his words. It takes a few tries, but finally, he is satisfied. That's when I notice Madam is beside us. Did he know she was here? She smiles as though relieved by the way Darius spoke to me.

Touching his back with her nails, she says, "I've got her now, Darius. Leave us."

He licks his lips, waiting a moment before turning to go. Madam's nails scrape up and down his side. I feel like vomiting. He finally leaves us.

"Yes," she purrs. "You are physically just as I want you. Turn."

I do as she asked, and she hums approval.

Madam is wearing loose red pants and a red-colored shirt, sleeveless and so tightly fitted that it looks like second skin. Her face is completely painted in cream-color, red lips drawn out. "I am sure Roshan and Darius told you, but I want you to remember." She grabs my wrist, squeezing hard. "Pretend to be mute. You can be coy. Drum interest. But no voice. If you lose your virginity, you will become worthless. Your only job tonight is to use your ears to listen to the way Roshan speaks and use your eyes to watch how she seduces her man. Roshan will show you the proper way of flirtation and movement.

"The Mafia Shqiptare are deadly. They make all other Mafias before them look like child's play. Never forget that. They are not religious men, as they like money more than all other things. Not that I mind that, of course. We aren't so different from them in that respect. Just remember to never, ever underestimate their crew. If one of these men sees you and wants you, it will be extremely difficult to stop him. Impossible. Those men take whatever they want, whenever they want it."

"Yes, Madam." I bow my head, my wrist beginning to go numb. The fear running through my veins is rampant.

And then they arrive. The Mafia Shqiptare is here, in clothes that look incredibly fancy. Black pants and matching jackets with crisp shirts. The women are all in position, casually lounging around, breasts bared, seeming to enjoy their nudity. Hookahs, tall and colorful, sit at every table, and the men immediately sit to smoke. They look like they own the world and have already landed in heaven, sitting with the girls and touching them as though it were their God-given right.

I see a few of them blowing out puffs of smoke and laughing. I have to hold myself back from staring. They are so different from the men I am used to seeing, whose bodies are darkly tanned and lined from outdoor labor. Their coloring is light, too. Now that I look closer, there is a resemblance between them and Darius. I want to laugh. *How could this be?*

I squint my eyes, focusing on a man who I realize is the tallest in the group. He's laughing, surrounded by a few of his friends. He's very handsome. His hair is cropped short around the sides of his head and then long at the top and parted to the side. It's different. Some of the other men have a similar haircut to his, but for some reason, I can tell he was the first to have it. The crew moves around in a way where he is always at their epicenter. He must be important.

A few of the girls move toward the bar, giggling. They present themselves like carefree beauties who happened to fall upon this spot.

For the millionth time, I wonder, *Are they as miserable as I am?*

I shift, uncomfortable and feeling somewhat impatient. I want this night to start so that it can end. Roshan materializes by my side, and I curl into myself. I hate having another body so close to mine. I hate the noise. Even the smell of this place, like vanilla smoke and candles, burns my nose. Still, I take a seat on the couch's edge, just like I was told, and force myself to study Roshan.

The man I assume is Abdyl brings her down beside him, so they are both lying on the couch, tangled up. She laughs with him. Then, he touches her breasts, whispering words in her ear. Her expressions are one of embarrassment, but at the same time, it's obvious she isn't shy. Is she playing? I want to avert my eyes, but everywhere I turn, there are nude women who the men are enjoying. There is nowhere to hide.

One of the lights flickers, and the girls migrate to the back of the room. Darius nods at me, and I scurry over to where he stands.

"They will perform now," he tells me.

That's when the music turns on. This is the dance the ladies were practicing. But now, under the dim lights and with their costumes, it's like an entirely different show. I'm mesmerized as Roshan takes the center position, twisting her body in ways that have every man's eyes wide. Each woman does her part, taking center stage at different times. They all have different body types, but all are equally gorgeous. With their legs spreading, eyes twinkling, breasts shifting, it's impossible to turn away. It's so sexual, and yet their clothes are still on their bodies. The heat of the room rises. I'm transfixed.

I feel Darius behind me. He's so close but not touching me. I swallow hard, wishing he could be closer. It's dark where we stand, in this corner.

"Would you like to dance like that," he whispers, "for me?"

Chills rise over my arms, and suddenly, I can feel the space between my thighs dampening. Darius steps so close that our bodies are flush. I can feel his hardness pressing against my behind. And suddenly, the realization hits me straight on. Darius wants me. He doesn't want the other girls who are dancing in front of him. I know this because he could have them anytime he wants, but he doesn't. He has been among beauties all his life, but I am the one he has chosen.

Shaina steps to the center of the open circle and drops to her knees, spreading them apart and swinging her head around and around so that her long black hair flies in circles. Finally raising her head and panting, she lifts a finger, summoning one of the men up to where she sits. He laughs, at first, with his friends, but eventually, he takes the stage beside her. Slowly, she unbuttons his pants. I can't help my eyes that are glued to the scene. And I'm not the only one. The entire room quiets down. She pulls out the hardness from his pants and licks it from the base up to the tip. On my word, I never knew this was possible. I watch as she takes him into her mouth, so deep that it disappears. It must be at the back of her throat!

That's when another one of the men walks up to the stage. He unbuttons his own pants before dropping to his knees behind her. He grabs her hips so that she winds up on all fours, still with the other man's member in her mouth. He lifts her skirt and pushes into her from behind. She lets out a long groan, and worry flashes in my chest.

Darius whispers in my ear, "Don't worry, Gini. She likes it."

She confirms Darius's opinion by impaling herself back onto the man, her moan no longer a yell but a long, guttural sound.

The scene is nothing short of pure debauchery. I'm so scared, and yet Darius's heat behind me is taking this scene to an entirely different place. I close my eyes, wondering how it would feel to put him in my own mouth. How it would feel to have him behind me.

"And you?" He pushes my hair to the side, whispering into my neck, "Do you like what you see?"

I shake my head, eyes still screwed shut. "N-not with them."

"How about with me?"

His hands span my stomach, and I have to exhale to keep myself standing. I tell myself that none of this is real. The last thing I want is to have my morality step into this universe I'm living in. Right now, I just want to feel.

"I remember the look in your eyes when I lifted your skirt that day in your home. You were afraid, but you liked it. You liked my eyes on you. And my hands."

I'm breathing heavy, my head rolling back onto Darius's hard chest.

"You were never completely innocent, were you?" His lips graze my ear. "I felt the need inside you. I felt the want, too. You're a good girl." He chuckles, his voice dark. "But there's more to you than simply saying yes to elders and authority. There's more to you than that. And, Gini"—he pauses—"I can smell it. And Allah forgive me, but I want to taste it, too."

Onstage, the noises get louder. She's moaning, and the men are panting. I open my eyes again to see the man behind her grip her hips, pushing into her with a roar.

Darius's hands roam to my front, cupping my breasts and slightly tweaking my nipples. He alternates between pinching and smoothing them down. I want to moan. Scream. But I can barely breathe.

Help me ... don't stop ... this ...

I can feel myself incinerating, the tingles in my core turning into a punishing heat. My hips push back into his. They seem to know something my brain can't understand. His hardness feels like heaven.

My mouth drops open as both men yell out, snapping me out of my trance. Drawing back, white cream drips from Shaina's face. My entire body turns to stone. All the heat drains out from my body, through my toes.

Is she okay? How could they do something so awful to her? I feel ill.

"We never force these situations," he whispers, holding me to his chest. "Shaina knows what she is getting herself into, and so do the men. We like to always have a girl in The Mansion whose job it is to keep things interesting. Men come here, and sometimes, they want to be a little wild. They always tip her extra."

I turn around, finally facing him. So many questions battle in my mind.

He tilts his head to the side. "What do you want to ask me?"

He holds my head in his heavy hand, and instinctively, I lean my cheek, nestling into his palm.

I look up, locking our eyes. "Is that what Madam will eventually do ... to me?"

"Never," he whispers, his face a mask of seriousness. "I will never allow anyone to do that to you." His fingers graze my face.

This man. My chest expands, drinking in the air he breathes out. Darius makes me feel like a goddess, as opposed to what I will become. A tool for a man to use.

I turn my head to find Shaina, but she has left the area, likely to clean herself up.

The lighting changes, and he steps backward, away from me. I want to tell him to come back, but he's already gone.

I look around the room. Now that the dance is over, the girls are continuing to lounge about. A few men rush up to take a girl straight from the stage. Others sit and wait for the women to come to them. Legs crossed, smiles on their faces, like they can't wait to be satisfied.

Roshan sits back in her place by the white couch, and I force my legs to move to where she sits. A shadow cannot separate from its body.

Abdyl comes beside her, the first two buttons on his shirt undone. He reaches the table, picking up a cluster of fat purple grapes from inside a circular glass bowl. He feeds Roshan grape by luscious grape, alternating between giving her the fruit and his own tongue. In a nearly imperceptible way, there is a difference between the two of them and the other couples around the room. Roshan and Abdyl look in each other's eyes. They seem to truly see each other.

I see Madam staring at something from the corner of the room. She stands beneath a red canopy, arms crossed and head held high. I follow her train of sight and see Darius. Something about her gaze isn't right. It's almost possessive.

I hear loud laughter and turn toward the commotion. Shaina is standing with Diya, one of her closest friends. They are touching each other's breasts and kissing with their mouths open. A few of the men rush up and surround them, seemingly excited to see another show.

That's when the man I noticed before—who is extremely handsome, tall, and dark—sits next to me.

"Hello," he says in English.

I blink, turning to Roshan. She is supposed to speak for me, but she is indisposed. *Should I reply or not?* I do not want to anger him. He is the king here. I look left and right, fear sinking into my chest. *Is he going to grab me, like Madam said?* My hands start to shake. *Should I yell for Roshan's attention? Darius? Where is he?*

The man notices my distress. He shakes his head, about to speak, but before he can get a word out, a throat clears.

"Can I help you?"

My heart leaps. Darius. I want to fall into his arms. I look between the men, my hunch affirmed. The Albanian and Darius look so similar; they could be brothers. They are both tall and extremely strong. Darius is younger, and his hair is darker. But the resemblance is uncanny.

10

Darius

"THIS GIRL"—THE man points—"where is she from?"

"She is not for sale this evening. She is in training only."

I look at Gini, whose beauty has me barely standing. I want to drop to my knees in front of her. The thin film of her dress against her creamy skin has my heart pounding. *Can this rich, entitled asshole see what I see?* Her exterior beauty is only a small sliver of her worth. *And this motherfucker thinks he can take her? Fuck him!*

I look him up and down, noticing the fancy suit and crisp white button-down shirt beneath a tailored jacket. He even has a red pocket square perfectly tucked into his breast pocket. This asshole probably has a chauffeured Rolls-Royce. A man like him is used to buying anything his imagination can dream up. If he thinks he can take my woman—

"Oh, I do not want to take her." He shakes his head, responding to a question I didn't ask. "But I would be lying if I said she did not interest me—for other reasons."

"I'm sure she does," I sneer.

Gini stands and places a delicate hand at my back, and immediately, I notice my stance is aggressive. I exhale, take a step back, and try to calm down.

Gini isn't my woman. She is to be sold. She is leaving. I need to get a grip.

He looks between us a few times before his eyes light up. I'm not sure what he sees, but it makes me want to blow his brains out. I feel the heat rising up again.

Gini, Gini, Gini. What are you doing to me?

"She does not look Indian, like the others. Actually"—he looks me up and down—"neither do you."

"This is my birthplace." I clench my fists, opening and closing them.

"Are you sure about that?" He pulls out a silver cigarette case and carefully opens it, offering one to me before taking one for himself.

I shake my head once, refusing.

He lights his cigarette with a matching silver lighter, taking a deep inhale. "You are the man of the house, am I right?" He exhales up into the air. "Darius?"

"Yes." I step to the side in an attempt to shield Gini from his prying eyes. I can't help myself.

"I'm Nico. These men"—he gestures around the room—"answer to me."

"Good thing I'm not one of your men." I hold Gini's wrist, needing to touch her. Needing this asshole to know that she isn't his to look at.

He chuckles, again looking between Gini and me. "Come, let us talk. There is some important business I would like to discuss with you."

We both look over at Roshan and Abdyl, who are kissing between whispers on the couch. His hands cover her breasts, mouth against her throat. In Urdu, I tell Gini to sit beside Roshan. Her eyes look alarmed.

"I won't let you out of my sight. Do not worry."

Finally, she nods and takes her seat. I make my way to one of the bars with Nico.

"First, this girl of yours, Roshan, my boy wants her. How much do you want for her freedom?"

The Madam and I have already discussed the amount. I tell Nico the number, expecting some sort of shock.

Instead, he says, "We will pay cash. Tomorrow, Abdyl and I will come with the money, and you will give us the girl. Also, I want a contract signed. It needs to say that she is no longer the property of your Mullah Omar. I don't want the fucking *caliphate* on my head a year from now when someone changes their mind. The moment we pay, she must be free."

"Mullah Omar will take a cut from the amount. If you need his signature, I can arrange it."

"Very well then."

I nod, liking the way this man does business. He is clear, without any bullshit.

"It will be done." I put out my hand, and he shakes it.

Shaina comes in front of us, a platter of tequila shots on a large silver tray, matching her silver sari. The top is loose and cropped, showing her flat stomach. "Anything interest you?" She plays timid with Nico, lifting and then lowering the tray to play peekaboo with her body.

Nico only laughs at her game. "Sure."

She bends her knees, keeping her back straight and not spilling a drop. A real pro. Nico takes two drinks and hands them to me and then takes two for himself.

"Cheers," he says with a wink as he drinks them in succession.

I do the same.

"Which girl do you want tonight?" I ask, taking the empty cups from his hands and putting them on one of the small tables beside me. "I can arrange it."

"That beauty. The one in training. How much—"

Before he can finish speaking, I grab his neck. In a twist I don't see coming, he ducks and pulls out a knife from his pocket, pressing it against my side.

In my ear, he whispers, "I just wanted to confirm what I already knew. Does the Madam know you're in love with one of her girls?"

I spin away from him, pulling the knife right out of his hand. He looks at me with surprise.

"I'm not in love, motherfucker." I put the knife to his neck. "But I am a killer. And I will not hesitate to fucking gut you if you ever try to threaten me again or look at what is mine."

"What is yours, huh?" He tries to move, but I keep him locked in. "If you hurt me, there will be hell to pay."

I slowly pull away from him, knowing that this isn't going anywhere.

"Do you train? You're strong. Almost as strong as me." He puts out his hand, and I give him back the knife. He lifts his hand in the air, and I notice that his crew is watching us, ready to pounce. With a nod from Nico, they all go back to enjoying their evening.

This might be my home, but I'm definitely outnumbered.

"Yes, I exercise regularly." I pull out my own smoke, lighting up to calm down. "These women are the property of the house. It's my job to protect them."

He laughs, looking around the room. "Your stock is beautiful. Hey"—he looks into my eyes—"you don't touch the girls, do you? I would assume it would be bad form to use what you sell."

"Never," I tell him with a straight face. "There must be respect between these walls."

"Interesting." He shrugs, looking pleased. "And do you have a wife? More than one wife?"

He must know that Sharia law is quite generous to wealthy Islamic men.

"If a man can afford many wives, he is expected to take them. But as of now, I have no wife. Not one, not many."

"Why is that?"

I shrug, not saying anything more. From the corner of my eye, I see Amma watching me. She is always watching me, more and more as the days go by.

Nico clears his throat. "My men and I don't subscribe to Sharia law. I find that it doesn't work for my sensibilities. There is one woman I am waiting for. And once she's mine, there will be no others."

"Once she's yours?" I chuckle. "Doesn't sound promising."

He laughs. "In the next year or so, my bachelorhood will be over."

"You are powerful and privileged. And you are choosing to take only one wife?"

What I've been taught tells me that he's ridiculous. I always assumed that, eventually, I would marry. Afterward, I would take as many wives as my pockets would allow.

"Yes." He smiles. "There is one woman who is meant for me. Only one. Jealousy breaks relationships between men. It also breaks relationships between a man and a woman. I want my marriage with her to stay whole. Do you follow? When the time comes, I will have her and only her. And our marriage will be holy."

I rub the center of my chest. I know this way of life is how the Western man operates. *Could it be the way I operate, too? If I could have only one woman, would I be happy?*

I turn my head to see Gini. She is watching me with a worried look. I smile at her. Her lips part expectantly, gorgeous gray-blue eyes widening. I imagine having her and only her. Nico is right about jealousy. When there are many women and one man, a competition always arises. There is never comfort in those unions. But is that what marriage should be for? Comfort?

He clears his throat. "You are strict with Islam?"

"I drink alcohol. I don't pray. But certain rules are good for business. Other rules are just good. I understand them."

He chuckles. "Tell me, Darius, how did you end up here?"

Not wanting to answer his question, I quickly divert. "What do you want to drink?"

He leans his side into the bar, telling me, "I'll stick with tequila."

Divya comes toward us from the other end. Her dark hair is done high in curls, showing off her beautiful, doll-like face.

Before she can ask what he would like, Nico lifts his head and starts, "Don Julio. Rocks with lime."

Divya practically melts for him, her lips pressing together excitedly. I guess he's a decent-looking guy.

I order the same thing. Instead of replying, Divya looks between
us, back and forth, the expression on her face something like confusion. I look back at Nico before looking down at myself.

"I'll get your drinks," she says in perfect English.

I smile, proud of her language skills. She took quite long to learn,
but she has finally mastered it.

"These girls. Wow." He's clearly appreciative. "How do they speak
so well?"

"I teach them."

He nods. "You are good with languages?"

"I guess you could say that."

"So, you were about to tell me how you wound up in this place."

"Was I?" I scoff, annoyed at his presumptuousness.

Divya leaves the drinks on the table in front of us when a group of
men on the other side of the bar whistle at her. I take my glass and lift
it to Nico before taking my first sip.

"Yes, you were." He picks up his own glass.

"None of your business."

"What do you have to lose? For all you know, I know something."

"Know something? About what?" I scoff.

"Possibly"—he pauses—"I might know something that you are
blind to." He shrugs, "But before I speak, I need to know how you
came to be here. At The Mansion. With Madam."

I look out across the room, taking a moment. The girls walk with
sways to their steps, smiling on the outside. The act can be riveting.
I've known it all my life, and I have seen these same women suffering
on the inside while looking completely carefree on the outside. My
eyes zero in on Shaina, who, just two months ago, had a baby ripped
from her womb. That was the third time and will likely be the last
time she will conceive. I know she cries at night, and yet here she is,
playing the part like a professional.

Nico steps closer, waiting for a reply.

"On one hand, what do I have to lose by telling you about my history? On the other hand"—I take a sip of my drink—"my privacy matters to me. And who the fuck do you think you are, prying into my personal business?"

"Your choice." He shrugs. "But are you willing to ignore something that might be important?"

I finish my drink and decide, *Why not?*

Without being too specific of any details, I give him the general outline. He listens intently to every word I say, humming at the important parts.

"So, Mumbai is not necessarily your birthplace."

"No." I shake my head. "It might have been. But maybe not."

"Has anyone told you that you look Albanian?"

I laugh out loud, swallowing quickly before I can spit out my drink. "No. Definitely not."

He doesn't seem to find it funny. "You were found by Madam when you were, how old?"

I shrug. "I assume I was between four and six. Old enough to remember, but not too well."

"I see." He blows smoke out.

And then he starts to sing. At first, I'm confused. I want to ask him what he's doing. But suddenly, one of the notes resonates. I listen to the entire song in a trance, his voice more elegant than it has any right to be. The song travels somewhere into the recesses of my mind. I know this song. I ... know it. He repeats it over and over again. Each time he gets to the middle, my heart knocks. My mouth, of its own accord, begins to sing along. The language feels foreign on my lips. I have no idea how I know this, but I do. *Holy shit.* I have to put my drink down before I drop it.

He smiles. "It is called 'Baresha'. You're Albanian, brother." He taps me on the shoulder. "What people are noticing is our resemblance. Personally, I'm offended." He laughs.

"How ..." My voice trails off, my heart thumping. I can feel sweat gathering at my temples.

"Every child in Albania knows this song. Mothers are always

singing it. Yours did, too, apparently." He takes another heavy swallow.

I lift the drink back up and finish it.

"When my guys came here to do business a few months back, they told me about this place. And you. They saw our resemblance, and it got me curious. Kosovo in the '90s was ravaged by war. Many people ran away to other countries. Some died. Lots of displacement."

I want to speak, but the shock has closed my voice box.

"I've been looking for some new blood to join my crew. The streets here tell me you are lethal. That little knife trick you pulled makes me think that maybe they're right. I'm also glad to hear you're not some religious fanatic. That shit doesn't fly with me." He slowly shakes his head.

My jaw clenches. This asshole comes into my home, and within minutes, he manages to turn me inside out. I'm trying not to lose my shit.

"The world is big but small. I know you are connected very tightly to Mullah Omar. How did that connection come to be?"

"He brings rich Islamic men to us. We supply his friends with girls, who are not only beautiful and English-speaking, but who also sign contracts for short-term pleasure marriages that are acceptable under Shia Islam. Sometimes, he finds girls himself and sends them to us to train."

"I see. So, for you and Madam, religion is not so important."

"No, it's not. Money over *jihad*."

We laugh together.

"Same with us, brother. Same with us. But you know," he continues, "sometimes, we as men want to rise. We want to question and ask and wonder. It's the human spirit. Within this world you've created for yourself"—he opens his hands, gesturing around the room—"you've managed to sleep comfortably with the concept of supporting Islamically legalized prostitution." He shakes his head before spitting on the floor. "Truth? You buy women and force them to sell themselves for sex. Me and my crew? We do lots of shady shit. But never selling girls."

I shift, wanting to argue, but he beats me to it.

"Mullah Omar and the wealthy in places like Iran and Saudi love this situation, don't they? The rich can grow their very own harem, passing girls around as young as nine, and all of it is acceptable. And he's got you and Madam as his pawns, gathering up girls to sell and training them for their benefit. That motherfucker Omar has personally crossed me in the past. Not only do I hate him, but I also hate what he *does*. You understand?"

I swallow hard. "Who do you think you are? You don't like it? Get the fuck out then."

I want to take his knife and slice his throat. Tell him that, on top of everything else, he's a heretic. I might not be so religious, but I'd never go against the Word. *How dare he!*

Through my teeth, I tell him, "These marriages are part and parcel of Sharia law. And aside from that, even for a nonbeliever, there are girls who are hungry. Their parents cannot provide for them. This is the best they can do. Omar has his faults, but he isn't doing anything illegal."

"Is that right?" He tilts his head, completely unafraid of me.

He laughs. I'm listening so intently that my ears might burst.

"You're still in your prime, Darius." He leans in, voice darker. "Maybe you have dreams outside of this life, eh? Maybe you aren't always okay with the"—he pauses, pulling out another smoke and lighting up—"system. Maybe there is a girl here who you want for yourself, eh? Would your Mullah Omar or even Madam allow you to be happy? To have a woman of your own to love?"

I can't speak. Suddenly, my legs feel weak. Almost paralyzed.

"I recently lost my biggest muscle. My guys told me about a huge fucker here, in this brothel, who looked like my little brother. I had Abdyl talk to Roshan about you. She told him everything. How you teach the girls English and how you, yourself, speak many languages. How you're both incredibly lethal and the most loyal. That Madam has you tied up here, as though you owe her something." He lifts his hand, slicking his hair back. "If you're interested in living your own life, call me. Hear me out, though." He points at my chest. "There can be no selling girls under my watch. My boys want to buy from time to time? I get it. But we don't trade. You come over to my crew? No more girls. Mullah Omar is a sick fuck. If you leave this house, you leave him behind."

"You shouldn't speak that way about Mullah Omar. He is a very powerful man, Nico. I'd be careful if I were you." Why I'm sticking up for that bastard is anyone's guess.

"You afraid?" He laughs. "Omar has power, true. He's also got you under his thumb, training these girls and taking care of them so he can sell them to his own highest bidder. But I've got more strength than he does. And money. Freedom doesn't only have to be for Roshan, you understand me? I run a tight ship. Loyalty is what floats my operation. If you come over, I'll make sure that Omar doesn't touch you."

"I assure you"—I clear my throat, clenching my teeth—"I am good here. This is my life. This is who I am. You might not understand why we do what we do, but that's fine. Madam and I do like the money. Who doesn't? But we also protect these girls. And more often than not, we save them from far worse situations. So, don't fucking lecture me."

"This is who you are, huh? Ask yourself, how can you support a set of laws that cares so much about sex for rich men in mut'ah marriages and yet be so dismissive of women and their rights?"

"Their rights?" Now, it's my turn to laugh. "Trust me, no woman thinks of her rights when she's hungry, living in the slums, and asking for money without hands because a crew chopped them off to make her look more pathetic when she begs."

"If these girls had protection and rights, they'd be able to get out of this mess. You think you're helping them. Instead, you're just perpetuating their situation."

"I'm not perpetuating shit!" I grit my teeth. Somewhere deep in my psyche, I know he's making sense. But I can't face the idea that I've been fucking up all this time.

"You know, Darius, you don't need to stay here. You aren't one of these girls with no options. You can have freedom, if you want it. I'm not sure what Madam has on you, but it can't be worth your life." He hands me a small cream-colored card with gold lettering.

I blink. Stunned. I want to reply, but I can't.

He taps my back before rising, not bothered by my emotional change. "Think about our conversation. You seem intelligent. I don't agree with what you do, but clearly, you use your brain. You're also Albanian. I bet we could find out who you were, before this. Good luck, brother." His eyes move to Gini before coming back to me. "I have a feeling you're going to need it." He nods and then leaves.

The rest of the evening goes off easily, although I do take a few more drinks. My stress level is giving me a huge headache. I know that his words will take time to filter through my body, but now isn't the time to think on them. My eyes stay on Gini the entire evening, ensuring her safety. I stand in the corner, away from the crowd, watching and waiting. If any man goes near her, I will tear his head off. My temper is sizzling, but there is nothing I can do about it.

Everyone continues to party and engage in sex, either here in the room or behind the red curtains.

Nico and I do not speak again. Sometime later in the evening, I notice him leaving the house with three large men, one before him and two trailing his back.

I move near Gini, wanting to be closer to her. In some strange way, her presence calms me.

Amma struts through the room and sits beside Gini, coming straight between us. She bends herself to whisper something in Gini's ear. I can see Gini squirming and trying to make eye contact with the floor, but finally, Amma holds her chin, forcing her to watch a sexual encounter. Gini has entered a life where a man's dreams, regardless of how perverse, will rule her life. The girls who understand that concept fare the best. Again, my stomach rolls.

Nico's condescending voice barges into my head.

Is this right?

I look at Gini, face frozen as Madam whispers again in her ear. I want to do something. Pull her out of here. But I can't. I just … can't. Years I've spent accepting this life, and my mind doesn't want to let it go. It's all I know.

Nico is right about one thing. I have shackles on my legs. Not only because I owe Amma my life, but also because this life is all I have ever known. *How can I leave? How can I just break away from this?*

It feels like there's a hand around my throat. I need air. I can't breathe! With long strides, I make my way to the door and quickly step out of The Mansion, dropping myself onto the bottom stair. It's nice and dark. Finally, I exhale.

The air is cleaner tonight than usual. I let my gaze adjust to the darkness as I focus on my breathing. I turn around to look at The Mansion, lit up in lights. This is my world. For all intents and purposes, Islam is my religion. And Amma is my mother. She is the one who saved me from the slums and fed me. I'm not one to turn my back. Freedom? I have freedom! I'm here because this is my destiny. The girls here don't live free, that's true, but in the system in which we live, this is often the best option.

Nico was wrong. When rich men take on many wives, they are doing the girls a favor. Most of them cannot be fed. Their parents hand them off, knowing they will be taken care of. What would become of them otherwise? Men like Nico are so Western. They think everyone lives in a land of plenty. They say words like *freedom* and *rights*. But they don't know what it means to starve. It might have been a long time ago, but I still remember hunger's burn. And when I take a girl off the streets, one who has no future other than death, I'm helping her.

My heart chimes in, adding that Gini wasn't near death and she wasn't starving, either. My head falls forward into my hands.

When I feel calmer, I take a look at my arms, trying to make out the color. Me, Albanian, huh? I wonder who my father and mother must have been, and I make a mental note to check out what happened in Kosovo in the 1990s.

I pull Nico's card from my pocket and stare, wondering how deep this man's connections lie. I finger the corners. Inhale and exhale.

What do I want most in this world?

Gini's face flashes in my mind's eye, but really, it's what is within her that entices me. She has so much love in her heart. She is kind and thoughtful. She is warm and intelligent. Still, she isn't mine to want.

Finally, I tear the card in two and stuff the pieces in my back pocket. I need to put this nonsense behind me. Who I was before Amma found me in the gutter doesn't matter. The only thing that matters is who I am today. The man of *this* house. Nico doesn't understand me or the life I live. *Fuck him.*

I stand up and walk back inside my home. Entering the kitchen, I open up the refrigerator, wanting to take out something good. All I've eaten tonight are grapes, and I'm hungry.

Finding nothing interesting, I go into the pantry. Most of this closet is filled with bags of basmati rice, but sometimes, the girls hide chocolates on the bottom-left corner, beneath the bags of salt. I flip on the light and find Gini sitting on the floor, her back to a sugar bucket. She is crying silently, unable to stop the tears when she sees my face. An old blanket of mine is draped over her narrow shoulders.

"Gini?" My instincts have me dropping to my knees beside her and holding her face in my hands. Every thought I just had on those steps evaporates into thin air.

She looks up, gray-blue eyes full of water. "Darius," she whispers. "Don't tell them I'm here. I just needed a moment."

Just as I love, she has a completely clean face, devoid of anything but tears. No black makeup falls from her eyes. No face powder is streaked. She looks like an angel.

"I don't want to stay in this place. Please, Darius, find a way out for me. I can't be like those girls. I can't."

I sit beside her, wishing I could fix this for her. But she is already promised. I can't pull her out without severe consequences.

"Why don't you make me food? I'm hungry."

"What?" She furrows her eyebrows.

"You heard me. Work helps to resolve disappointment. The cooking will occupy you, and also give you a reason to be away from the party if Madam comes in. And I'm speaking in Urdu. Don't make me regret it, eh?"

She nods and stands, taking some onions and potatoes before leaving the room. It only takes her a moment or two for her crying to stop. She cooks with laser focus.

How will she keep herself busy when she is in Iran? I will miss everything about her. I wish I could take a drive with Gini in the seat beside me. We could watch the sunrise. *Would she love me, if I allowed her to?* I know in the depths of my heart that if I could have her, I would never want another woman in my bed.

I stare at her form. My heart pounds. I take a seat at the table, entranced.

She puts a plate in front of me, watching to see if I will accept it. I recognize it as village food.

"Sit," I tell her. "Eat with me."

"I only made enough for you." She wipes her cheek, some dark oil smearing beneath her eye.

"Then, we will share." I swallow heavily, taking the moment to stare at her face. I can't help the urge to memorize her. That long, silky black hair and those stunning eyes against her creamy-white skin. I don't think I could ever get used to her. Not that I'll ever have the chance. I can't have her for long. But I want her now.

She looks at me with sadness in her eyes. "Darius—"

I press my finger to her lips, not wanting her to point out anything that would ruin this moment. I'm being stupid. I want her too badly. We eat together quietly, in silence. She is unbothered by sharing a plate with me. Likely, she is used to sharing a plate with her family. I, on the other hand, never do this. It's so intimate. More intimate than maybe any moment I have ever had. How many women have been in my bed? Countless. And yet, never have I had this urge to share. Not with just anyone, though. It's an urge to share with *Gini*. To feed *Gini* with my own hands.

"Take your hair down." It's not a question.

Without complaint, she pulls the ribbon out, staring at me. *Is this what you want?* her sweet eyes ask.

I exhale, pulling her closer to my chest. She sets her head on me, and I smell her hair. Her neck. Her cheeks. I want to kiss her rosebud lips, but I know that if I do, I won't be able to stop.

I dip the bread into the stew and put it into her tender mouth. She eats everything I give her, and I watch, enjoying the movement of her lips. I love feeding this woman.

Finally, I lift her into my arms and take her downstairs, to her room. I place her on the mattress outdoors. The air is balmy, evening completely dark.

"Come," she whispers.

I sit down beside her, and she raises herself up onto her knees, taking my neck in her hands. That is all it takes for me to finally press my lips against hers. The night is so dark that I can barely see. But I can feel her. I can feel the panting of her warm breaths against my lips. I move to kiss her cheek. Her neck. She tilts, giving me access to her entire body. My hands can't get enough. They roam around her breasts and down to her waist, lifting her into my lap, caressing her bottom.

She shivers in my arms and I tell her, "I feel it, too. I feel it, too."

She can't get a word out as I inhale her.

I want to bring her to ecstasy. My hand slides inside her shirt and moves upward, letting me cup her breast. The gasp she gives me has me pausing.

This is new to her.

Her body is begging for more, but her mind hasn't caught up yet.

"Don't worry, Gini. Not too much."

"Oh," she moans, hugging me. "I want it, but I can't. I'm scared. What they did tonight ... Darius—"

I sit up a bit to adjust myself before placing her back on top of me.

"Darius," she says my name like a plea.

"Yes," I reply, holding her head in my hands so I can stare into her eyes. "Do not worry, Gini. I will never hurt you."

"This thing between us, I wasn't sure—"

"I have felt it the whole time. From the moment I saw you. The way you loved your father. The way you cared about your life." I drop my hands to my sides. "I'm so sorry I stole you, Gini." My voice cracks. "Maybe I just didn't know better. Maybe I just never asked the right questions. Maybe there's a way out for us."

I think about Nico and the things he said to me tonight. Something like shame creeps up my spine as I imagine tearing Gini from her home. My eyes slightly adjust, and I can see the outline of her face. Her body, so soft, folds into mine as she cries. I love this woman, so much.

"I'm going to find a way, Gini. I swear it."

She nods, tears filling her eyes.

We spend the entire evening in each other's arms, kissing, holding, and finally falling asleep.

The next morning, I wake up with the most beautiful girl on earth curled into my chest. Allah help me, but I can't let her go.

I let myself touch Gini's hair and the soft skin on her arms.

She opens her gentle eyes, smiling. "Oh," she croaks, "it wasn't a dream."

"You are unlike anyone I've ever known. You make me laugh. You manage to teach me, just as I teach you. I love being near you. Your thighs." I bring myself down, kissing the soft skin between her legs.

My blood roars as I scent her, my nose inhaling at her neck, but my mind refuses to listen. She isn't ready for that. Not yet.

She giggles, trying to close her legs. I hold them open, nuzzling.

"Darius!" she squeals as I lick the soft skin behind her knee before blowing warm air over the wetness.

I ENTER Roshan's room to tell her the good news. I spoke with Amma just a few moments ago, and she was glad for the income her sale will bring. While we are losing our best girl, we are making more money off her sale than we ever would with her living at The Mansion. Amma couldn't be happier.

"Darius, hi!" She sits at her small dressing table, applying cream to her skin.

I cross my arms over my chest, trying not to smile even though I'm happy for her. "I have something to tell you."

"Tell me I'm being bought. Darius, I'm shaking, here. *Shaking!* Abdyl told me last night that our time had come. Has it? Has it come?"

"Yes."

She screams, jumping into my arms. "I'm really going to be free? Truly free?"

I nod my head. "Say your good-byes, Roshan. You leave today." I place her back down on the floor.

Something passes over her face before she bites her lip self-consciously. "Today? But that's not long enough. I need to prepare." She scurries around the room, lifting perfume bottles from her night-stand before placing them back down, muttering words to herself that I cannot hear. Tears well up in her eyes.

I watch her for a few more minutes before asking, "Hey, what's wrong?"

She turns to me. "Darius, I have been here, in this home, for three years. Before this, I was living with my parents and five siblings in a clapboard house in Dharavi. Freedom? What does that even mean?" She laughs, but it's clear she doesn't think anything about the situation is funny.

"It means, being able to come and go as you please. It means, deciding how you want to live. Your body and your mind are your own, and no one else can control you. When you want to leave your house, you can leave. When you want to return, you can return."

"He told me last night that he was getting an apartment for me on the Upper East Side of New York City. How will I survive there, Darius?"

"You will survive in the same way you always have. With your head held high. You are not only beautiful, but you are smart, too. You speak English, so you will have no trouble communicating. I trust you will figure out the rest."

"Have you been there? To New York City?"

I shake my head. "I've been to London. And Paris. They are

gorgeous cities. New York will be just as beautiful. And America is different—in a good way. At any age, if you want to be, say, a doctor, you can apply for school, and if you get in, you follow your dream. No one shuts the door on you. Rich can become poor. Poor can become rich. It's a kind of ... mobility. True freedom."

She looks at me, her eyes glassy. "You are more than this life, you know? I think—"

Amma walks into the room, and Roshan immediately quiets.

"I trust that Darius told you the good news." She lifts a brow.

"Yes, he has, Madam. Thank you so much for allowing my sale." She swallows hard. "I never thought I'd be so lucky."

"No need to thank me. We're making very good money. Other-wise, we wouldn't have said yes." She steps deeper into the room, her long blue sari draped around her tall, thin frame. She puts her hand on my shoulder, and I stiffen. "Just remember, even with this alleged freedom, you can find yourself in chains and indebted to him. Make sure to always keep money aside for yourself. If he hands you cash to shop, put a portion away. Any chance you get, save your money and hide it. Men in America can bore of you just as easily as any other man in the world. And if he kicks you to the curb, you need to have something to fall back on."

"Yes, Madam." Roshan drops her head.

"I tell you this in all seriousness, Roshan. Right now, he might be enamored by you. But when he tires of you, you will have nothing for yourself unless you plan for it. Remember this"—she lifts Roshan's chin up—"you need your apartment paid in full. For gifts, cash is always best, but diamonds or designer jewelry have decent resale value. Never trust a man to the point where you have nothing and he has everything. From the moment he takes you, begin to save."

"Okay." She nods, listening intently.

"You might pack up any gifts you have acquired from the men over the last few years. But everything else, down to your perfume, belongs to The Mansion."

Roshan moves to the side of her bed, her fingers glossing over a beautiful golden sari.

"And that includes your clothes," Madam snaps. "Narmada will check your luggage before you leave to make sure you didn't take anything ... by accident. Nico and Abdyl will be coming shortly. Upon the sale, they will take you away." And with that last word, she exits the room.

"She cares, you know." I lean against Roshan's desk. "In her own way." I pull out a wad of cash from my back pocket. "Take this."

Her mouth drops open, and I push the wad of cash into her palm. I know she has nothing, and I don't want her to be without.

"Darius, look. What we were talking about before. You're more than—"

"Don't say it." I clench my jaw. I want to be able to leave, but I still don't know how to make it work. I have all the girls under my roof to feed and house. I have Amma, who I am indebted to.

She exhales. "I have a phone. Take my number. If you ever find yourself in New York, will you call me?"

I pull out my own phone. "Sure. Give me the number."

FOUR HOURS LATER, Nico and Abdyl sit in our living room. They are both wearing dark blue suits, looking serious and imposing. I lean back against the couch cushion. In the light, I can finally get a good look at Nico. I'll admit, we share some strange resemblance. I smile, knowing that even with our similarities, I could kill him with my bare hands. I go through the different ways I could end his life, and for some reason, I'm comforted. In some ways, I'm decent. In others, I'm fucked up. There's no other way to describe it.

Gini appears with a silver tray filled with steaming hot chai. She makes her way around with a straight back as the men choose a glass, taking a fresh date with it.

When she stands in front of me, a blush rises up from her neck and into her cheeks. In Urdu, she asks, "Would you like a glass of chai?"

"Say my name, Gini. And ask me in English."

She rolls her eyes, smirking. "W-would you like a chai, Darius?"

"Hmm, that's good. Just bend down a bit, so I can see the glasses better. I want a full one."

She lowers her knees slightly, so her breasts are at my eye-level. "So perfect," I whisper, my eyes flitting between her chest and eyes. I take a tea and place it on the table beside me before adjusting the cups to make the weight more even.

"Thank you, sir," she whispers.

I nod, and she places the tray in the center of the coffee table before making an exit just as Amma glides in, fully made up. Abdyl sits at the edge of the antique couch, clearly nervous for Roshan to arrive.

"So"—Nico pulls out a cigarette and puts it into his mouth before nodding toward a suitcase beside his feet—"here is the money. Feel free to count it."

Amma smirks. "We shall. If you don't mind."

Nico hands her the case, and she grabs it, taking it out of the room. I can imagine her hauling the case into her bedroom, shutting the door behind her with a slam, and spilling the cash on her bedspread. Counting the money with relish. A man like me loves being the best at what I do. The money is nothing but a small result after tackling a mountain. But Amma? She just loves the money.

Abdyl twists his hands together.

"Don't look so nervous," I tell him, not unkindly. "She's just as you left her last night."

As if on cue, Roshan walks into the room, a small yellow purse in her hand. She is wearing a green sari, her long, dark hair shining against her clear skin. Abdyl immediately stands up, and she runs toward him. He lifts her in his arms, and they both start laughing.

Nico gets up with a smile on his face, shaking my hand. Quietly, he asks, "Have you given any thought to what we talked about last night?"

"A bit," I reply honestly.

"I'm sure. You'd better think quickly, or your spot might be taken. I almost never take an interest in new blood entering the core of my operation. But from the moment I laid eyes on you, I saw the potential. Make the right choice, Darius. You've outgrown this place."

The happy couple leaves the room after Nico, and I walk behind them, leaving The Mansion. Nico opens the backseat of his black Mercedes, getting in, and Abdyl and Roshan enter an identical car right behind his. But before they take off, Roshan sprints out of the car and runs to the top of The Mansion steps.

"I used to dream of you," she tells me, breathless.

"Oh yeah?" I want to laugh.

"Yeah. To find a man like you. So strong but with a soft heart." She looks down before bringing her face back up to mine. "I see the way you look at her. I noticed it right away."

I don't reply, keeping my face straight, although inside, worry courses through my veins. If she noticed, who else has? I turn my head to The Mansion. Amma watches us from her bedroom window.

"You'll text me, right? If you ever come to New York?"

I look back down to her. "Sure I will."

With a final exhale, she screams up to the second floor of the house. "Good-bye, girls! And good luck!"

The girls cheer, waving out of their windows and watching as she reenters the car.

And then she's off.

11

Darius

I COME BACK into The Mansion after a breakfast for Arman's birthday. All of D-Company surprised him at the Taj Hotel, which has a morning buffet that is second to none.

There will always be a line between me and Arman's crew because I have never taken their oath. But over time, they've come to trust me as much as an outsider can be trusted.

I take a seat at the kitchen table and adjust my pants as Narmada sets a steaming mug of coffee in front of me. Just as I lift *The Mumbai Times* to my face, I hear Mullah Omar's voice booming against the walls. Something is wrong. I did not even know he was scheduled to come.

I run down the hall, entering the great room. "What's going on here?"

I pause at the arched doorway, Omar's mocking grin turning my decent mood into something like a simmering rage. The air in The Mansion feels like it just got twenty degrees hotter.

"Darius," he states plainly, sitting comfortably in one of our chairs with his ankles crossed.

Amma pulls out one of her signature, long, thin cigarettes and places it between her red-painted lips. "We have a surprise visitor. Aren't we lucky?"

Her fingers shake as she tries not once, but three times to light it up. I walk inside, pulling out my own lighter from my pocket and helping her.

She takes a hard inhale. Exhaling, she whispers, "Thank you, my darling." She smiles tightly, worry etching her face.

For the first time, I notice the darkness under her eyes, seeping through her heavy makeup. It is highlighted by the black chador she is forced to wear when Omar enters The Mansion.

I give her a level stare, telling her with my eyes to get a grip. *What did he do to elicit this kind of reaction?*

She inhales and exhales again, the smoke blurring the contours of her face.

"So, Darius," Omar starts, "the girls you have here are special. I have to give you the compliment and tell you that you've really managed to perfect the art of finding the rarest beauties. Still, with the economy slowing and less business travel in Mumbai, times have been rather tough for your little house parties, have they not?"

"They have not. We have a great flow. Our girls are doing just fine, and so are we. We recently sold Roshan and made quite a bit off of her. Your portion of the sale is already on its way to you." I cross my arms over my chest, feeling defensive.

"You sold her?" His jaw drops. "I never gave you—"

"I don't need your permission. Acquisitions and sales are within The Mansion's domain, even for the girls you have bought yourself. However, as you were Roshan's purchaser, you will receive a cut of twenty percent."

I've reviewed the numbers recently, and they worry me. While we have profit each year, nikah mut'ah marriages are the dominant way we stay afloat. I wish it weren't the case, but it is.

"Money, like money does, gets spent." He shrugs. "And the party flow is not what pays your debts. The short-term marriage contracts that I procure are what make the real money for your house. And those contracts are attained by no one else but me." He points to his chest, black-diamond eyes aglow. "If I were to stop bringing men to you, The Mansion would be nothing more than a regular, run-of-the-mill brothel."

"Our girls are not run of the mill," Amma points out. "They are special. Intelligent. Beautiful. They dance. Speak English, even. This house has created generations of the most gifted tawaifs in India." She lifts her nose in the air, her old pride and arrogance in full force. "With or without your contracts, we are good enough to thrive."

He laughs. "Doubtful, my dear. It is with my connections that the men with the deepest pockets even know about this house." He looks me straight in the face and adds, "Don't even bother arguing this point, Darius. We all know that I'm the one who injects necessary cash to this operation."

I take a deep breath, my mind turning with the ways I can kill Omar.

My hands.

The knife in my sock.

The two guns inside the waistband of my pants.

Instead, I plant my feet into the floor, letting the churn in my chest run its course. "Why don't you just tell us what it is you want?"

Why Mullah Omar wants any more control over The Mansion than he already has is anyone's guess. The man is already extremely powerful and rich, owning businesses all across the globe. In his grand scheme, we are nothing but a sure way to satisfy his business associates. I can feel the sweat bead on my temples, but I refuse to show him how much power he has on my mental state. My only hope is that he gets out of here quickly, before I lose my mind.

"What I want?" He smirks. "You realize that when you throw these little sex parties, you're going against Sharia law. It disgusts me that you sell girls like prostitutes, without any contract to go with them."

"Oh, please." Amma chuckles, waving a hand in front of her face. "These parties we throw are the bread and butter of what we do and have always done. The first time you came to us was for one of our parties!"

He clears his throat. "Those days are over. I have high hopes for myself, but I cannot ever be connected to a ... a brothel. I want complete control over the entire Mansion and every item in it. Just as I have complete control in my other businesses. You see"—he rubs his hands together—"I'm essentially a king. Known far and wide as a brilliant and devout businessman. I am getting ready to rise. Politically."

Amma presses her lips together. "And what do you, in your infinite wisdom, suggest we do with the girls?"

"That's simple. Every single woman in The Mansion will be mine. I'll take care of all of you. I own many buildings. I can use one of them to house you all. Even Darius." He smiles. "I'm sure I can find good use for you, too."

I picture myself jumping forward, strangling him, when Amma puts her hand on my chest. "Settle."

Turning back to Omar, she asks, "You want us to close down The Mansion and move into your personal harem?" Amma tilts her head, as if she were a confused little girl. "Why don't we simplify this? You can tell me which of our girls you want to keep, and you can have them for ninety-nine years." Madam's smile is all innocence. "You choose any of my girls, and we'll figure out a price. Perfectly acceptable under Sharia law."

"You aren't understanding me," he spits. "I want every single one of them. Including you."

Amma smiles seductively, her way of softening a situation. "Mullah Omar. Please, if you want to take a few of my ladies, by all means. But let's not become greedy now. Taking over The Mansion," she repeats his words, laughing, as though this whole conversation were just a joke.

"Listen!" he shouts, standing up. "I don't want the women for ten years. I don't want them for ninety-nine years, either. I want total control of each of your minds and bodies for this life and the one hereafter. The Mansion will close. I'm not a bad man, which is why I'm telling you to come with me, back to Iran. I shall care for you all."

Madam's eyes flash. The truth has finally surfaced. "So, you plan to turn us all into your slaves?"

I grit my teeth, finding myself migrating closer to him. I imagine bending down to pull out my knife and gouging his eyes out.

He nods, a crazy look marring his ugly face. "That is exactly what I want. I want every single man in Iran to know that I possess the most magnificent slave harem in all the world. I no longer want to be the one connecting fat, rich pigs to the girls. I want those men to come to me and beg for a taste of what I own."

"How convenient," I add. "You can tell your community that you took infidels who engaged in sexual prostitution and shut down their operation, forcing them into slavery instead of killing them, as you could have." I slowly clap my hands together. "Heart of gold."

He chuckles. "Well done, Darius." His eyes sparkle. "You always were a smart boy."

"Let's get something straight here. You are an acquaintance of ours, who brings business to The Mansion. And as such, you receive a share of profits for connections you make. Under no circumstances are we planning to shut down. We are not your property and never will be. Ever. If you aren't happy with the situation between us, you can leave."

He smiles. "The question is, Darius, how long could you last without me bringing my customers? Your girls had better be ready to lie on their backs quite frequently to keep the money flowing in, and even then, it would be a pitiful sum. Why wait for your impending doom? Why not come to me of your own volition and bring the girls with you? Less pain that way, don't you think? At least then, you could without the chains."

I crack my knuckles, wanting him to leave before I smash his face in.

"We shall see." He shows me his teeth. "The offer is on the table but for a limited time. I'm sure you understand that I won't be bringing in my friends any longer. In which case, you will lose your cash flow. And when you have nothing left, I might change my mind about taking you all in." He looks around the great room, as though it were already his. "I guess you could always sell The Mansion and move into the red-light district here. I have heard that it's quite ... animalistic."

Amma clicks her tongue, turning toward me. "Let's not be so rash, Darius. Mullah Omar is a great man. A smart man." She spins around to face him. "We appreciate your kind offer and understand that following Sharia law and keeping us all as good Islamic citizens is always at the root of your words. You see, Darius"—she looks over to me, anxious but covered with a phony smile—"we really ought to discuss our options. If the great, magnanimous, learned Mullah Omar decides to stop sending us men for proper mut'ah marriages, where would that leave us?"

I can tell her words are only meant to pacify, but it angers me more than I thought possible. I will never bow to this fraud!

"That's right." He puffs up his chest, eyes scanning Amma's body like a man starved. "I'll be leaving back to Iran in a few hours." He points a fat finger at me. "Next time I return—and it will be soon—I shall come with Navid Soltabian. Gini had better be ready, as she just might be your last chance at earning any meaningful income. And at that time, I expect an answer from the two of you."

"Soon?" I state so quickly that Madam Amma's brows rise.

"Will that be a problem?" Mullah Omar questions, annoyed.

"Of course not!" Madam smiles. "We are delighted that you chose one of our girls to satisfy your client. Sharia law is good to us, praise God! She's been studying every single day under Darius, and she is ready."

"Just remember"—he points to us both with eerie calm—"the money Soltabian pays for Gini will be what floats The Mansion for the foreseeable future. Once that flow of money stops, or he decides he's done with her, you'll be without any decent income. I think it's safe to assume that sigheh has come to an end in this house."

With that, he leaves, taking long strides down the hall to the front door. The maids run after him to get the door, but he ignores them, letting himself out.

The door slams, and Amma's face crumples as she pulls the *hijab* off her platinum hair. "Is he right? Are we so low on funds?"

"Yes." I press my lips together.

"Darius—"

"I will come up with a plan, Amma. Do not fret. That piece of shit won't live to see the day this house crumbles."

We stand in silence until she breaks it. "I saw your face." A dark shadow moves over her. "Do. Not. Fall. For. This. Girl."

"Don't be ridiculous, Amma."

"You shouldn't teach her anymore. You must have nothing more to do with that girl. I heard a commercial the other day. Rosetta Stone. She can learn English, using that program."

"Amma, you are being absurd."

"Don't you speak to me that way!" she yells, cutting me off. "Love is the antithesis of our world. I saw it in your eyes, Darius, when he mentioned her. And the truth is, I have seen it in your eyes ever since she came."

I open my mouth to reply when she stomps her foot on the ground.

"Don't you lie to me! I took you from the gutter. Raised you. You think I can't smell the lies on you? You want that girl, and I won't allow it! If Gini can keep Soltabian happy, that can keep us afloat for years without Omar's connections." She breathes heavily. "This girl is the one who will save our home. Our lives. If Soltabian isn't happy with her, this entire house will fall into Omar's claws. The only answer is for Gini to enamor Soltabian and to stay with him for as long as possible. It's a hundred thousand dollars a year! Not rupees, but dollars. Do you understand this? You cannot get in the way of our goal, Darius!" she shrieks.

"Calm down, Amma. This instant. I will figure out a plan to save The Mansion. Trust me."

She turns her face upward, as though her mind were already elsewhere. "We will rot if you don't figure something out. Is that what you

want for yourself? Or for us? I have grown this business on my back!"
She begins to pace, her shoes clicking against the floor. "I need to do
more research on this Soltabian. See his likes and dislikes. Gini
cannot fail. She has to make him happy and get that ninety-nine-year
contract ..."

I grit my teeth, trying not to picture Gini's beautiful, innocent
face. I just promised her a way out. And now, the doors of opportunity are closing.

Suddenly, Amma's mania calms. She turns to me, her voice soft. "I
know I'm not always kind. But I do it for their own good. Think of all
the girls, Darius, who, truth be told, we have saved. Sure, we expect
them to sell sex. But the life they have here is millions better than if
they were on the street, begging. Or, God forbid it, as Omar's slave.
Think of the world we've made here. You and me, together," she
whispers her last word, her nails grazing up and down my arm.

I step back, hating the feel of her on my skin. "I will never give us
up to that maniac."

"That's right, darling. *Us.*"

～

I START to run down the steps into Gini's basement. I have a million
things to tell her. I want to explain the predicament and let her help
me think of options, but I'm worried that being truthful will hurt her
in the end. I stop, pausing before opening up the door to her room. I
can't see her. Not yet.

Fuck! I need to think. Pivoting, I make my way back upstairs.

Twenty minutes later, I find myself running on the treadmill,
sweating as my mind moves faster than my legs ever could. I have to
figure out how to both save The Mansion and take Gini out of here. I
can't run away with her, leaving Amma and the girls to fend for
themselves.

I finally stop the machine and hold the handlebars, dropping my
head as my heart beats through my chest. The answer is sitting at the
edges of my psyche. If I just dig deep enough, it will unfold. And then

his face flashes in my mind's eye. Nico. He said to call him if I ever needed anything. Calling in a favor with Nico would mean selling my soul to the Albanian Mafia. That's not something I want to do unless I'm desperate. A last resort.

Arman's crew, D-Company. An idea begins to take shape as I remember my conversation with him over drinks months ago.

Sweat drips from the ends of my hair and down my entire body. I drop to the ground and do a few sets of push-ups, needing to get my stress out.

Still out of breath, I walk upstairs to my bathroom, peeling my clothes off as I move.

I get into the shower and shut my eyes beneath the hot spray. *Am I ready to leave The Mansion, Amma, Mumbai, and everything else I have ever known?* Gini and I, we could go to America. Live free. I'm able-bodied and young. I believe that I can find work and make a life for ourselves. But how could I leave comfortably, knowing the destruction I left behind? The plan with D-Company needs to work.

I turn off the shower. After I'm dressed, I dial Arman and tell him my thoughts, finally spilling about Gini and wanting to leave.

"Listen, like I told you that night at Aer, it's a good idea to sell part of The Mansion to us."

"And you guys would protect the girls, too?"

"That's right. I know they have a decent life by you. We wouldn't change that. Also, I've got a cousin who lives in the Bronx. He can set you up with an apartment and work when you arrive."

"That's good," I exhale. "Real good."

"Listen." He clears his throat. "I'm not going to lie. I'm upset to hear of you leaving. But I'm not totally surprised, either. If anything, the most surprising thing of all is how long it took you to fall for one of these beautiful women you train. For a moment, I thought Madam had something to do with that."

"Madam?"

"Yeah. She has always been so obsessed with you. Come on, man. You know what I mean. I assume you aren't telling her about your plan, either."

"No, I'm not."

"Good. Because she wouldn't allow it. She'd find a way to stop you from leaving, no doubt."

I can't reply. I just can't. I change the subject. "I hope Devan agrees. Otherwise, I've got nothing left."

"Pray he's in a good mood when you meet with him. And you realize, time isn't on your side. You've got to get it squared away before the Iranian comes for your girl. When is he coming?"

"I'm not sure. I think in a few months from now. He won't take her until I say she's ready. I can stall. Will you set up the meet for me and Devan?"

"Of course."

We hang up, and I feel relieved. Nothing is decided, but it's good to have a plan.

A knock at my door startles me. I open it. Gini. I pull her inside, hugging her into my arms and smelling her hair. I don't want to tell her anything about D-Company or get her hopes up. Not yet. Soon, when things are more concrete.

She giggles, trying to get out of my hold. "The girls are dancing and Madam is out. But we don't have long." She thinks I'm playing by not letting her go, but the truth is, I need her. I just have to feel her against me.

12

Gini

THE BELL RINGS SO LOUDLY that the book in my hands drops to the floor. Not even a moment later, Narmada comes flying into my room.

"Get up here this instant." Sweat beads from her temples. "Madam wants you right away. And you have tea to brew!"

I stack my books and stand up, following her out the door. Before I cross the threshold, I take a quick glance at my work. When I'm not cleaning or mending, I'm always down here, learning. I never realized how spectacular it was to push your mind in such a way. Now that I've felt the feeling of mental accomplishment, I wish it would never end. It always seems that as soon as I find a stride, someone interrupts me.

We make our way upstairs and enter the kitchen.

"Make the chai. Six glasses, just as Roshan taught you. Then, take it all upstairs, on the silver tray, and offer it to Madam in her bedroom. It will be heavy, so keep your back straight!" She puts a small crystal bowl onto the tray, filled with fresh dates. "Offer her one, as well, with her drink. And this"—she puts another glass bowl onto the tray—"is hard sugar. Anytime someone asks you to bring tea in Iran, this is how you do it."

"Yes, ma'am."

I brew the tea just as Roshan taught me. She left just the other day. And although I will miss her, I couldn't be happier for her. Careful not to spill a drop, I make my way up the narrow staircase and into Madam's quarters. Part of me feels worried to enter her bedchamber, but another part of me is curious. I have been admitted into all of the women's rooms to clean, but Madam's has always been off-limits.

The light is dim, but I can still see the color of the walls, which are painted a creamy pink. Or maybe white? Two chairs and a couch face each other with a wooden table between them. Finally, I turn toward the bed. It is quite grand but old, made of wood with four large columns on each corner. It's imposing.

"Kutta, is that you?" Madam croaks. "Can't you see my room is boiling? Open the windows! Get some light and air in here!" She mumbles something else, but I can't catch it.

I gently put the chai down on the table by the seating area and make my way around the room, opening the heavy curtains and pulling up the windows. Narmada taught me how the windows open, and not for the first time, I'm so glad I listened when she gave me instructions.

When light filters through the room, I take a look and see Madam lying in bed, her pasty-white toes peeking out from a heavy, dark wool blanket. I try not to, but I can't help myself—my eyes trail up to her face. She has no makeup on. Heavy and stark white dots mar her yellow face. She looks like she's been drawn on.

She snaps, "What do you think you're staring at?"

I can see her small teeth grind against each other.

"I-I'm sorry, Madam. I almost didn't recognize you without your makeup."

Sitting up and leaning against her bed's headboard, she orders, "Bring me the tea."

I lift one cup of tea and walk it over to her.

"What are you doing?" she screams. "You offer me tea with the entire silver tray! It's silver, isn't it?"

"Yes, Madam." I scurry back to the table, put the glass down, and lift the entire tray in my hands.

When I bring it over to where she sits, she glances at each individual glass, as if checking to make sure the color is correct. I say the English alphabet in my head to keep my hands from shaking. She chooses a glass from the side, making the weight of the tray uneven. Still, I hold my back up so that it doesn't collapse. Her long, bony finger pushes the dates around their bowl until she chooses one to her liking. Lastly, she takes a piece of rock sugar and drops it into her cup. It falls straight to the bottom with a clink.

She takes a sip, and I find myself holding my breath. "This is cold. How could you serve me cold tea? I ought to whip you for this!" She spills the tea onto my shirt. It's so hot.

"I'm s-sorry, Madam." I put my head down, looking at the other glasses. "Would you like to try a different cup, perhaps?" I lift the tray forward again, offering them all to her.

"Absolutely not," she huffs. "All of these were made together. The same batch. Do you think I'm stupid or something? If one is cold, they are all cold!"

I stand there, unmoving, and then she changes her mind, taking another cup. Bringing it to her lips, she drinks a long sip before biting into a date.

"What are you staring at me for? Put the chai down, you idiot!"

I do as she asks before moving back to her bedside. When she is finished, she puts her glass out. I take it from her hands.

"Set it down over there," she commands, pointing to the table by her bed. "I want to tell you about this Iranian man I once knew. He was a billionaire, you know. Bought me this entire bedroom set. The pink fabric on the chairs was made in France."

She clears her throat. "Now, massage my feet while I tell you about him. Use your thumbs and press."

Using both of my hands, I rub the arch of her sallow, wrinkled foot.

"Just like that. Oh. Okay. That's nice," she exhales.

No matter how awkward this feels for me, I wouldn't dare move an inch.

"I was twelve years old, and he came to a party right here, at The Mansion," she starts. "Madam told him I was nine. I guess he had a thing for young girls, and luckily, my body was only in the start of its bloom.

"I danced for him, of course, like I danced and sang for all the men at that party. He was smitten by me." She looks up and out her window, as though she were floating elsewhere. "The group brought a cleric with them, so he could marry us before taking me into his bed.

"After our evening together, he told Madam that he wanted to prolong our contract. He handed her a fistful of cash before taking me to Iran, where I was part of his harem. There were maybe twenty-five women and girls living there, but it did not take long for me to become his favorite. I had three maids, all dedicated to my care. No one else had as many maids as me. They helped me dress and put on makeup; they cooked and fed me. I had my own seamstress, who brought me fabrics from Europe. Really, he treated me like his queen. I lived with all of the other ladies, of course, in a grand mansion down the road from his home. His wife was so jealous; she became blind with it. Eventually, I grew a few years older, and I thought he and I had become closer. In many ways, I became content with my place in his life."

She becomes quiet.

I squint my eyes to look closer. *Has she fallen asleep?*

"One night, he called for me. There was a huge party, and all of his business associates from Saudi were in Iran. He wanted to show me off. But I refused to go downstairs. I was tired. It was that time of the month for me, and my flow was heavy. I felt bloated. And my skin was horrendous."

She touches the side of her face, as though remembering. "When the maids ran upstairs and begged me to come out, I sent them all away, telling them to take someone else." She shakes her head, breathing turning shallow.

"His associates laughed and made fun of him. 'How could a woman lead you by your balls?' they joked. 'And a whore at that!' They laughed.

"He asked his advisors, 'What should I do?' They told him that if he let me get away with disobeying his orders, all the women in the country, from sisters to mothers and wives to whores, would think that it was acceptable to say no to a man's wishes." She shakes her head, eyebrows furrowing. "They told him that it was his job and his right to show everyone just what happens to a woman who disobeys her master.

"That night, he brought me to the foyer of his mansion, and in front of everyone, including his wife, he threw acid in my face before banishing me from his home. These spots"—she points to her skin —"were my punishment. I came back here, mortified. And hideous!" Her voice speeds up. "Madam had me lie on the table, nude, like a cooked chicken, so all the other women could see what had become of me. Apparently, The Mansion had been earning a huge yearly sum during my temporary marriage, and the end of it was a blow to its finances.

"Madam had me on my back more often than not, wanting me to earn what I had given up. She was tough but did what she could to survive. But I grew stronger, too. I learned how to live, using my mind. And in the end, I would like to think that I prevailed. She died young, and by the age of seventeen, I took her place."

She shifts her body so that I switch to massaging her other foot.

"I tell you this because you are my property. If you do not do as commanded, you might not be as lucky as I was. And if you die, I will lose my investment in you."

She shakes her foot out of my grip, and I rear back, startled.

Leaning forward, Madam grabs my jaw with her hand. I can smell her acidic breath. "Survival is not all I expect. You must carry yourself with dignity, beauty, and grace. Most of all, in any public setting, you bow to your master. He says *bark like a dog*, and you get on all fours and howl."

She pushes my face away from hers, and I fall onto the floor.

"Don't disappoint me, Gini. Or it will be your dead body I splay on the dining table for all the girls of The Mansion to see."

She shows me her teeth, slowly licking them. "While you're here, we should also talk about a small complication I've noticed."

I can hear my own breaths as fear leaks into my bloodstream.

"Darius." She speaks his name like he's her own. Her eyes narrow like those of an animal. "If you entice him more than you already have, there will be consequences. He belongs to me. His blood is mine. Every hair on his head is mine. The air he breathes? Mine!"

My mouth feels like it has been stuffed with cloth.

"There is a very wealthy man who lives in the outskirts of Saudi. He is known for his extremely wild nature and specific tastes. He frequently calls me, asking if any of my girls can be sent to him. I haven't agreed because why would I want to have any of my girls mutilated or killed for sexual sport? But for you, I might have to make an exception." She spits, and it lands directly on my face. "Now, get out!"

I catch my breath and sprint from the room, shaking, running down the steps into my quarters. *I must find a way to get out of here!*

I reach my room and find Darius sitting on the floor, books spread out around him.

I leap downward, into his arms. "Oh, Darius. You're here. You shouldn't be. You can't be."

He shushes me, holding me tighter.

I push back from his chest. "Madam's face. She showed me. She-she told me everything about her story. And she threatened me over you. Please—"

"Nothing and no one will ever take you from me. Ever. I have a plan, but you'll have to trust me." With his thumbs, he wipes the tears from beneath my eyes.

"A plan? Tell me," I beg. "I need to know. But we have to stay apart. She'll kill me."

I continue to tell him all about my encounter with Madam. He listens to every word, concerned. And when I'm finished, he kisses my head, my cheeks, and my lips.

"I don't want to give you details until it's done, but we will leave for America."

"America?" My heart beats so hard that I'm sure he can feel it.

"Yes, Gini. But I must tie up loose ends here before we go. I can't leave Madam without making sure she and The Mansion are secure. After all she's done for me ..." His voice trails off, and he presses his lips together, like he's conflicted. "Just hope that my plans for us solidify quickly. Time is not on our side."

I nod. "And in the meantime, you will stay away from me?"

He kisses the top of my head. "Trust in me, Gini."

Simmering on my tongue are a million agonizing words. A chance exists that I will have to leave regardless of how hard he tries to get us out. I know he wants to make it work, but sometimes, we try to make things happen, and they fall flat. Still, my hope of us leaving to America is stronger than my doubts.

"Life is too short for misery, isn't it?"

He holds my head in his hands. "Yes. Soon, all misery will be behind us. But you're right. We will have to be more careful. We don't want anything interrupting us."

"Careful," I repeat, praying into his eyes.

Under the flickering light in my bedroom, we kiss.

13

Darius

TO THE WEST OF MUMBAI, at one of the most famous restaurants in all of India, I find myself waiting at a square table for two. I am meeting the infamous boss of the D-Company, Devan Ibrahim. Arman set up this meeting after we spoke. All I can do now is pray that the deal goes off without a hitch. Every inch of my body wants to pace the room and maybe turn over a table or two, but I won't. He'll be here any minute, and the last thing I want him to see is my anxiety.

The table is clothed in white with gold plates and matching silverware. It's European elegance at its best. Even the background music spells wealth, an orchestra playing classical music as though we were at an opera and not a restaurant.

People quiet to a hush as waiters run to the periphery of the room, making way. With their backs straight and their gazes forward and center, they look like a group of subservient peacocks. Devan struts toward me with the confidence and grace of a man double his size.

"Hello, Devan." I stand, shaking his hand. "It is good to see you looking so well."

"Darius." He takes a seat, and I follow suit.

Devan is dressed in his usual daytime attire—a pair of khaki slacks, a white silk shirt, and a black belt with a large golden buckle in the center. His hair is jet-black and full of oil, slicked back. Even with the lines around his eyes—or maybe because of them—he has an air of seriousness.

Arman and I have known of Devan since we were kids. We used to fear him. Stories about his tough character and the deaths he had ordered were always filtering through the slums, all the way down to the kids. He's known as the most ruthless man in Mumbai, and frankly, I'm lucky to now call him a friend.

"So, I must tell you, I was quite interested when Arman told me about this sit-down." Two waiters fly over to where we sit, setting down ice-cold glasses and pouring Kingfisher beer. "I hope you don't mind, but I already had my men order for us beforehand."

"No problem."

"I like Kingfisher," he adds. "It's an Indian beer, brewed in Bangalore. You know, Heineken now holds over forty percent equity shares."

"Interesting. It's always good to support our countrymen." And in that moment, I realize that despite Nico telling me of my Albanian heritage, India is my country.

"Yes, it is." He nods.

We both look up, noticing the waiters are still beside us despite the fact that we do not need him. They notice our confusion and bow good-bye so many times that I begin to think their hats must be stuck to their heads with Velcro.

Devan growls, "For fuck's sake, that's enough!"

"Yes, sir. Y-yes, sir." He walks away backward, still bowing.

"The people at this restaurant are extremely ... accommodating," I add.

"Zero concept of personal space in this country." He clears his throat. "Talk to me, Darius. I've known you since you were a child, running around the slums with Arman. Always wished you would join D-Company."

"It would have been an honor to be part of your crew. But I owe my life to Madam."

I lean forward, praying that Devan and I can make this work. I'm not stupid. I know the man came to power because he's merciless. But right now, he is my only option.

"Well, sir"—I look at Devan straight in the eye—"I know you've always had an affinity for The Mansion and the girls we have there. It seemed you really enjoyed your time there a few weeks ago with the Parisienne businessmen."

"I should thank you for that night." Devan smiles, pointing a finger at me. "We had some work to do with them the following day. And let's just say, all of us were quite relaxed." He chuckles, moving his body forward to whisper, "That Shaina. My God. The things that girl can do with her mouth!"

I wink. "Yes. And I assure you that she enjoys it—tremendously."

Three waiters descend upon our table, filling it with appetizers. They make quick work of it, leaving the moment the plates are down.

"So, tell me, what is it *you* want?" He immediately digs into the food, using large serving spoons to shovel rice and stew onto his plate.

I take food as well, wanting to keep the conversation as friendly and relaxed as possible. And then I tell him about my situation— from Mullah Omar wanting to shut down The Mansion and taking the girls as his own slaves, to wanting to sell my stake in the business in order to avoid the mullah's plan from succeeding. If The Mansion had an injection of money from a new partner, it wouldn't be reliant on Omar. I leave Gini out of this because, frankly, she's none of his business.

"What's in it for me if I become a partner in The Mansion? I understand you need me to buy you out, but what else?"

"Well, The Mansion would become your turf. Another lucrative business in Mumbai to add to your portfolio. It's also an all-cash business—and who doesn't love cash?"

He chuckles. "Cash *is* king."

"Madam would continue to handle the girls. All you'd have to do is show up on occasion and collect your money. Maybe have Arman or some of your other men stand as guard during parties. Take my place."

"And with my name on the business, you think that'd be enough for Mullah Omar to step back?"

"I do. If he were to try to take The Mansion from you, it would be devastating to his reputation. Imagine"—I pause, putting down my fork—"with your money, you could keep The Mansion in its glory. You could own the most magnificent brothel in all of Mumbai. It's a spot for international business. Business that you could have a hand in."

He swallows his food, nodding. "I jump in, taking your partnership interest. Instead of keeping your rightful money, you are going to have me put the cash directly into The Mansion's fund, and you walk away, free to leave. Am I getting this right?"

"Yes, sir, you are."

"Truth be told, I'm not sure how I feel about you leaving like this. I have to assume that Madam has no idea of your plan; otherwise, she would be here right now with you. She has been good to you, and I must say, what you're doing feels ... disloyal."

I sit up taller. "I would never ruin Madam's life. Not after everything she's done for me. She saved me when I was a child and gave me a roof to live under. She fed me. Clothed me. She did not have to do that, but she did. For those reasons, I must respect her and take care of her in return. That doesn't mean I must be her slave for all eternity, but it does mean that I would never leave her high and dry. By all accounts, after selling you my portion of the business, I should take that money. I have earned it. But I wouldn't. I guess that is my penance. Leaving isn't an easy choice, but leaving her with money and without Omar's chains around her neck feels like the right one. I'd explain this to her before I left."

"I see. So, tell me this." He takes a sip of his beer. "Where are you planning to go?"

"Away." I lean back into my seat. "I'm ready for a change."

"That's all you're going to give me?"

I nod before pulling out a folder from my bag on the floor. "Here is the accounting for The Mansion."

He lifts it up and starts scanning the pages. "It seems that sigheh set up by Mullah Omar is a huge part of the current cash flow." He closes the folder. "Without those temporary marriages, The Mansion is a loss."

"Well"—I clear my throat—"I'm sure you can come up with ways to make it profitable. For a man with your business acumen, the sky's the limit. Fourteen beautiful women who are all fluent in English and yours to handle."

He nods, pressing his lips together. "Very smart woman, your Madam, isn't she?"

"Quite. The Mansion has done nikah mut'ah for years, and you can decide to continue that path, if you wish. Our business with Mullah Omar started slowly and then, suddenly, became completely encompassing. He brought us men who were much wealthier than we had ever before gotten. I guess you can say, we became reliant on his connections. Other Islamic men used to come, wanting to take a girl as a wife. But Mullah Omar had our girls lined up so quickly and his acquaintances offered so much money that no other men had a chance. Before we knew it, the other men stepped away. And then we were left with only Mullah Omar to connect our girls to men."

"Are there any women out right now on contract?"

"No. They are all home." I think about Gini being the next one in line. Swallowing hard, I know that I have to close this deal and take her away before Soltabian comes.

He lifts his glass, taking a sip. "You know, we hate Omar's fucking guts. Just to spite him, I might say yes." He pushes his plate forward, reviewing the paperwork again. "You should know, Arman and my boys love The Mansion. If it were up to them, they'd all vote yes." He raises a bushy eyebrow.

"If you left it up to Arman, he'd rename The Mansion, The Bada Bing!"

Devan laughs out loud. "It's true. He does have a thing for *The Sopranos*. Good man, that Arman. Okay, Darius, I've seen enough. Let me talk to my financial guys and get back to you with a number of what I think your shares are worth. Hopefully, it'll be enough to help you sleep at night after you leave."

We shake hands, and then he's gone.

I take my time, finishing my meal when I get a text.

Arman: It's as good as done.

You know me. I need complete confirmation.

Arman: Will do.

I GET BACK to The Mansion in a good mood, and yet the uncertainty has me uneasy. I make my way downstairs to Gini's room and smile when I find her there, bent over books.

"Hey."

"Darius." Her smile is the sun. I let my eyes move over every inch of her face. "How has your day been?"

"I want to tell you about the plan. I think we're close enough to something."

She sits up, but I maintain some distance.

"I'm going to have Devan, the head of D-Company here in Mumbai, buy my shares in The Mansion."

I tell her the whole story, feeling relieved by unloading the news. A nagging worry still sits at the back of my head, but seeing her smile, I push it down.

She hugs me. "We're going to be free? Together?"

"Together. We'll head to America with nothing. I'll have to find a job." I lift the ends of her dark hair, letting them stream through my fingers. "But the good news is, Arman has a cousin in the Bronx, New York, who can help us."

"We'll figure it out—together."

"Together." I pull her back into my chest, kissing the top of her head and saying a prayer.

And then, for days, it rains.

14

Gini

I SEE Darius from the corner of my eye. He's shirtless with white linen pants hanging from his waist, drinking a glass of water. He's watching me clean the floor, eyes raking in my body. I'm still in my usual uniform, but the way his eyes burn, you would think he had special vision that could see through clothes. I know he prefers to walk around the house without a shirt, but I'm still not used to it. He's so built and beautiful.

The clock ticks until the time I should be taken to Iran. Has the deal gone through with Devan? I'm stressed, and I have been waiting for an update for days. And yet, when Darius is near me, it feels like a fire has been lit inside me, burning every thought that isn't centered around him until Darius is all I can see. Smell. Taste. In every corner of The Mansion, I find bits and pieces of him. I wish I could be bolder, like some of the girls here, and take what I want when I want it. But I can't be someone I'm not. I'm strong but not forward.

"Come."

He nods his head for me to follow him, and I rise, trailing him up the narrow stairs. It's so hot. I can feel hot sweat bead on my skin beneath the fabric of my shirt. I pause, biting my lip. Maybe this isn't a good idea. I continue. Of course, I continue. I'd follow this man anywhere.

"No one is here now," he says, still climbing up, step by step. "The ladies are out shopping, and Madam is gone for the day."

He opens the door to his bedroom, and immediately, I catch his scent. It's woodsy, masculine, and clean and so, so good.

He shuts the door behind us. The last time I was in here, I barely had a chance to look around. The furniture is just as I thought—large and heavy. A gorgeous silk rug in swirls of red, green, and blue lies flat on the floor in the center of his room. And of course, his enormous wooden bed. A matching desk and chair sit by the window, papers neatly organized on top. A tall bookshelf is beside the desk, filled with books.

"I wish you'd let me clean your room."

The blankets look so soft in cream and white. If I could spend all of my days taking care of this man, I think I could be happy.

"You like it?" He moves to the desk, turning the chair around and taking a seat. His legs are spread open. I can see the ripple in his abdominal muscles as he leans forward.

"Yes." I nod, fingers trailing over sheets. "I like this room."

He stands up, moving behind me and bringing me in his arms. With his mouth on mine, he holds me so close to his body. I wish I could control it, but my heart palpitates.

Licking my lips, he sucks my tongue. I can feel my body incinerating. In such a short amount of time, this man has become my heart's desire. His fingers find the skin of my lower back, and slowly, he caresses me.

He touched my breasts the last time, and now, I'm hoping for more.

"This is killing me," he groans.

My stomach twists because I know he wants more, too. I step away from him, nervous but wanting. "What can I do for you?"

He hesitates, and for a moment, I'm worried that I did something wrong. That's when he unbuttons his jeans. He doesn't take them off, but thrusts his hand inside and down. His eyes stay glued to my face.

"Take off your shirt. Let me see you." His voice is gravelly and dark.

He goes ahead and pulls his member all the way out. My eyes widen at the sight of it. Of course, I've seen one before. I have brothers. But this. So huge. It's thick, and pink. The tip glistens. My mouth waters.

Slowly, I raise the shirt above my head.

Before I can register embarrassment, he groans, "Come closer." With his free hand, he cups one of my full breasts. "I want to show you everything." He strokes himself as I give him access to my body.

"Yes," I reply.

"Touch your breasts for me. Just like I'm doing." He nods, tugging on my nipple.

My heart bumps around in my chest, but I touch myself. For Darius, I would do anything. I think about getting on my knees and taking him in my mouth, just like Shaina did onstage at the party.

"What is it you want?" he groans. "I see the way you're looking at me."

"You," I croak. There is so much more to say, but I don't have it in me to say it. Something tells me he'll drag it out of me.

"Yeah?" He strokes himself harder. "You want to do this for me?"

Our gazes lock, and my yearning burns.

His eyes inhale my body. "There we go, Gini. So beautiful."

He takes my hand, putting it on his hardness. The skin is so hot. Like silk. I hold it and move my hand up and down, just as I saw him do.

"Oh, Gini. That's it. That's right. Harder, now."

His eyes shut as he places his hand over mine. Together, we stroke his long, hard shaft. Up and down.

"I'm going to teach you everything. Just how to please me. Just how I want it and like it. Would you like that?"

I'm in a trance. "Yes."

"Yes who?"

"Yes, Darius."

"That's right. When you touch me, I want to know that I'm the one you're thinking about."

He finishes with a drawn out moan, and cream spurts in my hand. I freeze, shocked.

Panting, he opens his eyes and smiles like I just gave him a gift. "Don't worry. Just wait." He walks away before returning with a warm towel, cleaning off my fingers. He kisses each piece of my hand from my palm to my fingertips. "There is so much I want to do to you. For you. But let's take it slow."

I exhale, relieved. My body is pulsing for him, and yet I'm still afraid.

"Let's lie together now. I want to hear your voice."

He curls me into his arms, and we fall together, laughing, onto the bed.

"Hmm."

"Hmm?"

"Just speak. I like when you speak. Tell me what you thought of what we did just now."

"Well, it was interesting."

"Was it?" He turns his head, staring at me.

"Mmhmm." I nod, resting my head on his chest. I've been dreaming of doing something just like this.

"Good interesting or bad interesting?"

"I'm not too sure ..." I tease. "It was definitely ... large."

"You!" he cries, peppering my face with kisses. He exhales, pausing, and my heart soars. "Gini, you know we're not supposed to do this. Actually, I've never done this before. With any of the girls at The Mansion, I mean. I want us to wait to be intimate. To wait until we are free."

"And until then?"

"Until then, we can enjoy each other." He pushes an errant hair from my face.

"Any way I can have you, Darius, I want you."

"You know," he says, pausing, "I need your goodness in my life. I want it like I've never wanted anything before."

"You can have it."

"Please, Gini, swear you won't let anything break who you are."
He presses his lips to my chest. "This part of you is light. Swear it,
Gini."

"I swear."

We spend the rest of the day laughing together as I tell him
village stories and jokes, making fun of my neighbors. For a little
while, we forget who we really are.

THERE IS ANOTHER PARTY TONIGHT. This time, it's D-Company, a crew
of very powerful Indian men from Mumbai. Apparently, all the girls
know who they are, as they often conduct business here. No one is
worried about it. Ananya, who I have been shadowing since Roshan
left, told me the girls love to "test out dances" with these guys because
they aren't discerning.

"Whatever we do, they're happy," she said, smiling. "They just
want to see us naked, shaking our asses. Indian men are good like
that."

The space tonight is set to look like a nightclub. I've never seen
one in real life, of course, but I have to assume one would look like
this. There are the same bed-like couches in white along the edges of
the room, and the three large bars are filled with drinks. The lights
are dim.

I am wearing a beautiful white sari, embroidered with red flowers. I look up and see Darius entering the room in dark pants and a
black button-down shirt. He looks incredible.

The lights in the room flash on and off, signaling that it's ten
o'clock. The event begins at ten thirty, but Madam always gives us a
thirty-minute warning. Some girls stretch, and others have a drink or
use the bathroom.

And then the men enter all at once, and immediately, the air in
The Mansion thickens and warms. It's sultry with the scent of candles

burning. Ananya tells me she has a few things to fix on her outfit, and she runs off, leaving me alone in the corner of the room.

That's when Darius and I lock eyes. He gestures to the corridor that leads to the girls' bedrooms. I start walking.

I can feel his heavy body behind mine, moving like an animal. He's graceful, silent, and intelligent, and he's ready to pounce. All I can hear is the beating of my own heart, urging me forward. I need this man so badly. I can't lose this moment with him.

Moving through the hallway, he steps ahead of me into the last bedroom on the right. I follow him inside. It's mostly empty with nothing but a large bed sitting in the center of the room.

"Gini," he starts and then pauses as his hands move around my face, framing my features in his palms. Moments tick with warmth, but suddenly, something changes in his features. His touch ceases to be gentle. I can feel his thick, hot fingers digging into my skin, his eyes darkening. "I wish I could, but I can't be soft with you. Not now."

I shut my eyes, screwing them closed. "I want to please you, Darius. So, so much."

"If I had you in the way I want you ..." He grits his teeth, like the truth is painful to utter.

"I saw it that night with Shaina onstage and heard it from the women. I know there are other ways to be sexual and to be had without vaginal penetration."

A few weeks ago, Ananya told me how much she enjoys it—with a new man who frequents The Mansion, just for her. He hails from Dubai and loves to spoil her with rubies and gold.

I tighten my fists and finally blurt to Darius, "Aren't there other ways you can have me? Other parts on my body?"

He groans, pressing his hard, thick length between my legs. An electric jolt has me suddenly light-headed.

"Don't you know?" He presses against me, again and again, and pants, "I can't do this to you here. We can't. Your first time will be with me, but not here. I want you so bad, more than anything. Gini, my love, what have you done to me?"

His hands caress my face and hair, and his nose moves behind my ear and beneath my neck. His staccato breath grazes so close to my lips that I can practically taste him. He keeps pressing against me, and like the beat of a drum, a pounding within my body focuses low in my stomach, pooling downward. My hands shake and wrap around his back, which is heavily muscled and hot.

His lips brush against mine. The warmth of his mouth settles over my mind like a cloud. He's so big; my entire body is encased in his. His hands trail down my sides. Chills roam down my body as my legs shake.

"You want me in your ass, is that what you're asking?"

I try nodding my head, but who knows if it works? Wetness leaks onto my thighs.

"I won't do that to you. Not yet."

"Please—" My voice cuts off. I'm begging. What I'm begging for, I'm unsure. But I will take anything I can get.

"I know what you need. Just promise me you'll moan. I want to hear your pleasure, so I can keep it as my own."

He drops to his knees before me and lifts my skirt. I look down, confused.

"Hold my shoulders and don't let go," are his last words before he raises the front of my white skirt, bunching it up in his hands.

Suddenly, I'm panicked. "What—*oh* ..." My head falls back as his hot mouth presses against my covered mound, inhaling. The heat! "What ... what ..."

"Yes." He fists my panties, painfully twisting them to the side as he looks up at me. "I'm going to eat you," he growls, dark and deep. "Drink you. I'm going to take so much from you that your juices will be in my veins. And I'm not stopping until your essence is in my blood."

His hands move around my panties before tearing them in two. My mouth drops open, and then he's on me. His mouth. His tongue. He eats me like a starving man would. Moaning and grunting. Half-animal. All animal. I tug out the tie holding his hair and grip the strands at their roots, pieces falling through my fingers like silk. He pulls my thighs closer to his face. I'm panting so hard; it's as though the blood in my body has doubled. Tripled. I can feel the weight of it. So heavy and thick. I can't survive this. He keeps going, hard tongue alternating between deep licks from my back to my front and then darting deeply inside me in the place that, now, only he knows.

"Darius. Darius," I chant his name.

He's not simply the king of my universe. He is the universe itself.

With an intrusion of his thumb into my back entrance, he sucks, and I scream and then explode. Behind my eyes, liquid gold splatters across my vision. His thick palms cup my backside. Without them, I would collapse. He brings me down into his arms, pulling off my shirt above my head. We're skin to skin, heat on heat. My breasts cradle against his hard muscles. I blink, willing my tears to stay hidden behind my eyes.

How could something feel this good, this perfect? This man, who has both ruined me and loved me. Stolen me but saved me. I'm his.

I begin to cry, although I'm not sure the reason exactly.

He kisses my forehead before he sits back on his knees, brows knitting together. "No tears."

"I don't want to hide. I can't keep living in this fear—"

"Devan got back to me. We will leave tomorrow and wait at the Taj Hotel until I can get visas for us." He uses his thumbs to wipe the wetness pooling beneath my eyes.

"Tomorrow?"

"Yes," he exhales, kissing me and smiling. "He just told me an hour ago."

"How about tonight?" I shiver, wishing more than anything that we could leave right now.

He whispers, "It's okay. Hang in there, my love."

He shifts our bodies, and we both move to stand.

I nod my head, wishing things weren't this way. "How will we leave tomorrow?"

"I'll tell you everything when I know."

He presses his forehead against mine again. Something flows between us, and my heart moves.

"I'd like to see a library."

He chuckles. "Would you?"

"Yes. In the news show you have the girls watch, I saw a huge library in New York City. One day, I'd like to see that."

"On my life, I will take you there."

I nuzzle my face into his neck, wishing with all my heart that he speaks the truth.

The door swings open. I jump back, away from Darius, as though I'd been whipped. It's Shaina in the doorway, wearing a stunning golden sari with jewels sprinkled throughout her hair and the fabric of her dress. A mocking smile spreads over her face like a mask.

"Look. At. This." She punctuates her every word, glaring as she crosses her arms over her chest, as though confirming something she already knew. "I smelled something disgusting floating across the halls. I had to leave the party with D-Company to find out what the awful stench was." She lifts her nose in the air and takes a whiff before screwing up her face in disgust. "Like a dirty, wet dog. Or maybe ... like a man fucking a nasty animal."

My entire being freezes. Her words are so awful that they shrink me in my own skin.

Darius grinds his teeth as he steps toward her. "If you were a man or if your face didn't add value to The Mansion, I would beat you within an inch of your life for your comment. If I find out that there are no parties in the near future, I might just go ahead and do it anyway. There is nothing to see here." His voice is a dark menace.

She flinches as he towers over her, his thick neck pulsing as he gets right into her face.

"Get the fuck out." Darius is capable of violence. Terrible, terrible violence.

I drop back, afraid. Of course, he told me about this dark side, but watching this part of him unfold is the scariest thing I've ever seen.

"The two of you should come outside," she stutters. "There's someone very special wh-who has come for Gini."

I think I see confusion pass over Darius's eyes, but it passes so quickly that I'm unsure.

"For me? Who is here?" I look at Darius, hoping for an answer.

Shaina lets out a small chuckle. "Why don't you two leave this room and go into the library, so Gini can see for herself what you and Madam have planned for her?"

She cocks her head to the side, smirking as she sidles beside Darius. He drops his head before lifting it back up again. It's like they know something I don't know. How she managed to align herself with him after their altercation is miraculous. But that's how it feels—like I'm on the outside, looking in.

We leave the room side by side, but his strides so long that I have to practically jog to keep up. My insides vibrate with confusion and fear. But Darius doesn't touch me or even turn his head. As we drift down the hallways with Shaina behind us, I wait for a word from him … but nothing comes.

I need to ask him a million questions. *Where am I going? Did Madam find out about us? Am I being punished?* My breathing turns shallow and quick as my thoughts darken. He's being distant.

Is he somehow in on this? Is the joke on me?

Shaina trails behind us, the glare of her evil eyes against my back. Her heels click in a measured rhythm, and I swear, hatred emanates from her. My anxiety grows so strong that I feel sick. Before turning the corner, I pause.

"Don't be afraid," Shaina whispers close to my ear. "Animals can get used to almost anything."

"Enough." Darius silences her, but her smirk remains as she scurries off, happily leaving us to our fate.

In the doorway of the wood-paneled library, Madam awaits. "Gini. Welcome." She gestures for me to walk inside, smiling as though she had a special gift for me.

Darius falls behind me. The mullah from the day I was brought to The Mansion is here. He stands, rubbing his hands together. Sitting in the corner is another man, who I have never seen. He stands to greet me, and I immediately notice his crisp clothing, dark hair, and neatly trimmed beard. He wears navy pants and a white shirt with a collar and buttons down the front. A piece of navy fabric pokes through his breast pocket.

"Gini, darling," Madam begins, kinder than I ever thought possible. "This, here, is Navid Soltabian." She turns to the man, much younger than I would have imagined. "Isn't she just the most beautiful creature?" Madam beams.

"Quite." He smiles with straight white teeth, body like an erect statue, his face like an impenetrable mask.

I can't feel anything from him. Not good, not bad. All I know is that he is *wrong*.

I turn to Darius, our energy from moments ago so distant that it's as if it never happened at all.

"Welcome to The Mansion." Darius smiles as he steps forward and exchanges pleasantries with both Navid and the mullah, shaking their hands.

Darius is calm and seemingly clearheaded, strong feet planted heavily on the floor as he laughs out loud at something the mullah said. I should focus entirely on Navid, but when Darius is near, all I can see is him.

"Gini is a very good girl," Darius says. "I am sure you will enjoy her company. Tremendously." He raises his eyebrows, implying something lewd.

My heart sinks. *Did my ears betray me?* It's as though Darius is a completely new man. A man I don't know. I turn my face to find Madam staring at me, a smile on her thin lips. She walks toward Darius, putting an arm through his, and joins the conversation.

"As luck would have it," Madam says loudly, "I was recently informed that a routine check was conducted just this evening. She is clean, pure, and ready for anything."

"Very well." The mullah nods to Navid. "Come here, Gini."

Madam smirks, and I make my way beside the mullah, my head bowed.

"Darius, do you give your permission for Gini to enter into this marriage?"

No. Say no. My chest tightens.

"Yes, I grant my permission," he replies with a clear, steady voice, wasting no time.

It's like a knife has been pressed into my heart. I look up to him, needing to see his eyes. Needing a *sign*. But he doesn't turn.

"As far as the time period, Navid, what do you propose?"

"Let us start with six months. By that time, I will know if I would like to renew." He looks over at me, his gaze assessing.

"Six months?" Madam shakes her head. "Trust me, you will not want the headache of renewal. Begin with one year. You won't regret it."

The mullah raises a pointed brow. I grip the chair by my side, trying not to fall over.

Navid looks me up and down, squinting his eyes. "Let me speak to the girl, first. Then, I will decide how long I will need."

"Oh," Madam drawls, "we couldn't possibly leave her unchaperoned. She's a defenseless creature. Innocent!" Her words are exaggerated, as though rehearsed.

The mullah shifts. "Soon enough, she won't be. If you want a few moments, Navid, we shall give them to you."

I blink, and the mullah, Madam, and Darius flee the room.

"Hello." Navid sits down on the couch, tapping the place beside him.

I sit on the edge, my back straight.

"To make a long story short"—he clears his throat—"I am here for a few reasons. I conduct business around the world and need a woman by my side. I have three wives. But all of them are quite serious about their Islamic beliefs. I need a woman who, when the circumstances allow, is willing and able to remove the hijab in a public setting, in front of other men. I also want a woman to travel and"—he clears his throat—"have fun with me. Parties and dancing at nightclubs. Wearing a bikini at my pool and indulging in alcoholic drinks with me. I want to have fun, you understand? With you. But of course, our relationship must be halal."

I ignore the fact that he is explicitly asking me to do things with him that, as I've been taught by Darius, are haram—or forbidden by Islamic law.

"Mullah Omar tells me the girls are trained in both Western ways as well as Islamic ones. I will need you to play both roles, do you understand?"

I raise my eyes to him, understanding clearly. "Yes."

He stares at my face, as though trying to read me. "You are very beautiful. I think we can have a great time together, you and me."

I risk a close look at him, noticing that he might not even be a man. *Could it be possible that I have more years than him?* Beneath the beard is a baby face. Still, I know the expectation is for me to submit to him regardless of age.

"How do you wish for me to speak with you now? As a West woman or Islamic?"

He chuckles, squinting his eyes. "Western," he corrects, raising his hands. "Do not worry. I understand you very well. Right now, I need you to speak to me as a Western woman might."

"I can play both roles." I imagine Darius telling me how this man expects me to act, and in a measured voice, I repeat the expectation, "In Iran, on the street, I will cover my face and my body. But when we are in private, we will be free to ... enjoy life. Yes?"

I give him a shaky, sweet smile. I feel as though I were a light switch, simply turning on and off with the pull of a line.

He nods, grinning. "Very good." He shifts forward, putting a finger on my upper thigh and dragging it around in circles. "The thing is, Gini, I want you to derive pleasure from what I give you. I already have an entire wardrobe set up for you in your quarters. Maids to wait on you. Your entire existence shall be as if you were a queen. But if I say we are to leave in five minutes to London, I expect full compliance. If I tell you to join me for a walk in town, wearing a full hijab with only a net for your eyes to see, I expect full compliance. If you please me, your life will be good. My friends and I, we're fun. We're nice guys, you see. But I want it to be pleasant for you, not torturous." His hand stops moving. "If you displease me or if it seems that you are cloaked in misery, I will promptly send you back here. Do you agree to this arrangement?"

My mouth dries out, my body feeling parched. And yet I know I should be relieved. He is affording me honesty.

I look at the closed door. *Is Darius behind it, listening to our conversation?* Minutes ago, I was in his arms. *Is all of that over?* With that thought, my blood turns heavy.

Navid stares at me expectantly. Not agreeing to this marriage would mean death.

I open my mouth, and the words leave my lips. "I agree."

"Very well, then." He grins. "Let us begin with a year. I know that you are innocent in all things, which I appreciate. Requested it, actually. I look forward to showing you what the world has to offer." He stands up, smiling.

He calls everyone back inside and tells them the news.

Darius shakes his hand. "You won't regret it. I have trained her myself. She is intelligent in all the ways you will need and innocent in all others."

"Very well." The mullah nods. "And the *mahr*, Navid?"

Roshan taught me that the mahr is the gift that must be given in exchange for the marriage.

I hold my breath as Navid says, "I have a present for you." He steps close and hands me a large black box. He smiles. "Open it."

Staring at the box, I am unable to make my fingers work. Slowly, I lift the top. My stomach drops to my toes as I see a large round blue stone, sparkling on a thin golden chain. I want to touch it, but will it break?

"It is ten carats of sapphire. After I saw your photo, I knew this would look magnificent on you. It matches your eyes." He steps close to me, lifting the box into his hands and removing the necklace. "It would make me happy for you to wear it now."

Madam chimes in with a clap, "How generous and kind!"

Navid clasps it around my neck. His breath is minty against my ear. "Perfect."

I press the stone against my chest, feeling the delicate facets. Looking up again, I try to catch Darius's eyes. But they are on the mullah, ignoring my existence.

"One hundred thousand US dollars will be wired to your account upon her signing," Navid states plainly. "And when she completes the year, I will give her the remaining sixty thousand in cash—US, of course."

I ought to be shocked, but I can barely move. Madam's entire body, however, lights up upon hearing the number as something like excitement electrifies her. I close my eyes, imagining my father receiving sixty thousand dollars. He, too, would feel electrified. With that money, my entire family would prosper.

The mullah clicks his tongue. "Let us recite the mutah, in English." Sweat pours down his thick neck as he smiles, yellow teeth gleaming.

"English," I repeat, feeling like I'm moving toward my execution.

The mullah clears his throat. "Very well. Now, repeat after me. *I marry myself to you for the known period of twelve months and the agreed-upon dowry.*"

He speaks quickly, but I repeat it as well as I can. I look up, and Madam looks pleased.

"I accept," Navid says, his face still a mask.

"Now"—the mullah clears his throat—"you must sign the following agreement. When traveling together within Iran, the morality police might stop you. As I'm sure you have been taught, men and women are not allowed to be seen together unless they are married."

He pushes a piece of paper my way. I stare at it. Time seems to slow.

"Sign." Madam's voice is pleasant, and yet there's an unmistakable edge.

I turn my head to Darius, and he nods calmly. "Go ahead."

The mullah laughs. "You've trained her quite well, Darius. Navid, I must say, you are very lucky to have this flower to do with as you please."

With a shaking hand, I grip the pen and sign my name on the dotted line.

15

Darius

NAVID SOLTABIAN TAKES Gini with him in his chauffeured black-and-tan Rolls-Royce. She leaves The Mansion in a trance.

When that bitch Shaina came into our room, I knew there was trouble. But I had to rein myself in. If anyone knew that Gini and I had a relationship of any kind, it could result in her suffering. And if her virginity were in question, it could mean the end of her life. There was no choice but to plow forward and play the game in front of Navid and Omar.

But the look on her face, the agony I saw in her eyes, was unbearable to witness. I couldn't look at her for more than a split second at a time. If I had, they might have seen something that would cause alarm.

A pain so acute swells in my chest.

From the window in the sitting room, I stare so intently at the darkened drive that I do not notice Amma coming up to me until she is already by my side.

"Well, Darius"—she clears her throat—"good riddance! I know, right now, you're angry with me. But what choice was there? One more day, and you might have taken her virginity. Then, where would we be? It's for your own good that she's gone."

I face her. "You had no right to send her out without my knowledge." I grit my teeth.

"Is that so?" She straightens her spine. "I have every right on earth to do as I see fit. This is my house. I paid for the girl." Lines crack all around her face as she fights to maintain composure.

"Every right, huh? Gini was not ready. If she cannot rise to his level of expectation, he might kill her."

"Well"—she shrugs a bony shoulder—"it's a risk I'll take. A well-measured risk, too. Now that we have D-Company as a partner, we should no longer worry about money." Her hands move to my bicep, gliding up and down as she glares. "I will forgive you for going behind my back and negotiating a deal without me. I understand you were only trying to help The Mansion, am I right? But luckily for you, you will not have to leave just to save us." She lifts an eyebrow, as though giving me an out to a truth she knows too well. "You can stay and remain as a partner—under my name."

I rip her hand off of my skin and look closely at this pathetic woman, who I have called Mother since my childhood, straight in the eye. This woman, who went behind my back in such a conniving way, who was willing to send an innocent girl—potentially to her death—just to keep her away from me. As I stare at Amma now, my fingers ache to rip the black scarf off of her face and to strangle her with it until her brain scrambles.

I wanted to do this the right way, damn her! To leave The Mansion and make sure Amma was left in a secure situation. But that idea is done. I'm leaving, and I don't give a shit what she does with herself or The Mansion. Not anymore.

Without another word, I exit the room. Do I want to scream and shout? Yes. But there is no reason. My mind is made. The deal with D-Company is done, and I'm leaving.

I head up the stairs to my bedroom. I pull out a duffle from the closet and pack some clothes. I know that if I have any chance of getting Gini back, I will have to find someone stronger and more powerful than myself. Devan and his crew are no match for Mullah Omar or Navid Soltabian, both of whom have wealth, influence, and world-renowned power. I take a moment to stare out the window, and I know, without a shadow of a doubt, who it is that I must contact. There is only one man who has the means to help me.

When I'm done packing, I take out a duffel bag of cash that has been stored beneath my floorboard. I count the money quickly but efficiently, noting close to half a million US dollars. Moving into my closet, I pull out my gun rack, removing my firearms and sliding each one into its own sock before setting them into my duffel with the cash.

With my car keys in my back pocket, I say good-bye to my room and begin the trek out of the house. I will stay at the Taj Hotel while I organize my life and my future. *Gini should be by my side, damn it!*

Passing through the kitchen, I hear a shrill, "Darius!"

I refuse to pause. Amma chases me as I take long strides, wanting to get out of here before I kill her. Out of respect to her, I will not physically harm her, no matter how badly my hands shake. But by God, I want to.

To my back, she pants, chasing me. "You're angry because you thought there was something between you and the girl."

I pause, breathing hard.

"You were wrong. She was nothing to you. She means nothing to you. I'm the one who loves you, don't you see?" She grips the back of my arm until I turn around to face her.

"That is enough," I tell her with gritted teeth. "I'm finished with this life. I'm not your slave, to be bound to you for eternity. You crossed me, and I won't allow that."

"So, you admit it, now? You loved her?" Her voice cracks.

"Yes, I admit it. And so what? Why should I be ashamed of that? Am I not a man who is deserving of a woman?"

"She wasn't yours to keep! I'm the one who belongs to you, not her!"

"Are you insane?" I yell. "Why the fuck should that be true? Why?" Saying it out loud, just like this, makes the injustice clearer.

But Amma isn't looking at me now like a mother would. She stares at me like a woman in love. I knew in my gut that Amma would never allow me to take a wife. She would have had Gini killed before permitting any woman in my life who could potentially mean more to me than she did. All this time, I resisted in coming forward to Amma. I did not tell her that this girl was for me. I did not tell her that this particular woman I wanted to keep. Because deep down, I knew she would never allow it. I knew that she would get rid of her, just as she did. The truth is a painful rock to swallow, but there is no way to deny it. Not anymore.

"Please," she moans, eyes skating between my face and the bags I hold. "I'm the one you love. I'm the one you love above all others. Say it to me, Darius. Tell me I'm the one you dream of at night. You and me, we are meant to be. And we always were. This is nothing but a quarrel between lovers."

I tilt my head downward, appalled at her delusions. I knew they were always there, sitting at the surface, but never could I have imagined how deeply they ran.

"I know you have seen me as a mother for all these years," she continues. "But you must have felt it. You must have known as you grew that you and I became much closer than a simple mother-and-son relationship. I was so young when I brought you into this home. We are barely fifteen years apart in age, Darius"—she bites her lip, as a child might—"imagine what we can achieve together once we finally consummate our love. All of those women you've had in the past, they were toys. But you and me? We're the real thing."

"We?" I pant. "We are nothing!" I readjust my bags and sling them over my back. As I look at this woman, it's as though I barely even know her anymore.

"Everything you are today is because of me." She grinds her teeth together, chest puffing out. "I raised you to be the man you've become. Lethal. Strong. Dependable. You owe yourself to me, Darius. Every breath you take belongs to me!" Her eyes move to slits. I can see the puffs of air moving in and out of her nostrils. "We are meant to be together. And if you can't see that now, I will make you see!"

She pulls a small black handgun from beneath her *burka*, sweat sliding down her temples as she raises it high, aiming at my face. "You think I did not see the way your eyes lit when you saw her? The moment she entered this house, there was a change in you like a tidal wave. I tried to ignore it, but you wouldn't let me. I watched as you taught her. With all your heart"—she looks up, voice pulsing—"you taught her. Did you think I would just allow your love to bloom? Your eyes never left her side. But, Darius, you are confused by what you saw. Women like Gini, they come, and they go. But me? I stay. A girl like Gini, she would steal from you. She would brainwash you. I'm the only one who is real. She wants your money and your power."

I grip the muzzle of her gun, stepping closer. "I will never, ever be with you. As Muhammad as my witness, I will never lie with you. Marry you. You are sick and deluded, Amma. I will spare your life because you once spared mine. But this idea you have of the two of us?" I laugh darkly. "Dispel it from your brain. Because we will never be. I am also no longer your partner. You'll have to find another man to take my place."

I let go of the gun, but not before pushing it away, out of my line of sight. She falls with it, dropping onto the floor.

"Darius, do not speak this way. I trained you to be the man I love. I created you! Don't you speak this way! The things I have seen in my miserable life are beyond what you can imagine."

"And yet, you have created a business with me at the helm, forcing these girls to do what you have done. For years, I told myself that this was the only way and that this was the path chosen for me by Muhammad. But the truth is, we sell women's bodies in this house. We trade them to the highest bidder after teaching them to spread their legs. And I'm done. What you did to Gini—sending her off before she was ready, just to take her away from me—was the final straw." I cut my hand through the air, stating, "We're through." The words leave my mouth, and it's like a weight has been lifted. "And I don't care who sanctioned what we do. It's no longer the life I'm living."

"Done? But you are my light. Your hair. Your eyes. I saw you as a child and felt the truth in my gut. My body *stirred* upon seeing your angelic face. I have waited so long for you to notice what you and I could be together ..."

I shake my head angrily. Disgusted.

"Don't judge me!" Tears stream down her face, streaking her skin. "If you leave, I can't go on, Darius."

Her body on the floor, I can see her thin bones poking through the tented fabric. She looks like a corpse.

"I'm leaving, Amma. I gave you all the years of my life so far and organized The Mansion so that you would not be indebted to Omar. But the deal between us is over now. You sent Gini away just to spite me. If she dies under Navid Soltabian, her blood will be on your hands." I look up and exhale, praying to any god who will listen that I reach her before any harm befalls her.

"Leaving? No." Slowly, she stands, her chest quivering. "It cannot be over. You will see soon enough that she is just a dog. A nobody from a village ..." Her eyes seem to glaze over as she continues, "You are like a god, Darius. That girl won't rise to your level." The red from her lips bleeds onto her chin. "Okay, you want her back? I can call and say she is soiled. Maybe they'll return her—peacefully."

I laugh out loud. "You think I'm fucking stupid?" I bend down, gripping her arm so hard that she shivers. "If you try to spread that rumor about her, I will come find you when you sleep. And I will kill you."

I turn my back, ending that chapter in my life. It's over.

16

Gini

WE ARE silent in the large, spacious car. I stare out the window, remembering the last time I was in a vehicle—with Darius. The car smelled damp and thick with stale smoke. I was perspiring myself, afraid. How innocent I was. How little I knew of the evils that lurked.

"Are you hungry?"

I turn my head to face the man who is now called my husband—for a limited duration. "No, thank you."

"The flight is about four hours. It will be very late when we land. You will have your own home for the term of our agreement, and I trust it will be comfortable. It is very nice."

I nod kindly before looking back out the window. *Flight?*

AFTER LANDING IN TEHRAN, I'm taken in my own car without Navid to Elahiyeh. In English, the driver tells me my home is exceptional with a swimming pool, garden, and fountain in the back. I want to ask him what a swimming pool is, but I will see it for myself soon enough.

"The wealthiest in Tehran stay in Elahiyeh throughout summer. You will be happy," he adds.

My stomach is still upside down from flying in the airplane.

NOTICING *I wasn't feeling well, Navid gave me a tablet dissolved in water.*

"Alka-Seltzer. It will help you."

He was kinder than I'd thought he would be.

He had something in his ears that played very loud music, and it kept him occupied. I looked out the window at the dark night sky, where stars could not be seen. I held my seat and tried to breathe calmly. Thought about the strangeness of life. And then we landed.

WE FINALLY PULL INTO A LONG, winding driveway. The trees around the house are lit up, casting a yellow glow over the house. It is two stories with many windows. The driver opens my car door. When we enter the house, one lady waits by the staircase, covered in black dress from her hair to her toes. Her round face, however, can be seen.

"*Saalam.*" She smiles, waving good-bye to my driver and ushering me inside.

"English, yes?" She smiles, taking off her head scarf. "I am Maryam."

Her smile is wide with two deep indentations on either cheek. With her eyes that glow dark brown, my immediate impression of her is kindness and warmth.

I nod, unable to get my mouth to work past the shock of where I am or how I got here.

"I will take you to your room, where you can wash your face and hands. I have put out sleep clothes for you on the bed. And then you will come downstairs to eat. I have set out food for you. During the day, there will be a few other women who clean and cook, but I am here to oversee the home and take care of you."

We walk upstairs and enter a hallway, where she opens the door and turns on a light.

"My daughter is in France now. Since she left, I have missed her so much. It will be nice to have a friend here with me." She smiles, and then she leaves.

The bedroom is so startling; it takes time for me to step onto the beige-carpeted floor. A large bed sits against the wall with what looks like twenty silver pillows over fluffy white sheets. A seating area sits in the front of the room with two small couches facing a glass table. The most incredible part of the room is the bookshelf, filled with hardcovers. Suddenly, I remember that I forgot to take my book. I made it through the first quarter and want to know what happens next. I step forward, finding the strength to walk and scan the titles. I cannot recognize any of them. I shut my eyes, imagining Darius handing me my first Urdu-English dictionary and later on *The Da Vinci Code*. Tears threaten, but I refuse to let them come. I'm not ready for that yet.

I use the bathroom after removing all of my clothes and hesitantly turn on the water at the sink. I clean my face and wash my hands with a floral-smelling soap. After drying my skin with a soft pink hand towel, I realize that my days of being treated as a kutta are over.

Looking in the mirror, I see the large blue stone set against my chest. It's heavy. It's also stunning. This is the life Darius told me about when I first arrived at The Mansion. I am to become a woman who exchanges sex, enjoyment, and pleasures with a man who, in return, will give me riches and the spoils of life. I touch the stone with my thumb and forefinger, noting in the mirror how its color looks against my eyes—a perfect match. *Should I run, or should I accept this life?*

I move to the bedroom, lifting the clothes placed on the bed. The pants and shirt are loose and soft in white. A pair of white undergarments are here, too, in that same fabric. I put it all on, immediately feeling better. Never in my life have I worn something so smooth. The clock on the bedside tells me that it is two o'clock in the morning.

Carefully, I make my way downstairs. I am exhausted, but hunger has me light-headed. At the foot of the steps, Maryam waits.

"Hello, Gini," she says kindly. "You look refreshed. You must be so hungry. Please, come with me. I made sure the chef prepared food for your arrival."

Together, we walk down a hallway into what I assume is the dining room. I want to look around, but everything feels hazy. The one thing I notice? The entire table is filled with fruits, salads, cheeses, and eggs. The food looks similar to what I'm used to but with less color. I eat quickly, not allowing myself to think about how bland it all tastes.

"How was your trip?" She pours me a hot tea, the steam curling around the glass.

Before I can formulate polite words to reply, tears, like a torrential downpour, drip down my face. Maybe it's her gentle demeanor or maybe it's because I feel like I have nothing left to lose, but I cry for everything I have lost. My father and my siblings. Darius, who had me so deeply in love with him before throwing me out the door. I sob, unable to speak, until my entire body feels brittle and my eyelids heavy.

Maryam watches me silently. When my crying has slowed to a small whimper, she takes my hand and guides me upstairs. "Don't fret, Gini. I know this is difficult for you. We are together now, and I will guide you and help you. Life is not always what we expect, but we must carry on with what we've been given." Pausing in front of the bedroom door, she adds, "I have known Navid since he was a child. Trust me when I tell you that he will not hurt you. He is spoiled but not cruel. He has his negative traits, but none of them are devious. There are worse places to be than here."

I hiccup, wanting to believe her.

She touches the door handle when I ask, "Would I be able to have a particular book?"

"Sure you can." She smiles, glad to help. "There are many in the room, and I can bring anything you need. It would be my pleasure. And when you are settled, we will go into town and visit the library, too, if you would like."

"There is a book called *The Da Vinci Code*. I forgot to bring it with me."

She looks panicked, her large eyes widening. "Do not say that name! That book has been banned."

"Banned?"

"Yes. It is illegal to read it here, in Iran."

My conversation with Darius over the newspaper comes back to me. The press is not allowed to give any opinion that is against the foundation of Islam. That decree must include books, too.

"The laws here can be tricky, but within these walls, there will be freedom. The books I can obtain for you without risk of arrest, I will surely get."

"Okay," I whisper.

"Good night, sweet girl. We will talk again in the morning." She closes the door.

I take ten steps to the huge bed, unsure of what to do with all of these pillows before finally giving up and settling onto the floor. I draw my knees up to my chest and let my body adjust to this new ground. Closing my eyes, I whisper good night to my family, imagining their warm bodies surrounding mine. How will my father feel when he is able to pay for a doctor to visit our home or when he realizes that he can feed all of his family indefinitely? They drift away when Darius kneels down beside me, pointing out the night sky. I want my imagination to continue, but my mind stops it in its tracks.

He's gone. They're all gone.

I'm truly alone.

17

Darius

THE LOBBY BUSTLES with British tourists. The restaurant here at the Taj Hotel is one of the best with five waiters to every patron. It took years and over forty million dollars for them to rebuild the hotel after the 2008 terror attacks, but I must say, they did the hotel justice.

Am I nervous that Nico of the Mafia Shqiptare is coming to meet me? Yes. I'm not afraid of him, but I am afraid of what he will say. If he doesn't allow me to join his crew, I've got no other options in saving Gini. If I could take her out of Iran on my own, I would. But I have no doubt that she travels with security detailing her every move. Those men wouldn't hesitate to shoot both of us dead if they caught us trying to escape. I need backing. I need Nico. Luckily, the business card that I split in half was still in the back pocket of my pants. I thank my stars that I not only found it, but could easily put the pieces together to read his number.

He walks into the restaurant, and the waiters seem to part. People whisper, as though a celebrity had entered the room. The air around Nico is unmistakable—power.

"Darius." He smiles, sitting down, and leaning forward, he shakes my hand. "Let's order. I'm starving." He lifts a glass of ice water while picking up the menu.

I wave to the waiter before asking Nico, "Do you just want me to take care of the ordering?"

"Sure." He sets his menu down, placing his elbows on the table.

The waiter approaches, and I list items off the menu that I know are excellent. Nico looks as large as I am, and I am sure that he can eat.

"So, talk to me."

And so I do. I tell him the truth, too, because I know that there can be no secrets between us. If I have a hope of joining his crew, there must be transparency. I tell him about the change I need in my life and how he was right about questioning my path. I also tell him about my love for Gini and how much thought I gave to his words about monogamy and the sanctity of marriage.

I sit closer, wanting—no, needing him to hear me out. "I must save Gini from the life she's in, but I cannot get to Iran without your help. I'm not sure if you understand Sharia law, as it is so different from what you know in the West. Sharia deals with all aspects of day-to-day life, including everything from banking to marriage and sexuality. It also allows a woman who was raped to be killed and a woman without full covering in public to be flogged. It isn't safe for her there." I can feel sweat break out on my forehead. "She wasn't properly educated in their lifestyle—she needed more time. She could make an error. Ask a wrong question. She is a curious girl. If she were to express any doubt of any word in the Qur'an—"

"Doubting any word of the Qur'an or Muhammad is a sin." He shrugs sadly. "I know the deal, Darius. I understand how it is in that part of the world. Kosovo, where both of us are from"—he gestures between us—"was actually the most recent Muslim nation to emerge in the world. Of course, we wear our faith lightly. But I understand everything you speak."

The food comes, giving us a much-needed pause.

I fill his plate, and he eagerly takes it from my hand.

"I love Indian food." He smiles. A few minutes later, he sits back in his chair. "Listen, Darius."

I put my fork down, taking a sip of water and shifting closer to him.

"I understand your predicament," he tells me. "I've seen how you handle yourself in this world, and I think you'd be a good addition to the Mafia Shqiptare. I really do. But the truth is, I do not know you. I cannot trust you as I trust my own men. Not yet. When a man joins my crew, he spends time working at the bottom level. I run various businesses, above and below ground. Through dedication and hard work, I might allow him to rise in my ranks. I offered you a position in my inner circle because I could tell from meeting you that you have what it takes.

"I've asked around about you, and you have an excellent reputation. Devan told me he has wanted you to join his crew since you were a kid. He described you as dependable, honest, and lethal. Smart, too. Roshan, who lived with you, also had excellent things to say about your intelligence and ability to speak many languages. Frankly, men like you are harder to find than you would think. The problem is, I still need the proof. Once you show me your loyalty, you and I can become brothers. And once we are brothers, there is nothing I wouldn't do for you. Even if it means putting myself and the Shqipe in danger to save your woman."

I clear my throat, my heart rate picking up. "How long are we talking here?"

"I will need at least one year. In a good scenario. I won't risk the life of my brothers for a man who hasn't proven loyalty. Busting into Iran and taking another man's wife is serious business. And if Navid Soltabian is related to Hooshang Soltabian, it would be an even bigger hill to climb. Hooshang is the top member of the Basij, the Iranian militia operating under the Islamic Revolutionary Guards Corps. President Khameni uses them to enforce any alleged threat to the government, and they're very powerful."

"Sure, I know about the Basij. They're the ones who recently opened fire on student protestors."

"That's right." He nods solemnly. "I fought in Kosovo for my freedom. Similarly, there is a great plight of Iranians who are crying out for a regime change and liberty. But the Basij keeps them under the current regime's thumb."

It's obvious that Nico feels passionate about the situation in Iran. Still, I can't help but ask, "So, one year?" My leg shakes. "Nico, with all due respect, I need to act faster than that. I understand that there might be obstacles, but Gini—"

He raises his hand, silencing me. "I have to know where your allegiance lies. I have to know that you would protect me above your own life. Nothing short of time can prove that to me. You are coming to the Mafia Shqiptare because you're ready for bigger and better things. Also, because of the girl. But I need to know that you will stay within my ranks, with or without the girl, because of loyalty to me." His face is hard and serious.

There is no negotiating with this man. I know it, and he knows it.

"I've grown this business with my bare hands. Intelligence is necessary, as is blood. Waltzing into Iran for you, a man who hasn't proven himself? Never."

I swallow hard, the food sitting in my throat like rocks. "What will the process be like for me to join the Mafia Shqiptare?"

"At first, you hang around. Come with me and the boys wherever we go. You'll be by my side. I'll need you to show me what you're capable of, and there will be plenty of times to prove your worth. The men in the Shqipe are strong and decent, but truth be told, not all are smart enough. That's what I want to see from you." He taps his head. "Muscle? Fine, you fit the bill. But what else?" He takes a drink, eyes never leaving my face.

"I have the brains. I am also a man of my word, Nico. If I pledge allegiance to you, I would never let you down."

"That's good." He nods. "Because no one leaves the Shqipe unless they're in a casket. You're also going to have to learn the language. Albanian isn't easy."

I chuckle at the irony, shaking my head. "Yeah. Sure. That won't be a problem. But, Nico"—I clear my throat, pressing my lips together—"I need some sort of guarantee that if I join you, I can get my girl back. If something happens to Gini. If he were to hurt her ..." I grip my napkin, my knuckles tightening. "I'm looking forward to working for you, but I'm being truthful. I have to get Gini out of Iran. I can't spend my time with you in comfort, knowing she suffers."

"We will check on her. Do not worry. I have eyes and ears all over the world. And we will not ignore her. She'll live in Iran under the Mafia Shqiptare's watch."

I exhale, rubbing the back of my neck before looking back at Nico's hard face. Deep in my gut, I know this is the only path that guarantees Gini coming back to me safely.

He stands up, offering his hand. With no other choice, I shake it.

"We leave tonight for New York," he says. "I'll pick you up at five."

Nico's private plane is like something out of a James Bond movie. It's high tech with all the gadgets you could imagine and seats in such soft leather that it feels like melted butter against your skin. Nico and I are not alone. There are a few stewardesses laughing, pouring drinks at the bar. They are all in matching uniforms of short navy skirts and navy jackets.

Nico and I sit across from each other in the center of the plane. Sitting opposite from him with a clear view of the plane's entrance, I feel comfortable with my view. If I'm working for him, I need to know everything there is to know. From his mannerisms to his habits.

Two pilots walk onto the flight next, nodding and saying their hellos before entering the cockpit. A few minutes after that, I hear laughter. Four men walk onto the flight in single file, joking in a language I assume is Albanian. I've never seen these guys before. They're big and burly with dark hair. They're each wearing comfortable clothes with designer names in bold on the front of their sweatshirts—Gucci, Balenciaga, LV. Man, I hate that shit. Any man who spends that much time on his clothes has his head in the wrong place. I turn to Nico, noticing his dark jeans and black T-shirt. His clothes look like they're pricey, but they're quiet.

Three of them sit together on a leather bench situated in the corner of the plane, but one walks straight to me. I remove my seat belt and stand to greet him.

"Valon." He nods, looking me up and down. Clearly, he's sizing me up.

"I thought your name was Gucci." I point to his stupid sweatshirt.

Nico laughs out loud at my joke.

"Come on!" Valon complains to Nico, holding the bottom of his shirt. "This shit is hot. Expensive, too."

I put out my hand, wanting to keep things between us cool. If I'm joining up, I can't make enemies. "Darius."

We shake, but then I step back, hearing a loud boom.

"Don't worry." He smiles, friendlier than I would have guessed. "It's just the door. We come on first, make sure everything is clean. Then, we stay outside, making sure the pilots and stewardesses are all clear before entering. Normally, Ezra walks on with Nico. Was always by his side, but he's gone now. I guess, now, that's your job."

"I knew Valon back in Kosovo," Nico adds. "Since he was just a little kid, hanging on my ankles. Let me tell you, Darius, he was annoying as fuck then and still is now."

They both laugh, and Valon playfully tries to hit the back of Nico's head. Nico ducks, grabbing his arm.

"Yeah, annoying, my ass." Valon chuckles, taking his arm back. "I was a cute kid," he tells me pointedly. "You see this dimple? Everyone goes crazy for it."

"Yo!" Nico yells to the front of the plane. "Can we get going, please?"

"Nico's got no patience, let me tell you. Come." He tilts his head, as though asking me to follow. "Let's sit together in the back. I'll fill you in on what you need to know."

I look to Nico to make sure he's cool with this. He gives me a slight nod before pulling out a laptop from a black bag by his feet. I take that as my cue to follow Valon.

We sit together on a couch in the back of the plane, buckling up. He gives me the general ins and outs of the Mafia Shqiptare.

"You'll have to prove yourself to all of us. Many men in the Shqipe were with Nico back in Kosovo, during the war. A lot of us are blood-related, too. Nico was a beast then and is even harder now. I love the man, but his work ethic is second to none. If you fuck up"—he shrugs —"you might not live to see your mistake corrected."

I nod in understanding.

"The man who came before you, Ezra, brilliant guy who fought for Nico's life. Big shoes to fill."

"I get that." And the truth is, I do.

I know about the life these men live. And it's not just because men from different countries frequented The Mansion. From the time I was a kid, crews ran the streets. The brotherhood feeds you and takes care of you and your family. In return, you owe complete allegiance to the boss. Even with the most violent guys, there is always one man they all follow. And in this case, it's Nico.

"Nico's a good man, though. Very fair. The Mafia Shqiptare works hard and plays hard. Welcome aboard."

We spend the rest of the flight talking about football and who'll win the cup this year. He's not bad. Not bad at all.

18

Gini
Three Months Later

THE POOL WATER ripples from the breeze. I sit up to take a sip of my iced strawberry drink before adjusting my pale pink bikini. It's Saturday—also known as the weekly barbecue with Navid and his friends. He never shows up during the week to say hello or share a meal, but every single Saturday, without fail, he comes over to party and eat kabob. His friends are twenty-something men who love music, dancing, and smoking opium.

At the start of my stay, I was incredibly shy and frightened. Their world was like an alternate universe, different from both how I had been raised and also from life at The Mansion. Luckily for me, Maryam, my aid who also runs the house, has been tutoring me in the ways of Iranian culture and law.

She told me a story when I first arrived. A few kids, who were school friends of her daughter, had posted a video on the internet. They were dancing together to a song called "Happy" and telling the world they were proud to be from Tehran. Within days, the group had been arrested for violating laws that prohibited dancing with the opposite sex. Over ninety lashes apiece and jail time. Suffice it to say, dancing can only happen behind closed doors.

"Among other things," she added.

To my amazement, Maryam also supports my learning and has procured many books for me. None of which are on the banned list, but many others. The parallel life I am forced to live is becoming a strange sort of normalcy. When she and I leave the house to go for a walk, we dress in full hijab and sunglasses. Inside the house, with Navid and his friends, I am expected to drink wine, dance, tell jokes, and laugh at theirs.

I hear the engines of what sounds like multiple cars entering the driveway and I jump up, adjusting the music. The men do not like to arrive with silence around them. Apparently, it *kills their buzz*.

I put on a mix featuring Axwell, who Navid has taught me plays "progressive house". The beat is fun and exciting, the likes of which I had never before heard. And the men love it.

Navid's best friends Arash, Dumani, Bobby, and Sam walk in together, wearing bathing suits and button-down shirts, calling out, "Hey, Gini!"

I stand up to greet them, kissing each man twice, once on each cheek. I know that Navid and his friends never touch their own country's women who aren't their wives, sisters, or mothers, but when they're in this house, all bets are off.

Anita and Sonia trail the guys—sisters from Brazil, who partied on Dumani's yacht during a summer trip to Saint-Tropez. After many gifts and phone calls, where he begged them to come join him in Iran, they agreed.

"We couldn't possibly say no!" they gushed, eagerly telling me the story. "And since we've come, we've gotten two diamond Rolex watches, a beautiful apartment to stay in, and two black American Express cards with no limit on spending. And we're going to Paris tomorrow!"

Smiling and waving to me, they immediately show off their new Chanel bags. "Summer 2020. Like?"

I nod. "Love." Touching the fabric and recognizing it as rare and expensive, I smile at them. In this world I've been thrown in, access to the best material items reigns supreme.

The girls put their purses down on a side table and take off their ruffled dresses. Beneath, each wears a bikini, similar to mine. While we're all nice to each other and might seem interchangeable on the outside, there is a feeling in my chest that separates me from them. A knowledge, I guess, that I'm different. I play the part, but it's all an act. If I can just finish up my time with Navid, I'll receive the money I was promised. Sending it to my family would mean that my work here wasn't in vain.

When Navid surprised me a few days after I arrived with an entire wardrobe of fancy clothes to wear beneath my hijab when I was in public, I smiled graciously and acted as though my life had been made. In reality, I couldn't care less. But for Sonia and Anita, clothes and jewelry make life worth living. Darius wanted me to think like they do. And in a sense, he was right. If I had the same mindset, my life would be simpler and easier to bear.

"Oh, that drink looks so good," Anita croons, her lips pursing like a duck.

With her black hair twirled in a high bun, she looks both effortless and made up, which I've learned is the preferred style here. The girls get together every few months and have a doctor give them fillers in their cheeks, foreheads, and lips. Even Sonia's jawline has been filled to make it look more angular.

I, on the other hand, have refused. If Navid hasn't complained about my face, I wouldn't unanimously decide to change it. What if he decides it's ugly? Would he send me back to Madam? A large part of me wishes I had the guts to do just that. To make my face so hideous that he wouldn't be able to look at me anymore. And then he would send me back to The Mansion. I would do almost anything to go back to Darius. But a much larger part knows that it's futile. Darius made his choice when he sent me out of The Mansion with dismissive eyes. We'd had the most intense moments together before Shaina entered the room. And when we walked out, it was as though the man I had known disappeared into thin air.

If I went back to The Mansion now, would Darius be happy or angry to see me? Maybe he has already taken a new girl under his wing to tutor, and I have since been replaced. The truth is, I can't trust my memory any longer. Shame pervades my chest at random times. I was so naive and innocent, trusting Darius, a man who is nothing more than a slave dealer. And while he tried to warn me about who he was, I ignored his words and instead believed in my own innocent wish—that he saw me the way I'd always ached to be seen.

As time passes, I have become unsure if any conversation between us was natural or choreographed. Maybe it was his way to harden me or to break my heart so that I would perform better for men in my temporary marriages. Perhaps he believed that if he could turn me away from love, I would finally accept my role. I was simply a distraction for him. Despite our moments of closeness, maybe he never actually loved me.

I rub my chest as an emptiness settles within my ribs. There are phones in the house that I could use to reach my brother Aadi, to connect with my family who I miss desperately. But the shame of my current life is too great. I don't want to lie to my family about the course of my life. I would rather them think I were dead than know what has become of me. When my time is up, I'll anonymously send them the money I have earned. At least then, I'll be able to sleep at night.

Sonia waves her arm in the air, and Arash's servant comes running over.

Flipping her hair to the side, Sonia clears her throat. "Can you make us two more of what Gini is having?" She points to my drink.

"Of course." She nods, walking away.

Sonia pulls out a black net to cover her tiny bikini bottom. The swimsuits the men like us to wear, at first, felt indecent. It's half the size of my undergarments. But with the help of Maryam, I learned to dismiss my fears. This costume is not only the way Western women dress at the pool, but it is also the only route to keeping Navid and his friends content. I am to wear these clothes with a smile and be thankful for all he gives. And in return, he gives me shelter, food to eat, and Saturday barbeque parties, where the food is plenty and the smoke never stops billowing.

Navid eventually comes outside, joining his friends. They laugh together immediately before he calls out, "Gini!"

I quickly walk over, not wanting to make him wait.

"Get the board for *takhte*," he commands, not unkindly.

I blink, confused.

"You know backgammon?" Arash asks, smiling.

I shake my head. "No, but I will ask one of the maids."

"Ah, our sweet Gini is learning who to speak with to get things done." Sam rubs his hands together. "Bring us the green board. It's my lucky one."

I run into the house, finding Maryam and asking her for the green board for *takhte*. She immediately understands what it is they want and brings it to me, reminding me to offer them chai as they play. Although there are many housekeepers in the home and men to cook, Navid still likes it when I put myself out for him and his friends. Brewing tea myself and serving it along with fresh fruit makes him feel taken care of. As luck would have it, Maryam has known Navid since his childhood. I listen to her advice like the Word. She hasn't steered me wrong—yet.

When I bring out the game board, the guys are already sitting comfortably together beneath the blue-and-white canopy to the right of the pool. A table is set between them, and they are ready to play. For Navid and his friends, who are the sons of the most powerful men in the country, their entire life's purpose is enjoyment.

"Iranians are very academic but also like to party like no one else," Arash says, smiling with pride. "No one is as smart as Iranians," he adds.

"You know, Gini"—Navid pulls me to his side—"America thinks Leif Erikson discovered their country, but that's a lie. Iranians did. So self-centered, those Americans." Navid places a cigarette in his mouth.

"Wow," I reply enthusiastically, moving to pick up his gold lighter and matching ashtray from the table behind him. Lighting his cigarette, I have no idea what on earth they're talking about. If there is one thing I've learned about Navid and his friends, it is that they love to teach me things. The more amazed and full of wonder I act, the bigger they feel.

"Go sit with the girls. Thanks for the board, Gini." He taps my butt, and I walk away.

In front of his friends, he makes a big show to act tough and dominant. But when they're gone, he's anything but.

Since I've come to Iran, Navid has yet to ask me for any sexual favors. I believe it's because opium is his primary choice in mistress, and I'm thankful for it. Sonia and Anita also handle the men's desires with ease, and neither Navid nor his friends seem to notice or care that I have yet to partake in their escapades. When under the opium influence, they don't have any idea who is who. For the first two months of my stay, I worried endlessly that he would come into my bedroom at night. Now, I realize that he simply isn't interested in anything more than a girl to call his own, who is willing to wear a bikini in front of his friends, bring chai, and dance seductively when they're smoking opium. I can manage this life.

After a delicious barbeque of kabob with plenty of doogh to drink, we are all full and relaxed, listening to music and lounging about. The sun begins to set, and the men walk inside to relax in the opium den. I go back into the house, as well, boiling water for tea and making sure the fruit plate is in the refrigerator. Before bringing it to the men, I change into my costume. It's a red skirt and short top, showing my freshly pierced naval. Navid requested it to be done with two small diamonds, and so it was. A red mask also covers the front of my face, showcasing my eyes.

I gather the drinks and food and walk into the den quietly, so as not to disturb their smoking. The space is filled with ornate, colorful pillows over a huge couch-like bed. Orange and gold fabric tents the ceiling. A large carpet in riotous colors lines the floor.

"The best tea I've ever had," Navid exclaims, exhaling a huge puff from the bamboo pipe, forming red clouds.

It makes me ill to smell, but it also takes Navid away from me and my bed. For that, I will forever be thankful to the red smoke.

"Gini"—Navid coughs—"we're going to Paris soon. My father has some business to do there with the Albanians, and I want us to go and enjoy. You will love it." He casually leans back into a group of plush satin pillows.

"Of course," I reply quietly, offering a cup of tea to Sam.

When the men are all situated comfortably with Sonia and Anita topless and lying about, I turn on "Cheshmat" by Mehrnoosh—my favorite Iranian song to dance to. It's sexy, slow, and sultry. Shutting my eyes, I dance for them. My hips sway from side to side, swiveling to the beat. I lift my ringed hands up high, twirling round and round so my skirt floats. As usual, I imagine Darius sitting before me. He's smiling, legs open, with his elbows resting on his knees.

Dumani says something, and I suddenly remember where I am.

There is no Darius here. The moment that thought hits me, my dancing changes. It's slower, my movements darker.

I imagine leaving my family, kissing my father good-bye. I find myself thinking, too, about the moment I was robbed a second time —losing my love. The song ends, and I drop my head, weighed down by grief. A new song begins, and I try to continue my movements.

There are only these men, addicted.

There is only my life, enslaved.

They smoke and lie back, enjoying the erotic scene as I move to my knees to a pillow on the floor, my hands touching the silk carpet. I roll my head in circles, just like Shaina used to do. Navid asks me to remove my top. It makes me cringe. I switch my mindset again. This time, it is to the money I will earn. For my family. I slowly pull the shirt off over my head as dumb smiles fill their ashen faces.

It doesn't take long for the men to close their eyes, falling into a drug-induced trance. When the second song ends, I gather my top and leave.

19

Darius

IF SOMEONE HAD TOLD me three months ago that I would be living in an apartment in New York City and working for Nico Shihu of the Mafia Shqiptare, I would have laughed.

At this point, I have one singular goal. And that is to prove my loyalty to the shqipe so that, in return, they will help me retrieve Gini from Iran. Night after night, I worry about her safety and wellness. In New York City, despite the distance and time, there is no escape from my thoughts of Gini. The fear in my stomach has become not unlike an ulcer. How long can I wait in worry, waking up in sweat? I dream of *his* hands on her skin. His lips on her lips. His fingers caressing her throat. His ears listening to her beautiful voice. I have to get her out of there, no matter what the cost.

Nico helped me to dig up information on Navid Soltabian, and it turns out, his initial assessment was right. Navid is the son of one of the most powerful men in Iran. Taking her will not be a simple task, but one he guaranteed we will embark on when the time is right. Waiting has become a physical burden.

Nico's days are filled with work. His businesses, both legal and illegal, are incredibly expansive. From pizza shops on the East Coast to underground arms and drug-dealing worldwide, the work never ends. Unfortunately, neither do his enemies. And each time one set dies off, another rises up in its place.

That's where I come in.

Monitoring these lowlifes and making sure they die before they can infringe on the shqipe's business has become a full-time job. My computer skills are not savvy, but my ability to speak so many languages gives us a huge leg up in taking down our enemies—or at the very least, pressuring them to stay beneath us.

Last month, we hacked into the computer system of one of the largest cartels in Mexico. With my ability to speak Spanish like I do, we were able to take back two hundred pounds of heroin they had previously stolen from one of our commercial ships. To finish the job, Nico made sure every man on the boat was slaughtered. I went with the guys, of course, who are known as the Mafia Shqiptare's cleanup crew. Nico told me I didn't have to get used to it, but I should go a few times to toughen my skin.

No one fucks with the Mafia Shqiptare. *No one.*

Nico has since asked me to not only pick up the Albanian language, but also Russian. Apparently, having one of his men fluent would be "huge for business".

Sweating from my morning run around Washington Square Park, I take a quick shower, drink a protein shake, and begin my studies in Russian. After a lunch of eggs, grilled chicken, and salad, I suit up and strap myself with weapons. Today, we're meeting with a group of outlaw bikers who run our guns across state lines.

They do dirty work for us that Nico isn't willing to risk his own men over. The bikers seem to be happy to make money, and they also don't give a shit about potential prison time. Nico, on the other hand, does everything he can to shield our organization from lockup. We operate like a family, and as I've learned, a lot of the men within the Mafia Shqiptare are actually related by blood. Sending one of us to prison is not on the agenda.

I walk outside my apartment building and enter the car. Alek is driving.

"Hey, man."

I shut the door.

"We're picking up Nico."

"All right." I look out the window, giving myself a moment to think about Gini and to pray for her safety. Anytime I feel doubt about my criminal work with the Shqipe, I remind myself that it's all for Gini. There is no other woman for me and no one to replace her in my heart. Would I kill for her? Yes. I would do *anything*.

"I spoke with Maryam." Alek looks into his rearview, making eye contact with me.

I immediately perk up.

When I first arrived, Nico assured me that Gini lived in a beautiful home in Elahiyeh—an upper-class neighborhood in Tehran. It turns out that her aid, Maryam, has a daughter studying in Paris. Alek was charged with threatening her daughter and pressuring Maryam to keep us updated on Gini. She won't give details out of respect for her employer, but she checks in monthly to let us know that Gini is safe and sound.

"What did she say?" I move to the edge of the seat.

"She said the same thing she always says. Gini is okay. Reading books, entertaining Navid and his friends, and is comfortable and safe."

I curse, happy that she is okay but angry that it's taking so long to get to her. I previously asked Nico if he could get Maryam to give messages from me to Gini, but he insisted it would be too dangerous. Maryam, herself, is a safe bet, as her love for her daughter outweighs all other things. But if Gini were under questioning and if she were to tell Soltabian that she and I were in contact, it could be catastrophic.

The car door opens. It's Nico.

"We have a lot coming up," he tells me, buckling his seat belt. "First stop, Paris to meet with Hooshang Soltabian and his network. Then, some enjoyment in St. Barts."

My heart leaps into my throat. "Soltabian—"

"Relax, Darius. Not the son. The father."

I clench my teeth, and he continues, "The country is in dire need of some medical equipment." He pauses to light up a cigarette, offering me one before exhaling.

I shake my head, and he takes another long drag.

"There is a rare flu overrunning the country. Iranians are dropping dead like flies, and all of this is amid a serious recession. The government tells its people, 'America sent this virus over to kill you', blaming the United States for its suffering. Meanwhile, Iran needs aid. They are desperate for medical equipment and supplies. That's where we come in."

I nod my head.

"By the way, the US offered help, but the Iranians refused it." He shrugs. "Good for us. We're going to buy masks, ventilators, and hospital beds. Then, we'll sell it to Iran for millions." Nico winks, blowing smoke upward. "Such an incredible country, filled with so much promise. Oil. Natural gas. Very intelligent people, too. But an oppressive regime is a cancer, Darius. Cancer to the people but good for the black market. We will help them out and make money from it. Win-win for the Shqipe."

"Definite win for the Shqipe." I nod. "Looking forward to St. Barts?"

"That's right. I'm bringing my woman with me."

I remember back when I first met Nico, and he mentioned a woman he planned to have forever. "Is this *the* woman?"

"Elira." He smiles, trying to hold it back but failing. "I expect you to keep an eye out on things while I'm with her. We won't work, though." Pulling out his phone, he furrows his eyebrows and intently stares at the screen, probably reading something important.

I look back out the window when Nico clears his throat. "Hey, you know that new hang-around, Agron?"

I turn toward him. "Sure. The kid with the drug problem?"

He scoffs, thoroughly annoyed. "That's the one. That's Elira's brother. I want you to be on top of his whereabouts. I've got a bad feeling about him, but we have to be"—he hesitates—"sensitive."

I grunt in understanding. He goes back to his phone, and I know the conversation is over.

I drop my head, imagining Gini sleeping. I loosen my tie, wondering if I didn't do enough for her before she left. Was her English strong enough to help her communicate? Heat moves up my neck. I'm angry. So fucking angry. Gini is gone and in the hands of a maniac, and it's all *my* doing. For the millionth time, I ask myself why I didn't figure a way out for us sooner. Earlier. If I thought it could help, I'd beg Nico to go and get her. Now. But there is no use.

"How's your Russian going?"

I exhale. "It's getting better."

"Albanian?"

"It's good."

"We're going to need you fluent in both."

"I got you." I nod. "A month more for the Russian. Albanian, I'm already there."

"This language thing you got, it's fucking great."

"Yeah."

In Albanian, he tells me, "These bikers we're meeting today, the Angels of Hell. Nothing has changed since the last time we discussed the deal with them. Just giving them a simple route change. Alek, Daniel, Elio, and Abdyl will be joining us."

I nod. In Albanian, I reply, "I'm ready."

"How about that dog? Did he take his piss yet?"

"What dog?"

He laughs. "Good. Just making sure you understand me."

The guys have been doing this to me for weeks now, just making up random shit and saying it in Albanian to test if I actually understand them. I shake my head, but it only makes him laugh louder. Even Alek joins in.

We pull into a vacant warehouse in the Meatpacking District. When we exit the car, the rest of our men step out of theirs. We say hello and make small talk before walking into the seemingly abandoned building.

Two bikers in leather vests sit at a scratched-up wooden table with four guys in matching leather vests behind them. I recognize the two main men sitting as the president and vice president. Big and burly with tattoos from their wrists to their necks, they all look like they could use a decent shower and haircut.

"Hello." Nico walks over in his perfectly tailored suit. He shakes their hands, one at a time. "Slim. Hunter."

"Hey, Nico," they reply in unison.

The president, Hunter, pulls a toothpick from his pocket and puts it in his mouth.

I step slightly behind our group, my arms crossed over my chest as I look around at our surroundings. Just like I did at The Mansion, I prefer to have a spot that gives me a clear view of every player in the room and all exits. The men start with light conversation, talking about sports, before Alek steps to the table, putting down a map.

Nico immediately tells them that he no longer likes their route option. "You cross Russian turf when you cross this border," he says, pointing to the map. "And they don't like it. I want you to go this way instead."

Hunter chuckles. "That's our route. No other way to get your guns outta state. Friends of ours work out of here." His fingers move down to the map. "And we prefer to do our work with them at our backs."

"Friends?" Nico's laugh is dark. "You need someone to hold your dick, eh? This isn't a communal effort. If you can't handle it on your own, I will find someone who will. This is the route you must take."

The vice president, Slim, pipes up, "You gave us the job, and the rest is in our hands. The only thing you have to care about is that your goods get there in one piece. How we drive is our decision."

"I don't think so." I can hear the tightness in Nico's voice. The man is not happy. "The property is mine. The work is mine. I dictate how it gets to where it goes. I'm not going to risk my other businesses because your men can't handle shit on their own." He looks around at the bikers before resettling his gaze back on Hunter. "I told you how I want it done. This isn't up for negotiation."

The group quiets, and the tension suddenly thickens.

"You're real funny." Hunter stands, his chair grating against the concrete floor. From where I stand, the outline of his weapon is visible. "You gave us the job. How about a little trust? We ain't botherin' the Russians. We ain't sellin' on their turf, either. We're simply drivin' through, like the law-abiding citizens we are."

A few men chuckle behind him.

Nico turns his head, and we lock eyes. He wants me to get involved.

"Trust?" I walk forward to the table, taking a stand beside him. "You guys do your jobs like the simple machines you are required to be. We give you the goods, and you take them on the route we prefer. You say, 'Yes, Mr. Shihu. Thank you for the business', and get on with it. When the goods are delivered, you take your money. The end."

"Big man, here, thinks we're just machines, eh?" The vice president stands. "I don't think you know who you're messing with."

He squints his eyes, and I have the urge to punch him in the face.

All of the bikers shift, and from my height, I can see a formation taking place among them. They're getting ready for a fight. My blood turns hot, excited, even.

A man behind Slim puts his hand on what looks like a gun, and I know in my gut that if I don't take care of him, he's going to shoot. I pull out my piece and pop him in the arm. With my free hand, I push Nico off to the side to get him out of harm's way.

Hell? It breaks out.

Hunter tries to take me on. I tear his weapon from his hands and throw it across the room, wanting to engage in hand to hand. I punch him in the throat, and he crumples to the floor. Kicking him in the side with my boot over and over again, I know I'm dangerously close to killing him. Something tells me Nico wouldn't want his death, but I. Can't. Stop.

The fury I feel is cloaked in pain.

I allowed Gini to leave. In front of my own eyes! I blink, and a knife slashes my face, bringing me back to the present. I barely feel the pain, but I taste blood as I pull the next biker's ponytail and snap his arm.

The sound of motorcycles roars, drowning out his screams.

I look around the room. A few bikers litter the floor, and the men of the shqipe still stand. Staring at me.

In Albanian, I ask, "Did the bikers leave so soon?" I laugh, kicking Hunter in the ribs. "*Qiju.*" *Fuck you,* I tell him in Albanian, spitting on his bearded face.

"Hey." Nico points to my cheek before straightening his tie. He looks as though he just jogged down a street, clean if not a little sweaty. I touch my face, feeling ooze. "Let's go get you stitched up. Feeling okay?" He wraps an arm over my shoulders as we exit the warehouse.

"Sure." I clear my throat. "Just so you know, I saw one of them put his hand on what looked like a gun. Didn't want to take a chance. That's why I shot."

"Goddamn, Darius, but you're a good fighter. Really, really good. Proved yourself big time today. I think all of us are proud."

I squint my eyes at the sun shining so brightly. Making it to the car, I sit inside first. My hand is bloody from my face, and so is my shirt.

"Abdyl," Nico calls out.

I hear Abdyl respond, "Yo."

"Take care of the ones on the floor. Drop them off at their club-house and let them know they're off the job."

In the car, Nico sits beside me, pulling out a towel from a hidden compartment behind his seat. "Hold it on your face until we get to the office. Don't want you bleeding on the leather." He shuts the side door and gets comfortable. "Those assholes weren't going to keep the job anyway. It's good we fucked them up. Keeps them in line."

"Yeah. I didn't like them. The people who touch our cargo should be cleaner."

After a few minutes of silence, Nico turns to me. "After we get the medical supplies to Iran, you and I will take a trip to Tehran. First, we'll make sure the medical equipment has arrived. And then we'll get your girl back. Welcome to the Mafia Shqiptare, brother."

With blood spilling down my face, I smile. *Gini.*

We drive silently back to Park Avenue and 51st Street, heading to

Nico's office building. He rents out floors one through six but keeps the entire seventh floor for himself.

Arriving at the building, we quickly walk inside and move straight into the elevator. "The doctor is waiting for you upstairs. Elena is very good." Nico adds, "She is married to Mat."

Mat is one of Nico's closest, and he is spectacular on the computer. The man has been able to hack into systems around the world like a ghost.

The elevator opens, and the good doctor is waiting with a smile.

"Nice to meet you, Darius. Follow me." She's tall with short blonde hair. Very pretty and clearly very Russian.

Nico's secretaries sidle beside him, immediately updating him on the day's work. He reads his phone while he listens, and they walk off.

When he is out of sight, I ask in Russian, "What part of Russia are you from?"

"Moscow."

In Russian, I tell her, "I am learning to speak your language."

She replies that I have a very nice accent. "Mat is trying to learn, but he is awful. You, on the other hand, sound very good."

I understand her perfectly. "I have been teaching myself over the last three months."

"That is great," she exclaims. "It's not an easy language."

When she takes me through a door I never before noticed, I find a miniature hospital room.

"I'm a dermatologist, but I help out the guys anytime they need me. You can sit on the bed."

I sit down and take the towel off my face.

Her eyes widen. "I can stitch you, but this will scar."

"That's fine." I shrug, feeling happier than I have in quite some time. The scar will be like a tattoo—a reminder of what it took to get me my woman. For Gini, I would do it a hundred times over.

"Let me give you some pain relief first—"

"No." I shake my head. "I don't like taking medication unless it's necessary."

"You're sure?"

"Yes. I suffer from migraines, and often, medications bring them on."

"That is interesting. Well, if you want to do this sober, that's your choice. Lie down."

I do as she said, putting my head on the pillow and feet straight out in front of me. She bends down to wipe my face with alcohol. I can feel the sting down in my toes, but I welcome the pain.

As Elena sews me up, I imagine Gini's gray-blue eyes closing in ecstasy above me. Her soft breaths coating my skin. Her loving me.

I'm coming for you.

20

Gini

THE PARISIAN NIGHTCLUB IS EXPANSIVE, dark, and loud with pulsing music. I find myself hanging on to Navid's arm like my life depends on it. People walk quickly in every direction with overflowing drinks in hand, laughing, seemingly joking, and dancing.

We push through the crowd, a tall man with shiny black skin and bulging muscles leading the way. From the corner of the dance floor, we walk four carpeted steps into a roped-off, private area. There is a dark, round table and a blood-red couch beside it. Looking around, I notice other tables identical to ours surround the room.

"The drinks are on the way," the man yells over the music, shaking hands with Dumani.

Navid smiles wide. "Sit, Gini, sit. Let's wait for the champagne."

We drop down onto the couch, and he wraps an arm around my shoulders. He's possessive but in a friendly way.

The moment we arrived in Paris, it felt as though I entered a dream. Maryam and I share a two-bedroom suite at the George Cinq hotel, which is owned by a close friend of Navid's family, Al-Waleed bin Talal from Saudi. Navid was very proud of his connection to the owner, explaining to me that Al-Waleed spent close to two hundred million dollars to buy the hotel and another one hundred million to renovate it.

"The suite you're staying in is the best in the world," he said, smiling happily. After handing me his black American Express card and an envelope filled with cash, he waved good-bye.

This evening is the first we've spent together since arriving here over a week ago—and I'm not complaining.

Maryam and I have been thoroughly enjoying everything the city has to offer. Simply put, I cannot imagine a place exists on this earth with better food, more incredible museums, or more magnificently built streets.

Yesterday, Maryam brought us to the Louvre, where we wore headphones and listened to someone knowledgeable explain the art. I think our bodyguards were bored, but Maryam and I were enraptured. I'd never known life could be like this.

She and I have become so close. There have been many times when I wanted to tell her about Darius, but I know it would be a conflict for her. She has known Navid all his life and might be upset to hear that I dream of another man.

The music changes, and I'm brought back to this moment. Suddenly, four women walk to our table, holding gigantic bottles, flashing with fire!

Sam must see the look on my face because he says, "Those are called bottle sparklers. Fun, huh?"

We all stand up and clap to the blasting music, watching as the girls dance with the bottles overhead.

I turn to Navid, knowing the song we're hearing. "'Memories' by David Guetta, right?"

"That's right, Gini!" He laughs out loud. "Look at you, learning the greats so quickly!" He wraps an arm over my shoulders and pulls me into his chest, kissing the top of my head.

The men shout, making noise and hollering, inviting eyes and excitement from the dancing crowd to where we sit.

People point at our table, as if to say, *Wow, look at them!*

Sam takes the hand of each waitress, bringing them up onto our table to dance. There is barely any space with the drinks they just set, but they manage it by grinding body to body, dresses fitting like second skin, and they dance together like the girls used to do at The Mansion. It's seductive and eye-catching. The men's eyes glaze over with lust, but Navid barely notices them. He isn't looking at me, either. His gaze is in some faraway place. I rest comfortably, knowing I'm safe and that he wants almost nothing from me.

Navid turns, touching my face as if I were made from glass. He's sweating, looking at me with seemingly new eyes, like I am something special. "You're the queen of this club, Gini. My queen. How does it feel to have everything?" He kisses the palm of my hand. The lights swirl in riotous colors, at once illuminating the dance floor and camouflaging faces. "While we are together, you must enjoy and dance and celebrate. Life might not be so good for you one day. Make this last. Did you go shopping?"

I shrug. "I've been sightseeing."

"Please, do not taarof with me. I want you to shop. Buy clothes. Go to Cartier and get yourself a gold watch. Tomorrow morning."

I bite my lip, and he continues, "Say yes, Gini. I swear, sometimes, I think you're more Iranian than I am with the way you refuse things. Please, buy yourself clothes and jewelry."

"Okay." I shrug. "If it pleases you, then I will."

He laughs out loud, and I think of Darius teaching me taarof with the banana. I always think of Darius.

Navid pulls a small, clear bag from his pocket. "Try some of this."

Looking closely, I notice his pupils are extremely dilated. Other than speaking quickly and sweating profusely, he seems to be in his right mind.

"It's called Molly. Pure MDMA. I wouldn't give you something that could hurt you. I know how new you are to this world. But it's amazing. It will bring us closer. Trust me." He takes a rock from the plastic and crushes it with one of the glass cups on the table. Gathering the powder into his palm, he tells me to lick my finger and put it into the powder before swallowing it. "It tastes like shit, but it's amazing!"

"I'm afraid, Navid," I tell him with honesty, staring at the white dust.

"I know, my beauty." He kisses my knuckles. "Our relationship is not sexual. You might be wondering why. I just … like your company. My father always had many wives from sigheh, and I remember them crying after lying with him. They were so young! I told Mullah Omar, 'She must be old enough to understand but clean'. I did not want someone damaged or abused."

He moves closer to me, so our noses are almost touching. I should be afraid, but I'm not.

He whispers, "In fact, women don't pleasure me. I can enjoy looking at their bodies, but they don't …" He pauses, shutting his eyes and screwing them up tightly before reopening them. "I need to have you with me, Gini. So that my father and wives assume I am getting my fill with you. Do you understand?"

Sweat pours down his temples. He smiles, but his eyes are sad. There's something he is trying to tell me, but I cannot understand what it could be. Still, I won't push. If whatever it is stops us from becoming intimate, I will take it.

I press my lips together, and he takes my hand in his, squeezing, like we're sharing a secret.

"You have me with you, Navid. You can tell anyone whatever you want. I am here to please you."

He hugs me close to his chest. "Thank you, my beauty. My friend. I will be forever grateful. Forget sixty thousand. I will give you one hundred thousand dollars for the year."

I want to scream with joy. One hundred thousand? My father will be in heaven. I am shaking and trying not to cry.

He takes my palm, pressing it against his chest when he says, "Your dancing. Your eyes. Your kind heart. One day, you will make a man very happy. Now"—he shakes the baggie in front of my face with mischief—"try some. I want you to party with me tonight."

My body shrinks back.

"Just let go and be free!" he exclaims, pushing his hair back with his free hand. "I will not let anything happen to you. Trust me. My guards are all around the room, keeping an eye on all of us to ensure our safety. We can do *anything*." He sees my hesitation and presses harder, "Go on, Gini. Lick your finger and dip it into the powder."

With a shaking hand, I put my forefinger into my mouth, sucking as he told me to do. I know this is wrong, but I feel like I have no choice. Dipping it into the powder, I move it into my mouth.

"That's a good girl," he coos, licking the remaining powder off his hand.

It doesn't take long for him and his friends to leave the table and walk into the center of the throng, sweating, dancing, and jumping up and down. Women join them, but I stay in my seat, just watching the world around me.

What will happen to me?

Dumani throws what looks like hundreds of bills in the air. People look up.

"It's raining money," someone screams.

In a flash, the guys seem to be swallowed up by the crowd. I hear laughter.

I let my eyes scan the other tables, where wealthy and entitled-looking people sit. I squint, seeing an outline of a man with hair, long and down, shining beneath the lights. His cheekbones are so high, almost carved. He's smiling with the men beside him, laughing, looking happy. He stands up, and my eyes widen at his build. He's enormous with wide shoulders and a smaller waist, just like Darius. I let myself wonder how he is.

For months, I have tried to remove him from my mind, but there is no use. He sent me away, and yet I still question if the words he spoke were all lies. For the millionth time, I ask myself, *Could they have been truth?* I imagine his warm hands and the gentleness with which he used them. His gorgeous lips—*Are they on another woman now?* Those eyes, seeing me in a way no one else ever has. Is someone else listening to his brilliant words? And his body. It's like I've been conditioned to lose my mind when seeing a build like Darius's.

The man looks up, and our eyes lock.

My hairline breaks out with sweat, and my heart thrums. The music has entered my bloodstream. The man who looks like Darius stares. He is so beautiful.

I inhale a sharp breath. *Is it him? He's here. He has found me!*

I smile, remembering him picking vegetables with me, the sun shining. My heart. The thump is thunder. I place my hand on it, wondering if it could beat out of my chest.

Darius leaves his group, moving through the dance floor like he's dying of thirst, but sees a well of water in the distance. I hang on to the bottom of my seat, my body wanting to move to him. To sprint. But something in my veins fills with worry. He has disappeared in the crowd. *Is he gone? Yes. No. It couldn't be. Is my mind playing tricks from the powder?* Darius was on my mind, and so he appeared to me. *Can that be it? This can't be real.*

A thickness enters my throat, like it has been stuffed with cotton, and for a moment, I feel like I am about to be sick. And then it hits me.

Oh ...

A smile flows through my entire body. I lean back into the chair, hanging my head down and feeling my skin heat up. My pores sing.

Wow. I close my eyes, touching my face with warm fingertips, tracing my nose, my jaw, and then the outline of my lips. I imagine Darius's mouth on mine, and my body comes to life, warming and liquifying. My fingers move downward, grazing my thighs, and then go up my neck. I shiver, picturing his heaviness above me.

All I know is this moment.

I reopen my eyes, but I am alone. Standing, I can no longer see him in the crowd.

"Gini!" It's Navid.

I look down to his smiling face.

"Come dance with me!"

I shake my head. I desperately look around the room. Darius is here. He is on his way to me. I just need another moment to see if it's true. My eyes rove around, searching.

Navid walks up to the table, taking my hand in his. "Come with me. I need to dance with you. To touch you. It will feel so good. You feel it now, don't you?"

I want to shout that I can't leave, but he grips my hand so hard.

"Please, Navid," I beg. I look around, a pull in my gut that won't stop twisting.

He snaps, "Come now." His words are my command.

I leave the table, and he brings me into the dancing mob.

"Be free," he yells over the music. "Don't worry about who you were or who you want to become. There is no time for stress and worry. Right now, just be yourself. Listen to the music. Let it consume you."

It wasn't Darius. It was my imagination. *How could he be here? He couldn't be.*

I pull the tie from my hair, letting it glide across my back and shoulders. Everything feels magical. The beat of the music. The bodies around me, touching me. *Could it be true that, a few months ago, I was taken from my home and brought to The Mansion? And now, here I am, in one of the most incredible nightclubs in Paris, dancing. My heart continues to race. What if it was Darius? What if, for some reason, he is actually here?*

I look around the room, wishing I were taller so I could see the room better.

Navid moves to my ear, asking, "Are you searching for someone?"

Worriedly, I yell above the music, "No, of course not!"

The man wasn't Darius. It couldn't have been. I'm not in Madam's house, under her terror. I'm not learning beside Darius, looking into his smiling eyes. And I'm not in my small village, picking vegetables and gathering water. I'm in the middle of a magnificent world filled with stunning souls, who all understand me. *Everything in life is beautiful, and it will all work out!* Something tells me that the drugs are causing this euphoria, but it has been so long since I have been happy. Regardless of the reason, I'll take it.

I lift my arms in the air, twirling around and around. If he is truly here, he will find me.

Navid stops me from spinning, his arms wrapping around my middle as he pulls me into his sweaty chest.

I look up into his eyes. "You are a good man." I swallow hard, locking my hands around his neck. "I was scared, at first. But you are such a good, good person. Nice. And thoughtful."

He has beautiful, dark eyes. And thick lashes, fanned out.

He laughs. "Look at you. The drugs have really done a number. The truth is, you're the good one. We are all blessed by Allah!"

He reaches into his pocket, pulling out a stack of one-hundred-dollar bills and throwing them up in the air, laughing. "What is money?" he screams as people crouch to the floor, crawling to lift the cash. "Money is for memories. For love. For enjoyment. Tonight, we should all be free!"

The cheering drums in my ears, a smile filling my heart.

We keep dancing until he whispers in my ear, "Let's get some water."

When we get back up to our table, my eyes go back to the group I saw earlier. The table is now empty.

21

Darius

ALEK MAKES us all laugh with a joke about a girl he is sleeping with, gesturing with his hands to make the whole sordid tale funnier than it probably was. I lift the drink to my lips, smiling as the guys crack up. Sitting with the boys is great, but I still feel alone. The club lights shine all around me, and yet a feeling of utter exhaustion consumes me. The day I'd met Gini, I was full of strength. And now, I'm wounded and heart-heavy.

I grit my teeth, forcing myself to act as my old self would. Confident and strong. My new tattoo that I got with the boys last week, signifying my allegiance to the Mafia Shqiptare, is fresh on my skin.

Life is *good*. I am running with the most powerful crew in the world, and soon, I will have my woman by my side.

I crack my knuckles.

Light up my tenth cigarette of the night.

Take another strong swallow of my drink.

I look around the room, exhaling, when my gaze locks with the most beautiful pair of eyes there ever was.

Bathed by a canopy of silver light, in a dress full of sequins, she sits at a private table with her dark hair pulled back. Staring at me, her eyes are wide and almost afraid. My head fills with an electric static.

I forget about the men at the table. Forget about the bodyguards watching our entire party so we can get drunk with our eyes closed. I can only think about getting to her. I stand.

Mine.

Moving through the crowd, I push bodies aside to clear the way. My chest tightens as I practically run, my legs refusing to stop, my chest unable to take a breath, lest she somehow got away in the time it takes me to inhale.

When I am halfway across the dance floor, three men grab me, pushing me across the party until I hit a wall.

Zef, Nico's main guard, gets in my face. "What the fuck, man? You can't just run off like that. You're supposed to contact us before you run, guns fucking blazing." He shakes his head. "And how heavy are you? Two hundred fifty?"

Dren looks at me hard. "Who did you see? Who was there?" He lifts his phone, ready to contact Nico.

I clench my jaw. "I don't want to hurt you guys, but I will if you don't let me go right fucking now. No enemies. Just a woman I once knew and want to see again."

Dren grips my arms harder. He knows if he lets go of me, I will bolt.

Zef presses his lips together. "Listen, Darius, we don't want trouble with you. We've heard where you come from and why you rose to the top so fast. Just chill, and let's settle this calmly. Rules here are meant to be followed, eh."

Roan, another guard, pulls out his phone, typing out a message. "Nico's coming." He says it like that's the biggest threat he can bring. "And he won't be happy that you left the crew without notifying one of us. You know the orders. If there's a girl you like across the room, you tell us, and we'll bring her to you. You never run off on your own."

It doesn't take long for Nico to find us.

"What's going on, Darius? We're in the middle of finally letting off some steam, and then I hear that you're running across the floor like you want to kill someone. There had better be a good reason you're ruining my night." He's mad, putting a cigarette into his mouth and lighting up.

I shake my arms, and they finally let me go.

"She's here," I tell him.

"Who?"

"Gini."

He exhales in defeat. "I had no idea that little shit Soltabian was here. He must have come to ride on his father's coattails."

"I'm going, Nico."

"Darius, the place is full of their personal security. If you go near her, they will grab you."

"That's right, boss." Dren points up to each corner of the room, pointing them out.

"No." I shake my head, adrenaline pumping. "I don't care. Gini is here. I'm here. It's a sign."

Nico shakes his head. "You left our crew, and you were spotted in seconds. I know for a fact that Navid Soltabian doesn't take a step out of his home without an entourage of lethal protection. The guys up there aren't paparazzi; they're dangerous guards. Now is not the time. If our guys saw you, they saw you, too. You might already be on their radar."

"You can't tell me what to do!" I grit my teeth, ready to throw down and kill anyone who gets in my way.

Dren grabs my shoulder, letting me know that he's willing to put up a fight. "Chill, Darius. Whoever she is, you can find her another time."

Nico tells the guards to leave us. At his command, they walk off.

"Just think about it. If you went to her and you touched her? It could mean a big problem for both of us. What if his men took you and found out that one of the men in the Mafia Shqiptare touched their personal property—a wife? They would take it as a serious offense. I know you've got a few drinks in your system and you're feeling hot. But we have a plan. Let's stick to it."

"It will take too fucking long."

"No." He shakes his head. "We are so close, Darius. Next month, we will go to Iran to supply them with the medical equipment. And then, when you see her, we will negotiate a price. You agreed to it."

"No, Nico." I shake my head. "You can't do this to me. She's *here*. Here!" I clench my fists, wondering if I should just run over him.

Nico grabs my jaw, forcing my attention back on him. I'm shaking.

"I'm doing this for you. For the Shqiptare. We are your family. We are where you belong."

"Maybe this isn't where I belong."

"Believe me, Darius, where I am is where you are meant to be."

I drop my head, my voice cracking as I say, "I love her."

"Hey," he starts. "I understand what love means. But if you care for her, you will take her properly and not risk her life and yours. Let's just get the fuck out of here, eh?"

"What if she isn't okay? What if she needs me?" Painful thoughts barrage my head.

"I'll have Dren watch her all night."

"She saw me."

"Which table was hers?"

"Across the room." I point to where she sat, noticing it's empty.

He follows my hand. "She probably isn't sure what she saw. It's dark and smoky. Now, let's go before you get us into trouble. One more month, brother."

He throws an arm over my shoulders, and I swear, for the first time since I was a child, I feel like crying.

ST. Barts is at once casual and yet extremely high-end. Nico owns the massive home we're staying in. It's often used as a bed and breakfast-style hotel. Overlooking Flamands Beach, it's complete with fifteen bedrooms, each with their own bathroom, and it has been cleared out to make room for the inner circle of the Mafia Shqiptare. There is an expansive view of the ocean from the back of the house and a pool that looks as though it filters straight into the Atlantic.

On the flight over, Valon gave me a quick rundown of Nico and Elira. "Nico has known Elira since her birth. Back in Albania, her father was head of the Kosovo Liberation Army. After his death, Nico took over his position and managed to wage a full-fledged war with the Serbs, which led to our freedom."

It was clear that the loyalty of the Shqipe was based on Nico Shihu's legacy as a freedom fighter.

"Elira is in college now, studying in Tobeho. Beautiful, strong, and smart. Perfect for us." He laughed.

Watching Nico and Elira together is interesting. He's different when she is near. Warm, almost. I remember when he told me about her back at The Mansion. She is the only one he wants and will ever want.

The men are relishing every moment of this trip. Not me. At this point, every minute of my life feels like years. The clock is ticking until we get to Iran, and I'm dying to get there. I'll have plenty of time to party with the boys—once Gini is back in my life. Until then, I want nothing to do with fun. I can barely stomach it.

Did Gini see me at the club and know it was me, or was Nico right and she was unsure? I pray she did not think it was actually me. Because if she saw me and knew it, and then realized that I hadn't come for her? She'd never forgive me. I can barely forgive myself.

I finish unpacking in my room and change into a bathing suit, wanting a stiff drink and a cigarette. Before leaving my room, I hear some guys talking through the open window. I pause, listening.

" ... killed three men with his bare hands. He's fucking lethal." It's Alek.

Another voice chimes in, "How else could he just walk into New

York from India, barely even speaking Albanian, and within a few months, he is fluent in our language? I heard Nico has him learning Russian, too. He must be some kind of genius."

"Or mechanical supervillain." Laughter.

I open the door, noticing three younger cousins standing with Mat and Alek.

"Come on." I nod. "The killer genius wants a drink."

We all laugh and walk up the steps together to the pool, where a party awaits, filled with women and drinks. I spot Roshan by the pool and wave. She practically shrieks, running up to me in her high heels, hands shaking in surprise, long black hair down to her waist. We catch up quickly, not wanting to draw too much attention to ourselves. Abdyl doesn't seem bothered, but I'm sure he doesn't want his woman looking so enthused over another man. I explain that I am now with the crew, and she can do nothing but shake her head in shock.

"So good to see you. So, so good."

I have to pry her hand out of mine. I smile. "Let's catch up more later."

Luckily for me, Mat brought his wife, Elena, who has been helping me with conversational Russian.

A waitress brings me a hot cappuccino and a dish called avocado toast. Food outside of India tends to be very bland to my taste buds, but this is pretty good. She hands a black coffee and scrambled eggs to Elena.

Elena and I discuss everything we can—from the weather to current events. Mat sits with us and listens but claims that it's all "gibberish" to him.

She corrects me frequently, but I welcome it. The only way to learn is to practice.

Two women, who are staying here and happen to be Russian, as well, sit beside us, joining in the conversation. It turns out, they are from St. Petersburg. The shorter one, Anastasia, takes an immediate interest in me. She's comforting, if only because she's exactly the type of woman I used to create. Accommodating, talented, and very seductive. She asks me how I got my scar. Biting on her bottom lip, she draws attention to her mouth, like she wants to use it on me.

I tell her with a straight face, "It's none of your business," and she laughs, as though I were joking—I'm not.

Just the thought of a woman like her on top of me or beneath me makes me sick. I've had so many. Too many. Now, and for the rest of time, the only breath I will taste is Gini's.

Finishing my third coffee of the morning, I take a seat by the pool beside Alek and a few other guys, trying to be social. In some ways, they remind me of Arman and D-Company. I've wanted to call Arman often, but until things are sorted with Gini, I don't want to get anyone else involved in what's to come. All of these underground networks are connected, and I don't want any information moving that could potentially hurt my plan. It still burns how Amma found out—was it Arman or Devan? That information cost me Gini. I've since learned how necessary silence can be.

The guys talk shit and bring me into the conversation as scantily clad girls walk around, ready and willing for anything.

The Shqipe is crazy with inside jokes and laughter. Fighting enemies, fucking women, and doing huge business in between. They might not marry many women, but I have since learned that they *have* many women. They marry one wife, who gives them children, support, love, and respect. They keep one sidepiece, giving her a place to live and a car to drive, who they can enjoy and fuck in the ways they would never fuck their wives. And then countless hookers to screw for a night and then pay to disappear. Their lives might be different from what I know, but in the end, it's all somehow ... the same.

Alek kicks his feet in front of him as two girls pull off their bikini tops and dance for him. "The American dream." Alek smiles, causing us to burst out in laughter.

～

I STAY on the trip for two days before Nico asks me to return to New York City to check up on Elira's brother, Agron. After getting word from some of the guys back in the city that they haven't seen him in a week, Nico knows something is up.

I get home, exhausted but ready to work. Turns out, Agron joined up with a rival crew who call themselves The Albanian Boys. The kid also owes a shitload of money to some big dealers for meth. Turns out, that little drug problem of his isn't so little. I still need information, though. He can go fuck off, but desperate people make desperate choices. Plus, the fact that he is Elira's brother makes things trickier. I know how much Nico loves his woman, and he would be angry as fuck if I acted against her brother without knowing every single detail.

I pick up the phone, texting Dren. He wasn't invited to St. Barts, and I know he was annoyed about that. Some of the guys are still irritated that I walked into the crew and started at the top, but they need to get over it. Fast. Turns out, I'm here to stay.

Hey.

Dren: What's up? You still angry with me for pulling you off the hunt back in Paris?

Yeah, I am.

Dren: Don't be sore.

Fuck you.

Dren: Okay, now that that's out of the way ...

I need you to trace a number for me. Agron. 917-664-3279. I think he's up to something, and I want all the details.

Dren: I assume you have clearance from Nico?

Don't be dick. I left the trip to figure out what's going on with Agron. If you make this harder on me, I'm not going to be a little bitch and cry to Nico. I'll take care of you myself.

Dren: Okay. Chill...

Get me the information. Now.

Dren: On it.

I call Nico, letting him know that I'm going to figure out what's going on with Agron. It's their last day on the trip, and he tells me that he's sensing some weirdness from Elira.

"Get to the bottom of this."

"I will, Nico. I've got it."

He hangs up, and I get to work.

I don't stop until there is blood on my hands.

22

Gini

I HAVE OFFICIALLY BEEN in Iran for four months. Other than the one trip to Paris, I haven't been anywhere else. I don't mind.

My night in Paris at the club made things even more difficult. I'm not surprised my mind played a trick on me after taking the drugs. But as much as my heart wants Darius, part of me knows he is irrevocably gone. I have since made a promise to myself. I swore that whenever Darius comes into my dreams, I will force him out. Deliberately, I will pull his image and any thoughts of him from my mind. It hasn't worked so well but maybe in time.

Navid's obsession with the red smoke has become even more intense. Before Paris, he came to the house once each week with his friends. But now, he comes much more often, preferring to smoke alone with one of his male servants. He is thinner now, and his skin has a grayish pallor. I still bring them chai and fruit, but it's never eaten. He barely cares if I dance anymore, either. He just waves me away once he is settled in the satin pillows, the steaming cups of tea on the glass table beside them.

Maryam explained to me that some men find themselves happier to be with other men. I think I understand now that Navid prefers men to women—on all levels. On one hand, it's shocking, but on the other, I realize that the world is not the simple one I was born into.

I come downstairs to have breakfast of coffee, fruit, and cheese with Maryam, and find five thousand dollars in cash on the table—meant for me to spend on clothes or other lavish items. Navid does this each week. I tried giving him the money back, but he was offended. I've since been keeping the cash in a shoebox in my bedroom, using the money only sparingly so that if he were to ask what I bought, I would have something to show for it. At Sonia's and Anita's insistence, I only buy items that have resale value. I have amassed a beautiful purse collection from Chanel and gold jewelry from Cartier. Maybe, one day, it will come in handy.

After we eat and read the daily newspaper, Maryam and I go to our bedrooms to change. It is Wednesday, and every Wednesday, we visit the local library before shopping at the Grand Bazaar to buy the best dried fruits and caviar. It is so busy, filled with men and women selling their wares. Maryam also insists on haggling with the vendors, and I love to watch her get a deal. I can't speak Farsi well enough to negotiate pricing, but one day, I want to try.

After getting dressed in a beautiful navy blouse and matching pants, I cover my entire outfit with a dark blue tunic and wrap my dark hair and neck with a blue scarf. Hiding my body is paramount when leaving the house, and honestly, I like it. After what I have been through, I want nothing more than to hide myself from the world.

We step outside. The air is crisp but with a hint of warmth to come. Maryam tells the driver to meet us in town in five hours.

"We want to walk and enjoy the weather," she tells him.

We walk on the sidewalk, keeping close together. The community here is gated and filled with magnificent French-style mansions of the Basij, who enforce state control over Iran's society. I've learned they receive their orders from the Islamic Revolutionary Guard Corps and the Supreme Leader of Iran, policing morals and suppressing any gatherings that go against their laws. Whenever we see one of the men walking, we immediately drop our heads and make way.

When it seems like we are alone on the street, Maryam turns her head to speak to me, her eyebrows furrowed, whispering, "Gini, what is your connection with the Albanian Mafia?"

"Me?" I point to my own chest, confused. "Absolutely nothing."

She stops moving, lifting her sunglasses to look at me hard. "Lift your shades and let me see your eyes. Are you telling me the truth? You do not know them?"

I take the glasses off of my face and shake my head. "No idea."

"Well, they want something from you." She puts her sunglasses back down over her eyes and continues to walk, her arm in mine. "When you first arrived to the house, I got a phone call from a member of the Albanian Mafia, also known as the Mafia Shqiptare. He told me that I had to tell him how *you* were each week and to keep the calls a secret from Navid, his entire family, and you, or else they would find my daughter in Paris and kill her. I was shaken. He assured me that all he wanted was to make sure you, Gini, were safe. Ever since, I call them weekly, updating him on your well-being. I swore I wouldn't tell you I was calling. But by now, you and I have grown close, have we not?"

"We have, Maryam. But threatened your daughter? How—"

"There is more." She tightens her elbow, bringing me closer to her. "I overheard Navid on the phone with his father, Hooshang, mentioning something about medical supplies being brought to Iran by the Mafia Shqiptare and a dinner party they want to throw in their honor. And the last time I spoke with the unnamed man, he thanked me for my help, as though he would no longer be calling. It could all be a coincidence, but something in my gut tells me it's not. He calls weekly, and then after I overhear that the Mafia Shqiptare is coming to Iran, the calls miraculously end?"

I feel nothing but utter confusion.

"Listen," she whispers loudly. "They do not let the newspapers print it, but I know firsthand that Iran is suffering under a mysterious virus. America has tried to send aid, but our government refuses it. They'd rather let people die than accept help. In fact, our government believes it was the Americans who brought the virus to us. To kill us and weaken us."

I press my lips together, taken aback by her theory. "But I thought America was the land of the free. They wouldn't do such a thing."

"It's all about the oil. Where there is oil, there is money. And where there is money, there is corruption. Who even knows anymore who tells the truth? If Iran needs something and won't take it from America, they would use the black market."

"Still, I'm not so sure that I believe the connection. Okay, maybe the Mafia Shqiptare are bringing over medical supplies because of this virus. But I still don't understand what that has to do with me?"

Exasperated, she whisper-yells, "Because they have been calling for you!"

"I don't think so. I have no idea why they are calling for me. Maybe there is some mistake."

"The Mafia Shqiptare is very dangerous, Gini. Arguably the most dangerous Mafia in the world. It is hard to imagine how you, so delicate and so kind, could be somehow tied to that criminal organization. You might not know them, but they know *you*." She visibly shudders. "They are lawless men. And they have their eyes on you. And they are coming!" She removes her arm from mine, putting her hands over her mouth before lifting them up in the air. "Allah save you!"

I stop walking, looking upward toward the grand oak trees lining the quiet street. "The only time I knew the Mafia Shqiptare was through Roshan, a woman who lived in The Mansion with me. They bought her freedom from The Mansion. And Darius ... Darius has nothing to do with them."

"Darius? Who is he?" Her ears perk up.

I lick my lips, gripping her arm again with mine. And as we walk, I finally open my heart. I tell her everything, all the way down to the way Darius forsake me. I even tell her about the powder I took with

Navid in Paris and how I thought I saw Darius across the room that night at the nightclub. Throughout my story, she shushes me, reminding me that there are ears everywhere. I continue until it's done.

"Hooshang, Navid's father, was in Paris with us, although you have yet to meet him. He was doing business then ..." She pauses, eyes flashing. "Oh my, Gini! He must have been doing business with the Mafia Shqiptare! If Darius is with them, then you might have actually seen him. Maybe your mind was not playing tricks!"

"But he didn't come to me. If he were there, he would have come ..."

"How could he? You were there with Navid, your husband! The guards would have killed him on the spot for touching you. Now more than ever, I think the truth is clear. Your Darius is with that evil crew. And they have had their eyes on you. And now, they are coming to Iran."

I swallow hard, wondering if that was actually the reason he didn't come forward. My insecurity about Darius not wanting me hits me full force. "Or maybe he didn't come to me because he has no use for me anymore. I fell in love with him, but I am no longer sure he felt the same way."

"If he had no use for you, then why would he have been calling to check in?"

"You are assuming that Darius is with the Albanian Mafia. He isn't even Albanian!" I bite my lip, suddenly remembering the physical similarity between Nico and Darius. Could it be that he *is* actually Albanian? I stop walking, feeling shocked.

"You're sure about that?" She raises a dark eyebrow, and it stuns me silent.

"Oh, Gini." Tears fill her eyes as we pause in front of the library. "In some ways, you are still so naive. Darius *must* be with them. He loves you, and he has been keeping tabs on you. I believe he is with the Mafia Shqiptare. And they're coming, my dear girl. For you, Darius is coming."

The rest of the afternoon, I try to lose myself in books in the library, and we stay as long as possible at the bazaar, shopping and buying caviar and fresh dates and tomatoes. Basically, I do everything in my power to take my mind off the Albanians, the Mafia Shqiptare, and Darius.

It doesn't work.

23

Darius

NICO and I came together to Tehran last week to ensure delivery of the medical supplies. And tonight, we are going to Hooshang Soltabian's mansion for a celebratory dinner.

Nico assured me that Navid would come with all of his wives. "And even if he doesn't, we will tell him the truth—that you want Gini for yourself. He will give her up as a token of goodwill. He will not want to anger his father by insulting an important business partner, who might have saved the lives of thousands of Iranian citizens."

I put on my navy suit in the hotel room, my hands shaking as I button up my white shirt. Nico always insists we dress formally when doing business, and frankly, I agree. After wrapping my hair in a bun, I touch the buzzed sides of my head. I look clean and ready.

Twenty minutes later, Nico and I are in the back of a chauffeured Mercedes-Benz. The driver is a close cousin of Mat, who came straight off the plane from Albania to drive us around Tehran.

Nico trusts almost no one.

We drive in silence. Nico is focused on reading something on his phone while my mind spirals out of control.

Could it really be this easy—just walk into the house and arrange to take her, and then off we ride into the sunset? Maybe yes, but maybe not.

I can't stop tapping my foot on the carpeted floor. If Nico notices my nerves, he thankfully stays quiet.

We pull into the driveway of a magnificent French-style mansion. Lit up in lights and surrounded with large trees, it is an enormous three-story home. The facade is limestone, and the roof shingles are green. Black balconies line the windows on the upper floors. Nico and I step out of the car, and our driver declines the valet parking offered here tonight. He will wait in the car close to the house and come straight over when Nico calls.

We walk up the steps to the front door, and two men immediately open it for us. The entry of the home is shining white marble, the walls lined with gilded mirrors on either side. My eyes are drawn to two wide staircases with golden handrails. Carpeted in blood red, they curve upward to the second story. When I look up, I see a huge bronze chandelier hanging from the top of the ceiling. It must have at least twenty-four lights.

The thirty-plus men in the room welcome us like we're family, profusely thanking Nico and me for our help in the "small matter" of the virus.

Jokes. Small talk. The best food flowing from silver trays to hungry hands. Cigars from Cuba. The gardens in the back of the home. The magnificent art around Hooshang's mansion, often borrowed to rotate throughout museums in Iran. Iranians are known for their hospitality, and I can see now how true that statement is. Everywhere Nico and I turn, we are welcomed.

In the middle of a conversation with two business executives, I excuse myself from Nico's side and walk around the rooms, which flow seamlessly from one to the next. I pause at a wood-paneled bar, filled with at least three servers.

Where is she?

I order and take my Sanpellegrino with lemon and ice from the bartender. Hooshang is clearly devout, as there are no alcoholic beverages anywhere to be found. My eyes don't stop wandering—

they can't. There are a few women walking around the perimeter of the room, their faces completely covered in black chadors with only their eyes showing. My gut tells me she is here. I can feel it.

But where?

I continue walking, finding myself in what looks like a ladies' sitting room. It's slightly separate from the other living areas and painted in a pale pink. There is a white baby grand piano in the corner and a beautiful, round table covered in a white lace cloth in the center. A tapestry, in soft pink and shades of blue, hangs on the wall, spanning from the top of the ceiling all the way down to the floor. That's where I find large grayish-blue eyes blinking in amazement at what is surely a wonderous piece of art. She is in conversation with two other women, seemingly talking about the design. They are all in black chador and covered from head to toe, but I *know* Gini. I would find her anywhere.

The air simmers, and my past is gone. I have no mother, father, or siblings, and there is nothing I can do to change that. I grew up in the Mumbai slums. I was brought into The Mansion by Amma to buy and sell women. Now, I'm a member of the Mafia Shqiptare, and I kill for money and power. Over the extent of my life so far, I have been merciless. But when I met Gini, my heart awoke. It wanted a future. It began dreaming of what could be. Maybe I am undeserving. Actually, I know I am. But she offers me a salvation that I cannot live without. Watching her now, I know with as much certainty as I've ever known that Gini is my peace.

I stand tall, focusing my energy on her. I'm in a trance. Gini and I share a bond, made in the heavens. I know the men in the Shqipe believe that everything they do or not do is a matter of choice. But I know that we, as a people, are pushed by something divine to fulfill what has been written. The moment Gini and I met, we connected. She is my ultimate destiny.

I inhale, willing her to look up.

She does.

Water fills her eyes as she sees me watching her. She whispers something to the woman directly beside her. This must be her aid,

Maryam. The two say good-bye to the third woman and walk out of the room without a second glance in my direction. After a few moments pass, I leave as well, pausing at the edge of the dining room.

Maryam finds me. "Darius?" Her eyes are a warm brown.

"Hello." I am careful not to touch her or to get too close. We must maintain propriety.

With a small nod, she gets straight to the point. "Firstly, I need to know, are you here for her?"

"Yes."

"Do you love her?"

The glass is cold against my hand, and I'm thankful for it. "With all of my heart," I tell her in earnest.

She swallows hard, her face filling with resolve. "If you want her, you must discuss the terms with Navid—alone. He has a secret." She stops speaking, and I can tell by her eyebrows that she is wondering whether or not she should continue.

"I'm listening," I tell her, urging her on.

With her voice lowered, she tells me, "He is attracted to men. Particularly one named Hassan. To keep his relationship hidden, he would sell his soul. At the very least, he would sell a woman he adores. If anyone were to find out about his appetites, it would mean his end."

"I see." I want to hug this woman and thank her.

In Iran, being gay is punishable by death. To save himself, he would likely do anything.

Inside, my heart thrums. But I keep my body relaxed, as though we were discussing weather. We start to walk, pausing at the wall before three large, intricately carved silver plates.

"She is a good woman. She is more than just beauty. Very intelligent. You would be happy to know she continued her studies and speaks English fluently."

"I know." And even though it was never confirmed to me, I wouldn't doubt it for a minute. Gini is studious.

"And you are with a band of sinful, wicked men. You are tainted."

I cannot deny the truth. "That is right."

She walks off and speaks to Gini.

Feeling a hand at my back, I turn around. It is Nico.

"We will have dinner first. When Navid is full with food and relaxed with his chai, tell him we have business to discuss with him alone. I assume you remember what he looks like?"

"Yes." I look around the room, glad for my height. "He is in the corner now. With three other men. I've also learned that he has a secret. We will use it to get her back." I might seem stable on the outside, but inside, I'm burning. It's taking all of my energy to not grab Gini and walk out of here.

"Secrets are good." He nods.

Hooshang and another man I haven't seen before step up to us. Nico shakes each of their hands, saying hello in Arabic.

To me, Nico says, "You already know Hooshang from our business in Paris."

"Of course." In Farsi, I tell him, "Thank you so much for having us in your beautiful home. We are honored to be here."

"You speak Farsi?" He turns to Nico, a look of shock on his face. "No wonder you negotiated such a good deal for yourselves. You have a man in your ranks who understands us!" He shakes a finger in my direction, a devious smile on his mouth.

Nico chuckles, making light of the discussion. "The deal is already done, Hooshang *Khan*, and thankfully, we are all happy."

"Yes, but next time, I will know." He winks.

Another man steps over. Before I can see his face, Hooshang spins around, covering him and exclaiming, "*Saalam, Mullah! As-Salamu Alaikum.*"

The man lowers his head as he lifts his face, showing me those black-diamond eyes below a white turban. "*Wa-Alaikumussalam wa-Rahmatullah.*"

My level of shock is so enormous that I can feel it down to my toes. What is he doing here? I grip my cup, pressing it so hard that it's a miracle the glass doesn't shatter in my hand.

Mullah Omar looks at me closely, a million unspoken words on his lips. Still, he waits for me to greet him. After all, he is the esteemed Mullah Omar, for whom respect is paramount.

Nico says hello with utmost politeness, and I bow my head along- side his, as if to say Nico's hello is for both of us. The truth is, I cannot speak.

A bell chimes, thankfully interrupting our conversation. Dinner is on an enormous rectangular mahogany table, filled from edge to edge with meat and vegetable stews, rice in many colors with a deli- cious golden crust at the top, and other delicacies. Iranian cuisine is similar to Indian, but to me, it lacks any excitement or spice. People fill their plates, walking to different areas of the room to sit and eat. The dining room itself is magnificent with three crystal chandeliers hanging in a row above the table. Of course, an enormous Persian carpet sits on the floor. It is so intricate that I wonder if it is handwoven.

"I hate that fucking bastard," Nico mutters under his breath. "This might wind up being harder than we initially thought. What do you think he's doing here tonight?"

My gaze moves to the left, and there he is, arms crossed over his thin chest, tilting his bearded face to men who greet him, as though he is Muhammad's gift to the world. Omar is in my midst, and I know it isn't accidental. Does it worry me? Yes. Tremendously. I can see by the tic of Nico's jaw that he is worried, too.

"It might be about me. But maybe not."

"Wishful thinking," Nico adds.

I lift my eyes to find Gini. She is not eating. In fact, she is barely moving. Does she see Omar? I glance over to him. Not surprising, he is surrounded by many men. She could be angry that I did not come for her sooner. That I saw her at the club in Paris and left her—again. I know I should speak with Soltabian first. And not just him, but Omar, too. No doubt, by the way he glared at me, I know he wants to talk. But fuck them both! I need to talk to Gini. *Now*. I've waited long enough.

While everyone eats, I move to Maryam. "Where is the bathroom?"

"There is one by the front door ... and a more *private* one down the hallway behind the kitchen."

I look at Gini, hoping she understands that I want her to follow me. I quickly find the bathroom and step inside without locking the door. It's entirely made of black marble with gold fixtures. The light is dimmed.

Moments later, the door opens.

I wrap my arms around her, pulling her into the room and locking the door behind us. I'm here to speak ... but I cannot. My lips find hers immediately. My hands move up and down her body as I press her against the cold wall. She moans into my mouth. At once, I want to inhale her and see her. I want to feel every inch of her body against mine, but I also want to hear her voice. I pull her black cover to find another set of clothes beneath. I groan, my hands lifting the second set and finally finding bare legs.

Between kisses, I tell her, "Oh, Gini. My love. My heart. I will never let you leave my sight again."

She stops her kisses, leaning her head against my chest, listening to my heart. I can hear her breathing.

"Speak to me," I beg.

"If I speak, I will cry."

"Cry then." I pull off her scarf, touching her beautiful, silken hair.

She lifts her face to me, and I'm gone.

"I have been dreaming of you for months. I thought you sent me away without a care. And I saw you in Paris, and again, you didn't come."

"Forgive me." I lift her hand, kissing her knuckles. "When you left with Navid, I had to be concrete. If anyone thought I had soiled you or taken your heart, they could have hurt you."

"You're with the Albanian Mafia?" Worry passes over her eyes.

"Yes. In New York City. In America. I never told you, but the night I met Nico, we found out that I am actually Albanian. He told me to contact him if I ever wanted to work with his crew. I did not know Madam's plan was to send you away. She found out that I was trying to sell my stake in The Mansion to D-Company and put the pieces together that I wanted to leave. She sold you in an attempt to keep me there. After she did that, I left."

She presses her lips together, eyebrows furrowing. "I missed you, but I also hated you. Hated how you continued to have a hold on my heart, even after you threw me away. But no matter what I did, I couldn't shake you."

"Gini, I love you. When you left with Navid, I had to turn my face from yours. Otherwise, every single person in that room would have known it."

She angrily crosses her arms over her chest. "You could have at least tried to tell me. Shown me somehow. On our walk over to the room, where Navid and Madam were waiting, you didn't even turn your head to me. It's been awful, living in this limbo. Not knowing if you cared or if it was all a sham."

"A sham?"

She raises her voice. "Yes! How could I have known that you didn't break my heart on purpose? To toughen me up?"

I pull on the ends of my hair. "When we're together—"

"Together? No, Darius. I'm not even sure I want that anymore."

"Gini." I use her name like a whip, gripping her arm. "You are mine. Forever mine. And you can be angry with me if you want. But I'm what you're getting. From this day forward, I am the only man you will ever need or ever have. I know you're angry, but I swear to you, I will make it right. There is no choice here. You're mine."

She drops her head. "I've tried to keep busy, but—"

Gathering her into my arms, I press her against my chest. "Did he hurt you? We were keeping tabs through Maryam, but we never got details. Did Navid—"

She steps back from me, placing a finger over my lips. "He did nothing."

"Nothing?" I squint, barely able to believe it. I know that Maryam told me about his bent, but ... still.

"Nothing," she replies, swallowing. "I'm exactly as you left me."

I drop my head, pulling her back against my chest. "I see your pain. I will spend my life erasing it. Tonight, I will secure your freedom. We have a flight to New York City in the morning. This night-mare is—"

"Darius, there is something you should know about Navid."

"I already know his secret. And I will use it to get you."

WHEN DINNER IS FINISHED, servants walk around with large silver trays filled with chai. After being asked no less than seven times if I would like a glass, I finally relent. Taarof can force a man to do some-thing he doesn't want to do, even if only to stop the back and forth.

I catch Navid standing alone, and I mention it to Nico. It's time.

We walk over to him, asking if we could speak about a private matter.

"Of course," he exclaims. "I must tell you, Darius, I am surprised to see you here tonight. Have you been well?"

"I have been very well, thank you."

He looks into my eyes, and I don't detect anything negative lurking within them. "Let me take you into the private office."

We walk to the back of the home and into a dimly lit wood-paneled library. Navid takes a seat at a small area in front of the grand desk, gesturing for Nico and me to sit in the chairs across from his.

Nico clears his throat. "We understand that you have a marriage with Gini, who you bought from Darius's Mansion."

"Oh, yes. I know I signed for a year, but I just might keep her for longer."

Nico clasps his hands together. "Unfortunately, that cannot happen. We want her."

"You?" He looks between Nico and me, confused.

"Yes." I nod. "For reasons we cannot disclose, we want the girl. Our flight leaves tomorrow afternoon, so we would appreciate it if you would terminate your contract with her tonight."

"Tonight? Oh no ..." He shakes his head, looking between us nervously. Skittish.

I can't let him make a fuss.

"Navid"—I sit closer to the edge of my chair, and he moves back in his, as though he were afraid of me—"I know about your ... sexual tendencies. I don't think your father would take them lightly, eh? Let us do you a favor and take the girl."

From the door, a deep voice says, "What sexual tendencies?"

We all look up. Mullah Omar smirks, evil spreading across his face.

Navid looks like he might pass out.

Silence ensues until, finally, Nico speaks, "Hello, Omar."

"I wasn't sure, Darius, where you could have gone. The Mafia Shqiptare. Interesting choice. Did you think you could escape The Mansion and hide behind Nico and his men? Leave the girls behind?"

I stand up. "I hide behind no one."

"Hmm. You see"—he steps closer—"your Amma has committed suicide."

I swallow hard, shocked but maintaining my calm.

When he sees that I'm barely bothered, he continues, "The precious Mansion you built is now in shambles. The D-Company has set themselves up, keeping the girls for themselves. Devan told me you sold your shares to him. Something I simply cannot have. The Mansion was meant to be mine."

I shrug. "I guess you will have to speak with Devan about that. I am no longer part of that operation."

"Those women were supposed to be *mine*, Darius."

"They were never yours." I clench my teeth, breathing hard through my nose.

Under his breath, he yells, "You have two choices. Go back to The Mansion with your petty Mafia thieves and take back control before handing it all off to me or—"

"Or what?"

"Would you really go against me?"

My eyes move to Navid, who now looks green in the face.

But Nico? Nico laughs. Darkly. He shakes his head from side to side. "Unfortunately, Omar, Darius is now with me. And he wants Gini. That means, I want Gini. And what I want, I take."

With indignation on his face, Omar says, "It's *Mullah* Omar. I am a master of the Islamic tradition! You can't scare me."

Nico takes out a knife and puts it directly at his neck. Suddenly, he looks as frightened as if he were standing in front of Muhammad himself.

"You have crossed me in the past," Nico whispers. "I turned my head, choosing not to kill you because of your station. That was then. Now is a different story."

Omar opens his mouth to speak, but Nico presses the tip of the knife to his throat until drops of red blood seep down onto his distinguished cloak.

Omar's eyes move around the room. "Navid, go right now to your father—"

Nico presses harder, and he immediately shuts up. "Darius, do you want him dead?"

I walk up to where they stand, smiling. Looking down, I see he's pissed himself. I take the knife from Nico, pressing the blade to his throat and contemplating my next move. "I should kill you. For what you've done. And for what you will do." With my free hand, I tear the turban from his head. Somehow, he looks naked. "You choke people out for your own gains. I ought to hang you in public for your sins. Acid on your face, maybe—Iran's favorite torture device. That could work, too."

Nico looks straight at me. "You took care of my woman. I will gladly take care of yours." In Albanian, he adds, "Brother, if you don't want a mullah's blood on your hands, I have no problem with getting mine dirty."

I swallow hard, looking Omar in the eye. Over the last few months of living in America, my faith, or whatever it was I had, has been shattered. Sharia law no longer governs my every thought or action. And yet, my hand still shakes over the idea of killing a mullah. I press the knife forward and then pull it back, over and over. I just *can't.*

I nod to Nico, and he takes the knife from my hand, slitting Omar's throat without another word.

The great Mullah Omar crumples onto the floor, blood spilling everywhere.

Turning to Navid, Nico tells him, "Your secret is safe. Two of my friends will come through the back door to clean up this mess. Gini is now property of the Mafia Shqiptare. Tell your father we wanted her, and out of respect to us, you handed her over. As far as Omar's disappearance, play dumb."

He wants to speak but drops his head, vomiting all over the Persian carpet.

He moans when Nico asks, "Where's the closest bathroom? Got to wash my hands."

Navid lifts his hand, pointing to the back of the room.

Nico enters and then reemerges a few minutes later. "Let's go."

I pause at the door. "Oh, and, Navid? You still owe Gini money for her time with you." As much as I want to turn away and never return, I want to make sure Gini gets her dues. She has never lost sight of her family, and I want to make sure she can fulfill that promise she made to herself.

"Y-yes. Of course. Where shall I send it?"

Nico walks over to the desk, finding a piece of paper and writing something down. "My bank information is here. Wire the money tomorrow morning."

Nico and I walk out of the room.

Immediately, I find Gini and exhale, "Time to go."

24

Gini

ONCE WE ARE in Darius's hotel room, he closes the door. The lights are on. I stand, unsure what to do.

Before getting to the hotel, we stopped at the house in Elahiyeh.

NICO WAITED *in the car while Darius came inside. He helped me pack up my belongings in three large Louis Vuitton–monogrammed suitcases. I took the cash I had stored, along with the jewelry and purses.*

I went back and forth as to whether or not I should take the clothes, too.

Hearing someone enter my room, I turned around, finding Maryam.

"They were bought just for you. Take them." Her eyes were teary but glad.

This time, I would not leave empty-handed.

She and I hugged. It was amazing how much she taught and exposed me to in such a short amount of time. In my heart, I knew my life was just truly beginning.

Darius took my hand. "You will still receive your money from Navid.

He will wire it to Nico in the morning. When we get home, we'll arrange an account for you."

"My father—I plan to still send it to him."

He nodded in understanding. "We will bring it to him ourselves. You can tell him that you were my maid, and we fell in love and got married. Show him the money as what you had earned while you worked."

"Okay, Viraj," I joked, calling him by his false name.

He laughed with me, and I hugged him then because he just knew. To hug my family again and to bring them wealth? Nothing I had done was in vain.

HE TAKES OFF HIS JACKET, draping it over the chair beside the desk. Next, he slowly unbuttons his white shirt.

A feeling comes over me as he undresses, like a fever breaking. I wipe the back of my neck with my fingertips, feeling the dampness of my skin.

His chest comes into view. Broad and golden tan with a perfect amount of dark hair scattered around his muscles. My fingers skitter over the large tattoo on the side of his chest.

"Albanian eagle." He nods with pride. "Signature of the Shqipe."

Next, he unbuttons his pants, dropping them to the carpeted floor before stepping out of them. I pick them up, folding the pants before setting them beside his jacket and shirt. His clothes are so nice, and I don't want them wrinkled.

"Gini," he rasps.

I look up, blinking.

"Do not be afraid." He inches closer to me and takes off my head-scarf and tunic, unveiling me. "So many layers ..."

He turns me around, his front facing my back, and unbuttons my gauzy blouse, sliding it off my shoulders. He unzips my long silk skirt, his fingertips grazing my backside. It drops into a pool by my feet. Undoing the clasp of my bra, he kisses a trail down my spine before sliding the thin straps off my shoulders and down my arms. With strong hands, he turns me around to face him.

"So beautiful." He clenches his teeth together, groaning. "Your face. Your body. Most of all, your heart. Gini, you're mine. There is nothing I wouldn't do for you."

I press my palm to his face. "Back in my village, I used to dream of a man who would take me away from my life and turn me into a princess."

"No, you are not a princess," he breathes.

I tilt my head to the side. "No?"

"No. You are my queen."

Our kiss is so intimate; it's like all of the borders in my mind have burned to ash. My feeling of love for this man moves to utter desperation as he lifts me in his arms, his mouth all-consuming against my own. He places me in the center of his bed. I pull the tie from his hair, and waves fall forward, pouring into my hands. I moan against his tongue, loving the feel of his weight on my body. His heaviness. Darius calls to me, blinds me, and deadens me to everything in the world other than him.

I wrap my hands around his heavily muscled back. At once, he is rock hard and silky. He makes me crazy with lust. My shaking hands can't get enough. He cages me between his arms, running his tongue down my throat, sucking on my nipple. I fist my hands in his hair, lifting my body up to get closer to his, needing the friction.

With a strangled growl, he moves down the bed. His huge, hot palms move directly on my breasts as he sucks a trail down my stomach, moving downward still, licking a path down my belly button to between my thighs. "Been dreaming of this."

His thumb strokes between my legs. For Darius, they open. He kisses my sex, and a blind heat rushes through my body.

"I want you," I beg, loving his mouth but wanting more.

He brings his body up, lifting my leg and fitting himself in the space between my thighs.

"Darius ..."

"It's time. We're alone. Free and together. This is it."

"This is it," I repeat as he rubs his hardness up and down along my slit, making me so wet that I want to scream. No, I want to beg him to put it inside me.

I spread my thighs wider, hoping that it will somehow fall into place. He continues to move, pressing against me, making me shake.

Finally, he pushes forward. "Hold on to me," he whispers. "There will be pressure."

Before I can ask what on earth he is talking about, he surges inside me, taking my breath. My body locks, and he pauses. I can feel droplets of sweat drip onto my skin.

"Is there more?" My breaths are so hard.

"Yes, there's more." He slowly begins to move in and out. "Open for me."

I do as he said, feeling my body bloom. "Oh my ..." The pleasure hits me in an instant. I choke out his name as the thick ridges of him move within me. Struggling to adjust but wanting it more than I've ever wanted anything, I melt.

Darius murmurs, "You're beautiful. Perfect. Made for me."

"Oh ..."

"Keep your legs wrapped around me," he commands, filling me up, harder and faster.

He's impossibly huge within me. I want to scream. He moves a hand between us, low, lower, using his thumb to press against my private space, and I clench, the feeling so exquisite that it's mind-blowing.

He croons, "That's right. That's it. Let me in, Gini."

We're sweating. Panting. I look up into his face just as my body quakes—stars, every star explodes before my eyes. Darius roars, scooping me into his arms and pressing me against his chest until we collapse back together onto the bed. I can feel the pulse of him inside me. Squeezing my legs together, I want to keep him. All of him.

25

"You ready?"

"Of course. Open the door."

He unlocks it but doesn't push it open. "I read somewhere that, in America, it's customary for the man to carry his bride through the front door."

"I'm not your bride," I point out, trying to hold back my smile.

He drops our bags and lifts me up, cradling me in his arms. "We'll have to change that. And soon."

I wrap my arms around his neck, so deeply in love with a man who I could have hated. All of this with Darius so easily could never have been. I could still be living in my small village, bringing water, taking care of my father and siblings. Or I could be stuck in Iran, dancing for Navid in his opium den.

And yet, here we are. Together.

Kicking the door open, he walks us over the threshold. Flipping on the light, he gently places me on the floor. "It's the same one-bedroom I've been staying in over the last few months."

Confirming what I know to be true, I tell him, "We are in a condo on 45th Street and Park Avenue."

"That's right. Just two avenues and a few blocks from the New York Public Library."

I look at him, utterly incredulous. "Library?"

"When I first came over to the city, Nico asked me if I had any location preferences. With you in mind, I told him I'd like to be close to a library."

"We could arrange to meet at one of the large museums. Or shops. Or even a library. At a certain date and hour."

"You found this place for *me*?"

He chuckles. "Of course. I did not do anything without you in mind."

On the airplane before we slept, Darius explained that we would live in a high-rise building with a large gym for calisthenics, a large meeting room, a playroom for our future children, a rotating group of twenty-four-hour doormen, and a concierge service, who would collect our packages and make reservations.

"New York City is overwhelming, at first," he said, "but soon, you will know just how easy it is there. Groceries? Delivered. Not feeling well? A pharmacy on every corner. Need clothes? The shopping never ends. Restaurants? Every cuisine from every corner of the planet."

"Is there Indian food?"

"Yes. So many restaurants. And I have already learned of the best ones."

.   .   .

I walk around the kitchen, touching the appliances. They are similar-looking to what I had in Iran. Very modern. The chefs did the cooking, but I often made meals or snacks for Maryam and myself.

"Come. Let's see the big bedroom. And then I can show you something else that's big." Darius smirks, like he told me a joke. He's waiting for me to understand, but I don't.

I look up at the ceiling, wondering what he could—

"Oh! You mean—" I laugh out loud. "You're right; that is definitely big, too."

He shakes his head, laughing at me and not with me. He picks me up to sit on the kitchen counter, his eyes shining.

"Darius?"

"Hmm?"

He looks so genuine that my chest tightens. My pull to this man is so strong.

"You've changed since The Mansion. Not just your scar." I slide my finger down his face, wondering how much pain he must have been in. "I know you, but there is still so much to know."

His stare tells me he's here for me. "We will have to grow together, you and me, in America. There is a lot we've seen, but so much we haven't. We'll do it slowly, without any rushing. My work now is with the Shqipe, but you can do anything and be anything. After all, this is the land of the free."

A pause.

"There was a girl," I whisper, touching the back of his neck, "who wanted to run. Did she run?"

"Yes, she did. And Darius, the biggest goon of all, ran with her."

Darius and I are dressing for dinner tonight with Nico and Elira. We've spent a week in our apartment, making love, talking, and ordering an enormous amount on Amazon.

I slide on a silk skirt and a cream-colored sweater. The top was gifted to me by Elira. After arriving to the city, she sent over bags and

bags of clothes for me from a department store called Bergdorf
Goodman with a note:

Dear Gini,
I am not sure what you brought with you from Iran, so I thought you
might need some casual clothes to get you through the start of your new
life! Can't wait to meet you soon.
Love,
Elira

THE OUTFITS WERE BEAUTIFUL, but I quickly decided that jeans were
not for me. Maybe it's because I've spent all of my life in a sari, but
I'm uncomfortable in tight pants.

Darius moves behind me, wrapping his arms around my center.
"Elira is a good girl. Very tough."

"Tough?"

"She's strong. A good partner for Nico and the Shqipe."

His hand shifts downward, pressing against my skin. "I like this
sweater. So soft. Beautiful color."

"Please ..." I groan, my head falling to the side. I thought that
having him would satisfy me, but I only want him more.

"We have about thirty minutes."

"Is that enough time?"

His hands go directly to my skirt, unzipping. "Oh, Gini," he
moans, his hands wrapping around my hips and lifting me up onto
the bed. His heavy body slips between my thighs, making way, as his
tongue finds my mouth.

"I love you," I tell him between kisses, sucking on his neck like I
know he loves and pushing his pants down with my feet.

Sweating and straining, he takes me until I'm carried away.

We're barely breathing, my head against his chest, when Darius's
phone buzzes.

"Shit. We're going to be late if we don't hurry."

I stand up, holding on to the wall for a second to gather my bearings. I head to the bathroom to wash my hands and face, and I'm pleasantly surprised when I look in the mirror. My skin is positively aglow. I'm so happy.

We get redressed and leave the apartment hand in hand. A black car waits for us by the entrance to the building, and Darius helps me inside.

"Alek," Darius greets.

"So, this is your lady?"

I can see his smiling face in the rearview mirror.

"Hello. I'm Gini."

"I know who you are," he tells me.

Darius squeezes my hand, sitting flush against me even though there is so much space in the car. "Don't be nervous. They are really looking forward to welcoming you to the family. And that's what they are to me—family."

"In that case, they are mine, too."

He lifts my hand, kissing my knuckles.

It takes about twenty minutes to get to the restaurant, Cipriani Downtown. It is filled with people laughing and talking loudly. In some ways, it reminds me of Paris. There are huge photographs on the restaurant walls of horses, and round tables are pressed so closely together. I clasp my hands around Darius's hand as we walk through the tables, still unused to crowds such as this. Patrons look up to watch him. I know; he's gorgeous.

Sitting in the corner table by the window are Nico and who I assume is Elira. They stand up together, smiling. She has long black hair, pale skin, and green eyes. A real beauty.

Nico shakes my hand before Elira wraps her arms around me in a hug. I'm confused, at first, by her warmth, but I try to go with it. Darius told me that while New Yorkers are more reserved than most, Americans as a whole are very friendly people.

"Nico told me all about you. I'm still in school, by the way," she adds, taking her seat and gesturing for me to take mine. "But I spend Thursdays through Mondays here, in the city, with Nico."

"That sounds wonderful. Where is the school?"

We continue discussing education and possibilities for me while the men talk about business. Nico's hand never stops touching her. It is obvious they are in love.

Over appetizers of a creamy cheese called burrata, fried artichokes, and two colorful salads, I quietly ask the men, "Is it simply coincidence that the two of you look so much alike?"

They laugh.

Darius squeezes my leg. "It took some time, but we found out our mothers were cousins. After my father was killed in the war, my mom escaped from Kosovo. We are still unsure of how she wound up in India, but she did. Other than Nico and me, we have no other living relatives on our mothers' side of the family."

"And your father's side, Darius? Are they around?"

The waiter sets down another plate before walking away.

"I might have some family living." Darius takes my hand beneath the table, rubbing his thumb against my knuckles. "But we are not sure where they are." With his free hand, he lifts a plate from the center of the table. "It's called beef carpaccio."

I look at the raw, sliced meat in confusion.

Darius lowers his mouth to my ear. "A lot of these foods were confusing to me, too. It's delicious. Try it."

The rest of the evening is filled with laughter among friends.

After saying our good-byes, I tell Darius how surprised I am at Elira's friendliness.

A shadow moves through his eyes. "I did a big favor for her recently."

A black car pulls up to the front of the restaurant, and Darius opens the door for me.

I slide into the backseat. "Did you?" I look at him closely, wondering what it could have been. But I think, deep down, I know that it must have been something serious. Dark.

He is the man I love, and he has an enormous heart. But he also has another side to him. I saw bits and pieces of it in The Mansion, and I can only imagine how it's changed and possibly grown within the confines of the Mafia Shqiptare. Maybe I am crazy to close my eyes to it, but there is no other way. He is mine, and I am his. It was written.

He wraps a heavy arm around my shoulders. "For another night."

I lean into him and let myself relax. I am where I was destined to be.

WANT MORE?

Ready to continue reading about the men in the Mafia Shqiptare and the women who love them? All three books in the Mafia Kingdom series are available now and free with a subscription to Kindle Unlimited!

Light My Fire: A Dark Mafia Romance (A Mafia Kingdom Novel)

He saved me from war.
Fed me when I was in too much pain to eat.
Smuggled me and my family into America when it became too dangerous to stay.

But, Nico didn't flee with us.
While I began elementary school in the United States, he was building the greatest and toughest Mafia of the century.

The Mafia Shqiptare.

Nico is now King of all underground trades.
Sexy. Aggressive. Brilliant.

After years of nothing but silence, he's back in my life,
Ready to do whatever it takes to bring me into his universe.

He isn't leaving until he takes me with him.

Start reading Light My Fire: Light My Fire: A Dark Mafia Romance

Break On Through: An Arranged Marriage Mafia Romance (A Mafia Kingdom Novel)

Talia
My only goal in life is to play the cello in a world-famous orchestra.
Unfortunately, education, lessons, and connections don't come cheap.
So, when the most notorious Mafia boss in New York City offers me millions to marry one of his men, I have two choices: take the money and follow my dreams, or risk death.
I choose to take the money.
But if I had known who my husband would be, I would have picked death.
Leo might be gorgeous and lethal, but he has never met a woman who refuses to bow.

Leo
After being pushed out of my country, I lost my woman, my business, and my life.
The streets of New York City are dangerous but nothing compared to the wrath growing within me.
Joining the Mafia is a natural progression, especially when they help quench my thirst for revenge.
When the boss offers me a marriage that will help me reach vengeance, I jump at the chance.
I figure she'll be a sweet, quiet girl ...
Not the stuck-up musician from the club.

She thinks she can always get the last word, but I'm on a warpath that she can't derail.
She can either fall in line or fall into pieces.

Read **BREAK ON THROUGH** now!
Break On Through

Keep on reading for an excerpt of **Break On Through**

break on
THROUGH

a MAFIA KINGDOM *novel*

INTERNATIONAL BESTSELLING AUTHOR
JESSICA RUBEN

EXCERPT, BREAK ON THROUGH

Chapter 1: Leo

We smile at each other. The silver moonlight shines through Daisy's bedroom window, illuminating her pale skin and shining black hair. She turns to her side, so we're facing one another. Her creamy breasts are bared to me, the soft white sheet draping across the left side of her hip. She's a model in an Italian painting.

"You should go soon." Her delicate hand moves to my forehead, long nails scraping against my scalp as she brushes my hair back. "My father will be coming in an hour."

Dark eyes twinkling, she dares me to leave her. Or maybe she dares me to stay.

My gaze moves down to her breasts and back up again. "Father? What's a father?"

I kiss her deeply, the back of her neck in my grip, and swallow her laugh with my lips. My free hand wraps around the small of her back, bringing her closer to me. When we are chest to chest, warmth radiates between us.

"You know"—she lifts her lips from mine to speak, and mine

move to her neck—"my father, also known as the man who already wants to kill you?" she reminds me, giggling quietly.

I kiss her down lower, pausing on an area of soft skin above her belly button. I grumble, "Oh, that one."

"Leo, listen," her voice whispers in a slow and sultry drawl. "I want more. You know I want everything with you. But if you're going to ask his permission to marry me, it would be better if he changed his mind about you. Him catching us would be catastrophic."

"Just a minute more—"

"But he really is on his way." Kiss. "Only"—kiss—"one more hour." Kiss.

She has to push against my chest to force my mouth off her skin. This woman makes me feel drugged. I can't wait to spend my life with her.

"I love you."

She looks deeply into my eyes, and I swear, I feel the vibrations of her feelings. She's all I see.

"I love you t—"

The door opens.

There is a moment of absolute pause on all of our parts. No one moves. Hell, no one takes a breath.

Daisy's father is an enormous, hardened man. He spent years fighting in the Kosovo Liberation Army before settling down and joining the police. He's a good man. But right now, he wants to kill me. And I know this like I know my own name.

"You." His voice is so low and dark. With his feet planted on the floor, he points at me. "Get the fuck out of my house. I've warned you once before. You shame my daughter, you shame my entire family!"

I jump out of the bed, head bowed, thankful that I'm wearing my boxers.

"Daddy, no." Daisy stands up, dragging the white bedsheets with her body. I cringe at her obvious nudity. "It's okay, Papa. You know we're in love. Nothing we do is without my consent. It's been three years. We want to get married. If he gets into college in America, he'll save money and bring me there with him."

Her father is so mad that he can't even reply. Just angry breaths, like a bull. I won't look at him to find out what he'll say. I'm getting dressed like my feet are on fire. There's a madman in my midst, plotting my death, and there's nothing but his nude daughter between us.

I do my best to slide my pants on as Daisy, clearly out of her mind, walks in front of her father and begs him to stay calm. It's all a blur in my haste, but her hands are at his barrel-sized chest, the sheet tucked beneath her thin arms. I probably have just a few more seconds before he wakes up from this anger-induced trance and grabs his gun to shoot me in the head. My entire body shakes as I drop my shirt on and slide into my sneakers, forgetting the socks. I pull up on her bedroom window. Daisy on her knees before her father, begging, is the last thing I see. Her sobbing is the last thing I hear.

Walking home on the tree-lined street, I can hear him railing. He might hate my guts, but he loves his daughter. He's never raised his hand to her, and he never would. I remind myself not to be worried. I'll get back to my room and call her. She'll be okay. We'll convince him to let us marry, and even if he refuses to allow it, we will do it anyway. We are old enough now to make our own choices. No, her father never caught us in bed before. And, yes, he hates me, even before this moment. He's been telling her that I'm too tough and we wouldn't make a good match. But he doesn't know the real us. But it's all going to be different now.

"You're not the right match," her father explained as calmly as he could after we first asked him to allow us to date each other. "I've seen you with your friends, and I know your type. Sporty, physical, and tough. You will not make each other happy in the long-term. Daisy should have a man who is gentle. Not you. And if people knew she was with a man like you?" His heavy hand cut through the air. "They would imagine terrible things happening between the two of you. The answer is no."

She turned to me, worried, her lips pressed together.

Although I wanted nothing more than to put up my fists, I simply nodded at Daisy before turning back to him. "I understand, sir. I will try to change people's perception."

"I do not believe that will be possible." He stood up to leave, waiting for his daughter to join him.

That night, Daisy and I spoke on the phone for hours, planning the best way to change his mind. Nothing could stop us.

I am my own man, and I make my own choices. Once Daisy's father agrees to let us marry, I'll tell my mother. And if he never agrees, we will tell them both after the marriage is official.

My brother, Albi's, face comes into my head, darkening my mood more than I thought possible. He's the only one who knows that we continue to see each other without anyone knowing, and he holds it over my head as though the secret were a set of knives that he could use to maim me. But I love her. And I would do anything for her. Unfortunately, Albi knows this.

I kick a rock across the dark dirt road, cursing. Still, I have to believe our love will prevail. I imagine meeting her in history class and her small smiles to me when she thought no one was looking. Keeping our relationship secret, so as not to upset her parents, was a strange thing. Particularly for a man like me, who's had plenty of conquests in the past. But Daisy is different from other girls, and I respect her enough to not tarnish her reputation. A girl like her must stay pure to get married. It hasn't been easy, living without proclaiming to the world that she is mine and I am hers, but in some way, it's beautiful to have our love private, without prying eyes or gossip.

My friends figure I am busy, focusing on my studies and football; my dream of studying in America is something they all know. They would never imagine a girl had been taking up my time. No one would ever assume that the kind, beautiful, and religious Daisy would have a boyfriend. Particularly not one with a reputation for fighting.

I finally make it to the lower end of town, where my house sits. It is a good house. My father built it with his own hands. I have already planned the house for Daisy and me, and of course, I will build it. Large and white with blue shutters. A mansion for my queen.

Pulling the key from my front pocket, I open the door.

The lights are on, and my mother and brother stare at me. I look at my watch—10:07 p.m. Mother has tears in her large green eyes but not unhappy-looking ones. My brother though? He looks ecstatic.

"You're leaving for America!" He jumps off the couch and embraces me.

My body goes rigid, as I'm confused by his affection. My brother and I have a twisted relationship, if you could call it that. He was born seconds after me, and as my mother likes to tell the story, in the last moment before our birth, I apparently pushed myself ahead of him. Even though we are twins, we are completely different from one another. And while we have the same parents, have gone to the same schools, and have both been given the same course of studies, we simply have contrasting personalities and abilities.

My father loved me best, as I am the most like him. We both loved challenging the forces of nature and using physical skill to overcome obstacles. He was tall. Strong in both spirit and physicality. A fighter in the Kosovo Liberation Army. When he walked in the street, others would part. I grew up hearing countless stories about how he'd killed enemies and saved the lives of his friends. He taught me how to handle weapons and how to protect myself. How to stand tall when I needed to, and how to lower my head when necessary to show deference and respect. When the war was over, he opened a construction company to rebuild the city.

My father's death was painful for me, but it only served to push me harder to succeed. Everything I am today; I owe to him.

Our mother, on the other hand, has always loved Albi the most. Albi has patience to sit and read. He prefers staying home, writing in his journal. He likes to review numbers and comb out details, whereas I see the bigger picture of things. Most of all, he despises anything physical.

My father used to laugh, telling me that when I tried to walk, Mama would knock me down, insisting that I was not allowed to stand until Albi could too. Suffice it to say, I spent an extra six months on the ground when I wanted to run.

But at a certain point, there was no stopping my growth. I'm close to two meters in height, and Albi is a head below me. It's true that studies come more naturally to him, but I put in the work and succeed in my own way. The girls have always flocked to me while he has barely kindled a relationship with a woman. Why should I pay for his lack of skills?

Our father always wanted more for me than what Albania could offer, and over his lifetime, he encouraged me to go to America to study and learn American building techniques so that I could return to Kosovo with not just money in my pocket—the likes of which would be impossible to make here—but also with what I'd learned to help our company.

As I'm the firstborn son in my family, the business became mine after Father's death. Originally, I tried to tell Albi that if we both worked hard enough, we could leave for America together. But in typical Albi fashion, he couldn't handle trying for something if there was a chance he could lose.

"America?" I tilt my head to the side, stomach dropping with excitement. My immediate reaction is a smile, but I snap it back. I feel much emotion, but showing it to my brother would be beneath me.

"Yes, Leo." Mother nods, holding up a large white envelope. "You got this from New York University. They accepted you to their school for Arts and Sciences. You can study architecture!" Her eye twitches, and her breaths are labored. Sweat beads at her dark hairline. "I knew you could do it!"

Albi visibly bristles but keeps a smile on his face.

I take the letter from her hands and pull out the paper from the envelope. I read the first word—*Congratulations!*—over and over again, and the world around me blurs. Taking a seat on the couch, I review the letter. Normally, I would do this in my room. But I just can't wait.

"There is so much I must do," I mumble to myself, looking upward. I glance through the envelope again, surprised there isn't more paperwork. Still, I did not ever think they would accept me. My grades are solid but not excellent. "Was there anything else they sent over? About housing or the food hall? Scholarship?"

"That was all." My mother smiles encouragingly.

My brother looks happy. Too happy. "I'm sure once you get there, they will greet you and figure it out. We will make calls in the morning."

"Sure. Still, I'll need to secure my visa. And this is dated from last month! I need to act quickly."

Daisy comes straight into my mind. I'll need to find a good job to be able to bring her over with me. Of course I'll return, but I can't be away from her.

"I'll let you boys figure out the rest. I am so glad for you. Tomorrow will be a big day. The next few weeks even." With a last kiss on my forehead, she leaves the room.

My mother has never been affectionate with me. I guess she really must be proud.

I am alone now with my brother, but can't shake the feeling of Daisy. *I hope she's okay.*

"Oh no." Albi shakes his head. "Do not tell me that Daisy is giving you doubts. That look on your face is distraught when you should be over the moon. She's beautiful, but nothing more than dead weight. Leave her and move on."

"No." I put the paper down. "She and I will get married. I know her father doesn't approve of the match, but we believe that in time—"

"In time?" He laughs out loud. "You are leaving for America. You can't take the girl with you. For years, Papa worked extra hours and put money aside so that *you* could get this chance."

"You could have tried," I spit out. "But as always, you never stepped up to the plate."

"Oh yeah?" He tilts his head. Before I can get another word out, he says, "Let's put all the nonsense of Daisy behind us. What if Mother hears us? How it would break her poor, poor heart."

He is full of guile, and my stomach turns.

"Nonsense of Daisy behind?" I repeat his words, clenching my teeth. "I will go to America, and once I am there, I will find a way for Daisy to join me. We'll come back to Albania together, eventually."

"Join you?" He shakes his head. "Her father will never allow it. If you ask me, she'll be married in a month. Before anyone finds out that you took her virtue, of course. If anyone were to hear, she'd be shunned. Imagine what would happen to her if people knew how I'd found you guys, wrapped up together, in the field ..." He shudders, over-exaggerated.

I grit my teeth. "She won't be shunned because she and I will be husband and wife."

My brother shrugs casually before chuckling. "When you leave, she'll be here alone, without a husband and without her virtue. If she's smart enough, she has likely already planned to place another man in the picture ..."

One, two, moments pass, and my fist collides with his face. He falls to the floor, hands covering his jaw.

"Don't you ever talk like that about my woman."

He slowly sits up, his cheek already smarting. "Just go and be grateful. Let the rest of us live in peace."

I stand up to my full height, pointing at him on the ground. "I'm not letting her go. But I will live my dream. Papa's dream. And in time, I will bring Daisy with me. After I finish school and work to make money, I will come back here and grow my business."

"Your business?" He rubs his jaw.

"Yes. It was Papa's, and now that he's gone, it's mine."

He shakes his head, glaring. "I've been the one there after school, overseeing the books. I've been the one making sure Mama gets her stipend each week to pay for groceries. You've been screwing around with Daisy and playing football." He grits his teeth, angrier than I've ever seen him.

"While you've been sitting in the back office, I have been watching the construction on the new project Papa was building!" I point to his face. "I will return from America. And when I do, I will take what is rightfully mine. As the firstborn son, this is my birthright."

I point to my own chest before taking a step closer to him. He shrinks back, afraid of my shadow. Turning away, I walk into my bedroom and shut the door, the hinges rattling.

Hearing the freezer opening and closing, my mother chirps, "What did you say to him? Why do you anger him when you know his temper? Just like Papa. He can't help himself! How many noses has he broken in his life? Five?"

I take out my phone and call Daisy. After the tenth attempt at reaching her, getting nothing but her voice mail, I put my phone on vibrate and leave it on the corner of my desk.

I review the paper from New York University, confused by the fact that they barely gave me any information at all. *Maybe there is a second letter coming?* There must be. The mail took too long to get here. School starts in three weeks, and I don't have enough information. *What if they already gave my spot away?* I open my desk drawer, gathering all the forms that I filled out, just in case the opportunity arose. I even made a friend at the consulate, so that if the time came, everything for me could be expedited.

I fall asleep with my phone beside my face and clothes all over my floor.

***

ALSO BY JESSICA RUBEN

All of Jessica's books are available on Amazon and Free with Kindle Unlimited!

Mafia Kingdom Series

(Books to be read in any order)

Light My Fire: A Dark Mafia Romance

Love Her Madly: A Dark Mafia Romance

Break On Through: An Arranged Marriage Mafia Romance

Mafia Kingdom: The Complete Series (Box Set)

Vincent and Eve Series

Rising (Vincent and Eve, Book 1)

Reckoning (Vincent and Eve, Book 2)

Redemption (Vincent and Eve Book 3)

Vincent & Eve, The Complete Series (Box Set)

Standalone:

Warrior Undone

Holiday Springs Series, Co-Written with MJ Fields

The Broody Brit

The Irresistible Irishman

CONNECT WITH JESSICA RUBEN

Jessica Ruben is a Top 40 international bestselling author. She spends her days practicing law in New York City and spends her nights writing deeper romance. Jessica loves connecting to readers, so feel free to reach out on any social media platform or via e-mail at JessicaRubenAuthor@gmail.com

Check out all of her books and be in-the-know about all her new releases by following her **Amazon Author Page.**

https://amzn.to/2MwV7eF

Sign up for Jessica's **newsletter** to get all the news about new books, bonus content, and sales!

http://jessicarubenauthor.com

Interested in hanging out with Jessica and chatting all things books? Join her **facebook group,** Jessica's Jet Setters.

https://www.facebook.com/groups/jessicasjetsetters

ACKNOWLEDGMENTS

I am indebted to the following people for their help, love, and support:

To Jon—You're always my hero.

To my kids, who complete me.

To Autumn Gantz at Wordsmith Publicity, who supports me every step of the way.

To Jovana Shirley at Unforeseen Editing, who turns my stories into art.

To Nicole Bailey at Proof Before You Publish, who perfects my words.

To Sarah Hansen at Okay Creations, for the eye-catching cover.

To Leigh Raines, my master beta reader, who always tells me what I need to hear.

To my beta readers—Roxy, Jayme, Sandy, Lena, Sandy B., Keeana, and Caitlin—I hand my raw stories to you all, scared to death. I call you constantly. I harass you daily, asking if you're done yet. I value your opinions tremendously, and I thank you with all my heart for your help.

To the bloggers, bookstagrammers, and my ARC team—Thank you, ladies, for reading, reviewing, and spreading the word! I am so humbled by all you do.

To the readers—You guys make my dreams come true.

Thank you for reading!

Love always,
Jessica

www.ingramcontent.com/pod-product-compliance
Lightning Source LLC
Chambersburg PA
CBHW060851250626

47159CB00008B/2682